DEVIOUS OBSESSION

S. MASSERY

Edited by Studio ENP

Proofread by Paige Sayer Proofreading

Cover design by Qamber Design

To the devious ones who satisfy our dark desires

INTRODUCTION

Hello dear reader!

Devious Obsession is a dark bully romance. Steele is not a hero... well, not most of the time, anyway.

Please be aware if you have triggers that are common to dark romance/bully romance, this story checks quite a few of those boxes! (Including: dubious consent, consensual non-consent, somnophilia, primal play, mental/physical/emotional bullying, and voyeurism.) There are also brief mentions of child abuse.

Steele's message for you: he will not apologize for his actions. And he hopes you've picked a memorable safe word.

Thank you and happy reading!

xoxo,
    Sara

STEELE

I adjust my position in my chair by the window, exhaling smoke.

One of the graduated seniors is hosting his annual summer party at his parents' lake house. His last party *ever*, by the size of it. Like a final hurrah before he goes off and does whatever the fuck he's planning on accomplishing with his life. Because of that sentiment, it's chaos downstairs. Everyone is getting riled up by the alcohol, drugs, music. There's a free flow of all three.

This year, it coincided with my return from the summer intensive hockey camp. A month spent sweating and skating and working my ass off with some of my teammates—only to return to shocking news.

My dad got married on a whim. Almost *three weeks* ago.

So instead of going home, I'm here. Stewing on the woman who managed to steal my father's common sense. Because it certainly isn't love that has him captivated.

Is she a con artist? After his money?

But why did *he* do it? Does she have something on him? Blackmail? A golden cunt?

I take another hit and stub out my joint on the arm of the chair.

Getting high is a summer luxury. During the school year? Absolutely not. Hockey camp? *Nope*. The few weeks I'm free, though, I take full advantage. Dad would skin me alive if he knew I was ruining my body with weed. But it relaxes the constant worry in my mind. The part of my brain that never fucking shuts up.

Well, now it's quiet.

Ish.

The door cracks open, and Finch sticks his head in. "Erik wanted me to round everyone up for his game."

I raise my eyebrow, unmoving. Finch is a junior—well, fuck, he's going to be a senior now, just like me—at Crown Point University. He's one of my teammates. He's always had potential to be a starter, and after what Coach saw at hockey camp, he might just make it this time.

He's a good guy. Which is why we don't hang out much.

Me and *good* don't mesh.

"So...?" He shifts on his feet.

"Yeah, yeah," I say, standing and tucking the joint back in my pocket.

Except Finch steps farther into the room, twisting his hands together. "I don't normally stay once Erik starts rounding everyone up. I've heard the stories. Is it... worth it? To stay?"

I focus on him, my lips pressing into a thin line. Erik's *afterparties*, his games... there are rumors that float around, but it's one thing to hear about it and another entirely to live it. To experience the rush.

He creates nightmares and marries them with fantasies, and somehow it works.

"Do whatever the fuck you want, Hudson, but if you do stay, don't chicken out halfway through."

No one ever calls him by his first name, and it startles him into moving out of my way. I pull the door open wide, letting light into the dark room. The music is ten times louder in the hall, but I ignore the way the bass vibrates my chest and assaults my eardrums.

Finch follows me down to the basement, where Erik stands amongst a relatively even split of guys and girls. My gaze zeroes in on a girl who I've never seen before.

Long dark hair. High cheekbones. Full lips.

Full *figure*.

Tits. Hips. Ass.

Her gaze slams into mine, and we just stare at each other. My heart beats uncomfortably hard. Insistent.

I move toward her like I'm being reeled in, almost against my will. Until I stop just in front of her.

"Hey, babe." Amanda flips her hair off her shoulder. She's a graduated senior, like Erik. "Are you playing?"

I ignore her, staring at the new girl. Taking in more of her appearance. Her tight white shirt, long-sleeved and off-the-shoulder. It's cropped, exposing a slice of skin. Ripped high-waisted black jean shorts. Boots. Rings and thin neck-laces, a watch on her slim wrist.

A sense of style and a pretty face.

"What's your problem, dude?"

It takes me a second to register the guy who's slung his arm around her shoulders. Her green eyes bore into mine, and neither of us acknowledge the asshole trying to claim her. I inch closer and reach for her, running my finger along the slice of skin between her shirt and shorts.

Her breath hitches.

I smirk at the reaction, although I'm troubled by my

own desire to touch her. I shouldn't want some random stranger in Erik's basement. I shouldn't want anyone.

I'm on hiatus.

"Back the fuck off, dickwad," the guy growls.

I glance at him. It's one of the football assholes. We had trouble with the quarterback last semester, and we sent him a nice little message before the end of the year. Maybe this guy wants the same treatment?

My gaze goes from his face right down his body. He's built, stacked with a lot more muscle than me. A few inches shorter. But none of that is a deterrent if I decide to start a fight.

Which, honestly, wouldn't be the worst thing in the world. Some pain might be just the distraction I need...

But then my attention is swinging back to the girl. She's staring at me with these huge fucking eyes, like she's never seen someone like me before. And I haven't even *done* anything. But suddenly, I want to blow her fucking mind. I want to show her every shadow in my soul, just to get that shocked reaction from her again.

I lean closer to her, ignoring the football dick's grunt of protest. "What will you give me to make him go away?"

Her breath stalls again. Her eyes are light green, like sea glass. Her tongue flicks out, sweeping across her lower lip, and I fight back a groan. My cock stiffens, immediately on board with the fucked-up thoughts running through my head. The ones that say she'd look stunning on her knees in front of me.

"What do you want?" Her voice... *Fuck*. It's throaty and raspy and deep.

I fight my smirk. "Pick me for the game."

Her eyebrow rises, then smooths back out. The only indication that I've surprised her. "Okay," she agrees.

"Babe," the guy protests.

I shove his arm off her shoulder. "You heard her." I slip between them, grinning at him like I've lost my fucking mind. And honestly... I probably have. It's like I didn't smoke at all, wound tighter than ever. "She picked me."

The football guy squares up... and just as quickly looks away. He can see that I'm spiraling. Maybe he knows my reputation, and that of the whole hockey team.

Erik claps just as the dick shuffles off and finds another place to stand. I turn back around, my front now almost touching mystery girl's back. I put my hand on her hip, and her body jolts. I run my thumb along that sliver of skin again, eliciting another reaction.

A shiver.

My cock throbs, and I shift so she can't feel it stiffen against her ass.

"Tonight's game is all about our dark desires," Erik announces. "Guys have already drawn a card. Ladies... it's your turn."

He motions to one of the girls beside him, and she reveals a deck of cards. She spreads them faceup, letting us see what we're going to be picking.

Erik continues, "The higher the card, the more excitement you're willing to have and the darker your fantasies run."

"What's the joker?" a girl calls.

"Anything goes," Erik replies. "And aces are high."

My heart pounds harder. The card he made me choose when I entered the room is burning a hole in my pocket. The fingers of my free hand twitch at my side, wanting to pull it and shove it under the mystery girl's nose. So she knows exactly what to pick.

Erik hasn't unleashed this version of the game before,

not with the joker. With the lack of restrictions. There's a new restlessness in the air as everyone leans in toward the girl with the cards. Amanda and Paris both choose cards, surrounded by other girls.

The mystery girl in front of me hasn't so much as shifted, though.

"Having second thoughts?" I whisper in her ear.

She shakes her head, her jaw set. "Hardly."

"Pick high, sweetheart." I release her hip.

Automatically, she steps forward. Away from me. The loss of contact is sudden and chilling, and I grit my teeth against that feeling. I watch her like a hawk to see what she's going to pick. Partly curious, partly insane.

The girl with the cards swivels toward us, and my stomach drops when mystery girl's fingers drag along the remaining cards. Over the two of hearts, the seven of clubs. Pausing on the ace of hearts... then continuing on.

I bite my tongue.

"Steele," Amanda says, nudging my arm.

I glance at her. She's holding her card to her breast and smiling at me. When I look back at my girl, she's already drawn. And I missed it.

Wait. *My* girl?

I ignore that slip up and scowl at Amanda. "What did you choose? Let me guess... a four of diamonds?"

She frowns.

Amanda's one of the dance girls. She's nice, but she's very fucking vanilla, which is a damn shame. We had one experience that nearly made my dick limp before I could finish—and that's saying something. My mind just keeps getting more and more screwed up, wound tighter until I don't know which way to spin to release the tension.

It's not that I don't think she's pretty. She is. Nice tits, eyes, smile. She checks the boxes of what I *should* want—so I flirt with her. Or, flirted, until things got awkward. After that, I just avoided her. And hopefully this party will be the last time I have to fucking deal with her.

"Ready?" Erik calls. "Show your cards and find your partner."

He flips his own card, grinning at the king of spades in his grasp.

My heart skips as I try to find my mystery girl.

Amanda shows me the seven of spades, her scowl lodged in place.

I shrug at her. "Close enough to a four."

In truth, I don't even know what the fuck the difference between the four and seven is. My tastes run dark—which is why I picked high. The card is still in my pocket, and I slide my hand in to cup it against my palm.

"What did you choose?" Amanda demands.

I show her my card. Her eyes go wide, and I smirk. She moves away from me, her cheeks flushing.

"Anyone without a partner has to leave or redraw," Erik calls. He's got a girl looped under his arm.

Across the room, Paris has paired with Finch. A surprising match. And I'm mildly impressed that he chose to stay, after all.

The football player I scared away from my girl is with a junior with big tits and a short skirt. I peruse the room, glancing at the cards, and stop in front of the mystery girl. She brushes her long dark hair off her shoulder, eyebrow raised.

"Let's see it," I murmur.

She shows me her card, a small smile on her lips.

Fuckable lips.

The red joker stares at me.

I show my first true smile, revealing the other joker.

"Anything goes?" Her throat moves when she swallows. "What does that mean to you?"

There's a beast roaring under my skin to show her exactly how tonight is going to go. My dick is hard, throbbing against my zipper, in anticipation of what we're about to do.

"I'm going to take what I need from you," I tell her in a low voice. "And then we'll focus on the twisted shit you crave."

Her nod comes fast, her lips parting.

First... a public claiming.

Because I still feel eyes on her. The football player, pissed he didn't get her. Some of Erik's friends, their gazes lingering on her ass. Erik himself, only two cards off from her.

She's the bombshell in the room. Fresh blood, too, makes her all the more attractive.

Couples have already broken off, but others are lingering. Talking, discussing. *Boundaries* and all that. The sort of thing healthy relationships thrive on.

I wouldn't know.

I undo my pants, my fly going down and immediately relieving the pressure. Now all that's shielding my dick is my boxers, the thin fabric doing little to hide my length.

She eyes my groin, her lower lip working between her teeth. Bite any harder, and she'll cut it open. She doesn't make a noise when I force her to her knees and take hold of her hair.

It's embarrassing how hard I am for her. And how much I want to prove to everyone who wants to look at her that she's *mine*.

"Take it out," I order, my voice dark. "And I'll make sure no one ever looks at you twice."

She swallows and nods once. Her silky hair pulls through my fingers, and I fight the urge to tighten my grip.

Her lips part, and her gaze flicks back up to mine. There's dare a written there.

"Is this all you've got?" she whispers.

And then her mouth is on me, and it takes everything in my power not to physically react.

I brace my hand on the wall, leaning forward as she swirls her tongue around me. Tasting me. I push my hips forward, testing her reaction, and her throat closes around my tip.

Fuck.

She gags but keeps going, her hands creeping up to hold my thighs. That damn card is still in her grasp, her palm pressing it into my leg. It's taunting me, urging me to take whatever the fuck I want from her.

My hold on her head tightens, controlling her pace. Thrusting so deep she chokes again, then withdrawing. Relishing her little gasps of air before it's cut off again, the way her saliva drips down her lips.

And when her eyes flutter closed, I glance over my shoulder at the remaining people in the room. Erik is watching us—and he's not the only one.

The girl on my cock, however, seems to have read my mind... or maybe she likes the idea of an audience. Because her movements get more exaggerated, a moan humming through her throat. Her hands move higher. She digs her nails into my ass.

It turns me on, too. I meet Erik's gaze and sneer at him. His girl stands at his side, her focus on him. *Waiting*.

"Kind of busy here, asshole," I grunt, flexing my hips

forward and eliciting that lovely choking noise from her again. "What the fuck is your problem?"

"She..." His jaw works.

He's annoying. And a bastard. But he's not as sick as me or my friends. Greyson or Knox would've enjoyed the show. Probably.

Or maybe I'm the only sick one in that regard.

He shakes his head and turns away.

Doesn't matter—she's got a magic mouth. And as soon as I turn my attention back down to her, my grip on her hair tightens. I take over control, fucking her face. I half expect her to tap out, to shove me away, but she doesn't.

I come in her mouth. My balls tighten, my muscles tremble, and the release is mind-blowing.

"Swallow," I order.

Her throat works, following my directive automatically. It's either that or choke, I suppose. When I pull out of her, she sits back on her heels. I let go of her hair and trail my knuckles across her cheek. I wipe the corner of her mouth, then step back farther. I tuck my cock back in my pants like we don't still have an audience.

Instead, I take the joint out of my pocket and relight it with a flick of my lighter. The flame bursts to life in front of my face, and I inhale the smoke. It sears my lungs but lessens some of that extra weight on my shoulders by the time I exhale.

"Satisfied?" She climbs back to her feet.

Her voice scratches an itch deep inside my brain. I don't understand it.

In the dim lighting, up close and personal, I get more of her details. Her red lips are puffy. Her messed-up mascara illuminates her eyes.

I smirk at that. Everyone will know what sort of game *we* play in the dark.

She doesn't object when I loop my finger in the waist-band of her shorts and reel her in. Her chest hits mine, and she steadies herself by gripping my upper arms. Her touch is electric, but I focus on my mission of dissecting her.

She plucks the joint from my hand while I unbutton her jean shorts. She takes a hit, and I run my finger along the lace top of her panties. They're purple. *Cute*. Like she wasn't expecting to get laid tonight. She shudders at the sensation.

"Your hand is cold," she whispers.

I smirk. "Every part of me is cold, sweetheart. Better get used to that."

Her lips part when I slip into her panties. She's smooth, shaved, and the heat between her legs is unbearable. My cock twitches again, waking up for a second round, but I ignore it. I run my fingers through her wet center, over her clit and then farther down, until I am cupping her entirely. The heel of my palm rests against her clit. Two fingers push into her. She's tight, and her muscles squeeze at me.

She's going to feel fantastic when I fuck her.

"What was it that woke up your sweet little cunt?" I ask in a low voice. "The people in the room who watched you choke on my dick? Or me ordering you around?"

Besides the barest brush of her chest against mine, and my fingers inside her, we're not really touching. She's got her hand on my biceps, her legs spread to let me in. But other than that, she barely even looks at me.

I don't like that.

"Eyes," I demand.

Her gaze swings back to me slowly, a pendulum that crashes into my guard with enough force to rattle me. Her eyelids drop, until she's only looking at me through little slits. Her lips part as I rub her G-spot with my index finger.

I shift my hand, digging the heel of my palm into her clit. While she's distracted, I pluck the joint and inhale. I hold the smoke in my mouth, then grip the back of her neck and pull her to me. Her lips touch mine, and I blow the smoke into her mouth.

She inhales, trying to stifle her reaction to my fingers. But I can't help but picture her at my mercy. On her knees again or tied to my bed. Struggling.

The noises she's making, the way her cunt is clenching around my fingers—suddenly, I don't want her to come. Our game isn't over yet.

So I pull out of her entirely, cutting off her pleasure before it has a chance to spiral.

Her eyes pop open—and then her brow lowers.

Even her glare is gorgeous.

I put my face right in front of hers, my hold on the back of her neck strengthening. Anticipating her withdrawal.

"Your dark fantasies," I remind her. "You tell me yours, I'll tell you mine."

Her gaze moves away from me.

Embarrassed.

"Tell me."

"Force," she whispers.

Oh?

I take her hand and pull her up the stairs. There are people in the living room and on the second floor. The furniture in the bedrooms above us is thumping. The whole house will smell like sex by morning. We go outside, where we can see the lake. It's a calm night. Perfect for a midnight romp...

"I need more information, sweetheart," I say in a low

voice, backing her into the railing. I cage her in. "Tell me what you want."

She swallows and stares at my chest. "I keep having these dreams..."

I wait.

"I want to feel like I'm out of control. Afraid."

Fuck.

This girl is going to kill me.

I shift and twirl a lock of her dark hair around my finger. "You want me to make you submit?"

She closes her eyes.

And nods.

I'm not going to lie. Her words are Christmas morning and my birthday and winning the fucking national hockey tournament all wrapped up in one. If only I could fulfill her wish to the extreme—but I can't. The mere fact that she's told me tonight, and that she already knows the taste of me, ruins it for her.

"I'm going to give you a two-minute head start," I say softly, still pinching her hair in my fingers. "And then I'm going to hunt you down. You'll know *I'm* coming. When I catch you, you fight me. Do your worst. And I suppose you should pick a safe word..."

I pause and wait for her to fill in the blank.

"Fire," she says.

I draw back and stare down at her again, then take a step away. Her chest is heaving, her hands gripping the railing behind her. She's gorgeous like this. Anxious, captivated.

She'll look better when she's *my* captive.

"What are you waiting for?" I bark, my voice suddenly loud and cruel. "*Run*."

ASPEN

My heartbeat thunders in my ears.

My mouth is suddenly dry with my confession, and I fight the urge to cringe away from him. Because all my life, I've been told—*urged*—to be normal. To be the good girl, the straight-A student. To go along with the flow, to coast under the radar. To listen to my superiors, to those in power, even when they might be wrong.

And I never protested.

Never once rebelled.

But then my stranger's face changes, excitement lighting his dark eyes. His lips twist in a way that sends shivers racing up my spine, the mirth falling away from his expression.

I really need to stop calling him *my stranger*.

But then he tells me to run in a cold voice, and every part of me comes alive. I didn't even tell him all of the twisted depravities running through my head. Part of me wanted to, though. I have recurring dreams where I wake up from a sound sleep and someone's on top of me. Pulling my shorts down. Sometimes there's a gag in my mouth, sometimes it's my hands that are tied.

It always ends too soon, my heart pounding out of my chest and seeming to echo in my ears. And then I'm left to try and calm down enough to get back to sleep.

I release the banister and inch to the side.

Two-minute head start. I glance around, considering going back inside. Every horror movie ever made steers me away from that decision, though.

Except, I'm not fit. I don't run, I don't do sports. I play the piano, I study, I read. My sisters, mother, and I would do the occasional hike—but that was more for them than me.

So, five seconds into sprinting across the lawn, heading toward a boathouse, I'm winded. My lungs burn, every part of me is jiggling. I should've worn a better bra, but I picked a cute lacy bralette instead. No support.

I get to the boathouse and throw open the door, stepping inside. There's a boat—*obviously*—in its own little inside dock, and two more smaller ones lifted out of the water. A whole rack of kayaks.

The boathouse suddenly seems too obvious.

There's another door, and I move quickly toward it.

I've only just grasped the handle when the other door flies open.

My heart jumps, and a squeak slips out of my mouth.

His chuckle answers me. It's dark, low, curls right around my core and threatens to never release me.

There are those people who you just have a connection with immediately, and my stranger is one of them. In the most magnetic, damning ways.

Good girl falls for bad boy.

Cliche.

Avoid.

I leave the door ajar, not bothering to close it behind me in fear that he'll hear it, and rush toward the woods. I manage to get to the tree line and duck behind one of the larger trees, pressing my back to it. My heart is pounding so loud, I almost miss the footsteps coming toward me.

Then past me.

Holy shit.

I let out a slow breath and creep around the tree, then take off back toward the lake house. The air has a bite to it that's refreshing for mid-June. When I got the invite to this party, I leapt at the chance. I'm not living in Crown Point, but the drive over was easy enough. And getting my footing here has been rough.

Uncomfortable.

Mom's been urging my sisters and me to get into a routine, to put down roots. I had only just finished two years at our local community college, and I'd been accepted into a few different universities.

I picked Crown Point University for its arts programs, not realizing I'd *still* be trapped close to my family.

Don't get me wrong—I love them. But aren't you supposed to find your independence in college?

My few high school friends immediately went off to the big, fancy schools right after graduation. Not a single one stayed in our hometown.

Because of that, I sank myself into my passions and let the rest rot.

Which is why my lungs are literally on fire when I reach the steps to the raised deck.

But I'm too late.

Hands wrap around my waist and yank me backward. My fingers slip off the handrail, and my feet slide in the grass. I'm towed around the side of the deck, into its shadow, and thrown to the ground on my back.

My stranger has a punishing gleam in his eye.

I crawl backward, fear and anticipation sweeping through me.

He grasps my ankle and drags me to him, his hands inching along my legs. He forces them apart, kneeling in the grass between them.

Fight.

I shove at him, batting his hands away from my shorts. He pulls his belt off with a *snap* of leather and catches one of my hands. Then the other. Without so much as a hesitation, he wraps the belt around my wrists and cinches it tight. He uses it to drag me into a sitting position.

"That's it," he growls in my ear. His teeth score my neck, his nose brushing my jaw.

When he pulls away, I throw my head forward.

My forehead cracks into his cheek, and he reels back.

Momentarily stunned.

I lurch to my feet and stagger away from him again, a small smile coming to my lips. My wrists are bound, making my run awkward, but I still do it. Still force myself to hurry away from him.

Picking the joker was a gamble. Erik, the host, had already confessed to me that he had picked the king. Like he expected me to choose it just for him, or something.

If you want to stay, you have to play the game...

I didn't want to leave, so I picked a card. But I didn't want Erik, so I avoided that second king like it was poison. Besides, my stranger gave me butterflies the first time we locked eyes. Well before I chose the card and sealed our fate.

The football player who was hanging out with the girls

I just met, too, seemed to think I'd be interested in picking what he did. He went so far as to show it to me, the nine of spades looking impressively dull in his palm.

But then my stranger scared *him* away, and my heart did some weird skip and jump.

When's the last time anyone fought that hard for my attention?

He's behind me now, running just slow enough to avoid catching me. And I wonder why until we hit the tree line again, and suddenly he's on me. He crashes into me, driving me to the ground facedown.

My forearms hit first, then the rest of my body. The air *whooshes* out of my lungs. Before I can get my bearings, he has my shorts and underwear pulled down to my knees, and he straddles my thighs. I scramble at the ground, but all I manage to do is slide my bound hands forward. Over my head.

He grips the back of my neck, his fingers curling into my skin. He forces me harder into the dirt, completely stretched out underneath him. The cool air touches my bare ass.

A low groan slips past my teeth, and I feel him shift above me.

I give one more attempt to throw him off, and he presses more weight on my neck.

He leans down and bites my shoulder.

The pain is unexpected, blooming through me. It feels like he's going to rip a chunk out of me. And then he thrusts into me, and I almost scream. I should've expected the intrusion. I should've been ready for it, because I *asked* for this to happen. And yet, everything about this has sent me spiraling.

"You're soaked," he says in my ear. "You're a fucking slut for this, aren't you?"

He pulls out and pushes back into me, my legs forced together making him seem too big, too thick. Each thrust stretches me wide, splitting me open. His pace increases, and the way he grinds into me has me moaning. The noises escape without my permission. I'm glad he waited until we had the cover of the trees to do this, especially after our public exploit earlier.

The spikes of pleasure are intertwined with pain. The rocks under my body, the bite mark on my shoulder that my stranger keeps returning to. His hand on the back of my neck. The undeniable pulse between my legs that keeps getting stronger.

"You gonna get off like this?" His voice is in my ear again, his weight bearing down on my back. "I want to feel you come knowing that I can twist you any way I want and you're helpless to stop it. My cock sliding into you is the worst sort of intrusion. The one you want the most and the one you can't fight off."

Fuck. I squeeze my eyes shut, absorbing his words.

The pleasure is building, climbing toward the impossible.

Before I can get there, he stills inside me and comes. He hisses a breath out, pumping a few more times before pulling out. He doesn't climb off me, though. He seems to hesitate, his weight on my thighs.

And then his finger runs up my center, and I shiver. Everything is sensitive. My skin, my core. My clit aches for him to touch me.

"I didn't use a condom, sweetheart," he says, his finger thrusting back into me.

"What?" I gasp.

I knew.

In the back of my mind, I knew.

"First time for everything," he murmurs. "Are you on birth control?"

His finger stills inside me.

"What are you doing?" I squirm, trying to get away from him, but his weight keeps me immobilized. "I—"

"Quiet."

He flips me over, my back hitting the ground hard. I bring my hands to cover my chest, protecting my shirt from being torn off me, but he doesn't seem to care about that. Instead, he touches my lips. My arousal and his cum on the pad of his finger smears across my skin. My jaw automatically opens, and he pushes his finger inside, pressing down on my tongue.

I glower at him as he rubs his finger along my tongue, making sure I taste both of us. There's a certain pleasure in not coming. It makes the ache between my legs all the sweeter. He smiles, then retracts his hand. He drags me up by the restraint on my wrists and undoes the belt, shaking his head slightly.

"What?"

"That was fun," he says. "And now that you've shown me yours...."

I raise my eyebrow. "Your turn again?"

"Something like that."

I rub my wrists. He pivots, shielding his body slightly to tuck his dick back in his pants. I get my shorts back into place, then stand and quickly assess the rest of my body. My hair feels gritty, like it has dirt in it... which it probably does. I finger brush out a few leaves and pine needles. There are new grass stains on my white shirt.

Once I'm somewhat put back together—although my

heart refuses to calm down, plus that aching pulse between my legs that won't go away—I follow him back toward the house.

There are a lot of questions on the tip of my tongue. His name, for one. Why he comes to parties like this. If he normally chases girls through the woods and fucks them, or if I'm special...

Yeah, right.

I push that last thought away, the one where I'm allowed to think I'm *special* or *different* or *not like other girls,* and obliterate it. Because when we're taught to strive to be different, we're also taught that we shouldn't be. That there's nothing wrong with being like everyone else.

My stranger takes my hand, threading his fingers with mine, and I try not to let out a noise. Like something between a whimper and a gasp.

He pulls me close and grasps my chin, lifting it so I meet his eyes.

They search mine for a moment, but I couldn't begin to guess what he wants. Or needs.

"You're not from around here, are you, sweetheart?"

I wet my lips. "No."

"You don't go to Crown Point University."

"No." Well, that's a small lie. The decision of whether or not I'll show up for the first day of classes is still wavering on a razor-sharp edge, waiting for a strong breeze to push me in one direction or the other.

Give it a month, my mother said.

I'm holding out hope for my top school. To see if I'll be taken off the waitlist. Even though it's months past when I should find out, and far too long to be holding on to it.

Two long years of community college, of getting perfect grades and suffering through too many extracurriculars, all to be considered for the best of the best. And then I got waitlisted, and my summer seemed to crash and burn.

So I'm enrolled at CPU, but the wishful thinking part of my brain wants me to believe I'm not actually going there.

Instead of explaining all that, though, I let my stranger take the no at face value. And it seems to be the correct answer, because his grip on my hand tightens.

"Stay quiet," he says in a low voice.

He waits for my nod, then we slip into the house. Down the corridor to the stairs that lead up to the second floor. We go up and pause outside of the first bedroom. The door is open, and there's a couple on the bed.

Having sex.

He leads me into the room and pushes me against the wall, leaning against it beside me. His dark eyes watch the couple, who seem oblivious.

But they must be okay with it, if they left the door open?

Anyone could walk by...

I shift on my feet. It doesn't matter who the couple is. I don't know them, don't recognize either of them in the darkness.

The guy is on top of the girl, thrusting into her and grunting with every movement. Her eyes are closed, her arms stretched above her so she can hold on to the headboard.

My nose wrinkles.

"Not your scene?" my stranger whispers in my ear.

"Too vanilla," I whisper back.

"Amateur hour," he agrees, smiling.

"We can hear you, jackass," the guy calls.

He tugs me back out into the hall and to the next room. There's rope and candles and a mess of wax, and I back out before I can even register that the girl is writhing in pleasure, not pain.

"Door number three," he chuckles. "I'm gonna bet this is Erik."

We step inside the room. The primary bedroom, judging by the size of it. I recognize Erik as he leans over the bed, the girl lying on her back with her head hanging off it. It takes me a second to realize he's fucking her mouth.

But there's someone else, too. Someone between her legs...

I shudder and back up, but I bump into my stranger's chest. And he wastes no time slipping his hand around my waist, dipping into my shorts.

My gasp is blocked by his other hand, which clasps my mouth with surprising surety. The noise is lost in the girl's pleasure, which she voices around the cock in her mouth... *loudly*.

But my stranger's fingers stroking along my clit has me squirming again, bringing back our own escapade with vivid clarity. And as the girl on the bed arches her back, gripping the hair of the guy's head between her thighs, my stranger's cock stiffens against my thigh.

Holy shit.

I don't know what to make of it, but no one seems to register that we're in the room. It's dark, and I have a feeling no one gives a shit anyway. Not about us watching.

This is his thing.

I glance over my shoulder, but his gaze isn't on them... He's locked on me.

"Get out of here, asshole," Erik says suddenly. The sound is muffled, through his teeth. He grunts a second later, and the girl swallows around his cock and makes porn star noises.

I'm equal parts horrified and curious.

A bad combo.

My stranger is still staring at me, unmoving. I try to get free of him. His hand on my mouth, his other between my legs, gives me nowhere to go. The feeling of being trapped doesn't hinder my climax... it speeds it on.

I squeeze my eyes shut, but he pinches my clit hard, and I immediately open them again. Staring at him while pleasure sweeps through my body like a bomb going off.

"That's my girl," he whispers in my ear.

My knees almost give out.

And then he's pulling free and urging me out the door. Erik stalks toward us, his dick out and saluting us, and we almost fall into the hallway.

The door slams, ringing in my ears, and my stranger grins.

"That was fucked up," I breathe.

He lifts one shoulder. I follow him back downstairs, but it seems like he's done. With me, with the party.

My brows furrow. He snatches a set of keys from the drawer and goes out the front door. To one of the cars on the lawn.

I stand in the doorway until he's backed out of his spot and turned the car around, and it disappears down the long drive. I let out a breath as soon as he's gone.

What the fuck just happened?

SIX MONTHS LATER

When I was little, I wanted a white knight to come sweep me away from my terrible life. I wanted the horse, the shining armor, the sword.

The knight would slay my monsters and carry me off into the sunset.

But like most fantasies, that didn't happen. The monster had more kids. And it was my mother who was the one who carried me off—but it certainly wasn't into the sunset.

This, however... this feels like the start to something new.

"Are you sure?" Thalia, my best friend, asks me. "I mean, this is on a level of..."

I shrug. We're standing in front of one of the oldest performing arts buildings in Crown Point, only blocks from campus, and the stadium we're due to be at in less than an hour.

The thing is, the theater has been shut down for a month as it undergoes repairs, and rehearsals for the new show start next week. And I'm not a betting person, but I'd guess they won't let random people wander around once that happens.

"I'll be quick," I promise her.

I give the side door a test pull, and it opens easily under my hand. I smile at her, as if to say, *See?* and step inside. The darkness swallows me whole. And a second later, Thalia joins me. She turns her phone flashlight on, illuminating the hallway.

We go forward quickly, our footsteps light, until we find the main stage. There are tarps everywhere, the floor rough, but it's not the *stage* I want. It's what's below.

There's a staircase set off to the side, and Thalia lets out a groan when I gesture to it. Down we go, until I locate the piano. The live orchestra plays under the stage. The conductor is visible from the audience, and some of the front chairs, but the piano is tucked into the back.

When I find it, I let out a quiet cheer. I toss my phone to Thalia and carefully slide out the bench. She nods when she's started recording, and I take a seat. I stare at the keys for a moment, starstruck. Crown Point Theater has seen many, *many* orchestra members who have then gone on to do great and wonderful things. This piano is like a piece of history.

"Go," Thalia urges.

I nod, tossing her another smile over my shoulder, although my nerves are climbing up my throat. It's not like anyone is watching—it's just, I'd like to do this for real someday. With a full orchestra backing me up.

The time for hesitating is gone. I dive into a piece I know by heart, my fingers flying across the keys. The sound, though. The *sound* it makes goes straight into my soul. I lean in and play faster. This is the risky part, after all. If anyone is here, they'll know exactly where to find us.

Breaking and entering isn't a good look on my college résumé.

I finish and sit back, caught in a trance.

"You'll get here," she swears in a soft voice.

A door slams in the distance, and we both flinch. I jump up and rush past Thalia, grabbing her hand and towing her with me.

"Hey! Stop!" someone shouts.

We ignore them, sprinting down a maze of corridors and following the glowing red *exit* signs. We burst out onto the sidewalk and keep running another block before we slow down.

I glance at her and burst out into laughter.

She follows suit a moment later, then looks down at my phone. "Oh, shit. I didn't stop recording." She lifts it. "How does it feel to have played at Crown Point Theater for the first time, Ms. Monroe?"

I smirk. "Like a dream come true, Ms. Armitage."

"You'll get there one day." She hooks her arm around mine and hands my phone back to me. "Now, you ready for your first ever hockey game?"

Thalia and I met two months ago. There was an on-campus welcome event for incoming students before the official start of school, and a mixer for transfers. As a junior, I didn't know what to expect. My community college in Chicago didn't do *mixers*. Or functions of any kind, really.

Anyway, Thalia and I bonded almost immediately at that mixer, which was pretty lame compared to the parties the freshmen were having. We were both supposed to be living in the dorms, but we decided to take a chance and get an apartment together.

And she's been stuck with me ever since.

The stadium is up ahead, and we join the masses of blue-and-silver-wearing students filing in through the metal detectors. One of the workers scans my student ID and nods me through, and another peeks in my bag. And then we're in.

"We're meeting some of the dance team," Thalia says. "They're saving us seats."

She joined the dance team at the start of school and was immediately swallowed up by that crowd of girls. She's tried to take me along when they go out, and I keep wavering. Like I want to, but I can't. The only party I happened to find over the summer was insane. Obviously, it ended a bit differently than I thought it would.

Now, I prefer to stick to my pajamas and movies at night. And I've been keeping my head down as much as possible.

"Willow!" Thalia suddenly yells.

She pulls me forward faster, catching up with a blonde girl who's surrounded by others. My nerves buzz, a reminder that I have never had very many friends. So what if I socialize wrong? So what if they hate me on sight?

"Hey, Thalia!" The blonde hugs her, then seems to realize that Thalia is still attached to me "Oops, sorry. I'm Willow."

"This is my roommate, Aspen," Thalia introduces.

"Nice to meet you, Aspen." Willow gestures to the girls around her. "These are Violet, Jess, Amanda, and Michelle."

They all nod their greetings, but Amanda's gaze stays on me. Recognition floods through her, and my stomach twists. She was one of the girls I was talking to before we all drew cards.

"You were at the party," she says.

"I..."

"Erik throws some ragers, huh?"

We start walking toward whatever section they have seats in, and I glance at Amanda. The last time I saw her was just before the card draw. Although she doesn't seem to harbor any ill will that my stranger seemed more interested in me than her. Even after she went all gooey-eyed over him.

My stranger.

I bite my lip. I haven't thought about *him* in a while, although I've been keeping an eye out. Crown Point University seems to be just big enough to grant me the grace of avoiding him, though. The last thing I need or want is to see him and have that night thrown in my face.

"Are you a freshman?" Amanda asks. "I thought you were older..."

"I'm a junior." I frown and try to recall what I told her. "I transferred in this year."

"The dick was that good, huh?"

She says it so quietly, I have to do a double take. But she just smiles at me. And then her pace increases, until she's joining one of the other girls at the front of the group.

"Did you meet Amanda before?" Willow glances over her shoulder at Thalia and me. "She graduated last year, but she got a job on campus."

I force a smile. "Yeah, we met over the summer."

Thalia nudges me. "You good?"

"Perfectly fine."

We get to our section and head down the stairs. We're just off-center, to the right of the penalty boxes. The group keeps going lower, and lower, until they file into the first row.

Holy shit.

"Did these tickets cost anything?" I ask Thalia. "The student area is free, but that's..."

Not close to here. Nowhere as good as these seats either.

She chuckles. "Violet and Willow are both dating guys on the team, so they pulled some strings for the first game. Don't worry—after this game, we'll be slumming it in the student section. Unless we find guys to date who want to hook us up..."

I snort.

We take our seats, and I'm on the end. Which is totally fine, but I'm still fucking reveling that I'm this close to the action for my first game. I listen to Thalia chat with the other girls about the dance team and whatever practice they have coming up. That usually keeps her out of the apartment late some nights, but I'm glad she's finding her footing here.

Unlike me.

The players skate out onto the ice to begin their warm-ups, and one of the Crown Point Hawks players points to one of the girls in our row as he skates by.

"That's Greyson Devereux," Thalia explains. "He and Violet are together."

"Who else should I know?" I ask, leaning closer to her.

She hums and looks around. "Um, Knox Whiteshaw is the center, he and Willow are dating. Those four are seniors. Miles, his brother, is a junior. He's the goalie."

My gaze goes to the goalie, covered head to toe in gear. He seems comfortable catching the pucks flying his way, dropping them out of his way almost as soon as they touch his glove, or batting them aside with his stick.

"They had two seniors graduate last year who were starters," Willow says to us. "Knox said that a senior and a sophomore are starting tonight. Hudson Finch and Tony Rodrigues."

I met Finch. Briefly.

"And Steele," Amanda adds. "But you know him, Aspen."

I wet my lips. "Do I?"

Her eyes narrow. "Do you not remember? You guys pulled the cards..."

Oh, no.

"Steele O'Brien?" I question. "That's who..."

I'm going to be sick.

And then his jersey, with *O'Brien* across the back, flashes past me.

My stomach turns, and my skin goes clammy. I jump to my feet, thankful that I'm on the aisle. I rush up it and into the bathroom, barely making it to a toilet before I lose my dinner.

"I haven't seen that reaction before," Thalia says when I exit the stall. Her gaze stays on me as I cross to the sink and rinse my mouth out, spitting a few times. "Are you okay?"

"Yeah, um..." I straighten and turn to her. "I just wasn't expecting *him*, you know?"

"No, you lost me at your rather insane reaction to his name." She crosses her arms. "What's up?"

I shake my head. Nope, not going there. Not now anyway. My secrets will come out in due time. And Thalia already knows part of the story. I just don't feel like admitting to the rest of it at the moment.

"Let's pretend that didn't happen," I suggest. "And we can watch the game like nothing's wrong."

She sighs, twisting her long, light-brown hair in her fingers. She's got a Crown Point University blue sweatshirt on, same as me, and black leggings. Where she's petite, perfect for the dance team, I'm all curves. It doesn't really matter to me—it is what it is. I exercise when the mood strikes me, I eat just fine. The weight doesn't shift, though. No matter if I starve myself and exercise four times a week or fourteen.

So, the curves are here to stay, judgmental bitches be damned.

It's fine.

But it makes online clothes shopping a pain in the ass.

Anyway—besides *that*, we could be sisters. My two sisters already look more like her than me, pulling my mother's complexion. I got Mom's nose, and the rest seems to come from Dad's side of the family. Dark hair, pale skin with the tendency to freckle, green eyes, height...

We return to our seats, and Thalia murmurs something to her friends, an excuse for me rushing away. I ignore Amanda's questioning glances and remind myself that she's graduated. She's just here for the game.

So am I. And once it's over, I'm never going to another hockey game.

2

STEELE

"I'm pretty sure you're seeing things," Miles mumbles, following me into Haven.

We lost our game. Fucking spectacularly.

My plan is to get fucking blasted and go home. I could've just skipped the going out part and drank at home, but Miles and Knox are convincing assholes.

Knox and Greyson are ahead of us, first in the door, and they're greeted with cheers of support. More subdued than if we had won, but *damn it*. Our first game of the season, and we were as jumbled as newborn kittens.

"Coach is going to have our ass tomorrow," I warn. My job is to stop the puck before it gets to Miles, but it felt like getting hit with a freight train. Repeatedly.

"We can't win them all," Finch says, ever helpful. "They're one of the best teams in the league, it's just bad luck that we got them first..."

Miles groans. "Which makes it *worse*."

We get to the bar, and I lean against it until the bartender reappears. She smiles at me, sliding a beer my way. Then one to Miles, who definitely isn't old enough to drink. Not that anyone gives a fuck.

Haven isn't as thoroughly packed tonight. There's a sea of blue and silver, sure, and there are fans gathering around each teammate already. Less than five seconds after we walked in. And I'm really just sick of trying to put on a good face.

I scout out Greyson, who's having none of the bullshit either. He's in a corner booth with Violet and her friends, so I take my beer and head their way.

A weird sense of déjà vu washes over me a split second before I arrive at the table.

"Join us, O'Brien," Greyson offers. He points to the end seat across from him.

The horseshoe-shaped booths are nice for cramming in as many people as space will allow, and the girls dutifully shift to make room for me.

"Have you met our two new transfers, Steele?" Amanda asks, batting her eyes at me.

"I thought you graduated." I sip my beer.

Still, I take the bait and look at the girl sitting beside me. Long, light-brown hair. Blue eyes. Petite.

Then the other, sandwiched between Violet and Willow, is *her*.

My heart picks up speed, but I don't know how to react. She's not looking at me. Her eyes are glued to the table, to the pink drink in front of her. The harder I stare, the more she seems unwilling to acknowledge me.

Doesn't matter.

I know her all the same.

"Thalia Armitage," Violet is introducing, although her voice is registering like bees, but it snaps to surprising clarity when she says, "And Aspen Monroe."

Aspen.

Monroe.

A name I would never fucking forget.

And a face I *could* never forget.

Immediately, the hatred rises in my chest. It's fucking suffocating, but I don't know what to do. My instinct is to drag her over the table and out the bar, throwing her to the curb.

That instinct is contained—*barely*.

I need to leave. I need to get the fuck out of here before I do something stupid.

But then she looks up at me, and those perfect green eyes of hers burn into my soul. And she's just as magnetic as the first time I met her. It's not meant to be like this. I shouldn't be attracted to her and want to hurt her in the same breath.

"Can I get out?" she asks Violet, her voice so fucking raspy.

It goes straight to my dick.

Violet nods, and her and Greyson rise to let her slide out.

I turn and watch her stride across the bar, in the direction of the bathroom. Her full ass sways with every step, looking damn good in those jeans.

"You okay, man?" Greyson asks me.

I shake my head slowly and stand. I know something similar happened between them. Violet and Greyson. That damn bathroom is where everything started for them.

But that's not what's going to happen with Aspen. I'm going in there to fucking finish it.

I follow her without a thought and push into the women's bathroom. She's at the sink, scrubbing her hands, and her head shoots up at the sound of my entrance. I duck down to check for feet in the stalls, then lock the door.

"What are you doing?"

I hate her voice. I hate her voice. I hate her voice. Say it enough times, and it may become true.

"You remember me." I stalk forward. "Yes?"

"Y-yes." Her eyes go all wide, darting around. "From the party. From—"

"The lake house," I finish. "But you know me from somewhere else, don't you?"

She winces.

It's confirmation enough.

I reach out and wind my fingers into her hair at the base of her neck, more surprised than anything when she doesn't bat me away. No, she lets me grip her and tilt her head back.

"Tell me," I whisper in her ear. "What was it like living in my house? Enjoying my family's money?"

Her breathing is her giveaway. It's rough, shallow. Her chest rises and falls too quickly. And I'm fucking turned on by her, by her reactions.

"Are you a student here, Aspen?" I asked her the same question over the summer. If she was a student. If, before I showed her my secrets, I had any chance of seeing her again. Because if she had said yes, it would've been an entirely different night.

There's still a possibility that she's visiting friends. But from the CPU sweatshirt hiding her tits from me, and the blue makeup on her eyelids, I'd say the evidence that she's a student here is damning.

"I transferred in," she whispers.

"Why?"

"B-because..." Her gaze crashes into mine, and some of her fight comes back.

I don't know where it comes from, or why, but suddenly she's pushing back against me. Her silky hair slips through my grasp, and she forces me back a step.

"Your daddy is paying for it," she finally answers, her lip curling. "In exchange for watching out for you."

I laugh. Because it's fucking *funny* that Dad marries a gold digger with three kids, and now one of them is going to be shadowing me. Feeding back information to him? About me, and what I do, where I go?

"A spy," I repeat.

She lifts her chin. "Don't say I didn't warn you."

I sneer. "I'll give you a warning in return, then."

I step closer, knocking her hands aside. She's pinned between the sink and my body, and she grips the edge of the counter instead of touching me. Except for where my hips press into hers, my thighs on her legs.

"Every day you stay at CPU, your life will get worse." I run my finger down her jaw, and a spark of pleasure goes through me when she jerks her head away. "If you leave, it all stops. But if you stay... I'm going to have so much fun tormenting you, sweetheart. Fucking count on that."

I step back, and she sags against the sink. Her gaze is hot on my back, but she doesn't seem inclined to snap back. Maybe my threat will be enough to hold her at bay.

But I do know this much: she's going to be begging to drop out by the time I'm through with her.

3
ASPEN

I tell Thalia everything. That my mom spontaneously got married at the beginning of the summer to a guy she met in Vegas, that she moved me and my two sisters into the rich fucker's house. That her new husband has two sons, neither of which showed up over the summer... and then the worst part.

That he offered me the chance to go to CPU, which wasn't exactly a dream school of mine, but he was offering to *pay*. Mom urged me to take the chance, because I worked my ass off to pay my way through community college. She said graduating from college debt-free is a gift that not many twenty-somethings get, and I should take advantage. Especially when I never got off the waitlist from my top choice.

But this gift came with strings:

That I should find my way into his son's good graces.

That I should answer when he calls, answer his questions, and... well, *spy*, as Steele so elegantly put it.

It made me sick, and that was before I ever set foot on the CPU campus.

"Wow," Thalia says, flopping back on my bed. "That's twisted."

"They clearly don't have a relationship," I mumble.

She grunts her agreement.

"So... I have to spy on a guy who hates me."

She glances at me. "Do you think he meant the part about tormenting you?"

I shrug. If he did, I'll just have to bear it. Steele's a senior —he's graduating this year. Which means *my* senior year will be easy. I just need to get through two years of college, and then I'll be home free. If I can get a job with an orchestra before then, I'll drop out and leave everything behind.

Except...

"He said his goal was to get me to drop out."

"And?"

I frown. "Now that he said it, I want to do the opposite."

She laughs. "Of course you do. Okay, we should get up. We're going to be late." She pats my leg and sits up.

I heave another sigh—dramatic, yes—and follow her into the bathroom. We do our makeup side by side, and she moves over so I can brush my teeth. My nerves are a mess. I don't do well with threats, I never have. He makes me anxious.

Which is probably exactly what he wants.

Back in my room, I grab dark jeans and an olive-green sweatshirt. I put in little earrings and clip up the top half of my hair, pulling the loose ends over my shoulders. A neck-lace, a few rings, and I'm ready.

Thalia waits for me by the door, her bag slung over her shoulder. "Ready for battle?"

"As I'll ever be," I answer lightly.

The nerves get worse when I'm on campus. But I make

it through my first two classes, then the last of the day. Everything is... normal. No weird looks, no out-of-the-ordinary texts.

It isn't until I get to the student center with Thalia that the dread picks up again. Because Steele is lounging against the entrance to the dining hall, an apple in his hand. And when he spots me, he slowly straightens.

"Uh-oh," Thalia murmurs. "Um, do you need backup?"

"Nope, let's ignore him."

I get as far as holding my ID out to the dining hall worker—but before she can take it, he snatches it out of my fingers. I turn to him, my jaw dropping. He's already striding away.

Gritting my teeth, I face the worker.

"Sorry, honey, I can't let you in without swiping. It's policy." She seems apologetic... but completely unmoving.

Thalia is already inside, and she takes a step in my direction.

I hold up my hand. "It's okay," I call. "I'll go get it."

He's disappeared through the doors to the stairwell, and I march after him. I hear his footsteps on the landing above me once I'm in it, the sound echoing down to me. I hurry after him and round the landing between the floors.

I almost bowl right into him, and he grabs my shoulders.

His smile is alarming. On the edge of cruel. And he walks me back to the edge of the step I just walked up, until my heels are off it.

"Maybe I should just push you down the stairs and be done with you," he muses, almost to himself.

I grab his wrists. "You wouldn't."

He shoves my shoulders back, and I yelp. Only my grip

on his wrists keeps me from tumbling. The noise bounces around us as he drags me forward again.

"I could, though." He sneers. "Right now, you're at my mercy. Wouldn't you agree?"

"Nothing compared to you at mine," I counter.

"Is your rags-to-riches story worth a year of suffering?" He tilts his head. His fingers move up, catching on the strap of my bag. And in an instant, he has it off my arm.

I lunge for it, but he blocks me. He seems completely unbothered as he unzips it one-handed and tips the contents out.

Books, sheet music, notebooks. Loose papers from class. Pens and pencils I had just left at the bottom, not bothering to shove them in a case. It all comes tumbling out.

The notebooks and books slide down the stairs, thumping with every step.

The papers go *everywhere*. Some slip through the railings and flutter all the way down.

He steps on one. One of the pages of sheet music I was planning on learning this week. He picks it up and squints at it, a scowl forming.

"What do you play?"

"Piano," I say, crossing my arms and backing away from the ledge. I only stop when my ass hits the railing against the wall. "Why do you care?"

He shakes his head. "I don't. Just gathering ammunition."

My throat closes. His gaze lingers on me, dropping down to my breasts.

"Show me your tits," he orders.

"What?"

He drops the sheet music and moves toward me slowly, his fingers deftly undoing his belt.

"Show me your tits, Aspen, and I won't piss on your backpack." He points to the bag at his feet. "Clock's ticking..."

I close my eyes and shove my shirt up. Anyone could come into the stairwell and witness this.

"Bra," he says, but it comes out on a sharp exhale. "Take your fucking bra off."

I open my eyes—and my mouth, ready to retort—when I notice that his cock is in his hand. And his hand is currently sliding up and down its impressive length. His thumb runs over the tip with every pass, smearing the precum that leaks out.

Why is he turned on by this?

Better question—*why am I?*

My fingers shake as I reach behind me and unclasp my bra. It takes a second to get it off my arms, then it falls to the floor. He stares at me with an intense expression, all the fire in his gaze that I remember from the party mixed with anger. He's closer to me, too. If I wanted, I could reach out and touch him. But I don't, so I curl my fingers around the railing and wait.

My nipples pebble in the cool air, and a chill sweeps up my back.

He tugs harder on his dick, and I open my mouth to ask what the fuck the reasoning behind this is. But then he groans, and his cock jerks. His cum spills out, hitting my bare skin. Ropes of it cross my stomach, my bare breasts. He gets it on the waistband of my jeans and on my shirt, not that he gives a shit.

He smirks, nodding to me, and before I can move, he has his phone out.

He takes a picture of me.

I make a noise in the back of my throat and tug my shirt

down, ignoring how it feels to slide against the wetness on my skin. The fabric immediately sticks. I pull my sweatshirt down, too, and reach for my bra.

Steele's foot lands on it a second before I can grab it.

"That's mine," he says.

I scowl at him, but he bends down and snags it, folding the material and tucking it into his own bag, which sits out of harm's way on the stairs above.

"I need my ID back," I finally say, because I don't even know *where* to start with him. The picture, the backpack, the complete insanity of this moment...

He pulls it from his pocket and tosses it at my feet, a smug smile secured on his stupid fucking face. He blows me a kiss and heads down the steps, kicking more of my things down as he goes. Above us, the door on the second-floor crashes open.

"We should do this again sometime," Steele calls over his shoulder.

"In your dreams," I retort. Because, damn it. I walked right into this—and then let it happen. Like a freaking moron.

Next time, I'll be smarter. I'll do better.

I've got to, or else he really will run me out of this school.

Hours later, I trudge into the dining hall for dinner with a mixture of foreboding and anticipation. The dance team and hockey team both have practice, which means this is the perfect time to sneak in, eat, and run back to the library.

This afternoon, I made the disgraced walk back home, hoping that no one could tell that my bra was missing, or that I smelled like a cheap whore. I'd never taken as hot of a shower as I did today, scrubbing my skin eight times before finally getting out.

The embarrassed part of me wanted to stay home. But unfortunately, I have a paper due that requires more than just a textbook. Which means: library.

"Can I sit?"

I look up from my plate of food. A guy stands in front of me, plate and drink in hand. He's cute and vaguely familiar...

"We met at the party at Erik's," he offers.

I snap my fingers. He's the one Steele scared away.

"Sure," I agree.

He sets his stuff down and drags the chair out across from me, dropping into it with a smile. "Chase King," he introduces, extending his hand. "Aspen, right?"

"Yep. Monroe." I take his hand and shake it, my cheeks heating. When's the last time a guy shook my hand? "What brings you to my neck of the woods?"

He grins. "I saw a beautiful girl sitting by herself. Isn't that reason enough?"

"Nope." I set down my fork and lean forward. "Pretty sure that's just judging a book by its cover, don't you think? That was outlawed a few years back."

He's got blond hair and piercing blue eyes. The type of guy who girls like me are *supposed* to fall for. The popular football player with the heart of gold, or whatever.

"I hate to break it to you, Aspen, but everybody still judges books by their covers. It's simple marketing." He braces his forearms on the table. "But *why* are you sitting alone, is the question?"

"My roommate is at dance." *And I haven't made any more friends*.

He nods. "Yeah, mine decided to hit the gym after practice. Our coach was not pleased with their performance."

"But he was with yours?"

"Of course." He pauses and glances around. "This is a little off the cuff, but I was wondering if you'd want to get coffee with me tomorrow morning?"

I sit up straighter. "Why?"

"Because we had a conversation going at Erik's party before O'Brien snatched you away." His eyes darken. "And I was hoping to reignite that conversation..."

The blush that is probably taking over my whole face is hot. I swallow carefully, not sure how to respond. Did I have an okay time at the party before Steele showed up? Yes. Did the little card game with Steele make it better? Yes. Did I *like* that Steele scared him away? *Unfortunately, yes.*

"You let Steele scare you off," I reply instead. "What happens if he tries again?"

Chase shakes his head. "I was a dumbass. It won't happen again."

I extend my hand again. "Okay, deal."

"Deal?"

"I'll get coffee with you tomorrow as long as Steele doesn't *chase* you off."

"Puns," he murmurs. He takes my hand again. This time, he doesn't shake it. He just holds onto it and squeezes gently.

And it's nothing like how Steele O'Brien would touch me. The exact opposite, if we're being honest.

Why does that disappoint me?

4
STEELE

I can't stop thinking about her.

What she's doing.

What she's thinking.

What she's wearing.

Her fucking glorious tits, her wide eyes—

I punch the bag in front of me harder, driving into it with everything I have. As if that'll make it better. As if that'll solve my problems and make my brain stop working in overdrive. But now I've started dreaming about her under me. The feel of her neck in my grip, the little breathy sounds she made when she struggled.

My dick is hard in an instant, and I stop moving. I look down at it, clenching my jaw.

She was made for me. Her reactions, following my orders, her fear. She's made to *tempt* me—it's like my father fucking knew that when he married her mother. When he brought her into the house that my mother lived in, the house my mother raised me in, and let her take over.

That's why I didn't go home this summer. Because I

sure as hell didn't need to see evidence of that woman's takeover.

And now he's sent her siren daughter to spy on me. To feed information back to him, because apparently my communication with him isn't enough. Our relationship is too strained, too muddled from our past for anything like trust to exist between us.

Bet he's regretting giving me access to my inheritance at the humble age of eighteen.

My brother, Blake, is nineteen. Two years younger than me. He's at school on the West Coast, playing football for a division one school. We haven't been close in a long time, but I imagine he took his money and ran, too.

I straighten, an idea bursting into existence in my brain. The spy can be threatened, tormented—but I need more dirt on her. More than just a photo of her breasts on my phone.

When I told her to show them to me, I didn't think I'd do much more than take a picture to distribute. But then I *saw* them, and the fury in her eyes as she did what I said, and I changed my mind.

Coming on her wasn't part of the plan either, but if I need to assure the world she's a whore, this would do it. The stairwell is dim, but it's obvious where we were. And what we were doing.

I unwrap my hands and leave the stadium gym. It's almost two o'clock in the morning, and the moon is high. Sleep is a long way off, per usual. I don't know what it is about the darkness that's so alluring—and what it is about sleep that's so repulsive.

Exiting the stadium—the gym here is better than the one on campus—I head back toward the hockey house. But my feet carry me past it, to the quiet row of brownstones a few blocks over. I stop in front of Aspen's, my lips curling at the light on in one of the bedrooms.

Is she a night owl like me?

Or is it her roommate?

I followed her back here the other day, knowing she'd scurry home to change and get my scent off her. She's got a first-floor apartment—nice for moving in, not so good for security purposes.

The light goes out, and her form passes by the window.

I give her an hour to fall asleep and then I push away from the shadows across the street. Her window is cracked, letting in the breeze. The screen pops out easily when I slide my pocket knife along the edge of the frame, loosening the catch. I put it on the ground and drop my bag beside it. I peer into her dark room, eyeing the shape of her, in the bed against the wall.

Luckily, the space in front of her window is clear, and I vault in with ease.

My footsteps are light on her rug, but I pause nonetheless.

Her soft breathing fills the room.

I stride closer and stare down at her. I can barely make out her features in the darkness, even with the streetlights illuminating her room with a pale, warm light. I reach out and run my finger down her bare arm, and she shivers.

My stomach swoops.

My cock goes hard, pressing against my shorts.

Instead of doing exactly what I want with her, I step back and glance around her room. I turn on the flashlight on my phone and shine it around. A desk and chair, which seems to be a catch-all for clothes. Her backpack that I threatened earlier, once again packed with whatever she carries around.

On the desk are her keys.

An idea occurs to me, and I carefully pick them up. There's only a few keys—probably one to the front door of the brownstone, then the apartment, and who knows what else—but I go to the window and drop them out to collect later.

She lets out a breathy sigh, and my willpower fractures. I slide the blanket down her body, stopping at her hips. When she doesn't move, I lift her shirt. Her breasts are plump, round. Her nipples immediately stiffen, and I run my finger over one of them.

I wasn't going to...

My control completely shatters, though, and I yank the blankets the rest of the way off. She's not wearing shorts or pajama bottoms like I would've guessed—just fucking panties.

I roll her onto her back, somewhat surprised that she doesn't wake up, and part her pretty legs. I drop my shorts to the floor. My heart is pounding out of my chest, tight with anticipation, as I crawl over her. I slide her panties to the side, and the tip of my cock touches the apex of her legs.

She's wet. *Soaked*. For no fucking reason.

She's asleep.

That pisses me off.

She should only be wet when she's thinking about me —not whoever is starring in her dream. I look down at her cunt. Did she rub herself to orgasm before she fell asleep? I pick up her hand, lifting it to my nose. Her fingers curl around mine, and I sniff. Then lick the pad of her index finger, just for the hell of it.

Aspen squirms, her hips shifting, and my dick rubs against her clit.

I move it lower, notching at her entrance. Pushing in

just enough to keep it in place as I capture her wrists in one hand and cover her mouth with the other. So slowly, so carefully, that she doesn't wake up.

Until I drop my full weight on her, my hips pinning hers into place. My fingers dig into her cheek, and she inhales sharply when she registers what's happening.

Her legs try to close, but I'm right there.

"Do you remember your safe word?" I look into her wide eyes.

She's still for a moment, maybe still trying to piece together what's happening. But then her head jerks up and down.

"Say it." I lift my hand from her mouth, wrapping it around her throat instead. "Tell me."

She licks her lips. "Fire."

I never understood why she picked that—but I'll ask another time.

Right now, I need to be inside her.

"Do you want me to fuck you?" I ask her.

She shakes her head. *No.*

Good.

I thrust forward, and her pretty eyes roll back at the sudden intrusion. Her body bows up off the bed to meet mine, but it's her cunt that I'm focused on. The way her hot, silky muscles clamp down on my length.

The last girl I was inside was *her*. Over the summer. Six fucking months ago.

I draw out and ram back into her, judging her reaction. She seems caught between anger and lust, and she's not doing enough to make me stop.

"Fight me," I growl in her ear. I drag my teeth down the side of her neck. She smells sweet. As delectable as a dessert. "Come on, little viper. Fucking *fight me.*"

My teeth sink into her neck at the same time that I rock my hips forward again.

She groans. The sound is music to my fucking ears, but I don't give a shit about her own pleasure. Especially if she already got off tonight without me.

So this has to be more unpleasant for her. A punishment instead of a reward.

I pull out of her so fast, she cries out.

But I'm not done.

I haul her up with me and shove her toward the window. She catches herself on the sill and meets my eyes over her shoulder, her eyes hooded. The window is open. The screen is off. It's the middle of the night, but who knows what noises are going to come out of her mouth?

I smack her ass.

She jumps forward, and I haul her back again. My grip on her hips steadies her, and I strike her again. My palm fucking stings, but I keep going until her knees buckle. She sinks to the floor, and I follow her.

Always fucking following her.

My hand on her back, between her shoulder blades, forces her the rest of the way. We're in the strip of light coming through the window from the streetlight, and her pale, smooth skin is glowing. Her cheek touches the carpet, her hands press to the floor on either side of her head. She makes a low noise when I slide into her again, my cock now so hard it's painful. There are marks on her ass. Handprints.

She never answered my question about birth control.

I thought about that after I left the party. How I asked and she didn't reply.

Guess we'll find out.

My balls tighten, and I lean farther over her. My weight keeps her pinned, and I chase my release. It's pleasure to the point of pain, and I groan when my climax hits. I still inside her, filling her with my cum.

"No condom," I whisper in her ear, when the residual tremors have subsided. When I can form words again.

I pull out and find my shorts, dragging them up over my wet length. I have half a mind to make her lick it clean, but she hasn't moved from her position on the floor. I stare down at her for a second, my head tilting.

"Roll over," I say.

She moves slowly. Methodically. Muscles bunching, weight shifting. She ends up on her back. Her eyes are filled with tears.

She looks so fucking perfect like that. With my cum in her pussy, already leaking out. Her expression is broken.

"I'll do this to you every night," I promise her. "I'll be your own personal demon."

"Why?"

"Because you're the enemy." *Simple.*

I step over her and straddle the windowsill, casting one long look back at her. This is the last time I'll take the window, that's for fucking sure. Because this is the last time she'll leave it unlocked.

But that's okay. I have her keys, and I'll make copies. I'll sneak in when she's away and imprint myself in this entire fucking apartment, just to make sure she'll never escape me.

I put the screen back, leaving her to close the glass from the other side. I pocket her keys and sling my bag over my shoulder, and I smile to myself. Satisfied for the first time in six fucking months.

5
ASPEN

I miss a note for the seventeenth time. The same fucking note.

I slam my hands on the keys, and the sound is harsh. Loud in the small practice room. I do it again, trying not to flinch this time. It doesn't work, so I let the sound fade into silence. The room is still, everything paused, except for my ragged breathing.

Steele has me rattled.

I check my phone and scan the email I received this morning from his father, asking for an update. He hasn't received a reply back from his last two emails—because I'd been too busy avoiding any mention of Steele O'Brien without actually knowing who he was. But now, if I don't give him something, then he'll have no choice but to stop payments next semester.

I'm an *investment*, and those often get cut if they're not turning a profit.

The threat isn't even fucking veiled.

But I can't tell him something about Steele that I don't know, so I type a quick reply to give him the basics. He goes to hockey practice, he goes to classes. He doesn't flirt with any girls or go to any parties.

It's not going to be enough.

I toss my phone on top of my bag, out of my reach on the floor, and take a deep breath. And then I run through the piece again, from the top.

And I miss the note again.

I rise suddenly, the bench tipping over. I grab the sheet music and rip the pages from the stand. They flutter to the floor around me. Tears burn my eyes, and a lump forms in my throat. Before I know it, the sob wrenches out of me.

"Aspen?"

I whirl around.

Chase stands on the other side of the door, visible through the glass.

I wipe hurriedly at the tears on my cheeks, but it's too late. I open the door for him—you have to fill out a form for access to the music practice rooms, and I wouldn't suppose he has that. He frowns and enters the room, kneeling and righting the bench.

"Sit down," he murmurs.

I follow his directions. My eyes still feel wet. I pull up one of my legs and wrap my arms around it. He picks up the papers, stacking them and setting them on top of the piano. He stays on his knees, his brow furrowed.

The longer I look at him, the more I realize something is wrong with *him*, too.

"What happened?" My voice comes out hoarse and scratchy. I've always had a deeper, raspier voice, but this just makes it worse.

"Your knight in shining armor."

I flinch.

He scoffs, rising and brushing invisible dust off his

jeans. "O'Brien is tactical. He's just implemented another move in his war, and the same probably goes for whatever he's done to make you cry."

Breaking into my room and fucking me is *tactical*? I open and close my mouth, then shake my head. It would be insane if I blurted that out—and it would lead to questions about the party. Drawing the joker was stupid, I thought it then and I know for certain now.

Why did I do that?

When Chase showed me his card, the black nine, my gut reaction was that it was *boring*. That nine is middle of the road. Not high, not low, just... there. Not kinky, not vanilla. And I really didn't want that.

I still don't.

But when Chase sits beside me and wraps his arm around my shoulder... I don't mind it so much. I don't mind that he's safe—even if he doesn't feel safe.

I let out a shuddering breath, and my tears stop, and finally, Chase releases me.

"Dinner?" He stands and waits for a moment, then holds out his hand.

I hesitate. I can't even look him in the eye, focusing on his white shoes. They're really white. Impressively so. Like he's never accidentally stepped in a puddle, or cut across the quad after it's been freshly mowed, or stepped off the sidewalk. Ever.

So maybe that's why, ultimately, I lie. "My roommate and I are going off campus, otherwise I would."

He nods and moves backward. "No problem, Aspen. I'll let you get back to practice."

The door clicks shut in his wake. I take a deep breath. I stare at the keys, the music, for another minute. Completely still. It's like I'm locked into place, my muscles turned to stone.

Music has always been my source of comfort. My safe place. When I'm sad, when I'm lonely, when I'm scared. If I can play, if I can listen to it, then everything else fades away. It's been my retreat for so long.

But it's not working today.

Playing anyway.

I collect my things and shove them back in my bag. I have rather excellent headphones at home. The kind that go over your whole ear and block out the rest of the world. I'll put on my playlist of instrumental music that doesn't drive me crazy, I'll lie on my bed... and I'll try to forget.

I'm halfway home when my spine tingles.

I glance over my shoulder, my gaze sweeping the street. It's getting dark—the sun is setting earlier now, and even though it's only six o'clock, the sky's light is fading fast. The streetlight over my head flickers on, and I check behind me again.

A car pulls out of its spot on the curb, and fear sweeps through me. It doubles when the car rolls to a stop parallel to me, and the passenger window lowers.

My uncle sits at the wheel. He leans onto the console to meet my gaze, and his eyebrow lifts.

"What are you doing here?" I shift my weight, deciding how best to play this.

Best way to describe my uncle? He's from the bowels of Chicago. As the stories go, he grew up fighting on the streets, running drugs, making friends with gangs. He's a mobster's worst nightmare and best friend, because he can do things that ordinary people can't.

When I think of monsters, I think of my father first, and my uncle second.

There's a *clunk* of the car's locks opening, and he shoves open the passenger door. "Get in, babydoll."

"I…"

"Don't make me force you, Aspen." His voice has gone cold.

I obey, sliding into the car. The seats are black leather, the windows tinted. As soon as I'm in, the locks reengage and the window climbs upward. It darkens the already dark interior.

"Your daddy wanted me to deliver this to you. Said he owed it to you." He reaches in the back and withdraws a brown paper sack, setting it on my lap. It's heavy, but the edges are rounded. Whatever it is, he must've wrapped it in something to protect it.

"I don't talk to him, Uncle," I say in a low voice.

He huffs. "You're older. You're as safe as can be from him. Now that you're at a fancy college and being bankrolled by a corporation."

I grimace.

The car is moving. I barely grip the package in my lap, just enough to keep it from sliding off. After a moment, he stops at the curb in front of my brownstone.

"Get going," he grunts. "I'll be in Boston until the end of the week, then the city after that. You need anything, you call me."

"Got it." I reach for the door handle.

His hand comes down on my forearm, and I automatically freeze in place. But then the overhead light floods on, and he grips my chin with his other hand. Pulling my face around, staring into my eyes. His are a deep blue, his hair dark brown like mine. He looks like my father, so I guess in turn he looks like me.

"People giving you trouble?"

"No," I lie.

He narrows his eyes, and he waits a moment. Under his rough exterior, I think maybe he did care. Or does care. It's hard to tell—it seems to come in waves.

My father only pretended to care about my mother. He married her because he knocked her up, and then he showed his true colors.

I yank free from his grasp and step out onto the sidewalk, closing the door quickly behind me. I spare only a moment of worry that he knows exactly where I live. The car idles, and I dig through my bag for my keys.

Keys that are most certainly not there.

"Problem, Asp?" My uncle is out of the car, leaving it idling. He bounds up the steps to stop just below me.

Out of the car, he might be even more intimidating. Tall, covered in tattoos, with a hard set of his brow. The kind of guy who doesn't take shit from anyone.

I shift my weight. "I don't know where my keys are. But it's okay, I'll just call my roommate—"

He waves me off and nudges me aside. He has something in his hands, two slim silver tools, and a moment later, the door swings inward.

"Your apartment door, too?"

I eye him. His tattoos crawl up his neck, framing his jaw. He *looks* like he could be in the mob. He disappears inside my building, and I have no choice but to follow him. Definitely not if I want to get in without calling Thalia. We stride past the rows of mailboxes, the stairs to the upper levels, to my apartment door.

"Why are you helping me?" I blurt out. I've seen him more recently than Dad. He's kept tabs on us over the years, finding us when even Dad couldn't. I suspect it's because

Mom wanted to keep one of the Monroe brothers close. Better him than Dad, that's for sure.

He glances at me, then at the package in my hand.

My fingers tighten on it.

"You may think you're like your mother," he says carefully, not meeting my eyes. "But some would say you're more like your daddy's side of the family."

I grimace. "I'm not."

"Your sisters are not," he retorts. "Your sisters are soft. You..."

I'm the softest of them all.

He gets the door unlocked and holds it open, his arm high enough that I can duck under it. "First-floor apartments are dangerous," he says. "You should secure your windows."

Yeah, right.

"Did you leave your keys in here?"

"I'm sure I did." I spent about as long as I could waste this morning searching for them, but that didn't mean much. I have a habit of misplacing them. "Thanks for the ride."

He nods, still eyeing me funny, and releases his hold on the door. "Remember to call if you need—"

"I will," I assure him.

The door shuts between us, and I let out a breath. I lock it again, even though he just proved that's a useless endeavor to keep him out. Then I get to work turning on all the lights in the apartment. I set the package down on the counter, my bag beside it, and keep moving toward my bedroom. I'm tired enough to go right to bed, anything to do with my dad be damned—and dinner, too.

"Who was that?"

I shriek as Steele comes out of the shadows of my room.

He smirks, stepping up and helping me remove my jacket the rest of the way. He pushes it off my shoulders and lets it drop off my arms. It hits the floor with a muted thump.

My heart is going a million times a minute.

And then he's moving away, flicking on the overhead light. When he closes the door and leans against it, my stomach knots.

"What do you want?"

His eyebrow lifts. "I *want* to know who that was."

I shrug.

"Aspen."

"Steele."

His eyes narrow.

"Why are you in my room?" It occurs to me that *this* sort of behavior is what his dad might be interested in. What if Steele has a history of stalking? And that's why his dad was worried? "Are you stalking me?"

He laughs. "Yeah, Aspen, I'm stalking you. And doing a pretty poor fucking job of it, since you've 'caught' me twice." He pushes off the wall and steps into my space, his fingers curling in the front of my t-shirt. "Have you talked to my father?"

My hesitation gives me away.

His hold only tightens. "Who's the stalker now?"

"I didn't tell him anything good," I retort. "I didn't tell him that you snuck into my room and fucked me against my will—"

"You're into that, remember?" He runs his nose up the side of my face, into my hair. The action is so sudden, so surprising, that I let it happen. "You have a safe word, little viper."

"Why do you call me that?"

He chuckles. "Because you're going to be the death

of me."

My eyes shut of their own accord—until he releases my shirt and grips my chin instead. It's too similar to my uncle, and I shove against him.

His expression lights up.

I tear my face away and stumble back, holding my hand up. "Can you not be psycho?"

"You fight me and I like it," he answers. "It makes me want to hurt you."

Fear and a sudden burst of desire wind through me. The combination urges me to do something. To run, to flee. There's nowhere to go. Not here anyway, with Steele between me and the door.

"Why do you want to hurt me?"

He eyes me. "This isn't normal. You know that, right?"

"I know."

He hums. And then he opens his phone and shows me the photo he took. Of my exposed breasts, the cum across my skin. "I thought of sharing this around, but I'm too selfish for it. I don't want anyone else to see your breasts. I don't want them to see any of your skin, because they'll think of your hard little nipples. They'll think about palming your tits, pinching those nipples they can't stop staring at, rolling them between their fingers and tugging until you scream."

"No one's thinking about my breasts." I cross my arms and narrow my eyes, trying desperately to hide my body's reaction to his words. "It's not like I can control what other people think anyway. People should just mind their own business."

His eyes are dark. He's brimming with energy, and my gaze roves over him. Dark jeans, socks. He must've kicked off his shoes somewhere, made himself right at home.

White t-shirt that fits his chiseled body to perfection. The tattoos on his arm stand out, a flower on his biceps, a wolf on his upper forearm, a pine tree forest that finishes near his wrist. That's not to mention the linework that peeks out from the collar of his shirt. The ones on his chest that I haven't seen yet.

My mouth waters.

"Punishment," Steele suddenly says.

I snap to attention, my lips parting. "What? Why?"

He shakes his head. "Not now. If I catch someone looking at you like they want to fuck you—"

"No one is going to look at me like that," I snap. "Because I'm invisible. Because I'm not as pretty—"

"You're fucking gorgeous," Steele answers.

The volume shocks me into silence.

He shakes his head, muttering something. About a bad idea, maybe, I don't know. But then he lunges for me.

I squeal and try to dodge him, but it does nothing. He drives me into the floor like he's a freaking linebacker and pins me down. He straddles my hips and sits up, staring down at me with an intense expression.

He grips the front of my shirt, at the collar. His knuckles brush my throat. He winks—and then the *rip* sound fills the room.

My shirt tears in half, and I stare up at him in shock. His fingers go to my bra, to the front hook—*small prayers for a front-closing bra*—and undoes it like he's undone a million of them.

My breasts spill out.

He immediately cups them. My nipples are already hard, and he pinches them just like he described. The pain is nothing compared to the ache between my legs. If anything, it enhances it.

"Why?" I grit out, squirming under him.

"Because you're beautiful. Because you're sin. Because you're a distraction. And I've never hated anyone more than you," he confesses. He leans forward and presses his lips to my chest.

I suck in a breath. And I think of him. I think of my past. My parents—my mother. His father's threats. It's all confessions caught in my throat, but I don't want to tell him any of it. So instead, I unbuckle his pants. I push them down just enough to free his cock and wrap my fingers around it, tugging sharply.

He groans, his lips still on my skin. Lips, teeth, tongue.

I stroke him faster, letting my nails dig into his skin. Hoping it hurts him just a little.

Or a lot.

"I hate you, too," I breathe.

"No, you don't," he accuses. "You don't hate me nearly enough yet."

He shifts lower, and his dick slips out of my hold. He kisses his way between my breasts, down my sternum. When he reaches my stomach, I suck in my breath. My stomach is soft, round. There are stretch marks that stand out silvery against my pale skin.

"Breathe," he orders, glancing up to look me in the eye. "There will be a time when you won't be able to, little viper. Like when I force my cock down your throat. So take what oxygen you can now."

I don't want to breathe.

I don't want him to see me naked—all the way naked.

Somehow, that night at the party felt like a cheat code had been entered into my brain. And last night, I didn't think about how he may have been judging my body. But right now it's all I can think about.

He drags my leggings off my hips. I lift a little, helping him move the material past my bruised ass. He pulls them all the way off, my panties with them, and spreads my legs.

"What are you doing?" I sit up and push his face away. "Stop."

He growls. "What?"

"*Stop*, I said." I press my thighs together.

His face was right there.

My face is too hot.

"You're okay with me fucking you, but not going down on you?" He shakes his head. "Fine."

He shifts to his knees and grabs his cock, stroking it. He moves to the edge of the bed and parts his legs. Giving me an even better view of him. "Come here."

I start to rise.

"No," he interrupts. "No, Aspen. Crawl to me."

My face burns.

I watch him, waiting for the punchline. Or the smile. But it doesn't come. He just jerks himself off maddeningly slow.

"Crawl. To. Me."

Fuck.

There's no blackmail here. There's no physical force. But I feel the weight of his order sitting on my chest as clearly as his hand around my throat.

This is punishment. For not giving him what he wanted. For not lying there and letting him lick—

My heart hammers, and I drop to my hands and knees. My head stays down, my gaze locked on the floor, as I crawl across my room to him. I ignore that my panties are still caught around my ankles, that my shirt and bra are loose on either side of my body. My breasts hang down. It's embarrassing.

Shameful.

I don't stop until I see his socked feet, and his hand curls under my chin. He guides my face up, and I glare up at him from my position on the floor.

Then my lips part, and the head of his cock is slipping between my teeth.

I swirl my tongue around him, furious at myself for getting into this position. Furious for letting him humiliate me like this.

His hand leaves my chin and moves to the side of my head. His fingers slide into my hair, and he grunts when I take more of him in my mouth. I let my teeth trail along his shaft for a moment, and his grip on my hair tightens almost painfully.

I don't bite him, though. I suck, and my cheeks hollow out. He moves my head back and forth, fucking my mouth but forcing me to do the work. I choke and gag when he hits the back of my throat. Spit drips out of my open mouth, trailing down his shaft. He rocks his hips forward and goes farther into my throat. Then again, and deeper.

I squeeze his thighs. Dig my nails into his jeans.

His assault goes on and on, until my jaw aches and my mind stops working. Until I think he may keep me here forever.

But then he tugs on my hair—and that's the only warning I get.

He comes, lodging himself so deep in my throat that I have to swallow around him or choke. I hate every second of it—but I don't taste it until he pulls out and rubs the tip against my tongue.

As soon as he's free of me, I fall away and barely manage to snag the trash can by my desk. Before he can stop me, I stick my fingers down my throat. My stomach contracts, and I puke into the can. All his cum mixed with bile. I'd have more if I had eaten, but I feel strangely proud that I was able to eradicate him so quickly. I gag again and spit.

I set it aside and wipe my mouth on the back of my hand.

"Fuck," he groans. "You're so fucking stubborn."

He stands and adjusts himself, dropping something that was in his fist. With a start, I realize it was a pair of panties from my hamper that he used to clean his cock off.

"I came here to return these, since you lost them." He reveals my keys that were in his pocket and tosses them onto my bed, then heads for the door. "But that was so much better. Except, you're not angry enough, Aspen. You think you hate me, but you don't know the meaning of the word. If you did... you wouldn't have let me fuck you without a fight."

He's right. I gave up the fight when I knew it was him. Pretending just isn't the same, and it isn't like we can recreate the summer.

I wet my lips. "What are you going to do?"

He smirks. "I'm going to make you believe that I'm the Devil reincarnated. And I'm out for your soul."

6
ASPEN

Thalia slides into the seat across from me in the library. She drums her fingers on the table, and I glance up at her with a frown. She doesn't normally come to the library. Says it's too quiet for her type of studying—and judging from the way she's tapping, I'd agree.

She likes to move when she studies. I've seen her in action at our apartment, walking laps around our living room with a textbook in her hand, reading it aloud. Under her breath, sure, or sometimes in a strange accent.

I pull my earbud out. "Why do you look worried?"

She winces.

"Thalia."

"Oh, um, well..."

I glare at her.

"There's a rumor going around that you're..." She grabs my hand. "I'm just going to spit it out and I don't want you to freak out, right?"

"Right." My mouth is dry, and I can't help but think

back to Steele's visit last night. He promised to make me hate him, or whatever. Did he finally leak that photo?

"There's a rumor that you are a sex worker," she blurts out. "And I know that's not true, but there's a website—"

"A *website*?" I screech.

I glance around, garnering annoyed looks from other students. Libraries are not the best places for loud voices. They carry. But then Thalia slides her phone across the table to me, keeping her other hand on mine. Squeezing, as if that's reassuring.

The website reads like a sex toy résumé, boasting about certain *skills*. And then there's a photo of me. It's not sexy, really. It's been ripped right from my social media.

Then there's the contact form.

"Someone said it goes to your student email," she says in a low voice. "It's been going around online all evening."

"Fuck." I pull back and go for my phone, opening my email app. It takes a minute to load, and then—

Ping.

Ping.

Ping.

Ping.

I shut off my email notifications, then drop it facedown. I cover my face. I feel more than see Thalia take my phone and scroll through the notifications, and her silence means that I'm well and truly fucked.

"These are disgusting," she murmurs. "Some just sent dick pics, others are propositioning you. Who's Cillian Monroe?"

I snatch the phone. It's not an email—it's a call.

My uncle.

I answer it and stand, motioning to Thalia that I'll be

back. I hurry toward the stacks, away from people, before I whisper, "Hello?"

"What sort of mess have you gotten yourself into, kid?" Uncle asks. His voice is low, ominous. "And why didn't you call me?"

My jaw drops. "How—"

"I have eyes on campus." He scoffs. "You don't think I'd leave you unprotected? Your daddy—"

"I don't want anything to do with him," I interrupt. "So if you're doing this because of him, I'm going to say thanks but no thanks."

"My brother doesn't know any of this," Uncle growls. "He's out of pocket for the near future, which is why he gave you the money."

"Money?"

He sighs like I'm an absolute fucking idiot—and maybe I am.

"Did you open that package?"

"No."

Silence.

"Is it…"

"Cash, darling. Think of it as a monster repaying his debts. But now there's the matter at hand. You know prostituting is illegal. The website is being taken down as we speak. I've got someone going through your email, and they'll delete—"

"No." I shut my eyes.

"No?"

"I mean, thank you for taking down the website. But if you do any more, they'll know… And there's a risk. Dad doesn't know where I am, does he? He asked you to get me the package, but we both know you don't share information that's not vital. If you had, he'd be on my doorstep."

"At the library doorstep, you mean."

A chill sweeps down my back, and I look around. Which seems fruitless, because I'm alone in the stacks. I can barely even see the tables in the center of the room.

He sighs. "No. I didn't tell him, for the exact reasons you've described. And more that you haven't, but we won't get into those. What you need to know is that you're safe from my side of the board, and I'm hearing what you're saying. You'd like to deny the Monroe name altogether."

When he puts it like that...

"You're the only child who took our name," he says suddenly. "Because your mother refused to put his name on their birth certificates. Even though you were all living together."

Not married, though. I suppose that's the one good decision Mom made. If she had married him, she would've been tied to him in so many more ways.

"Yeah."

"So, when the Monroe family comes to collect, they care about you and you alone. You're the one who shares our name."

"If you care so much, why don't you do anything about my father?" I grip my phone hard, and part of me thinks he might actually give me an answer. *Part* of me has hope that he'll own up to everything Dad put me through as a kid.

It's why we left, after all.

It's why Mom is still running almost a decade later.

"The website is down," he says instead. "I'll leave your email to you. And dealing with the culprit."

"Thanks," I whisper. "I've got to go."

"Stay safe, Asp."

I tuck my phone in my pocket and head back to Thalia. I sink into my seat and watch her. She's pulled out some books, giving the library a solid effort. But her lips are moving, what she's reading just barely audible.

"We can go home," I offer.

She nods quickly and flips the book shut. "Are you okay? Should we stock up on some ice cream on the way home?"

"I'm fine." I don't mention that the website is down. But part of me wants to go confront Steele. To make a big deal out of this.

That's what he wants, though, isn't it?

We make it almost all of the way home when my phone rings again. This time, it's my mother. I pause on the sidewalk. "I'll catch up."

Thalia nods and continues on, while I glance around the quiet street. Then I swipe to answer it.

"Hey, baby," Mom greets me. "How are you?"

"I'm fine." My gaze stays on Thalia's back. I slowly drift after her. "How're you?"

"Oh, lovely. Lovely. Stephen is taking the girls and I to Spain!"

I stop in my tracks. "What? Why?"

She tuts. "Can't you be happy for us?"

It's like I can feel Mom's pout through the phone. Sometimes I think I'm more of an adult than she is. I mean, only one of us would get a shotgun wedding in Vegas to a near-total stranger. Right?

"I… Yeah, no, that's awesome. Are the girls around?"

She makes a noise in the back of her throat. "Dakota is in the back yard with Stephen. They're discussing building a tree house or something." Her voice shifts, getting louder as she calls to one of my sisters. "Lennox—your sister is on the phone. Yes, Aspen. Obviously. Okay, well, she wants to talk to you—"

"Hi," my baby sister says into the phone. "I miss you."

I smile. Lennox is joyful. Spirited. She's twelve. And although she's now at a new school, she's the type to adapt quickly. It's why she took to Stephen O'Brien so fast. Dakota is a bit like me. More reserved, slower to warm up. But the fact that she's outside with him right now, having a conversation without my mother involved, is a good sign.

Isn't it?

There's a tiny piece of me that doesn't want anyone to adjust or adapt, so we can go back to normal. But that's unrealistic—and a little cruel, too.

"How are you, Len? I miss you more."

I reach our brownstone and unlock the front door. Len chatters in my ear about school, her new friends. A lump forms in my throat, but I ignore it and make the occasional humming noise to keep her talking.

Thalia stands at the kitchen island, her gaze on a pile of money.

Like, more cash than I've ever seen in my entire life.

Hundred dollar bills wrapped in thousand dollar bundles stacked on top of each other. Some have spilled off, making more of a mound shape. And off to the side, the brown paper sack it came in with a piece of fabric piled on top of it.

"Holy shit." The words slip out before I can stop them.

"Hey," Len huffs. "You said a bad word."

Uncle said there was money from Dad... I just assumed it would be a few hundred, maybe? I don't know—I didn't have any expectations.

Not a few thousand dollars. *Or more.*

"Sorry, Len," I answer, finally. Once I've screwed my jaw back onto my face. "Can I call you back? Maybe tomorrow?"

"Sure. Love you, Aspy."

There's a *click* as the call disconnects, and I step up to the other side of the island.

"Where did this come from?" Thalia asks, her gaze lifting to me. "I shouldn't have opened it, but I was curious. And then it opened and all the money...? Is this illegal?"

I have no fucking clue.

But actually, it probably is illegal. Blood money, drug money...

I count the stacks, and a laugh bubbles out of me. There are sixty. Sixty thousand dollars sitting on my counter. From my *father*. My stomach turns, and my vision flickers. I suddenly feel hot and clammy. I grip the counter with both hands, but I still go down, my knees buckling and hitting the floor.

I close my eyes for good measure. It's better when I'm not looking at the cash.

"Aspen?"

"It's a payoff," I murmur.

Thalia comes around and kneels beside me. "What?"

"My dad's done some fucked-up stuff in his life. I'd be willing to bet that this is just a way to get in again. It's an apology, or something." One I can't stomach. I rise and grab the bag, shoving the money back into it. I'm going to put it in my closet and forget about it. I stuff the fabric into the bag, too, piling it on top. If anyone opens it, they'll just see that.

Not that anyone is going to dig through my closet, probably...

Thalia follows me into my room. "Are you okay?"

"Yeah. But I don't really want to stay here."

"Let's go get drunk," she offers.

I think on it. "That doesn't actually sound like a terrible idea."

She grins. I hide the bag up on the top shelf of my closet, and she flips through the hangers. I don't object when she pulls one off and pushes it into my arms. When I hold it up, I mirror her grin.

If anything, it'll cause a stir.

Which, at this rate, why the fuck not?

7
STEELE

I follow Knox, Miles, and Greyson into Haven. My mood is black. I've been listening to asinine comments about Aspen the whole fucking evening. Guys who think she's now fair game. Their wallets opened and their brains fell out.

Maybe I should let someone else try to fuck her and see how they do. She's a wildcat when she wants to be—the lake house party taught me that. But she seems softer nowadays. More inclined to be *nice* and take my dick like a hooker.

So I turned her into one.

"Oh, shit," Greyson laughs, glancing over his shoulder at me. "We're late to the party."

She's on the bar. Lying across it like it's a fucking bed. And she's got a shot glass between her teeth, and another cradled between her tits. Which are very well near exposed by how low she's pulled her shirt.

Dress.

Fuck.

I grit my teeth and storm forward, but Knox grabs my

arm. "Hey, chill out, dude. This looks like a meltdown in progress, don't you think? She's spiraling. Which means your plan worked."

I wanted her to be embarrassed to go out in public. I wanted her to be ashamed of being accused of having sex for money, that she'd swing completely in the opposite direction—like wearing turtlenecks and four layers to hide her curves.

Chase King, the football asshat who keeps talking to her, puts his lips around the edge of the shot glass in her mouth. He takes it from her and tips his head back, then removes it from his stupid, dumb mouth and smirks at her.

One of his teammates does the same to the shot glass between her breasts.

I'm going to beat the fuck out of both of them.

And I'll consider my next move with Aspen, because labeling her like this has backfired. Spectacularly.

Knox and Greyson drag me to one of the U-shaped booths, pushing me into the center to keep me from escaping. Unfortunately, it gives me an excellent view of Aspen. And the way the football douchebag—not Chase, the other one—lets his hands linger on her when he helps her off the bar.

She leans into him.

And then her gaze collides with mine.

Her smile is slow and wicked, and the tension that's been curling through me finally reaches a crescendo.

"Big fucking mistake." I shove at Greyson to move. "Let me out."

"You gonna show your cards now?" Greyson asks, his voice mild. "Are you going to storm over there and punch them, getting yourself suspended from our next game for fighting? And then Aspen will know that all she has to do to get a reaction from you is to flirt with someone else. How do you think your father will take *that* news?"

It's irritating that he's right. I sag back in the seat, and he nods.

"We'll get payback later," he assures me.

Knox orders us drinks. It seems like my gaze on Aspen only makes her behavior worsen. She smiles at every damn guy who walks up to her. She's perched on the bar stool in the shortest black dress I've ever seen, her hair in bouncing curls around her shoulders. Her friend sits beside her, soaking up the attention that sloughs off Aspen and hits her.

Seems like the friend doesn't care one way or another about how it comes to her.

"Look around," Knox adds. "Every girl in here is glaring at her like she kicked their puppy. She's diverting attention, and they hate it."

He's right. While the guys are attracted to her like bees to a flower, the girls around Haven seem like they want to stab her.

Aspen ignores them. Or doesn't notice.

I catalog every face. Every guy she puts her hand on, touching their arm, their hand, their waist. And every guy who touches her. Every place. *Her* waist, *her* arm, *her* thigh.

"See?" Greyson smirks. "Now retribution will be so much sweeter."

I drain my drink. Order another. Rinse and repeat, the alcohol blurring my rage. Aspen gets drunker, too. Her smile slips a few times, the mask cracking. I stare and stare, hoping that she feels the weight of it.

I flag down a waitress and ask for Aspen's tab. I pay it, because if there's one thing I'm *not* going to do, is let other assholes buy her more drinks. I order the waitress to deliver a message to the bartender: Aspen and her friend are cut off. Aspen's eyes are half-lidded even now, her movements slowing.

She's so fucking drunk—and they would've kept going, too.

Aspen seems bewildered that there's no bill to pay, and I relish the uneasy exchange between her and the bartender. Finally, they leave.

The guys and I follow them out.

Knox and Greyson are loud, unperturbed by my silence. They don't give a shit that I'm not joining in. Miles is quieter than usual beside me, too. I glance over at him, wondering what his deal is. But he doesn't so much as bat an eye under my scrutiny.

They leave me at the top of Aspen's street, heading for the hockey house. We have a game in two days, and Coach has been working us twice as hard to make up for our loss. If we lose again, we may as well kiss any hope of the national championship goodbye.

Aspen and her roommate are walking—stumbling—toward their apartment.

I stop outside and watch the lights in the living room go on. I settle across the street, the spot familiar from the last few times I've done this. The kitchen is at the back of the apartment, through the living room, and they're not clear through the curtains. But they're lingering, maybe drinking water to stave off a headache in the morning.

Eventually, though, the light goes off. Aspen's bedroom light turns on next, and I catch her shadow as she passes the window. Copies of her keys are burning a hole in my pocket, connected to the ring that holds my own. Seemed fitting to add hers there, since I plan on using them often enough.

I pull open my phone and go to the website.

A white window pops up instead.

Error, page not found.

I grunt and log in to the back end. It shows up there just fine, but there seems to be a glitch. Still, I can access the log of submissions Aspen received through that contact form. Some are creepier than others, and my gut churns. It seems the website caught a wider net of psychopaths than I intended.

What I wanted was for the girls at school to hate her, and the guys to be... intrigued, maybe? Or scared off of her. Who wants to date someone who would spread her legs for anyone? Allegedly.

I guess we'll find out the impact of that tomorrow, outside of the nasty looks she was receiving tonight. Damage done.

I delete the page and then the whole account. I go onto her social media and swipe through photos, my jaw tensing. Her most recent few, posted in the last two weeks, have blown up. A hundred comments on each.

That will be dealt with, too.

I chew on how to solve the problem of keeping assholes away from her. It takes a little while for me to come to a conclusion, but I smile to myself as I pull up another website. Once that's done, I give Aspen twenty more minutes to fall asleep.

Then I move. I get into her apartment with ease and lock the door behind me. I slip through the long kitchen and living room, to the short hallway that leads to Aspen's room, the bathroom, and her roommate's door. Both of which, except the bathroom, are closed. It's quiet in here, the silence seeming to echo inside my skull.

Without further delay, I step into her dark room. I don't

need a flashlight—I have the space memorized. But seeing her on the bed, on top of the covers and still in that fucking dress, spikes my anger again.

I'm going to mark her as mine. *Soon.*

But right now, my hands will have to do.

8

ASPEN

Something wakes me up out of a dead sleep. Even though the alcohol still buzzes through my system, and it delays my movements. And my thoughts.

Before my eyes can open, a weight drops down on my hips. I jerk, the reflex tensing my muscles hard, but my arms don't move.

And when my eyes open, I can't see. I open my mouth to scream, and a hand slams over my lips. Fear bursts through me, and I thrash before I fully register what's happening. Something bites into my wrists, keeping them stretched up over my head. A soft blindfold covers my eyes.

And the weight on my hips keeps me immobilized.

A soft whimper escapes me, and then I feel it.

A hand traces over my collarbone and dips down between my breasts.

Bare.

I'm naked.

My breathing comes faster, my nostrils flaring. His hand is still against my lips, preventing me from begging for him to stop. Until he pulls it away for the briefest moment.

Immediately, something is shoved between my teeth. The hand covers my lips again, and the fabric in my mouth muffles any noise I hope to make. The other hand is still trailing across my chest, avoiding my breasts. Down my sternum, across my ribs. My stomach, the stretch marks, around my belly button.

It's Steele.

I know it's Steele.

But he doesn't say anything, and I can't.

Not when he forces my thighs apart and thrusts into me hard enough to make my back bow off the bed. The slide of him into me is an invasion I'm not prepared for—and one I can't stop. No matter how hard I twist my body, he stays right there.

Holy shit. I groan through the gag.

He fucks me hard, gripping the back of my thigh with one hand and keeping his other over my mouth. He pushes my face to the side, into my pillow. I struggle to breathe evenly through my nose, half worried that he's going to pinch off that airway, too. It makes me wonder if every finger is going to leave a bruise on my skin.

I yank my hands, trying to get my wrists free from the bindings over my head. He's invading my senses, and I hate the hold he has on my face. I hate that he's silent. He's taking his own pleasure and ignoring mine.

He slams fully inside me and goes still, his low grunt the only sound he makes as he comes inside me. I feel the wetness immediately in his absence, because he doesn't linger. Doesn't put any of his weight on me except where his hands touched me, and his hips joining with mine.

Something light hits my stomach after he climbs off the

bed. I sense his stare like an ice pick. My chest is heaving, my nerves shredded.

My door clicks shut, and I lie on my bed in complete silence for too many seconds. He's gone. And judging from the pervading silence, he's not coming back.

I squeeze my thighs together, grateful for the lack of audience. Tears burn my eyes behind the cloth, but I refuse to let them fall—or to let out the sob that's climbing in my chest.

It brings back increasingly volatile memories. The silence, being naked and unable to move. My mind replays my trauma behind my eyelids, until it's hard to breathe. There's a weight on my chest, crushing me, that doesn't go away until I manage to get the blindfold off my eyes.

It takes a few seconds to blink in the darkness and let my eyes adjust, and I make out the belt that he used to secure my wrists to the headboard. I inhale slowly, counting in my head. I lick my lips, forcing my brain to acknowledge that I'm not gagged. My feet are free, too.

After a moment of staring at the belt, puzzling through it, I inch my body up the bed and use my teeth to release the buckle. The whole thing loosens, and I drop my head back to the pillow. Small miracles.

My inner thighs are wet, his cum seeping out and onto the sheets. He managed to strip me down completely—and immobilize me—while I was sleeping. I don't remember falling asleep. I barely remember the walk home. There's still a buzz of alcohol in my system, so maybe that aided him.

I climb off the bed, but I pause when I spot what he threw onto my stomach before leaving.

A folded fifty dollar bill.

I grab it. My eye twitches, and the *rage* I feel inside me is nearly unmatched.

I ball it up and chuck it toward my closet. The asshole wanted me to know that this was all him. The website, the stares that I'll inevitably collect tomorrow. The hate from the female population.

At the bar tonight, I had more attention than I ever have—and sure, maybe it was partly due to the dress. But I'd bet more of it was from that shitty website and the rumor going around campus. That's why I wore the dress. It's better to confront rumors like these instead of shying away. And then Steele showed up...

The look on his face almost made it worth it.

But the guys' attention made my skin crawl. The whole night was an act, and I hated every second. And then Steele paid for my drinks, the bartender confirmed it. Another act of possession? Or was he just trying to mess with me?

I tear everything off the bed, stripping it in the dark, and ball up the fitted sheet. Panic attack or not, I need the change. I need to remove all traces of Steele from my bed.

Are you on birth control? He asked me that at the party—and I never answered. And then he fucked me again, and he didn't repeat his question.

I'm glad I am. That I get the shot every three months. The last one I got was just before I left for college. It comes with headaches around the time of the shot, and occasionally they reoccur—but it's one of the easier forms of birth control, in my opinion. I don't have to remember to take a pill every day. I don't have to worry about a piece of plastic or copper in my uterus, or an implant in my arm. Then again, you're only supposed to be on it short-term, and my time to be on it safely is running out. Another year or two, and I'll have to figure something else out.

I remake my bed and check the clock. It's three in the morning.

Witching hour again.

First, I need something to soak up the alcohol in my system. There are dinner rolls in the pantry. I pull out two and cut them in half, spreading butter on each piece. I eat quickly, eyes half closed. Once I'm done, I shower. As hot as I can manage. I scrub between my legs, whimpering when the soapy washcloth grazes my clit.

I do it again and brace my shoulder on the tiled wall, my foot on the edge of the tub. I fall into the feeling, my hips shifting. Practically humping my hand as I rub myself to orgasm.

It breaks over me, and I groan at the sensation.

I almost fall over.

When I'm as clean as I can get, I turn the light on in my room. The belt, sitting on my nightstand where I tossed it, catches my attention. I wrap it up, tucking the tail into itself. It rests in a ball on my palm. It's definitely Steele's belt, so... there's that.

I climb into bed in the largest, softest t-shirt I own, and try to fall asleep.

The morning comes way too freaking fast.

I stagger to the bathroom and lift the large shirt to pee, and I almost choke on my gasp at the sight of my thigh.

Handprints. *Bruises.*

I thought his fingers might bruise, but my thigh has a perfect imprint of his hand wrapping around toward my ass. I rotate, trying to get a better look at it in the mirror. He must've dug his fingers in, because the spots where his fingertips rested on my skin are darker. Blue-black, where the rest of his hand is lighter.

Still totally obvious, though.

I shake it off and continue with my morning bathroom routine, emerging feeling somewhat better. Sleeping on wet hair was regrettable, and it takes a few tries to get it smooth. Thalia is in the kitchen when I emerge, already dressed and ready. She slides a giant mug of coffee my way, which I happily accept.

"Maybe not the best idea to get trashed on a school night," she confesses. "Sorry."

I sigh. "It's okay."

"What do you have planned for today?"

"Battle." I say it simply, even though it's anything but. I need to play my hand smarter, not louder. The idea of Steele getting the upper hand again makes me sick... even if some part of me last night was into it. Some little, fucked-up slice of my brain that is *not* making decisions around here.

Thalia eyes me. "Do you need help?"

"Nope. I'll see you for lunch, though?"

"Of course."

I smile and head back into my room. I turn in a slow circle. My gaze falls on the crumpled fifty, and I pick it up. Smooth it out. Put it in my pocket and smile to myself, because I get an idea that's bound to drive Steele absolutely insane.

9
STEELE

Knox and Greyson lean against the rooftop door, blocking it off for me. The football asshole who had his lips *way* too close to Aspen's breasts is on the floor beneath me. His face is a mess—bruised and bleeding and swelling. His eye is already swollen shut, with the other one soon to follow.

I may have broken his cheekbone.

"You get the message, jackass?" I growl, hauling him upright.

He stumbles away from me, his lips pulling in a grimace. "Yeah, yeah—"

"Good." I point to the door, which Knox hauls open.

My latest victim wastes no time rushing through it and down the stairs, practically falling on his face. There are two more downstairs, tied up in the boiler room, and Greyson goes to fetch another one.

My knuckles are sore, split open, but I don't give a shit.

The next one isn't an athlete. I'm not sure why he even thought he had a chance with Aspen, but here we are. He sat next to her and kept his hand on her knee. So that's where I'll start.

"Wh-what are you doing?" The guy is already blubbering by the time he comes to a halt in front of me. No doubt he heard another guy pleading and thought it may help.

It doesn't.

My lip curls. "You remember Aspen Monroe?"

He eyes me. "Y-yeah..."

"You think you deserve to be in the same room as her, let alone *touch* her?"

"Hey, man, she was flir—"

Crack.

I slam my fist into his mouth, and something breaks. I'm not sure if it's a bone in my hand or his face, but I'm hoping it's the latter. Either way, he goes down like a ton of bricks, sprawling out at my feet. Which makes it easy to stomp on his kneecap hard enough to snap it.

He screams.

Knox suddenly appears, his brows drawing together. "You know we're not trying to permanently maim them," he mutters. "Especially since this is technically on you."

I glower at my best friend. He's right—it *is* my fault. I should let them beat me up instead. Maybe that would take away some of this rage that's been hammering at the bars of its cage for far too long.

Aspen ignored me. Fully. Even at lunch, when she and her roommate sat at the end of our table with the dance girls, she didn't even look at me. Not when I called her name, not when I stood behind her like a giant freaking shadow.

Nothing.

She may as well be a stone wall.

And then I got a phone call from my father. *Apparently*, he's taken his new family on a spur-of-the-moment trip to Spain. They'll be gone until the new year.

Does Aspen know that?

I asked him what she's been telling him, the lies she's been feeding to keep herself afloat here at Crown Point University, and he had nothing to say. But he didn't throw anything in my face either. So I take that to mean Aspen is doing a shitty job of being a spy—or he's preparing for something big. With a lot of ammunition.

I jerk away from Knox and the idiot on the floor, pulling a joint from my pocket. I don't smoke during the school year, and especially not the night before a game, but fuck it. I'm so wound up, I can't even think straight.

"She's under your skin," Greyson says. "And the only way to make it stop is to get the whole school to believe she's yours."

I nod to myself. That's how it happened with them, wasn't it? One minute, his girlfriend's lips were wrapped around my dick, and the next, he was the only one who could touch her.

"You've sent the message you needed to send," he continues. "Both to her and to the guys... they'll spread the word that she's untouchable." He nudges the idiot in the leg. "Won't you?"

"Aspen's untouchable," he gasps, curling in on himself. "I'll tell everyone I know—"

"Good enough for me," Knox says lightly. He hauls him up and shoves him toward the door. "Get the other guy in the boiler room to help you the rest of the way down."

He hops toward the exit, the door slamming shut behind him.

I light the joint and suck in a lungful of smoke. I hold it, then slowly exhale. I pass it to Greyson, who wrinkles his nose and hands it to Knox. He takes a small hit, then exhales, too. I cross to the edge of the roof and sit on the ledge, looking out at Crown Point.

We're on top of the Administration building on campus, but it has a great view of downtown. To the right is the lake, and barely visible is the restaurant that serves as a visual marker for the point. We jumped off it once last summer, but we didn't get a chance to do it again.

And with the way the semester is going, I doubt we'll have a chance to do it before the lake freezes over.

"Party," Greyson says, his attention on his phone.

"Where?"

Greyson lifts his head, grinning. "The stadium."

I shake my head. "Coach is going to murder us."

Knox slaps my arm. "Coach won't find out."

Sure he won't. We follow Greyson downstairs and across campus, heading directly to the stadium. I guess he's not worried about drinking. Well, we have a game tomorrow, so we shouldn't be doing that anyway.

All that body-is-a-temple talk really is true during hockey season. Eating well, sleeping well—it all *matters*. And yet, I feel like I'm on the edge of self-destruction.

I stub out the joint and return the remainder to my pocket with the lighter. The side door entrance that the players use is propped open an inch, and we slip through it.

Voices draw our attention past the locker rooms, to the ice itself. The stadium is dark, the rink ominous. The ice seems to almost glow from within, catching the moon's glow through the skylights. The emergency lighting along the aisles is the only other source of light. It doesn't seem like any sort of party I'd expect. In fact, there's almost no one here.

Just two—in the center of the freaking rink, of all places.

I recognize Aspen immediately. She stands on the ice in plain boots, her hands planted on her hips. A player circles around her on skates, but I don't recognize him from here.

Greyson disappears for a moment. A second later, a spotlight flickers on. It hits Aspen, shrouding her in bright white.

She turns and raises her hand, blocking it from her eyes.

The player grinds to a halt, lifting his head to look at us.

"A Knight," Knox says, his voice hard. He stops in the open doorway, not stepping foot on the ice. "What are you doing here?"

The player shrugs, his grin arrogant. "It was a dare. Wasn't it, babe?"

He touches her hip, and she lets him.

She stares hard at me, then leans into him.

Greyson reappears, grinning like a Cheshire cat. He steps up beside me. "What are you going to do about that, O'Brien?"

I don't fucking know.

That's my problem. Indecision and misery and anger follow me like ugly shadows. The weight of this season is pressing down on me. I just want to kill something, I want to hurt, I want pain.

Pain.

I focus on Aspen's lips. She's sucked her lower lip between her teeth, which she does when she's not sure about something. She's shivering, too. The asshole beside her doesn't seem to notice, or care.

Why have all of my attempts to hurt her only made her stronger?

I practically handed her to Chase King—one of the only

guys I couldn't find tonight—and the others at the bar. Now him.

"How about a bet?" I call to the player, shoving past Knox.

Knox is the one who loves bets, not me. He's still fucking playing one, waiting for the payout.

He leaves Aspen on the ice and skates toward me, stopping just out of reach. The asshole's wearing jeans and a sweatshirt, which is more than I can say for Aspen.

"What's that?"

"You know she's not gonna sleep with you tonight." I cock my head. "She only fucks winners."

His eyes light up. But then he glances over his shoulder. "I don't know, man. She's with me right now..."

Her phone rings. We both watch her answer it, and she shakes her head.

"No, I'm not doing anything," she tells the caller. "Yeah, I'll be there in fifteen."

I chuckle and try not to rage. The high is helping a little, dampening the effect. *I think*. Either that, or I see through her charade, and Greyson's power move. Everyone wants me to make a damn decision.

This is her payback, and it's his way of pushing me into her arms. How the fuck he knew she was here, though, is another question entirely.

She strides toward us. She's like a freaking magician, not slipping or sliding or looking even the slightest bit unsure on the slick ice. She moves between us, not touching him—or me. Even as she squeezes beside me, her gaze flicking up to meet mine.

"See you tomorrow," she says sweetly.

And then she's past Knox and Greyson, too, and leaving the four of us with our fucking dicks in our hands.

Metaphorically, obviously.

"Whoever wins tomorrow gets her," the player says, appraising me.

"Whoever wins tomorrow gets first shot at her," I counter.

He nods. "Fine."

We shake on it. And then my friends and I go home. Because, fuck it—I need to be ready for tomorrow.

"**W**hat are you wearing?" Willow screeches and throws her hands up to stop me from coming any closer.

I snort, plucking at the Knights' jersey that Josh Maverick gave me last night. It's the one they wear when they play at home, so it's mostly red with white lettering. He's number seven. His name is on the back of it, making no mistake exactly where I got it.

The fact that Thalia's cousin goes to Smoke Valley and was able to get me the number of their best player is just another reason why I love her. And that he'd be willing to help me... although I heard what he and Steele were discussing afterward.

Luckily, I picked the best player for a reason. So even if Steele has some sort of vendetta, he won't be so easily crushed.

I hope anyway.

Coming to the game tonight in general might've been a bad idea.

"It's just a little motivation for O'Brien." Violet slings

her arm around my shoulders. "Greyson explained it. Right, Aspen?"

Oh, great. "Yep."

I have a picture saved on my phone that I took while I was getting ready, but I'm not ready to send it yet. I won't until just before the game, because the last thing I need is for Steele to try and get me to change.

Thalia is trying not to laugh at Willow's mortified expression. Amanda, Jess, and Michelle join us, too, and they have mixed reactions. But Violet explains again, and they all go back to looking semi-normal.

We sit, and I pull out my phone. I'm sandwiched between Violet and Thalia.

Violet glances at the image, and she chuckles. "You're dangerous."

My face heats. I thought so, too, when I took the picture in my mirror. I'm only wearing the jersey, which is long enough that it just barely covers my ass. My body is tilted to show off the number and name on the back, as well as the bruise on my thigh.

May as well hit him with a double-whammy.

Me: [image]

Me: Thanks for the fifty bucks, asshole.

The sad thing is, I actually did pay that much to borrow the jersey.

Worth it, though. It's not like it was my money. This is as much Steele's fault as mine.

And also, this is the first time I've texted him. I got his number from his dad before I left for college, and I never thought I'd use it. But then again, he wasn't supposed to be the guy from the summer either.

Everything just got screwed up.

Steele: You're going to pay for that.

Me: You already did, so...

Steele: Hilarious. Hope you're not too attached to his face.

Me: What's that supposed to mean?

I stare at my phone, but he doesn't respond. My brow furrows. A minute later, the players are bursting out onto the ice. Someone drops a whole bunch of pucks down, and they begin to warm up. They move like a beehive—somehow in sync without visibly communicating. My gaze is drawn to Steele. He's flicking a puck toward one of his teammates, paying no attention to the crowd.

All focus.

My heart skips when he skates by our section. Still, doesn't even glance at me.

Which... what was I expecting?

"He's pissed, huh?" Thalia whispers.

I laugh it off. They change to taking shots at the goal, the goalie leaving it wide open for them. There are two Whiteshaw jerseys out on the ice—Knox, one of the forwards, and Miles. The goalie. He's covered in padding, per usual. I haven't actually met Miles. Just his brother, who's dating Willow.

Speaking of... "Do you guys actually like dating hockey players?"

Willow and Violet turn my way.

Willow smirks. "Yeah, it's a rush."

Violet rolls her eyes.

"They just seem so..." I shake my head, not wanting to offend.

"Arrogant?" Willow supplies.

"Hotheaded?" Violet guesses.

"Hot in general," Willow adds.

"All of the above," I mutter.

They both burst into giggles.

Violet grabs my hand and squeezes. "Yeah, it's a little rough in the beginning."

"Doesn't help that my mom married his dad," I say on a sigh.

They both freeze.

Oh, shit. I wasn't supposed to say that.

"When did that happen?" Willow is leaning closer, almost in Violet's lap. "Why didn't you say anything?"

"Let's just talk about how Steele O'Brien is her new stepbrother," Violet murmurs. "Is that a forbidden fruit sort of situation?"

I frown. That hadn't occurred to me.

Well, shit. *Now* it does.

I've been looking at Steele as anything but *brotherly*.

When I turn my attention back out onto the ice, Steele is stretching. He's got both legs spread out on the ice, leaning forward and bracing his weight on his hands. He flexes his hips down, and *damn it* if it doesn't look dirty.

"I love that one," Violet murmurs to Willow.

Eventually, the players file off the ice and the Zamboni rumbles out. Violet glances at her phone, and her cheeks heat. I'm not that nosy, but I'm dying to know what sort of shit Greyson says to her.

"How'd Maverick look?" Thalia asks me.

I cringe. I hadn't even checked the other side of the rink, where the opposing team was warming up. "Fine," I lie. "Tip-top shape."

Thalia rolls her eyes. "Liar," she whispers. "Don't worry, your secret obsession with your tormentor-slash-brother is safe with me."

"He's not my brother."

Because, ew.

"Okay, okay, fine."

I snap to attention when the players come back out, just the starters, and take their positions. They're joined by a ref in the middle, and Knox and one of the Knights, in a white-and-red jersey, lean down.

The ref drops the puck, and the game begins.

My eyes lift to the suspended cube above our heads. It cycles through the players and statistics, with the time left in the period and scores underneath it in red.

The crowd is quieter than usual. The rough skating noises, the scrape of blades across the ice, is almost the loudest part. I find Josh, the Knight whose jersey I wear, and a second later he gets the puck. He skates furiously down toward our goal.

Steele comes out of nowhere. Josh passes it, but Steele still slams into him at full speed. They both crash into the glass on the opposite side.

I gasp.

Both players shove off each other and go their own ways—but moments later, the same thing happens. Josh gets the puck. Steele is right there, body-checking him. Maybe harder than is necessary—I don't know.

It gets to the point where I ignore the rest of the game and solely track Josh around the rink. Not because I'm fixated on him, but because wherever he is, Steele doesn't seem to be far behind.

By the end of the first period, my nerves are strung out.

The bell sounds, and I shoot to my feet.

"Are you okay?" Thalia asks.

Her voice sounds a million miles away. I wave her off and slip past her, hurrying up the aisle. Is Steele starting shit on purpose? Hunting after him because I'm wearing his jersey?

The thought is ridiculous.

The bet on who gets a shot with me, or whatever he said, is stupid enough. But *this*?

"How much for a blowie?" someone calls.

I ignore it and continue into the hall.

But then someone grabs my wrist and tugs me around, and I come face-to-face with... a complete stranger. Older, too. Definitely not a Crown Point student.

"I asked you a question." His eyebrow raises. "How much?"

"Fuck off," I snap and tug my wrist free. I hurry into the women's bathroom and lock myself in the stall, fishing out my phone.

One new message. Not from Steele, though.

Uncle: Your address was leaked online.

No directions after that, no advice. My breathing hitches at what that means. First the site, which must've gone viral before it was shut down, because I received about six hundred emails. Now this. Did Steele do this, too? I should go home and get the money. Thalia and I can stay in a hotel until we figure something else out.

If my address is out there, it isn't safe.

Especially on the first floor, where anyone could break in through the windows. We lock them now, but didn't Steele prove that it's easy enough to get the screen off? And then how hard is it to use a screwdriver or something to break the lock?

I'm not a burglar. Unless we're talking about the Crown Point Theater, obviously.

When I reemerge, the hallway is almost empty. The guy is still there, though. Lingering with a sick look in his eye.

My stomach turns, and I hurry back toward my section. I beat him there—barely—but he follows close behind me.

The second period has started, the crowd on their feet. I feel almost invisible, except to the man intent on harassing me. He keeps up with me all the way down to the glass, where he finally makes another move.

"Come on." He grabs my upper arm. His fingers dig into my skin. "You're not supposed to fight it, right? I'm offering you cash."

"Hey!" Something crashes into the glass.

The guy lifts his gaze, and his eyes widen.

I glance over my shoulder, too, surprised to see Steele there. He's slamming the glass with both hands.

"You get your hands off her," Steele shouts.

The guy, surprisingly, listens.

He backs up the aisle steps and turns around once he's far enough away, hurrying away from us. I face Steele again, and he meets my eyes for a second before skating away.

"Holy shit," Thalia says, standing to let me pass. "What was that?"

"Well, he was behind that shitty website that told the world I was a sex worker," I grumble, practically falling into my seat. I'm more rattled than I'd care to admit. "It shouldn't come as a surprise that more than just students saw it. That guy wanted to pay me to blow him."

"Well, shit."

Violet takes my hand and squeezes. "It'll be okay."

"I know." I lift my chin and gently pull away. I'm all for comforting touches, but really—I've got enough on my plate without Steele making it worse. And now I have to tell Thalia that we can't go home. That's going to extra suck.

I refocus on the game.

The Knights have the puck. Someone passes to Josh,

who dodges around Knox and Greyson. Someone tries to intercept him, and he leaps over their stick.

Steele is coming in fast, a look of determination visible even with the helmet blocking some of his features.

It seems that the Knight has had enough of getting smashed into, though, because he skids to a halt a second before Steele hits him. He gives Steele a check of his own, sending him into the glass in front of us. The wall shudders, and I try not to have a visible reaction.

The other defenseman tries to intercept, but for once, no one can touch him. Josh passes to another teammate, who flicks it into the goal.

It sails past Miles' glove.

The horn goes off, and the red-and-white-clad crowd erupts into chaos.

The first goal of the game, and it goes to the Knights.

W e're going to lose out on our chance at the championship before our season has even begun. This time last year, we were undefeated. Hell, we were undefeated for most of the year. But now, we're losing, and Coach is *pissed*.

He's throwing things in the locker room, taking it out on anyone and everyone. And as he rounds on me, I put up a blank-faced mask. Because I know what he's going to say. I let Josh Maverick get under my fucking skin, and he skated circles around me.

I stare at my skates as Coach rips into me, his face red. Spit flies out of his mouth. We all take it, though, because we know we're playing like asswipes.

All I want to do is punch the smug expression off Maverick's face. It's the least he deserves.

And that guy who touched Aspen.

How fucking *dare* he?

If she was wearing my jersey, no one would touch her.

But then Coach has run out of steam—for now—and it's time to go play the last period. I take one last gulp of water and run my hands through my hair, then grab my stick and helmet. I march after Knox, keeping my head raised.

We may be playing like garbage, but we're not so far behind that we can't pull this off.

Knox and the Knights' center face-off. Josh leers at me, his expression so fucking cocky, my grip on my stick tightens. He's fucking dead.

I glance over at Aspen, who's sitting squashed between Violet and her roommate in that fucker's jersey, and it pisses me off even more.

The ref drops the puck, and Knox edges out the Knight. He flicks it toward me. I take control for a second, the feel of the puck gliding along my blade pulling my focus straight back to the game. I drive it forward and slip around one of our opponents, then shoot it up toward Finch. He takes possession and sprints toward the goal. We're right there with him. I should be hanging back a little, but the urge to stuff Josh's face overtakes me again.

I block him from interfering. He's at my back, trying to get around me, but I skate in his way again. His arm is on my back, trying to shove me away.

Finch passes to Devereux, who sends it back to the right defense, Tony Rodrigues. He shoots it to Knox, who goes for the goal. He fakes the goalie out at the last second by feigning left. The goalie falls for it, reaching, and Knox sends it smoothly through his open legs.

Okay, great.

But Josh Maverick is still pushing at my back, and I'm fucking tired of him.

So I do the rational thing—I fist the front of his jersey to keep him at the right distance and punch him in the mouth.

He reels back, anger contorting his expression.

Yes, fucking fight me.

I almost say it out loud.

He lunges for me, coming for my face, and I struggle with him. We hit the glass, vying for control. I rip his helmet off and punch him again. His knuckles collide with my jaw, and pain explodes across my face. I lose my helmet, too.

No one is interfering. The whole stadium is quiet outside the buzzing in my ears.

I hit him again, and he wobbles. Without hesitation, I grab his jersey with both hands, my fingers wrapping under the padding at the edges of his armpits, and throw him to the ice. I land on top of him, drawing my fist back and punching him once, twice.

When I climb off him, I register the noise of the crowd.

Everyone is screaming, cheering. My gaze goes right to the siren in this fucker's jersey.

She's on her feet, too, and her green eyes burn into me from a distance.

I can't tell if she's happy or upset that I put him in his place—but it doesn't fucking matter.

"Penalty box," Coach snaps when I return to the bench. The refs are beside him. "And get your fucking stick, O'Brien, for god's sake."

I salute him and collect my fallen items. Devereux slaps me on the back, then Miles Whiteshaw. Then his brother. Rodrigues and Finch both pump their fists in the air. I smirk and skate to the box across from the benches. An official holds it open for me, and I step up into it. I sit down carefully, my muscles aching.

My nose is wet with blood.

The official hands me a towel, his expression stoic.

Power play for the Knights. But Josh Maverick is sidelined, hopefully for the rest of the game. Pretty sure his ugly mug will look hideous tonight, and that'll lessen any chance of Aspen going home with him.

Not that he'll get the chance. Because twenty minutes later, we score again. Two to one. And we hold them off until the final second ticks down.

I sit on the porch of the hockey house with Miles. We have tomorrow off, which means getting drunk is in order. And we're well on our way.

Inside, the party is growing bigger and louder. Miles and Knox own the house we live in, and they spent a good chunk of change renovating it over the summer. It's only right that the first party comes on the heels of our first win. We're christening it.

There's something nostalgic about the smell of beer, the sound of music and laughter, and the cool night air.

Miles nudges me, jerking his head toward the sidewalk. Violet and Willow are already inside, but I'd bet anything that they invited these two.

Aspen and her roommate, whose name I should probably find out. If only so I can stop calling her *the roommate*. It's a mouthful.

But Aspen is still wearing that fucker's jersey. Her hair is down, and the black leggings under the jersey hug her curves.

Still.

I rise and block their way onto the porch. Aspen doesn't seem surprised. She tips her head back and meets my gaze, her hands on her hips. I don't want her here tonight. I just want to get drunk and hang out with my friends and go to bed. Alone, obviously, since I haven't been able to get a hard-on for anyone except her.

And we're not doing that tonight.

"Sorry, no enemy fangirls allowed."

She rolls her eyes. "Come on."

"No enemy *jerseys* allowed," I correct, smirking at her. "You can remove it if it's that important for you to get in."

Her eyes narrow, and she seems to contemplate it for a minute.

Then her fingers go to the edge of the jersey.

My chest tightens as she pulls the fabric up, exposing the rest of her high-waisted leggings. Then the pale skin of her upper stomach, her ribcage... and then her bra. Black lace. Her nipples are fucking visible through it, hardening in a way that is intimately familiar.

If only we weren't outside with the world watching. What used to be a turn-on is now a curse. I don't want anyone staring at her, and she seems set on attracting all the attention.

"What are you doing?" I growl before I can stop myself.

She removes the jersey the rest of the way, dropping it on the sidewalk beside her. Now her hair looks just-fucked, and she stands in front of me in a bra and leggings.

What the fuck am I supposed to do with that?

"I'm going to the party." She bats her eyelashes at me. And she slips past me, dragging her roommate with her.

They go up the porch, past Miles, and into the house.

I turn and track her, my jaw clenched so hard my teeth might crack. Miles has his mouth covered, hiding his growing laughter.

"That backfired," he murmurs.

I'm going to kill her.

I storm after her, my feet moving before my brain can

catch up. She hasn't made it far—there's a lot of fucking people in the house, and they don't give a shit about two girls trying to force their way deeper inside.

But for me, they move out of the way.

I grab her hips and haul her over my shoulder. She screeches and flails, knocking the drink out of someone's grasp. I band her thighs to my chest before she can do anything else, and her hands land on my shoulders. She's more upright, hovering above me, but I shift her until her ass is higher up. Her balance betrays her, and she folds again.

The people get out of my way, their eyes wide.

I'm sure I can guess why.

I've never had an interest in girls beside the occasional fuck. But even then, I usually hit it and quit it. Never recycle the same girl twice, or else they'll start getting ideas.

Aspen, though... the thought of anyone else seeing her nipples is more than I can bear. We talked about this, and she broke the rules.

Again.

I bring her upstairs and to the first bedroom on the left. My room. It takes me a second to unlock it—a necessary measure for parties, if I want my bed to remain unsullied—go inside, and kick the door shut behind us.

My bed is made, my room mostly neat. It could be better, but I'm not ashamed of it. Or the clear message the lotion on my nightstand sends. That I beat my dick in here alone most nights. If I'm not sinking into Aspen anyway. Which is what it wants right now.

I toss her onto the bed and step back, eyeing her.

She shoots up immediately, her hands balling into fists.

Cute. She's mad.

"What the fuck?" she seethes.

I go to my closet and unzip my duffle bag. I was going to wash this, but fuck it. If she wants to wear a jersey so bad...

When I turn back around, she hasn't moved. I shake out the dark-blue material, adjusting my grip so I can put her into it. She doesn't even object when I put it over her head, then grab her wrists and guide her arms through.

It dwarves her.

My cock thickens, and the urge to take her like this is overwhelming. She looks good in my jersey—better than in red and white, that's for fucking sure.

"You wore his jersey to piss me off."

She lifts one shoulder. "You snuck into my room and fucked me without my consent, then tossed *money* on me. Which is exactly what that guy at the game had in mind, by the way."

Her green eyes are so intense, I can only stare at her for a second.

"Did you leak my address?"

Now that's new. "What? To who?"

"To the sick fucks who want to try and toss money on my stomach for a quick fuck." She crosses her arms.

I can't even blame her for being mad. A simple joke got out of control. How was I supposed to know that would happen?

But I suppose it *is* my job to make it right.

"You and your roommate can't go home?" I confirm.

She scowls at me. "We drove by it after the game. There were some guys waiting across the street... I don't know if they were waiting for me or not, but I can only assume."

I stiffen.

That *is* fucked.

"You'll stay here. And I don't want to fucking hear it,

little viper. You said it yourself—it's my fault. So you can sleep here until we get it figured out."

Maybe Jacob will have some solutions. He graduated last year, and he was one of our better players. He's off playing the big leagues now, but his dad is a cop. It's a long shot, and I have a feeling doxing an address is one of those things that you can't stuff back into the box.

"And Thalia, too?"

I nod emphatically. Really, I don't give a shit where her roommate goes. But sure, if it means Aspen will stay.

Wait, why am I suddenly so eager for her to stay here?

"There's an empty bedroom she can stay in."

Aspen's lips twitch. "And I can't stay in that empty bedroom with her?"

"No."

"Why not?"

"Because you're staying in here." I tilt my head. "Do you want me to show you why?"

"I want you to apologize for making me feel like—"

I shake my head and step forward. She stands her ground, which is new. New-ish. Reminiscent of the summer version of the girl in front of me. I run my finger down her jaw, which is clenched, to her throat, to the top of the jersey. Her breathing hitches when I curl my fingers into it.

It's the same way I held Maverick during our fight, keeping him in the right position.

But now I use it to drag Aspen into me.

Her chest hits mine, and her breath whooshes out of her.

"You look good in my jersey," I say in her ear. "But you look even better out of it."

"Maybe I should change, then," she offers lightly. Fake

lightly. She's just as affected by my presence as I am by hers. "Or I can go put on a strip show downstairs—"

"If you do that, a handprint on your thigh isn't the only thing you'll be walking out of here with."

She tips her head back and bites her lip. She reaches out and puts her hands on my chest. Her palms are hot, burning right through the thin fabric of my shirt.

"Promise?" she whispers.

12
ASPEN

Steele doesn't stop me from leaving his bedroom. I'm in his jersey, after all, and I'm ninety-nine percent sure that's the only thing he cares about. He follows me downstairs, but he keeps his distance after that. Like he's marked me as his, and now he's done his job.

Thalia is in the kitchen, talking to Finch and Miles. She's giggling, her hand on Finch's arm. Poor guy seems like he's never talked to anyone like her, because he's giving her a wide-eyed puppy-dog expression that says, *please have sex with me*.

Eh. She once confessed that the best boyfriend she ever had was a virgin. They're easier to train in the ways of women's pleasure, I guess. So maybe she's into the innocent vibes that Finch is throwing out. Although I saw him at Erik's party over the summer, so maybe he's not *that* innocent.

Miles has his gaze on someone else, although he's indulging Finch and Thalia in conversation. I try to follow his line of sight to figure out who he's watching, but there's a sea of people in the room. Including his brother and Willow, Greyson and Violet, and more.

I step up to the keg and lift a cup.

"May I?"

I glance up at Miles. He's holding his hand out for the cup, and I give it to him. He tilts it, pouring the beer without spilling a drop, and hands it back.

"Thanks. Did Steele get in trouble for the fight?" I ask him.

Miles smiles. "Nah. I think Coach told him to get over it, and sometimes you need to get over things with your fists."

Interesting.

This is why hockey is such a fascinating, terrible sport. They use their fists to solve their problems. They hit each other, slam into the glass. It's fast-paced, adrenaline-filled—

"You think you can handle him?"

I snort, focusing on Miles again. "Me? Handle Steele? Does anyone *handle* him?"

He raises his brow. "Not since this summer."

I stop short. Is he saying what I *think* he's saying?

"What do you m—"

"Miles!" Jess, from the dance team, rushes out and grabs his hand.

She, along with ninety-nine percent of the girls in here, is decked out in blue and white. Or silver. I can't figure out if people substitute the actual school color, which is silver, with white because it's too hard to find? Or pure laziness?

"Dance with me!" she demands.

He focuses on her and doesn't spare me another glance. Which is fine, because I'm still fucking puzzled by what he insinuated about Steele.

Someone stops beside me, and I look up at Greyson

Devereux. He must've stopped dancing with Violet when Miles was pouring my beer, and she's nowhere to be found. He gives me angry-boy vibes. Like some deep instinct is shouting, *Danger! Danger!* He's like Steele in that regard, I think, but more on edge.

Maybe it's because Violet isn't with him. Those two fit together better than any couple I've ever met.

"Congrats," I say to him, because I don't know what else to say. He scored the winning goal, after all.

"Thanks. So, what's up with your mom and his dad?"

"What?" My heart all but jumps into my throat. Cutting right to the heart of the matter, is he?

He glances at me. "I think you heard me."

"Um..." I shift away from him. "My mom likes spontaneous things."

Only a little bit of a lie. She likes a lot of things, being foolishly spontaneous is just one of them.

"And she found Steele's father...?"

He probably wants to know where. Or how. If only I had that information—or was willing to share it. As it is, I'd rather not. So I settle on, "It appears that way."

I spot Steele through the dancing crowd in the living room. He's across the room, leaning against the wall. And even though bodies come between us, somehow his gaze is steadfast on me.

"Excuse me," I say to Greyson, feigning politeness. I don't want to be polite. I'd like to just ignore him entirely. But he's friends with Steele, so it's the least I can do to be nice. My mom didn't raise an asshole, after all. Unlike Steele's dad.

I join Willow on the dance floor. She's got moves, but she snags my hand when I try to backpedal. She grins at me, tipping her head back and looking at me through half-lidded eyes. The fine baby hairs that frame her face are stuck to her skin with sweat. Her hands go to my hips, and she guides my movement.

"Like this," she yells in my ear.

I close my eyes and forget my fears. Forget that I'm probably being judged by a lot of people right now. But no one comes up and tries to grind into my ass. No one touches me except Willow... until her hand is replaced with another, larger one.

The hand slips from my waist to my stomach, and they pull me backward. Until I hit a chest that I know without even opening my eyes.

How's that?

I tip my head back, resting it on Steele's shoulder. I crack my eyes and confirm what I already know. It *is* Steele. His arm bands around me, and his knees bend until his thighs are against mine. He's touching me from my shoulders to my knees, and he takes over the dance. Slowing my motion until we're in sync.

He brushes my hair over my shoulder and leans down, pressing his lips to my bare skin just over the collar of his jersey.

I reach back and loop my arms around his neck, pushing a little more forcefully with my ass into his groin. When his teeth skim the crook of my neck and shoulder, I smile.

Do I like him?

Not particularly.

Am I attracted to him?

Too fucking much.

It's an awkward position to be in, caught between wanting to knee him in the balls and suck on them.

But then his mouth is moving up my neck, pausing at

my ear. "Two-minute head start," he says, his voice just barely audible over the music. "You know the rules."

The lack of rules.

I meet his eyes. He's not joking. There's one safe word, and that's the only thing that will save me from him. But also... we need this fight.

The night after the summer party, I stood in the bathroom of *his* childhood home, feeling like an outsider. My cheekbone was bruised, my skin scraped all over. My forehead had the slightest lump where I had headbutted him.

But I didn't hate it. In fact, the bruises made me feel proud, in a way. Relieved.

Someone saw me, and they didn't hate it. They reveled in the way I wanted to be treated.

My heart picks up speed, and I hurry away from Steele. Anywhere in the house is foolish, and it's not yet so cold that I'd freeze to death outside. I duck down and try to break his line of sight in the crowd, weaving toward the front door.

But also...

I like foolish.

So I head out the front door and jump off the porch, staying low as I head around the side of it. I keep out of sight of the windows, hunched, and make my way to the backyard. There are people out here, gathered around a fire, but I ignore them. I peek in the window and immediately find Steele.

He's looking down at his watch.

After another few seconds, his head lifts. He glances around, then goes toward the front door. I slip back in and weave amongst the people, finding my way to another room that I hadn't yet seen. There's beer pong set up on the dining table, two couples playing, and a couch in the corner with a game station.

I rotate in a circle, debating.

Then I catch sight of Steele coming inside, and my heart rate *triples*. I whirl around and bolt for the closed door, half hoping it will lead to a garage or something. Instead, it opens to stairs that descend into the dark.

I glance back.

Steele's spotted me, his dark gaze locked on me as he pushes his way through the people.

Fuck it.

I rush down the stairs, stopping short at the setup. It seems like just another party room—a pool table, a game console, a couch and chairs. The only light is coming from the electronics.

"Nowhere to run, is there?" Steele comes down slowly. "Now what?"

Well, backing down isn't an option.

When he lunges for me, I jump sideways. He misses and leaves the stairs open, so I do the sensible thing and bolt for them. But sudden pain sears through my scalp, and I'm yanked backward. He has my hair in his fist, and he drags me down the rest of the way. Until I hit the carpeted floor on my back.

He circles me and licks his lips. My eyes are adjusting to the light faster, the red tones from the gaming systems giving him an eerie, devilish look.

When he doesn't pounce again, I shove myself back to my feet.

This time, I fly at *him*, a small screech leaving my lips. I scratch at him, claw at his arms and chest until he captures my wrists. He slams me face-first against the wall. The air is forced from my lungs. He lifts my wrists, keeping them trapped at my back, and my shoulders burn.

"Fuck you," I spit, struggling to free myself.

He yanks my leggings down and reaches between my legs. I close my eyes when his fingers slide against my clit, then my slit. He thrusts two fingers into me and twists.

An unholy moan escapes me.

"Why are you so wet?" His voice curls like smoke in my ear, and he continues to finger-fuck me. He adds a third, and I widen my stance. "Why do you like this?"

I don't know.

I may be dripping between my legs, but my mouth is dry. I shift my weight, but he leans harder on my back. My cheek is against the cool paint, no doubt leaving a smear of makeup. He pulls out of my pussy so suddenly, I want to yell at him. Or scream.

But I refuse to give him that much.

Still, I'm not prepared for him to slide his wet index finger into my asshole.

I arch and try to escape it, but he doesn't stop. Not until I kick out at him, and my heel collides with his shin. His grip loosens enough for me to yank free, and I whirl around. Shove him back with two hands on his chest, my expression shocked.

"Why did you do that?"

"I wanted to." His eyes gleam. "Are you going to stop me?"

"Yes."

"Try," he goads.

I snarl, but he comes at me again. We go down in a heap, and I use all my strength to roll us. I straddle him for all of a single second before we're moving again, and I hit the floor hard. The pain gets my blood pumping.

He pries my legs apart with his knee, and his fingers are pushing back into me.

"What do you need, sweetheart?"

"For you to get off me," I growl.

He shakes his head once, and then his fingers are replaced with the tip of his cock.

I shove at his shoulders as he thrusts into me.

I scream.

His middle and ring fingers fill my open mouth. I gag when he hits the back of my throat, pressing down on my tongue. I could bite him if I wanted, I think, but then he shifts his hips, and his cock strokes something deep inside me.

I groan around his fingers. He's holding my mouth open, his palm against my lower lip and chin, the rest of his fingers fanned across my face. The two in my mouth move across my tongue with the same tempo that he fucks me.

At some point, I stop pushing him away and start pulling him closer.

The lights flicker on above us.

Steele freezes, glancing over his shoulder. We're off to the side of the room, having somehow drifted closer to the bathroom. It would be easy for us to get up and lock ourselves in there. Footsteps on the stairs send a spike of fear through me, and I can't see who it is. His body blocks it.

Oh hell no.

I squirm, trying to get away.

He uses his free hand to hike my thigh up, my knee bending. It can only go so far, my leggings still stuck around my ankles. But he thrusts into me again and rocks his hips harder.

I glare at him and close my teeth over his fingers.

"Don't," he warns. "Or I'll make sure you don't come for a week."

That... sounds like a threat he'd follow through on.

"Are we playing eight ball—oh, shit."

I close my eyes until Steele squeezes my jaw. I stare at him as he continues to fuck me. He's shifted upright, and my ass is half on his thighs. Off the carpet anyway.

I wrap my hand around his wrist and dig my nails in.

He smirks.

"You need some alone time, O'Brien?"

My attention slides to the guys who have moved into view.

More than just guys.

Amanda, Jess. Finch. Knox. Tony Rodrigues, the new starter. I don't think my face has ever burned so bad—until Steele removes his hand from my leg and touches my clit. Then my whole body feels like it's on fire, seconds away from combusting.

"Steele's a one-and-done kind of guy," Amanda says, her voice decidedly cold. "Let him finish, and then he'll be finished *with* her, too."

I focus back on Steele's face. His jaw tics.

"Don't mind us," he says over his shoulder, his voice sounding... *normal*. "I just can't resist when a girl wears my jersey."

Fucker.

There are a few snickers from the guys.

"Isn't that right, little viper?" His dark gaze finds mine, a smirk curling his lips. He's getting off on this, and what he probably assumes is my mortification.

Fuck all of them.

I wrap my legs around him and lift my hips in challenge. His eyes light, and he thrusts harder. He works me up until I'm meeting every piston of his hips with my own, surrendering to the feeling. An orgasm is right there, spurred on by his fingers on my clit.

And then it crashes into me, and Steele removes his fingers from my mouth. Releasing any hope of blocking the sound that comes out of my mouth. His name. *Oh, god*. A moan, a plead. I'm too loud.

He finishes a second later, stilling inside me.

We both stop moving, and I look down. I can't see his cock buried inside me—thanks, curves—but I can feel it pulsing with a heartbeat outside of mine.

He came in me *again*.

He sits back and tucks himself in, then pulls his jersey down around my hips, covering the apex of my thighs and my ass. When we stand, he drags my panties and leggings up, securing them into place.

The look he gives me...

"Wait, you're actually wearing his jersey?" Amanda scoffs. "I thought he was kidding..."

I face her. I don't know why her jealousy is getting on my nerves—except maybe I'm having fucking flashbacks to her throwing herself at him at the party. He picked me, though. Instinct says he'd pick me again, because at least I'm interesting.

"His jersey, his cum..." I shrug. "Bet you got neither when he fucked you, right?"

She stares at me for a long moment, her jaw working. Then she turns away and goes over to the pool table, yanking one of the sticks off the wall. Maybe she should go fuck herself with it—she'd have better luck.

Rude, Aspen.

Jess shakes her head, holding back a laugh. Finch can't look at us. Or won't. Tony's gaze bounces back and forth between Steele and me with a certain sort of awe that brings a smile to my lips. Because while I definitely wouldn't *choose* to get fucked in view of other people, their reactions are pretty telling.

Steele chuckles. He's right behind me. "Guess you told her, huh?"

He slaps my ass, and I jump. I glare at him, but he just pushes me toward the stairs. Which I climb dutifully, because, let's be honest, I'm not about to stick around in the same room as the people who just watched me get fucked.

Even I have my limits.

I wake up in Steele's bed. I know this because we're going to have to work on his pillows. And I'm cold, which hasn't been a problem in my own bed, simply because of the amount of blankets I keep available. We're going to have to work on that, too, if he expects me to stay.

Anyway, it's also sort of hard to forget that when I got tired, he led me away from the party and brought me upstairs. He gave me the key to his room, pulled out a toothbrush still in the packaging from a drawer in the shared bathroom, and then went back downstairs. To places unknown.

Leaving me alone... which couldn't have come at a better time.

I go to roll, but a hand on my stomach stops me.

My eyes open fully. I'm still in his fucking jersey, but the fabric is collected just under my tits.

And Steele's head is between my legs.

He's not touching me, though. My thighs are spread, his shoulders a hair's breadth away, and he seems to be... staring?

Counting the flaws?

His hand is hot on my stomach, and it occurs to me that this is why I'm cold. Because his comforter and sheet are forgotten off to the side, tossed off me with little regard.

"What are you doing?"

"Waiting for you to wake up." His voice is low and husky, mirroring my own. "So I can give you a good morning kiss."

"I—"

He leans forward. His lips touch mine. Well, *mine* being the set between my legs. Only his hand on my stomach keeps me from shooting away from him. He leans back and smirks.

"Maybe a French kiss," he suggests. "You know how they do it. Lots of tongue."

"Steele, no—"

But then his mouth is on me again, and his tongue swipes through my center. Over my sore clit. Little electric bolts zip through me, and I grip his hair. I yank him up enough to make eye contact again.

"Stop fighting, Aspen." He rolls his eyes. "This is supposed to make you feel good."

"Yeah, but it just feels like you're making fun of me." I release his hair and drop back flat, exhaling heavily. I didn't mean to say that. Sleep—or lack thereof, since I think I only caught a few hours—is clearly messing with my judgment. "Or you're just offering it so I suck you off or something."

He frowns. "Why would you say that?"

"Previous experience?"

His frown gets deeper, and he crawls up my body. I exhale when he drops down on top of me. "Let me get this straight. Some guy tried to go down on you, did a shitty job that made you not like it, and then asked for a blow job?"

I nod carefully.

"And did he come in your mouth?"

I shift, then nod.

His mood seems to visibly darken. "Okay, well, we're fixing that right now."

"Steele..." My voice is a warning.

Which he ignores.

He scoots back down and nestles between my legs like it's his favorite position. He slips his hands under my thighs, gripping them and holding them open. I rise on my elbows to watch him, forgetting about everything I'd learned about making myself smaller.

He doesn't care if my stomach rolls when I'm curled up like this... and I'm more curious to see what he's doing anyway.

This time, he doesn't hesitate to put his mouth on me. My lips part when his tongue sweeps through me, and I automatically want to close my legs. Which is why he's holding them open. His fingers tighten, and he sucks my clit into his mouth.

Stars.

Immediately.

I let my head fall back, fighting the urge to close my eyes. He flattens his tongue and swipes it against the sensitive nub again, then goes lower. His nose brushes my clit at the same time that his tongue stabs into me.

"Holy fuck," I groan.

He grabs my hand and puts it on the back of his head. "Show me what you need."

I dig my fingers through his hair and urge him up a little, back to my clit. He sucks it and swirls his tongue around, eliciting a whimper from my lips. And when his teeth graze it, the pain jolts through me. He continues working me higher and higher, thrusting two fingers into me and shoving me over the edge.

I twist and try to get away from him, but he doesn't move. Or lift his head.

"You're the sweetest fucking dessert I've ever had," he tells me. Or rather, his words seem directed to my cunt. Which is only slightly mortifying. And then his mouth is back on me.

"I can't," I pant.

Except, I don't really have a choice, do I? He continues to lick and suck until I come a second time. And then he's turning me over. Straddling my thighs. He grabs one of the pillows and leans over, stuffing it under my hips.

He palms my ass cheek.

I look over my shoulder at him just as he pushes into me. He lets out a breath, then pushes the jersey farther up my back. He stays fully seated inside me for a moment, and his hand traces the curve of my bare spine. All the way up to my neck, which he wraps his hand around.

"Remember?"

I grimace. "Are you going to—"

"No, I want you to remember. Because you fight me until I please you, and then you turn into putty. Would there ever be a time when you don't?"

"If you leave me wanting," I whisper.

I don't like the softness between us.

I don't like that I can't go home.

I shift my hips, trying to get him to move. He does a little, and the friction makes me sigh. Two orgasms, and I'm more sensitive than I've ever been.

"We go back to hating each other when we leave this room," he says, pressing me deeper into the mattress. "But right now, I just want to enjoy fucking you."

"Fine," I bite out. "But don't expect me to let you off without consequences. You made it so I can't go home."

He may have even leaked my address.

Wouldn't that be the icing on the cake?

First, he creates the danger—then he offers me a solution. And said solution brings me closer into his orbit.

He pulls out almost all the way, until just the tip of his cock is nestled inside me. Then he slams back in, grunting with the effort. He doesn't lighten up. He grips my ass and my neck and fucks me like he's trying to hurt me.

But I accept that, because if I had a choice, he'd hurt, too.

And someday soon, the tables are going to turn. I'll get him where *I* want *him*, and he'll be powerless to stop my onslaught.

By the time he's done with me, he's forced me into another orgasm. And then one of his own, buried inside me. He stays there and traces a new pattern over my back.

"Let me up," I say. I haven't peed, and the urge is getting insistent.

"What would you do if you got pregnant?"

I freeze. What *would* I do?

I'd probably go to a clinic. I'm too young to have a kid, so I wouldn't. In this state, at least, the choice is available to me. It's why I'm proactive with my birth control. And, until he came along, I never had sex without a condom.

He hums, shifting. Eventually, his cock slips out of me. But his fingers are right there, pushing his cum back into me.

"Too early to say," he murmurs, more to himself than me.

"Steele." I roll onto my back. I use my heel to shove him away, and he goes.

He laughs at me, at the way I probably look like an absolute train wreck. Instead of commenting, or acknowledging that I didn't answer his question, he tugs on pants and heads for the door.

I snag my leggings and grab a t-shirt from his closet. My bra is on the floor, too, so I add that to my pile. My phone, plugged in on his dresser, goes off. I glance at the door.

Steele is gone.

But there's a text from his dad, and my mood plummets.

Stephen: Call me now.

Oh, great.

I hurry to the bathroom and lock the door, dumping my stuff on the counter. I sent him an email—does he need more on Steele?

Or did he find out about the website? It was taken down in record time. It's all lies anyway. I need the weight of anxiety off my chest, which means calling him *immediately*, as ordered. I just have to ignore the sour taste that invokes.

My hands shake as I click on his name and press the phone to my ear. The ringing tone picks up. I wipe my other hand on my leg. Jittery nerves hit me.

"Aspen," Steele's father greets me.

"Good morning," I say in an attempt to be cheery. Like there's nothing wrong.

"Can you please explain to me why I'm getting calls from the Dean of Students about your conduct on campus?"

I go silent. Because no, I definitely can't. Not without throwing his son under the bus... which doesn't sound like such a bad idea. Why am I protecting him anyway?

"There was a prank that got out of hand," I hedge.

Stephen clears his throat. "I see. And who started this prank?"

I let my non-answer fill in the blanks for him.

"My son," he guesses.

"I suppose that would make sense," I agree.

"Thank you, Aspen," he says. "I'll take care of it."

The call ends, and I sigh. People are always *taking care of* things for me. Like my uncle with the website, and Steele's dad with whatever the hell the Dean of Students is moaning about. Probably the website, and me being painted as an on-campus prostitute. Or maybe Amanda decided to complain about public sex... even though it was in a house, technically.

Does that count?

And anyway, I've always been curious about how these things are handled. Do they just make phone calls to the right people, who then pull some magic strings, and the issue goes away? Or do they get their hands dirty?

I can't picture my uncle logging on to a computer and hacking into the website's host domain to blow it to smithereens. I'd *like* to see that. But in reality, he probably knows someone who knows someone who owes him a favor or six.

Steele's dad may pay off the dean. Or donate to the school... wouldn't that be grand. I spent the summer with him. So many problems can be solved by slipping someone some cash.

It's stupid, especially for the people who need that money, who would break the rules for some extra cash, or circumnavigate policy.

Isn't that how the rich get richer? It's why politicians are corrupt, and why cops take bribes, and corporations can get away with murder.

Someone knocks on the door, and I almost fall over. "I'll

be out in a few minutes," I call. There's a bathroom downstairs, I think. It shouldn't be that bad.

"Let me in," Thalia calls.

I smile and unlock it, stepping aside so she can slip in. Her hair is in a bun on top of her head, and she wears a borrowed t-shirt. From whom, I don't know. There are a handful of guys I would guess would be eager to lend it.

I relock the door and turn on the shower. "How was your night?"

"Great. As long as I don't think about the fact that Greyson and Violet probably fucked on the mattress I slept on, I'm good."

She pulls another toothbrush from the drawer, shaking her head at how many there are. Not a *lot*, per se, but more than a normal house would have. Someone clearly went out and bought a dozen toothbrushes for their conquests.

"Who do you think handles the toothbrush inventory?" she whispers.

I shrug, but I meet her gaze in the mirror.

"Knox," we both say at the same time.

Listen. He's with Willow, I guess. Honestly, it's a little hard to tell sometimes, because he's a *massive* flirt. Especially when she's not around. Thinking he'd plan ahead for his sleepovers to leave with fresh breath isn't a stretch of anyone's imagination.

I shed the jersey and duck behind the shower curtain. There's a good selection of shampoos and conditioners to pick from. The water was quick to heat, too. Plus the pressure...

"Are you going to tell me what's really going on with you and Steele?"

I crane around the shower curtain again. Thalia's sitting

on the toilet, the lid closed, with her leg drawn up under her. She raises her eyebrow at my expression.

"No," I decide.

"I'll tell you who I kissed last night..."

"I don't want to know that either," I lie.

She chuckles and flushes the toilet. My shower switches to icy cold water, and I scream. I step out of the spray until it returns to normal.

"I hate you," I mutter. "Totally unnecessary." She wasn't even peeing—just being an ass.

"Do we need to move?" she asks in a quieter voice. "Maybe we should call the police..."

"We could," I agree. "But the website was taken down, and I think the post with my address was, too. Besides some guys loitering on the street, what are the cops going to do? I say we just wait it out for a few days and try to go back. The guys might go with us to grab some supplies today."

"So we don't get stuck smelling like boy products," she agrees. "Okay, fine. What are you doing today?"

"Well, I need my sheet music." I frown. And probably the money, especially if the apartment isn't secure. But where would I put it? "And a change of clothes. So maybe the apartment first, then I can go to the practice rooms."

Thalia takes a deep breath. "Okay, I'll leave you to finish and try to wrangle some guys to come with us."

I was unsuccessful breaking into Aspen's phone. I tried in the middle of the night, when she was passed out in my bed, but it's locked down. Not a simple passcode—she has a six-digit one. Plus face ID, but it didn't register it with her eyes closed.

I'll get into it eventually. I want to know exactly what she's saying to my father. To make matters worse, they're not even in the country. They're on *vacation*. When's the last time my workaholic father took time off?

The only trips I remember are back from when my mom was still in the picture. When we were one big happy family. But that all changed in high school. Dad buckled down and became all about work.

My stomach twists. I check my calendar. It's mid-October. Mom's birthday is early November, and I need to arrange a visit. I'll have to tell Coach, too, but he might remember the situation from last year. How I usually have to dance around my father's demands and my game schedule.

Besides that, I'm fine missing classes. And Coach will excuse me from a practice or two.

Well, he might not *this* time, since we've been on thin ice since the first game. Even winning against the Knights did nothing to stave off his ire.

It's been three days since the game. Knox, Greyson, and Miles went over to the girls' apartment the morning after. I didn't go, but apparently there were some creeps hanging out that scattered when they showed up.

Good.

That's been a mess.

However, my new course of action has presented itself: since Aspen is still under my father's thumb, I'm going to make her an unreliable narrator. Which means warping Aspen's perception of reality a little. Twisting her around until she doesn't know which way is up. And then my father will have no faith in her, and it won't matter if she blames the whole thing on me.

The first order of business: the hallucinogenic in my pocket.

She and Thalia showed up at the hockey house with their packed bags, and she's since decided that she'd rather stay with Thalia in Greyson's old room than bunk with me.

That girl has a habit of twisting *me* up, so I let it slide.

For now.

But only because the guys in my house know that she's off-limits. If Thalia wants to fuck one of them, she can go to their room. She's got more options than Aspen anyway. The two of them sharing a bed actually keeps Aspen safer.

I put a few drops into a water bottle that I carefully manipulated. The cap and the safety seal stayed together, so it appears like it was never opened. I find Aspen in one of the practice rooms, leaning over the piano in the corner of the room. There are music stands stacked along the wall, with a few folded chairs for other instruments, I suppose. Unnecessary for Aspen and her piano.

However, the sound that comes out, the drifting melodic tune she's playing, is muted. The soundproofing in the room isn't *horrible*, especially since I'm sure it's loud inside it. But I can still hear her in the hallway. Figures the school wouldn't splurge on quality for their practice rooms.

That gives me another idea for another day.

Enough waiting. I unlock the door with my ID and stroll inside. Aspen stops mid-song and cranes around. Her eyebrows hike up, and her mouth parts. I like her surprise. But it's instantly replaced with wariness. She swivels to face me fully, opening her mouth to probably tell me off— or to get out.

I hold up the water and granola bar in my hands. "I'm playing nice," I lie. "Thought you might want some nour-ishment, since you've been in here for hours."

She frowns. "I've been in here for an hour, tops."

I scoff. "Whatever." I set the water and bar on the bench beside her, then unfold one of the metal chairs. I lower myself into it and cross my arms, propping my leg up. "Well?"

"Well, what?"

She reaches for the water and unscrews it. The satis-fying noise of the seal breaking fills the room, and she takes a sip. Then another. Her throat moves with every swallow.

She sets it back down and wipes her mouth on the back of her forearm, then turns back to the sheet music. Some of the edges are bent, which makes me think they're the same pages that I sent flying down the stairwell. Which means she didn't reprint them.

Interesting.

"Are you just going to watch?"

"Listen," I reply, closing my eyes. "Yes."

Pause.

I resist the urge to check if she's looking at me.

She lets out a breath and starts again from the beginning. I think it's the beginning anyway. I really don't have any idea about piano music. I don't know if she's playing classical or new age or a cover of a modern song. Maybe something from a movie.

I like it, though. It kind of has that haunting melody that sits in your chest.

Suddenly, she stops. Curses. After a second, she restarts again. The notes go all wonky, and she stops with a squeak.

I crack my eye open.

She's leaning forward, her head tipped to the side. Her fingers are pulled away from the keys like they bit her.

"Aspen?" I focus more fully on her.

The drugs went to work fast, judging by her expression. I wonder what her sheet music is doing. If it's talking to her or wiggling across the page.

She glances at me, and her eyes bug out. I slip my phone from my pocket and switch it to video mode, aiming it at her.

"What is it?" I ask.

She's staring at me with a horrified expression. "Steele," she whisper-yells. "T-there's a monster behind you." Her grip tightens on the bench, her feet leaving the pedals.

I glance behind me, then face her again. "Maybe we should get out of here? Get to safety."

She nods wordlessly and rises, leaving her bag behind. She hurries out into the hallway, and I follow. She seems to be walking like someone's hunting her, glancing over her shoulder at me with wide eyes.

I smile to myself.

Perfect.

15
ASPEN

I wake up in the music room, my mouth full of cotton. I look around, squinting in the dark room. The fluorescent light from the hallway comes in through the window in the door, slanting across the floor and giving me enough to see.

My bag is gone, as is my phone.

What happened?

I lick my lips and drag myself upright, tugging down on the hem of my shirt. As soon as I move, the motion sensor lights in the room flicker back to life. I close my eyes briefly against the searing pain of the brightness. It takes a minute for me to open my eyes again and resume taking inventory. My leggings are dirty, and there are grass stains on my knees. There's a rip in my shirt, too, right across my stomach.

A shadow appears in the window, and I scream.

"It's me!"

I take another look and wince. Thalia's brows are pinched, and she tries the door handle.

Locked, of course, unless you ask the school to give your ID access to these rooms.

I pull the door open. Her gaze quickly takes me in, and without warning, she drags me into a hug.

"Wh—" My voice cracks, so I just stop.

"Are you okay?"

I shake my head and clear my throat. "What happened?"

She pulls back a little, still holding my arms. "You don't remember?"

"No…"

"Let's just go home," she murmurs. "Where's your bag?"

I don't know. I don't know what happened, I don't know where my bag is. Or why I'm covered in stains and dirty, when I should've just been… I should've been here, right? Practicing?

The sheet music is gone, too.

She takes my hand and leads me outside, and I stop short.

It's dark out.

"What time is it?"

She shifts. "Nine."

"At night?" My knees wobble. "The last thing I remember is getting to the music room this morning." A terrible thought occurs to me. "It was this morning, wasn't it?"

"Yeah." She squeezes my hand. "Listen, we just need to get back to our apartment, and I'll explain everything there—"

"I know," I interrupt. "It's okay. Let's go."

At this point, it doesn't matter that there could be strange guys lingering outside the apartment. I'm ready to sleep in my own bed. Thalia is a fine roommate but not so good at sharing a bed. I have bruises on my shins from her wild flinging.

But it was better than staying with Steele.

My mind seems to be running at half-speed. We're already on our apartment's street. Thalia pauses and stuffs a ball cap on my head, muttering something to herself. I cling to her and let her unlock the door, not bothering to turn around. I can feel eyes on me, and I silently plead with her to hurry up.

"I'm going," she grumbles, getting the door unlocked and open.

Maybe not so silently pleading, then.

She makes sure the door latches behind us, then we repeat the steps at our apartment door. Once we're in, she motions for me to stay where I am. She picks up a bat—I'm not sure where we got it, or if one of the guys left it for us— and checks out the apartment.

It's silent, except for the clock hanging on the wall, ticking mutinously loud. Thalia returns and sets the bat back by the door, frowning at me.

"Water?" she asks. "Maybe food?"

I press my hand to my stomach. It gurgles on cue. "Do we have anything in the fridge?"

She shakes her head. "We don't have much, since we haven't been here. But we have frozen pizza."

I grab a cup from the cabinet. "Fire up the oven, chef. We're eating like royalty tonight."

She cracks a smile, but it doesn't last.

Which means she knows what happened to me, and it isn't good.

I heave a sigh and drink a full glass of water. It helps with my dry mouth, for sure, but it feels hollow in my stomach. While she gets the pizza ready, I head to my bedroom. It looks untouched, which is good.

Thalia steps into my room behind me, leaning on the frame.

"Can I borrow your phone to call mine?" I go straight to my closet. Half of my stuff is at the hockey house, but it wasn't like I moved everything in. I grab new leggings, a hoodie, undies. What I really need is a nice, long shower as hot as I can stand it.

"No."

I stop. "No?"

"No, I think we need to talk before you try to find your phone or go on social media—"

A chill sweeps down my spine. It's that foreboding feeling where I just *know* she's going to ruin my day. Or night. But there's only so much bad shit a girl can take.

"I'm going to shower first, then," I say softly.

She nods and steps back to let me pass.

Showering makes me feel more human, at the very least. I comb out my hair and take my time getting dressed, but all I'm really doing is procrastinating the inevitable. As soon as I go out there, Thalia's going to give me a slice of pizza and break my heart.

If it didn't have something to do with Steele, she wouldn't have taken me back here.

So, what did he do?

Or, better question: what did *I* do?

I try to think, but my memory is frustratingly hazy. I remember playing the piano. And... he came in. I think I kept playing while he sat there watching me, and I didn't like it. I felt too hot in my body.

I drag my fingers across my abdomen, pulling up my shirt. There are scratches there. My nails are jagged from picking at them—a nervous habit my mother tried to break. Did I try to claw my own skin?

Did I rip my shirt?

I shudder.

The smell of pizza reminds me of my empty stomach, and I quit procrastinating. I head out to the living room, where Thalia's curled up on the couch. She has a Christmas action movie rolling the beginning credits. Wordlessly, she hands me one of the plates from the coffee table. It already has two slices on it, and I take it from her.

She grabs her own, and we eat in silence.

Then she mutes the TV and turns to me. "Ready?"

"As I'll ever be."

She sighs. "This video was posted around lunchtime. It's been passed around..." She opens her phone and hands it to me.

I click play, my heart in my throat. It's me. Very clearly. I'm leaving the Administration building, hunched like I'm afraid. My steps are short and fast, and I keep glancing over my shoulder at whoever's filming. My lips move. Then...

My chest tightens.

It cuts to a new clip, and I'm screeching, screaming at nothing and ducking like I'm being attacked from above. In the center of the quad, with people *everywhere*. It cuts. I'm sprinting down a path between buildings and off campus, the filmer following me. Eventually, I fall and curl up into a ball. I've got tears streaming down my face, and I scratch at myself. My stomach, my arms. There's another minute left of the video, but I set the phone facedown between us.

I'm going to throw up.

In fact... *Yep*. I sprint to the bathroom and barely make it. My throat burns, and I sag back when the spasms stop.

"Shit, I should've told you before pizza." Thalia hands me a bottle of water.

I crack it open, then freeze.

The sound...

"What?"

I look down at the bottle.

"Steele..."

She kneels beside me and waits.

It sounds insane. "Steele came into the music room, and he gave me a bottle of water. I drank it, and that's when things get fuzzy. Did he drug me?"

I shudder.

He wouldn't, would he? I mean... no, actually, he *would* do that. But I have no idea why.

"They're saying you had a psychotic break," Thalia whispers. "But if it was drugs—"

"I should get my blood tested. Go to the hospital or something." I rise. "He can't get away with this. I mean—he should pay."

"The only paying that would happen would be his father taking away your spot at CPU and bribing whoever he had to at the hospital to bury it," Thalia points out. "You said it yourself, you don't trust the O'Briens. I think you meant his dad when you said it, but it applies to his son, too."

I grimace. She's right. It *does* apply to both of them.

Steele calls me the viper—but he's the snake.

"**A**spen," the man calls, standing at the door to the small lounge.

I rise and follow him down a hall, into an office. There's a couch, a chair, a desk. A window. For some reason, I go to the window first, peering out of it. We're on the fourth floor, all the way at the end of the Administration building on campus. From here, I can see all the students crossing the quad in that in-between period between classes or heading to the dining hall for an early dinner.

My stomach aches.

I haven't eaten all day. Every time I think I should, I think of that video and I get nauseous. I made the mistake of attempting coffee, only to lose it a few minutes later.

And then I got the email.

"Aspen, I'm Michael Hauser." The man who collected me from the waiting room closes the door. He's got to be only a few years out of college. His red hair is combed neatly and held immobile. "Thank you for meeting with me."

"I was told it was mandatory." My voice is tight, and I sit on the windowsill. "Is that correct?"

He looks down at the folder in his hand. "Well, ah, yes."

"And you're a...?"

"Counselor." He smiles. "I'm here to help with whatever you need. Especially after..."

I go still and wait for him to say it.

"After the past few weeks," he ends, somewhat lamely.

At least be up front and admit that I'm here because of that stupid video. It was taken down last night, and a little bird—*Willow*—mentioned that Steele told everyone to delete it. I guess the cat's out of the bag that our parents are married, so there's that unfortunate truth out in the world, too.

I've kept my head buried in the sand.

Still, no one was more surprised than me to get a supportive text from Willow, and another quickly followed by Violet. Apparently, an ugly video was passed around of Violet last year. She was quick to assure me that everyone will move on quickly when more interesting gossip comes to light, and to keep my head up.

Right.

The counselor takes a seat in one of the armchairs where I remain in his line of sight. Although he seems unperturbed by my choice of placement. Instead, he says, "Let's talk about how your week has been. What are you majoring in?"

"Just to clarify, you're not a licensed therapist, correct?" I lean forward and swing my feet. My heels hit the wall with steady, soft *thumps*.

He shifts. "That's right."

"So you don't have to abide by HIPAA?"

"Oh, everything you say here is confidential—"

"You can tell me that all you want, but there's no real repercussions if you don't, right?"

"You're right." He sets aside the folder and notebook, his pen on top of it. "The whole reason you're here is because the administration is concerned about you."

"It's mandatory that I show up here." I lean back against the glass. The cold permeates through my shirt, and I fight the urge to shift away. Instead, I keep my hands completely still in my lap. "But if I can't trust you, why would I talk to you?"

He nods, all understanding and serene bullshit. "Trust is a big thing for any therapist-patient relationship."

"I don't trust anyone," I mutter. "Especially since this is getting blown way out of proportion. I was drugged."

"You were drugged? By who?" He's skeptical.

"And they videoed it," I add. "Obviously."

He picks up his notepad and writes something. Maybe, *CRAZY!!!*

"You're saying you were under the influence of drugs?"

"I guess." I twist around to look out the window again.

"Have you ever taken hallucinogenic drugs before?"

My attention snaps back to the counselor. "Why?"

"Because certain kinds will stay in your brain. They can come back days, months, years later and send you into an unexpected trip."

My lip curls. "You think that's what happened?"

"I'm not here to pass judgment." He lifts his hands, like he's surrendering. "Although as I'm sure you're aware, CPU has a strict policy when it comes to illegal substances."

What I know is that Steele O'Brien wants my family separated from his by any means necessary... and he's hated that I've been spying on him. I mean, I all but admitted that his father wanted me to keep an eye on him when I first met him. How was I supposed to know that it was an abnormal event? Or something that Steele would freak out about?

"How about we talk about something else?" I suggest.

"Sure."

His amiability is getting on my nerves.

"How about your sisters? You have two?" He flips open the file beside him and scans it. "Dakota and Lennox."

I narrow my eyes. "Yeah..."

"They're quite a bit younger than you. Fourteen and twelve to your twenty. Did you take on more of a parental role with them?"

"Nope, my mom is an excellent mother. She managed to take care of all of us and herself just fine." I don't think I like this line of discussion either. I grit my teeth and glance at the clock. At this rate, I have a feeling he's just trying to get some—*any*—reaction from me.

"Where are they now?"

I force a smile. "With mom's new husband, I would imagine."

"Leaving you alone here?"

"No," I reply steadily, except my heart is beating faster. I'm not alone—I have Thalia. And if I really had to stretch, I'd say I had Willow and Violet, and maybe some of the other girls. I mean, we're not friends by any means, but they both showed compassion when that video went around. And if I had to stretch further, I'd include Uncle.

Not my father, though. Never him, no matter how much money he throws at me.

"Your mother mentioned you had a traumatic childhood," he continues. "In fact, it was noted in your school records by your stepfather to be on the lookout for resurfacing of such trauma."

I go completely still. Is that the truth? Did my mom and

Stephen tell Crown Point University that I was... traumatized? What my father did to me as a kid has nothing to do with Steele drugging me. That doesn't even make sense.

"Should we talk about your father?"

I cringe.

The big bad monster I so desperately needed saving from as a child? No, we shouldn't talk about him.

I stay silent, and the counselor continues his notes. He doesn't seem bothered by my unwillingness to speak. He exudes calmness, and it's driving me crazy. I sit there and stare at him writing god knows what. I fidget with my hands, pick at my nails. My heels drum into the wall.

Time passes so freaking slowly, until *finally*, his phone chimes.

He scans the screen quickly. His focus returns to me. "Our time is up, Aspen. Although I hope to see you again. If anything, I can refer you to a specialist outside of school."

Thank god it's over. I take a deep breath and rise.

I grab my bag and march out of the office without a backward glance. Mandatory counseling, my ass. Luckily, they're only making me go to one.

I've got an email on my phone from the financial aid office. I scan it, my stomach knotting. They want to see me as soon as possible. They're down a floor, I think. I wander until I find it, the glass-walled office sleek and efficient-looking. And cold.

The receptionist takes my name and points to a chair along the wall. My advisor will be out shortly. I've never met the person, so I'm not sure what to expect. It certainly isn't the matronly woman, her steel-gray hair pulled back into a bun, who comes bustling out from an office. She's got the classic chilly-all-the-time vibe, wearing a cardigan over her plum-colored dress, thick socks and boots hiding her legs.

She motions for me to follow, and we step into a small office. There's a space heater on the floor, directed at her chair, and she smiles warmly when we're both seated.

"So, Aspen. We're halfway through the first semester, and I was informed today that your funding for the second semester would not be covered." She frowns. "This is highly unusual, but nothing to worry about. We just need to know how you'll be paying."

I stop. "What do you mean, it's not covered? Did my—" I hesitate. "Did my stepdad call you?"

"Mr. O'Brien did let us know, yes." She has a sympathetic expression. "He tried to confirm your withdrawal from the school, but that's not our department. And unfortunately, there's not much we can do about the funding at this stage..."

My stomach knots, and I swallow down the bile rising in my throat. I should've expected this, but he moved a little faster than I thought. I mean, the asshole didn't even call me.

"What..." I clear my throat. "What are my options?"

She slides a folder toward me, with clear Crown Point University marketing on it. This is probably what they give all their accepted, prospective students. I open it and flip through the pages tucked inside. A guide to applying for financial aid, a list of 'helpful' tips for budgeting, et cetera.

"You can try to apply for financial aid—grants, loans— for next semester. However, most of our allocation is decided over the summer. I would suggest reapplying for aid next semester to cover your final year." She slides me a box of tissues. "It's okay if you're upset."

I stare at the tissue poking out of the top. "I'm not upset," I say slowly. "I'm *pissed*."

She sits back. "Oh. Um—"

"Not at you." I rise. "When do I need to pay?"

"Before the start of next semester. I can file for an extension, give you until the end of January—"

"I'll let you know." I swing my bag over my shoulder and book it out of there. Once I'm free of that cold, depressing office, I head straight to the elevator. With it being during a class period, it's quiet in the halls. The elevator arrives empty, and I stand silently in it until the doors close.

The scream that tears out of my mouth has been building for hours.

It echoes in the small space, bouncing around me, but it feels so good to let it out. I scream until my voice is hoarse and my throat burns. The elevator stops, and I lick my lips. My breathing is ragged, but I don't give a shit.

Steele's been targeting me since I told him I was passing information back to his father. His father, who told me that my way was paid as long as I was useful.

Does that mean I'm no longer useful?

Or... trustworthy?

I shudder. It seems awfully convenient timing. The website, my address being leaked, and now this. Steel's been making everything worse for me, but *this* seems to be the straw that broke the camel's back. The camel being his father.

The idea of giving in to the O'Briens makes my head hurt.

Letting Steele win isn't an option.

17
STEELE

Coach Roake follows me into his office, closing the door behind him. The window that looks out into the hallway won't shield the fact that we're meeting, but it will stop the passersby from eavesdropping.

"What's this about, Coach?"

I stay standing in front of the chair. I don't plan on being here long—I've got a paper due for my biology class tomorrow, and I don't plan on being in the library until midnight. Practice ended about twenty minutes ago, and he called into the locker room that he needed to see me. It gave me enough warning to finish showering and get dressed. My hair is wet, my shirt sticking slightly to my skin.

All's been quiet on the Aspen front. She's been keeping to herself the past few days, dealing with the repercussions of the video and waiting for the storm of attention to pass. The room she shared with Thalia in our house was cleared out yesterday while we were at dinner, which means she obviously knows I was behind drugging her.

I thought posting it would make me feel better. But instead, I feel worse. Like I betrayed her by sharing a vulnerable moment. Except, it was a vulnerable moment I created specifically to embarrass her.

Anyway, practice tonight was fine. We did drills and learned a new play, and Miles and the other goalie worked separately on stops. Not out of the ordinary, although all of us were exhausted by the end of it.

I've racked my brain for reasons why Coach would summon me, but I keep coming up empty.

He folds his arms over his chest, leaning against the wall. "You didn't mention you have a half-sister attending CPU."

"What?" I shake my head in disgust. "*Step*sister, Coach. I barely know her."

Lie. It tastes like ash on my tongue. I know her in all the ways that matter. The way she squirms, how fast to get her to come, her expression when she's cross, afraid, or in pain. I know exactly how to make her shiver or moan. And I know how to destroy her, piece by piece.

Coach clearly believes me as much as I believe myself, because he grunts at my answer. He sits at his desk and types something out on his computer. He swivels the monitor toward me, and the video that's been circulating of Aspen plays on the screen. It's muted, but I can still picture the words she mumbles.

There was more that I didn't film. Her helpless cries, her pleading with the shadows not to take her. The way her eyes went wide as tears poured down her cheeks, her sobs almost choking her.

My gaze stays glued to the screen, although I hate every second of it.

"Explain this, O'Brien."

I shake my head, suppressing my anger.

I took it down last night, and I told everyone else to, as

well. Obviously, I can't control everyone. The video was more for my father than anything, but it spread like wild-fire. That'll be the last time I underestimate the allure of Aspen Monroe.

Option 1: bluff my way out of it.

Option 2: own up to my part in this.

Yeah, right. "Not sure what you want to hear, sir."

Coach sighs and shuts it down, leaning back. "Listen. This is your senior year. Do you really want to go down for something petty like this?"

"I didn't—"

"Don't fucking lie to me, O'Brien," Coach snaps. "I'm not sure what you wanted to gain from exposing this poor girl's mental illness..."

I open and close my mouth, but ultimately, what the fuck can I say to that?

He seems disappointed.

I dig my nails into my palms.

But Coach is already done with me. He points to the door, his face redder than I've seen it. And it occurs to me that this may be taken as some sort of psychotic break, not drugs. Why would anyone think drugs when all the scary things our brain can make us see or do can be caused by malfunctions? By some deficiency of a chemical, or over-abundance of another.

Shit.

"I've already told people to take it down," I say suddenly.

Coach waves me off and turns back to his computer. I leave quickly, striding toward the end of the hall. I make it without running into anyone else, then dial my father.

He needs to open his eyes and actually see who he let into our family.

"What are you doing, Steele?" He doesn't even say hello. Always business with him, never pleasure.

I clench my jaw. "I'm trying to protect our family."

He's silent for a long moment.

"Okay," he finally agrees. "She's coming home—"

"I don't give a fuck whether she stays or goes," I interrupt, my stomach twisting. "It may be better that *I* keep an eye on *her*, don't you think? Instead of using a stranger to spy on your son. But as far as the rest of her family..."

"I love her mother." His voice is a bucket of ice water dropped over my head. "Do you want me to abandon her?"

Like you abandoned Mom? Why yes, yes I do. Drop this gold digger and protect our family better. Simple.

"I just want you to see—"

"Enough." Dad sighs. "If you had come home over the summer, you would've met them. You would know them like I do."

I don't want to see what he sees. That's the problem. I want things to go back to the way they were when I was a kid. And maybe Dad can tell, because he doesn't push for once. We just stay on the line in silence until one of us figures out what to talk about next—or how to break past this.

In the end, it's my father who does both.

"We'll be at your hockey game in New York next week," he says. "Make sure Aspen comes, too."

I bite back my laugh. If she lets me anywhere near her, sure. And even if not...

A thrill goes through me.

Why am I so fucking obsessed with her?

I get home and head straight upstairs. It's a bit weird now that Erik's not our basement dweller and Greyson's living on his own with Violet. Erik used to always be around, in the kitchen or hanging out in the living room. Knox and Miles must be elsewhere, because the whole house is unusually silent.

On one hand, I'm glad we got the extra bedroom free. It certainly helped out when the girls were staying here, although I was pissed that Aspen wouldn't stay in my room after that first night. Now that they're gone, though, it's right back to how it was at the start of the semester: depressingly empty.

Willow occasionally sleeps in Knox's room, although it seems like she might not be as into it lately. Or he goes to her... who the fuck knows what's up with them anyway. Knox just wants Willow to admit that she loves him. It goes back to a stupid, offhand comment that Greyson made, which devolved into a bet... which Knox won't let go of. He wants to win, and I guess he's fine with one pussy. For now.

All at once, I register that I'm *lonely*. Like a fucking loser.

I open my phone and flip through my contacts, but no one stands out. I open my bedroom door and drop my bag on the floor. I strip off my shirt, then toe off my shoes. Change of wardrobe, get my laptop, and I'll just go with my original plan: suffer at the library to finish that paper.

It's better than failing it and putting hockey at risk anyway.

I'm dragging a hoodie over my head when movement catches my attention. I pull it the rest of the way on and try to find the source, but there's nothing against that wall. Just my desk, which is painfully cluttered with papers. The chair is pushed all the way in so I don't try and cover it in half-dirty clothes.

Looking around the rest of the room, my gaze snags on a card on my nightstand.

I snatch it up and stare down at the front of it.

A little thanks from me to you... is printed on the front. It's one of those thank you cards you can buy at the on-campus store. I flip it open, and my gaze skips to the feminine print at the bottom.

Dear Steele,

Once a snake, always a snake. Enjoy your new roommate.

Love,

Viper

I stare at it, not comprehending the words—until something brushes my foot. I snap the card closed and look down, *almost* unsurprised to see a literal, actual snake making its way over the top of my foot toward my bed.

Holy shit.

I don't move until it's not touching me anymore, although my stomach is in my fucking throat. I hurry out of the bedroom and slam the door shut behind me, and I get all the way downstairs before I realize I should've put my stupid shoes back on.

The *only* saving grace is that my phone is still in my pocket and the card clutched in my hand.

She put a snake in my room?

Where did she even get a snake?

I grit my teeth and yank my phone out, calling Knox. He's the single most connected fucker at school—if he doesn't know someone who can catch a snake, I'd be shocked.

An hour later, Knox and a girl whose name I missed stand in front of me, the door to my room open. She has a bucket and a long stick with a hook on the end in her hands, and she steps in carefully.

Knox glances over his shoulder at me, then shrugs. Like he doesn't know what she plans on doing either.

And yet, in less than five minutes, she's got the snake in the bucket—lid screwed into place—and steps past us.

"Can I see that card?" she asks.

I hand it to her.

She reads it and laughs. "Yeah, okay. I know whose snake this is."

"It's a pet?" Knox asks.

"Yep. I'll take care of it." She smiles at him, like she wouldn't mind if he just leaned forward and pressed his lips to hers—

Instead, he pushes a hundred dollar bill into her palm.

Her fingers curl around it, shock opening her expression. But then she nods and slips past us, leaving us alone in the hallway.

"So, was it Aspen or not?" Knox asks.

"Who else would refer to themselves as Viper?"

He frowns. I snag my shoes and bookbag from my room and follow him. I should just give up on the paper, but I refuse to do that to myself. I'm on thin ice with my father as it is, and I know he watches my grades. Waiting for a single slipup.

"I'm going back to campus," I tell him.

"Have fun," he calls. "And give her hell!"

Oh, I definitely will.

"I'm going to go let them in." Thalia says, getting up from the couch and slipping her feet into my sandals by the door.

Tonight was supposed to be lowkey—and yet somehow, it's turning into a girls' night. She wasn't very specific, but she *did* come home with a bag full of those face masks and whatever else from the drug store on the corner. I didn't inspect it too closely.

She returns with Violet and Willow.

Violet holds up a bottle of wine. Which is fine, if we're going that route. But then I spot the tequila Willow has in her grip, and my expression must light up.

"Someone wants to get fucked up the proper way," Willow quips. She toes off her shoes. "We brought popcorn, too. And Thalia assured us that she has a good selection of rom-coms to choose from. Anything to keep your mind off the guy we're not thinking about, right?"

I smile.

Yeah, okay, maybe it's a good thing they came over.

Willow joins me on the couch, while Thalia plops into

the armchair. I'm suddenly glad that we decided to get more furniture than I originally thought was necessary. That's Thalia, though. She likes to be surrounded by people sometimes, and she knew we'd eventually have friends over.

So therefore, we got as much comfortable seating as we could find and afford.

Thalia grabs the remote, and Violet goes hunting for glasses.

"Wine or tequila?" she calls to us.

Willow and I decide on tequila, and she winks at me.

I relax farther into the couch and adjust the blanket over my lap. Violet returns with two wine glasses and two shot glasses, delivered with our shaker of salt and limes in a little plastic cup that is more likely used for sauces in to-go containers.

My brow furrows. Did we even have limes?

"What?" Willow smirks at me. "We stopped by Haven for the limes."

That damn bar.

We prepare the salt on the back of our hands, and she pours both of us a healthy shot. We cheers and take them together, then bite into the lime. It soothes the burn, and heat spreads from my center almost immediately.

"Do you want to talk about it?" Willow pours me another shot.

I take it and let my head tip back on the couch cushion. "Steele drugged me."

Violet chokes. "He what?"

"He put some sort of hallucinogenic in a water bottle somehow. It was sealed—"

'There are ways around that," Willow says, her voice dark.

Goosebumps rise on my arms. "He found me in the music practice room. I don't know, I just thought he was coming to be nice for once... then..."

Willow grips my hand.

I squeeze back. "I don't remember half of what's on that video."

"Because he's an idiot who probably gave you too much." Thalia shakes her head. "Trust me, I did my fair share of experimenting at my old school. It's easy to get the dosage wrong, especially if you're putting it into water. Did he think you'd just take one sip? Drink the whole thing?"

I shudder. I don't know the answer to that.

"Knox got Ruby to collect your present," Willow says suddenly, her hand still on mine. "She got a hundred bucks from him to go pick up her own damn pet."

I snort.

When I asked Thalia if anyone owned a snake, her first phone call had been to Willow. Who just so happened to know a girl who Steele had burned their sophomore year. Slept with her then iced her out, I guess.

While I didn't really relish the idea of having a girl who knew what Steele's dick looked like help me with a revenge plot, Willow assured us that Steele probably wouldn't even remember her.

And sure enough...

I smile. "He got my message, then."

"And he'll be coming for you." Violet meets my gaze. "I know his type, Aspen. He's..."

"Whatever he's got is nothing compared to what I'm going to do to him," I whisper. "He crossed a line—his dad pulled my funding for next semester."

Thalia eyes me. "What about the you-know-what in the you-know-where?"

She's talking about the cash in my closet. I checked it once we returned to our apartment but only pushed it deeper back on the shelf. The longer it sits there, the more I hate it.

I don't want to take anything from my father, but seeing as it's already here, ignoring it is my next best bet. He probably got it from somewhere illegal. And if I just waltzed into the financial aid office with that cash, they'd ask way more questions than I want to answer.

What if it's tied to bad people and I get arrested?

Or worse, targeted?

"It's not an option," I respond in a low voice.

Violet's gaze doesn't waver from me. She doesn't seem put off by our veiled conversation. If anything, her lips twitch up at the corners like she's trying to hold back a smile. I can only imagine her and Willow have that sort of shorthand, too.

"Game on, sister," Violet eventually says, then motions to the television. "I, for one, am ready for a movie. Popcorn, anyone?"

Five hours later, and we've finished two movies, eaten the popcorn, demolished the wine... and the tequila. *Oops*. My body and my brain are only faintly connected at this rate, which is fine by me. I'd rather not be connected at all.

And in fact, I think Willow feels the same, because she's snoring on the couch beside me.

Violet and Thalia are talking quietly, and I roll my head toward them. They look like shadowy figures from this angle, similar with their body shape and their hair pulled away from their faces.

I tug a lock of my dark hair in front of my face, frowning at it.

I wouldn't be mistaken for any of these girls.

Ah, well. My eyes drift closed for a minute.

Maybe longer than a minute.

When I open them again, Willow is covered in a blanket on the opposite end of the couch, curled into a little ball. I'm momentarily guilty that I'm taking up half of it, and I climb to my feet.

"I'll be in my room," I mumble to her, although I doubt she heard me.

Except there's a body in my bed.

Violet, I decide upon closer inspection.

I head back out and go into Thalia's room. She's asleep on her back, snoring, with her arm slung over her eyes. I climb in beside her and fluff the pillow, and immediately my body goes back into the relaxed, drunken zone.

This time when I wake up, it isn't because it's morning.

Nope, I'm being moved. Jostled.

Is Thalia having a nightmare? Thrashing?

I crack my eyes open and am met with... white.

T-shirt.

Chest.

I drag my gaze up.

Throat.

Jaw.

Lips, nose, cheeks, *eyes*.

Steele.

My brain's firing too slow for this. Am I dreaming? Am I that fucked up that I would dream about him coming to carry me away?

For the last time, Aspen, he's not your knight in shining armor.

And yet, I can't get that stupid image out of my head.

A door clicks behind us, and it takes a second to register that my eyes have closed again. Another door, and my stomach swoops. I'm being lowered, positioned, and yet my muscles are jelly. I really don't even care where I'm going right now in my dream world.

It would be a better dream if I could open my eyes all the way.

Heat blasts onto me, and my body shifts with my seat's movement. It's not bad either. In fact, it lulls me to sleep again.

Wait...

Can you sleep in a dream?

The next thing I know, I'm in a bed.

It's soft. Warm. And exactly how I was when I went to sleep next to my roommate.

See, brain? You were just dreaming about Steele, when you're really still next to Thalia.

I sigh and roll over. My arms are above my head, and they get all twisted with the movement. My eyes crack open, and I stare up at my bound wrists, although it's so dark, it's hard to see what's six inches in front of my face. Another minute passes while I try to catch up to what's happening.

Why would Thalia tie me up?

I blink and try to lick my lips, but something is in the way. Hard plastic between my teeth, keeping my jaw open.

A flash of fear storms through me like lightning, obliterating the last of the drunken haze.

Nothing will wake you up quite like adrenaline.

I swallow and attempt to sit up. Something holds me fast around my ankles.

Okay.

Okay, okay, okay.

I let out a little noise. A whimper in the back of my throat.

The room is dark, and it's silent, and I'm definitely not in Thalia's room, that's for sure. I pull at my wrists, my ankles, but I've got no leverage. When I spread my legs, something clicks—and then I can't shut them again.

Fuck.

I close my eyes and will myself to ignore the panic welling in my chest. Breathing deep only gets me so far before I revert right back to shallow huffs through the gag.

It takes me too long to register that I'm naked. That when the air moves, it brushes against my bare skin. That there's nothing hiding me from whoever walks through the door.

Whatever door it happens to be.

This isn't fun anymore.

This isn't a game.

I squeeze my eyes shut, blocking out the burning sensation and the lump in my throat. Instead of twenty-year-old Aspen, I'm a kid again. Trapped exactly like this, with only my heartbeat keeping me company. Waiting for the door to open and my nightmares to begin.

Or continue. Because they never really *stopped*, not back then.

I like to be in control. I like to be *out* of control with an emergency stop button. I like it to be *my choice*—and this isn't that. My childhood wasn't that either.

My breathing continues to come in short bursts. I stare at the darkness above me, my mind wandering.

You're okay, I assure myself. It's a complete lie, though. I rip at the bindings around my arms, jerk my feet. There's another click, the bar locking and keeping my legs in their new spread position.

Seconds pass.

Then minutes.

My panic doesn't ease. My heart doesn't slow.

The longer I lie here, the more I'm convinced that this is cruel and unusual punishment—and for what? For leaving a snake in his bedroom? For telling his father about him? Which, that point is bullshit. I never gave his dad anything actionable. Never told him about the worst treatment Steele has given me.

Fire, I think. That safe word that lives in the back of my head. I say it out loud, but my tongue can't get around the gag. It comes out as a muffled plea that could mean anything.

Fire.

Because we're taught as little girls that if you're attacked, no one will come running if you scream for help. But they will if you yell fire. People are selfish like that. They're drawn into action by things that may hurt them. But if it's you on the line?

Forget it.

I pant and twist and curl my fingers around the head-board, trying to get enough leverage to rip the bindings off my ankles. Or give my back some relief, because my ass is starting to go numb. I barely get my hips off the bed.

The door opens. It's a little crack of dim light coming through, and then it closes again. My breathing stops. It's a noise that was there, but now the room is entirely silent. Except for the footsteps that come toward me.

The bed caves. He climbs up over me and trails his finger up the inside of my thigh. I groan through my teeth. I can't even make out his face, or his shadow.

It could be Steele, or it could be my father. I'm waiting for the flash of a camera. For the searing sharpness to temporarily blind me further. And I'm mumbling nonsense behind the gag. A string of *no, no, no*s that fall on deaf ears.

Something heavy drops on my belly.

And then the bed lifts again as his weight disappears, and he retreats. The door opens, and he slips out, but there's still something on my stomach. A second later, the overhead light comes on.

I raise my head.

A snake sits coiled on my belly, its tongue flickering out.

I groan through my gag, and a burst of adrenaline burns through me. Tears leak out of my eyes. I can't stop them. The snake doesn't seem interested in moving, but it watches me.

The light goes out, plunging us into darkness again.

I lower my head and close my eyes, burying my face in my arm. My breathing hiccups, my nose blocks. I'm an ugly crier—always have been, always will be. My skin gets blotchy and red, I get snot running down my nose, my face contorts.

That's probably happening now.

Except with the gag, I can't get a good breath.

Can't seem to take in any breath at all.

On some level, I register the escalating panic attack for what it is. I've been slowly ramping up while I've been lying here, but this is the icing on the fucking cake. He *wants* to torture me—and he's succeeding.

"Fire," I attempt to say again. The safe word that's supposed to be my ticket off this insane ride. But nothing happens, and I stay exactly where I am.

I blink, and I'm a kid again. Anxious, scared. My brain is playing tricks on me, making me see my old room. The purple comforter under my body, the stuffed animals that lined the bed next to the wall. I used to think they'd protect me, too.

My breathing is still ragged when the snake uncurls. It

slithers lower, down over my abdomen. It drops down between my legs, and the feel of it sliding across my core is too violating. I shudder. My chest heaves, the fear dripping into my lungs icy cold. It freezes me from the inside out. My skin crawls—and my mind splinters.

I lean into the numbness, begging my brain to give up control. To not care that Steele is torturing me for his own sick pleasure, for payback. I just want to shut it off for a minute, or an hour, or a day. I just don't want to be here anymore.

And my brain accepts.

The tears stop.

The shaking stops.

I stare at the ceiling—or where I imagine the ceiling to be, since I can't see a thing—and wait. My body is cold, but I'm caught up in a floating sensation. Like I'm not really *here*, after all. I'm just watching this happen from far, far away.

When Steele finally reemerges, and the light flickers on, I don't really notice it. My eyes ache as my pupils retract, but I don't look away from the spot on the ceiling. It has a crack running through the paint, forking off in different directions. I can see it now, although I had already built the image in my head. I fixate on the cracks. Maybe the ceiling will split and come crashing down on us.

He leans over me, and I flinch when he touches me.

That's what he wanted, right? To break me?

I think he succeeded.

19
STEELE

Aspen doesn't respond to me. It's like she can't even hear me.

The snake is under the bed, but I ignore it. Its owner will be back to collect it later, and she can find it then.

I unfasten the cuffs around her ankles, tossing away the spreader bar and closing her legs. A shudder moves through her. I undo the gag next. Her teeth have dug into the rubber, indenting it, and she doesn't open her mouth to release it right away. I touch her cheek and rub my finger along her jaw, coaxing her mouth open. I pull it out, and she wets her lips.

"Fire," she whispers.

I go cold.

Fuck.

Fuck.

FUCK.

How long has she been trying to say that? How long has she been trying to bail out of this? I untie her wrists and let her cross her arms over her chest.

She's still not here.

We're in the extra bedroom. The empty one in the basement that Erik used to sleep in, where there are only high windows—easy enough to block with blackout curtains. It's noon, but it feels like midnight.

I snatch the blanket from the floor and wrap it around her. I help her into a sitting position, but she's like a rag doll. She leans against me, her cheek on my arm.

Her eyes are fucking vacant, and a chill settles into my bones.

"Come back," I say in her ear, like that's going to make any difference.

It doesn't.

She blinks slowly, and she draws her legs up. Wraps her arms around her knees. She makes herself as small as possible, a little naked ball.

I pick her up like that, with her trying to curl into a fetal position, and carry her out of the basement. The blanket that covers her—*barely*—flutters behind me, still half caught on her body. There's no one home today, I made sure of that. I pass by the couch in the living room, my tablet open to the night-vision-equipped video feed of the basement room.

I waited for her to snap, to struggle. I thought she would fight and scream—but instead, I think I watched her go into a panic attack. And I did nothing about it.

I grit my teeth and carry her upstairs. Her eyes are closed, her breathing shallow and quick. I set her down on the edge of my bed and grab a clean shirt and boxers. I do the shirt first, guiding it over her head and sliding her arms through the sleeves. She doesn't fight me, or help me, or anything.

Boxers are next. Her skin is cool under my hands as I

take each ankle and put them through, then drag the fabric up her legs. I help her stand and pull them the rest of the way up, and she sinks right back down onto the bed.

I guide her back and drag the covers up over her, tucking them in around her body.

And then... I don't know what else to do. Leaving feels wrong.

Staying feels wrong, too.

But I want to understand, so I circle the bed and crawl in behind her. I drag her into my side and brush her hair out of her face, then drape my arm over her hip.

And I watch her breathing even out, and she disappears into sleep. I try to join her, but I only manage a few hours before I have to get up. I leave her curled in bed and step outside, checking my phone.

It's blowing up. Texts from Violet, from Willow. Everyone demanding to know where Aspen is. I reply that she's fine, that she's with me, although my gut squirms. I'm not sure she is fine. Or that she's here with me, at all.

I grab a few water bottles from the fridge and head back upstairs. I can hear sound coming from Knox's room, and more from Miles'. Good to know they're back, I guess. I turn my phone off and head back into my room, setting the water within Aspen's reach. I keep the lamp on my side of the bed on, because if she wakes up in dark again... it just doesn't seem like the best idea. Then I settle in behind her and doze off, waiting for her to come back to me.

Because she has to.

Right?

When she eventually wakes, she panics. She flails, and it takes me a second too long to reach for her. Her knuckles catch my cheek. The force cuts my cheek against my teeth, and the metallic taste of blood fills my mouth. I catch her wrists and force her upright.

Her chest heaves, her eyes wild.

She snarls at me.

I shove the blankets off us. They slide onto the floor, leaving both of us sitting without protection. She curls her legs under her, and I mirror her. Until we're both kneeling on the bed, her wrists in my grip.

But then I release her.

"Show me how you feel," I demand.

She launches at me. I guess I should've expected it, but she bowls into me and knocks me off-balance. We crash to the side, and she propels us off the bed. I land hard on my back, and it takes a second for air to return to my lungs. As soon as I do, though, she's on top of me. She wraps her hands around my throat and squeezes, cutting off my air.

My heart thrashes as I look up at the gorgeous girl straddling my chest.

I rub my hand along her bare thighs.

Best not to tell her that I'm harder than a rock right now, and I wouldn't even mind this death.

My lungs sear. I resist the urge to knock her off me. She won't kill me—and I deserve this. She finally releases her tight grip, and I take a gasping breath. She drags her nails down my throat. Pain follows.

I can't seem to tear my gaze off her face. She's furious.

Rightly so.

I hold her hips and move her backward, off my chest, and my erection brushes her ass.

Her brows furrow.

"Show me how you feel," I say again. "Everything."

She lets out a little noise, a roar too small for the

animosity she feels, and tears my shirt down the middle. I stare at it, then her. There's blood on her fingernails. The wetness pools on my throat, and a drop of it slides down toward my neck.

I move my hands to her thighs. She inches backward and frees my cock from my sweatpants and boxers. She fists it and strokes me once, twice. She's fucking brutal, but my balls tighten in reaction all the same. The pain and lust feel good wrapped up together.

But there's something missing.

I grip her chin without warning, dragging her face toward mine. I sit up at the same time and force her mouth open.

I spit into her mouth.

She stares at me. Those green eyes are going to be the death of me, because her jaw works. Not swallowing, though. She rips free and leans down, letting her spit and mine drip onto my dick.

Now wet, her fist glides easier. She runs her thumb over the tip with every stroke, seeming entranced by it.

When my hips thrust, she stops.

"You know what I want?" she whispers, her voice so much deeper than usual.

I shake my head.

For now, I'm *her* captive. It won't last. Our power balance will right itself again, eventually. But if this helps her...

She stands over me and pulls the boxers down her hips. I get a view up her legs to her pussy—and an even better view when she kneels again. Fuck, I want her on my mouth. So I slip between her legs and drag her down over my face.

The noise she makes is cute—and she tries to lift off me.

But I've got her in my hold now, wrapping my hands around her thighs and urging her lower. She's still resisting, though. Her pussy is right there. She's wet, too. I see it, I smell it.

"Sit," I order her, licking my lips.

"Steele—"

"I swear to God, Aspen, sit on my face right now."

She slowly gives in, and I'm greeted with her cunt on my face. I tip my head back and lick her, groaning at the taste. She's like candy, which is fucking weird, but I can't explain it. I thrust my tongue into her, and she jolts. She's tense, her hand bracing on the bed, until I get to her clit.

Then she whimpers.

I'm fucking addicted to that sound.

I do it again, and again, swirling my tongue around the sensitive nub, until she gives in and grinds against my face.

I let go of her thigh and add my hand to the party, pushing two fingers into her. She cries out and moves faster, getting herself off on my face and my fingers. My cock twitches, wanting in on the action, but I focus on the sounds she's making above me.

All at once, she goes still. Her pussy clenches down on my fingers, pulsing, and I lick at her clit until she sags forward. She crawls off me and curls into a ball, staring at me with a mixture of hate and confusion.

I climb to my knees and fist my cock. It demands my attention, and I stroke it slowly. It's still wet from her spit, and mine.

Her gaze lingers on my neck. The scratches she left behind are burning slightly, so I can only imagine what they look like.

"Tell me," I order. "What do you need?"

Show me how you feel. Give me what you want.

Tell me what you need.

I'll get to the root of her.

When she shakes her head, it isn't good enough. It isn't enough. I shake my head back, frowning at her. She has to know that this is our fucked-up way of making things right, of figuring out a solution. Naked. Hot. Angry.

I don't do apologies—and neither does she.

Besides, an apology would be a lie.

"Aspen."

Her name makes her eyes close.

"I don't need anything from you," she says.

I scoff. I rise, my dick still pointed straight at her. Always at her, like a fucking beacon. I knew from that first day that she was special, and hell. She is.

"Yes, you do," I growl. I offer her my hands.

She hesitates, but she takes them.

I pull her to her feet and shed the scraps of my shirt still on my arms. I kick off my boxers that were trapped under my balls, not really hiding much of anything.

She plucks at the shirt she's wearing, and I wonder if she's trying to decide what it is she needs. And honestly, at this rate? I'd give her anything she asks for, do anything she said.

I'm a sucker, and the tears still on her cheeks are just making things worse.

"I need you..." She bites her lip and steps closer, her hand wrapping around my cock again. Fisting it and sliding her hand up and over my head, then pushing back toward the base.

"You need me to what, sweetheart?"

Her fingers touch my balls. Cups them with her free

hand while stroking me, and I don't know why the light suddenly in her eyes has me all twisted up.

"I need you to go fuck yourself, Steele." She steps back and grabs my forgotten sweatpants, dragging them up over her legs. She leaves me standing naked in the middle of my room and disappears out the door.

My uncle is waiting outside Steele's house. I climb in without comment, securing the seat belt around me and folding my arms over my chest. I feel... raw. I walked out without shoes, without my clothes. Steele's sweatpants are baggy around my legs, even my waist. He really is bigger all the way around, and that should make me feel good about myself.

But instead, I just feel sick.

"You want to talk about it?" Uncle asks.

"No."

"Because it looks like things are spiraling." He glances at me, then taps the lid of the coffee cup in the holder. "This is for you."

I lift it and wrap both hands around it, savoring the warmth.

The sun is setting, the sky a wash of cotton-candy colors. The clock on the dash says it's almost six o'clock. My stomach growls, and Uncle's jaw tics.

"Tell me why I shouldn't go back and kill that boy."

I hesitate, although the thought makes me nauseous. "Because he's..."

If I say he's an O'Brien, he'll look into him. Find the rumors around campus, sure, but also that we're stepsiblings. And wouldn't that be a fun explanation to my mother about how Dad found her location?

If I say he's just some boy, that's not really an excuse at all to stop Uncle from doing exactly what he wants.

"He's important to me," I end lamely.

He sighs. "Because his father is married to your mother?"

I glance sharply at him. "Who said that?"

"The marriage license I dug up in Vegas."

"Because my father—"

"No, Aspen, because I wanted to make sure your mother wasn't being an idiot. *Again*." He shakes his head and turns into a diner. "At least she never married your father," he adds under his breath.

I can't help but agree.

Once parked, he reaches behind my seat and grabs a pair of flip-flops. He sets them on my lap, and I stare at the cheap, dark-blue plastic. A few sizes too big for me, but whatever. I slip them on and follow him inside.

My footsteps thwack against the pavement, up the steps, and down the linoleum-tiled floors to a booth at the end of a long row. He takes the seat to see the rest of the diner, and I slide in across from him.

A waitress comes by with menus and takes our drink order —coffee for him, hot chocolate for me—and leaves again.

"Your daddy and I aren't speaking at the moment," Uncle says. "He's made some moves in Chicago that no one is happy with. It's why he gave me the cash... and an explanation. Said he'd only be able to make things right if he had his family back together."

Another chill goes through me. "That doesn't make sense. Who did he piss off? And how can *family* help?"

Uncle pins me with a hard stare. "The mob, darlin'. Only people in this world you should fear are the ones with no fear, themselves. And your father lacks any inhibition at all. As proven with what he'd done to you."

I reach for the silverware in the rolled napkin. Just so I can have something to do with my hands. "He's on the run?"

"Something like that."

I meet his eyes. "Is he coming here?"

"Here or to your mother..."

"That's why you haven't left yet." I frown. "You said I was safe from him."

Uncle was going to Boston. Then New York City. But instead, he's still here in Crown Point. Which at this rate, I'm not *not* thrilled about. Having someone watch my back feels a little better than being completely alone, or relying on my roommate...

He inclines his chin.

"How did you know where I was?"

Uncle shrugs. "You've got a boy who won't quit tormenting you. It was common sense."

Yeah, I guess so.

The waitress returns with our mugs, and Uncle orders enough food for four people. All breakfast food.

Wait.

"It's six o'clock at night, right?"

He raises an eyebrow. "What makes you say that?"

"B-because otherwise..."

"You lost a whole day." He glances out the window. "Sunrise is such a peaceful time."

Sure enough, the damn sky is getting lighter.

Fuck.

"Stress can do that to a person," he adds. "Too much sleep, I mean. If that's what you were doing."

He gestures to my wrists again, and I lift them for both of us to see the red marks. I bore those marks a lot when I was a kid, but Mom always insisted that I just wore those hair ties too much. She made a lot of excuses for my father out of fear.

"I slept some," I admit. "After."

Uncle's expression darkens. "You going to tell me what he did to you?"

Because when Uncle found out what my *father* was doing, he damn near put my mother through a wall. I still remember their hushed, angry conversation. About how she could be so blind, so ignorant. It wasn't until he pointed out that he could do it to my sisters that she freaked out. And we were gone a few weeks later.

"No." I pull my leg up, hooking my arm around it. "But his dad withdrew funding for my education. I owe for next semester if I want to continue at Crown Point. I've got to figure that out... but I want to give you that cash back. I can't accept it."

Uncle sighs.

"That's why you're here," I say, repeating my conclusion from earlier. "Because he stole that money from the mob. Right?"

Sometimes, monsters are about people.

Sometimes, monsters try to do what's best for their blood.

"Yes," he confirms. "Because I can't save your mother, and she'd want me to look out for you."

I shiver. Deep down, I know that my uncle cares more about my mother than he'd ever admit to himself—or her. It's more than a brotherly love. It's soul deep. And it makes my chest ache, because I'll be damned if I ever find myself in that position. Forced to watch the man I love endure a marathon of abuse and trauma and *still* not choose me. Or maybe... maybe Mom just can't choose him because of who he is.

Does she look at Uncle and see my dad?

"Don't go pouting, darlin'." Uncle sighs. "It's just a fact of life."

The waitress delivers our food, and we don't bother divvying up the plates. We have our forks and we attack everything. My hunger comes back with a roar, and I can see the relief in my uncle's eyes that I'm not so scarred as to have lost my appetite.

What Steele did to me was... terrible. Hard. Hurtful. But he wouldn't know about my past, about my limits, because we never talked about it. And foolishly, I made it seem like I was all sunshine and rainbows. There's some desperate part of me that wants him to know these things, and for him to understand that just because I couldn't handle *that*, doesn't mean I won't handle *him*.

Fuck.

When did I start wanting to handle him at all?

Because he can make me come with his tongue and doesn't seem put off by my curves—in fact, he might argue that they're a plus—and he's so fucking possessive, it actually makes me smile.

"Aspen?"

I crane around and find Thalia coming down the aisle.

She slips into the booth with me and throws her arms around my shoulders.

A lump forms in my throat.

"I'm okay," I assure her. I hug her back. "How'd you know—"

"Cillian texted." Her cheeks pinken. "He suggested that I come join you."

I raise my eyebrow at my uncle. It's unlike him—to put it nicely—to invite an outsider to join us. Not that I don't trust Thalia, because I do. I just haven't told her my dad's side of the family history, including what my uncle does for work. Plus, she's calling him by his first name? Not many people get *that* honor. Everyone has always called him Monroe.

"Well, I'm glad you're here," I tell her.

The waitress comes by to clear some plates. There's enough food left for Thalia, and she picks at some of the pancakes smothered in syrup. The waitress brings more coffee for Uncle, plus another mug for Thalia.

I sit back, angling in the corner to see both of them.

"I'm sorry for worrying you," I say to Thalia. And really, to both of them.

Her brows furrow. "You're sorry? For Steele literally kidnapping you out of our apartment and holding you hostage? That's not your fault, Asp. Like—that's bordering on criminal—"

"One could say it *is* criminal," Uncle interjects with a frown. "Were you free to leave?"

I bite my lip and shake my head.

His jaw tics again. "Give me one reason, Aspen."

One reason not to go back and murder him? I reach across the table and grab his hand. I pull it toward me so I can put both my hands on his. His fingers curl, our palms pressing together. His hands are calloused, rough from work. The opposite of mine.

I've hardly done anything with my life, except play the freaking piano.

"Because I'm not..." I shake my head. "It's just our thing."

"Your thing," Thalia repeats.

"We push at each other." I eye my uncle, careful to word this in a way that won't send him flying off the handle. "We like to hurt. But usually with limits."

His eyes light with understanding, and I withdraw again. Message received. Whatever notions he has about my life, and what it should be, we can agree that my past has fucked up my future.

And sometimes that means doing extreme things in pursuit of happiness.

"How's the piano?" Uncle asks.

I smile. "I'm going to apply to orchestras. If I can't afford the tuition for next year, then I need to get a jump on my career—"

"Use the money." Uncle frowns. "I'll deal with the fallout."

My smile fades. "I won't do that."

He exhales but thankfully drops the subject.

When we're done, he pays and motions for both of us to follow him. Thalia must've caught a ride or walked—we're not far from campus—because she doesn't hesitate to climb in the backseat of Uncle's car.

"Where are your clothes?" she whispers to me before Uncle gets in.

I stifle my sigh. "No idea."

"Oh my god," she groans and leans back. "I don't know how you're not wanting to kill him."

Uncle, now in his seat and slamming his door, glances back at her. "Your friend has the right idea, Aspen."

I shake my head. "I think I just want to go home. Please."

That scraped-out feeling returns. Food helped. The company helped. But now, as we lapse back into silence, the darkness creeps back in.

Still. I ignore it as Uncle parks on the curb and follows us inside, making himself at home on the couch. I go right into the bathroom and lock the door. I turn the water on as hot as it'll go. Some therapist in high school once said burning-hot showers were a way of self-harm, but... in this case, I feel like it's warranted.

Anyway.

I shower until I feel somewhat human again. My room is just as I left it. Well, except I left when Violet was sleeping in it—and luckily, she's not still in it. That would be weird.

It appears that she changed my sheets and made the bed. My phone is on the charger, and I open it to a slew of messages from yesterday morning. When they realized I was gone, but before they found my phone?

A new message comes through as I'm holding it.

Steele: Our parents are going to my New York game. You're coming, too.

Bossy.

Are they done traveling Europe? I hadn't heard anything...

Me: Is that a question, or...?

Steele: No.

Me: Your tone is a little off-putting. I'll pass.

Steele: Either get on the fan bus with some friends, or I'll hogtie you and leave you to ride in cargo with our bags.

Steele: Your choice.

I gape at my phone, then toss it down.

He's *infuriating*.

I get dressed quickly and find my binder of music. I'm skipping classes today—but I think I'm in need of some music therapy.

My uncle rises from the couch when I enter the living room.

"You should consider moving," he says. "At the very least."

I shake my head. 'There's no place that's going to rent for a semester."

He watches me.

"It's fine."

"I'm changing your locks," he adds.

Well... that's not a bad idea. Better than continuing to give Steele unfettered access to my apartment, to me.

I face him. "I should just... keep being a college student. Don't you think?"

His lips twist, then he nods.

"So, with that in mind, I'm going to sign up for the fan bus for an away game this weekend. I'm going to pretend that everything is fine, and that I don't have a crazy family, and that my stepbrother doesn't secretly want to kill me." *Or fuck me while he terrorizes me.* "And I'll pretend that everything is just going... *swimmingly.*"

He rubs his eyes. He looks tired for a thirty-five-year-old. I guess that's what happens when a thirty-five-year-old has taken to sleeping on a college student's couch. Which he's done sporadically for the past week, minus the girls' night gone wrong, in some misguided effort to keep us safe.

"I don't suppose I could talk you out of that," he responds.

"No."

He lifts one shoulder. "Okay."

Not that I expected his permission—and certainly not that I need it—but that was surprisingly easy.

I leave him standing there and head to campus. I'm not prepared for the amount of fear that settles on my shoulders. Like every car I pass is going to open up and someone is going to drag me in. Or every window is filled with a hidden face staring at me, judging.

All I want to do is lose myself in the piano.

Except when I get to campus, every practice room is filled.

I find one of the theater professors and ask if there's anywhere else I could play. He shrugs, then points me toward the stage.

My jaw drops, but I don't argue.

Hell. I'll play on the gorgeous baby grand piano in the auditorium. I've wanted to do so for a while, and who am I to miss out on that?

Of course, I didn't think I'd be doing it in the dark, with just a lamp clipped to the music stand, lending my pages and the keys enough light to see by. For some reason or another, they've moved the piano from the orchestra section up onto the stage. I sit at it and take a second to run my hands over the keys.

"This isn't anything insane," I murmur to myself. "Just pretend you're at the practice room piano."

I count to eight in my head, then begin.

It's a piece I know intimately well. I play it almost without looking at the sheet music, because it mostly lives in my head. I run through it once, then play it again with a variation. The last few notes fade into sweet silence, and I flip the pages to the next piece.

Again.

I'm playing the good stuff first, the ones that I don't mess up. The ones that are so ingrained in my muscle memory, I could play with my eyes closed.

In fact, my eyes do close at one point.

When that piece ends, the clapping starts.

I spin around and find the professor I sought out earlier coming onto the stage.

"Beautiful," he says. "Do you mind giving this a try?"

He stops beside me and sets the new music in front of me. I'm a good sight reader. It hinders me when I'm trying to bullshit myself out of practicing, because I know that for the most part, I can get away with it. And yet, that skill is going to come in handy now.

I adjust my hand position and skim the music. It's in E flat minor, one of my preferred keys. I nod at him once, and he takes a step back. My attention stays riveted to the music. My fingers know where to go, how to find the correct keys. That's part of the training—it's like typing. Once you're proficient, you don't have to look at where the letters are.

The piece is sad and somewhat familiar, and it ends with a drifting, lasting note.

The professor waits until it's faded away to step back up and collect the pages.

"We need a pianist for the spring musical," he says. "Normally the orchestra is hired outside of the school, but we also haven't had much luck sourcing a committed pianist. Would you be interested in working with Crown Point Orchestra on this?" He holds up his hands. "Before you say yes, because I see that smile, you'd have to audition with them, as well. But my recommendations are taken seriously, and your playing is beautiful."

My eyes burn, and I nod wordlessly at him. Because I don't know what the fuck else to say. *Yeah*, I'll take a recommendation on top of an audition to Crown Point Orchestra. That's... that's insane. And a dream come true? And—

"Here," he says, offering me his business card. "Email me your information, and I'll set it up. Your name?"

"Aspen Monroe." I rise and extend my hand.

He shakes it, smiling widely. "Nice to meet you, Aspen."

His business card says, *William Wilcox, Professor of Theater and Music Theory*.

As in... the perfect guy to know.

I nod to him, and I stay standing until he disappears back offstage. The door to the hallway beyond closes behind him.

Holy shit.

21

STEELE

I follow Aspen from the music rooms to the dining hall. She doesn't know I'm following her, that I've been lurking in her shadows since she stopped replying to my texts. She's gone radio silent, and we have two days until the game in New York.

She joins up with Willow, Violet, Greyson, and Thalia. Knox comes over, too, and they all head inside for dinner. I come along slower, dragging my feet.

I'm all twisted up inside.

Aspen and I need to get back on track—simple as that.

But when I finish getting my food and go into the section with the tables, I find Aspen sitting toward the end of the table. Across from Chase fucking King.

That football asshole really has no idea who he's messing with. I should've beat him up when I had the chance, consequences be damned.

He pats her arm, and I almost drop my plate. I make a beeline for their end of the table and sink into the empty chair beside her. She sucks in a little breath, and I allow myself to enjoy her surprise. I spread my legs under the table until my thigh connects with hers. The connection eases my anger a touch.

I glower at Chase, who seems mildly annoyed. But not afraid.

I'd prefer if he was afraid. Too bad he's got a daddy who rivals mine in terms of power and money. That's why he's almost untouchable. Because if *he* makes a phone call, I'll get the heat for it. No escaping that.

Fucking bastard.

"Hey, O'Brien, you ready for your game on Saturday?" Chase grins, leaning back in his chair.

"I'm always ready," I reply. I mirror his position and drop my hands to my thighs. Food forgotten.

Aspen doesn't look at me. She spears salad with her fork and eyes Thalia, a little farther down. Miles is beside her, with Violet and Greyson beyond them. Willow sits on Aspen's other side with Knox. It's very couple-y, how they've decided to pair off. Except Thalia, who seems to be a free agent, and Miles. Who definitely doesn't have any attachments.

Are they trying to matchmake? I wouldn't doubt Willow's and Violet's interference in that regard.

"You know, Aspen," Knox leans over Willow toward us, "Steele here is usually the quietest son of a bitch on the team. And then you come along, and he won't shut up."

"Is that so?" Chase asks.

Aspen eyes me, then raises her eyebrow at Knox. "He doesn't seem to have a lot to say at the moment."

My hand lands on her thigh on instinct.

And as a warning.

She's wearing a tight black shirt that gives everyone at this table way too good of a look at her cleavage. Her hair is down, her makeup is nonexistent. She's the type of girl who guys *say* they want, but then they go for the puck bunnies or the easy lays.

Hell, I'm guilty of that myself.

It's simpler. Less drama... sometimes. I mean, we all saw what a fucking complication Paris was last year, although Greyson handled that with finesse. He played Paris like a cheap recorder to get Violet to pay attention to him.

Hmm...

Nah.

I slide my hand up Aspen's leg. It's easy to feel the way her skin heats through her leggings, and she shifts. Trying to escape me, maybe. But she doesn't push me away. Even when I inch between her thighs and brush her center through her leggings and panties.

"I have a lot to say," I finally answer. I stroke the inside of her thigh, missing the mark on purpose. To get a rise out of her. "I just find more creative ways to say it."

"Do you?" Her voice comes out higher pitched.

"Yep." I smirk at her.

Her legs open wider.

Naughty thing.

"Like... I'm going to put you in my jersey at the game." I lean into her side and whisper, "And then I'm going to fuck you in it. *Again.*"

Chase makes a noise of protest. Or disgust.

Aspen meets my eyes, and her mouth opens.

I grip her thigh and tug her whole chair closer, wrapping my other hand around the back of her neck. And I take advantage of her surprise, pressing my lips to hers. My tongue immediately slips into her mouth.

The kiss goes from shock to filth in an instant.

She *moans*, and everything in my body goes haywire.

Every instinct begs me to go caveman on her, to take her somewhere private and ravish her the way she deserves. But this public kiss will have to do.

And I find myself wondering if it's going to heal her reputation, too.

Or damage it.

Either way is fine, honestly, because in a year we're going to be so far away from this place.

Wait.

We?

Never mind that she'll still have a year of school after I graduate, but I have two options... one, I can lean into the crazy and just fucking go with it. Or two, I can backpedal in my own head, pretend to recover from kissing her like it wasn't my idea to stick my tongue in her mouth, and then do this whole thing again in a month.

Option one.

I release my grip on the back of her neck, but she doesn't automatically pull back. Her teeth catch my lower lip, and she tugs. The little bit of pain doubles the urge to maul her right now. Then she sits back entirely, her face turning red.

"We're together," I inform her... and the rest of the table.

Her brows lower. "Um, I don't think—"

"You're not *going* to think about it." My stomach grumbles. I've got practice in an hour, and I'm fucking hungry. So I turn back to my food and dig in, ignoring everyone's looks.

Including Aspen's.

"When you say together," Willow starts. "Do you mean..."

"Whatever the fuck together means," I grit out. My food is getting cold, and Knox was right—I don't usually talk. I don't like to draw attention to myself. Can I seem to help it with Aspen around? Nope. "Exclusive. She's not seeing anyone else. Neither am I. So you can get lost, King."

Chase snorts. "And miss this show? Nah, I'm good."

"Steele—"

I round on Aspen. My expression is probably pretty dark, because I feel like I'm gonna lose it. Which I need to *not* do, and save my crazy for practice. And better yet, harbor more of it for the game.

"Come to practice," I say quietly.

Confusion mars her expression. "What? Why?"

"Just come." I lean forward and touch my forehead to hers. "Okay?"

She pauses, then nods. "Yeah, yeah. Okay."

I don't know why the fuck that fills me with some weird relief, but it does. So I back off and return to my food, and she does the same.

And that's just fine for now.

Turns out I'm not the only one who watches hockey practice. Violet and Willow accompany me, sitting high above the ice opposite the players' benches.

"Coach will close practices sometimes, but other times he likes the motivation that those girls bring the guys." Willow points to the section diagonal to us. The group is mostly girls, all decked out in CPU Hawks paraphernalia. Some hold signs for the players, although I can't quite make out the words through the glare of the glass.

"Puck bunnies," Violet murmurs. "It's infuriating to watch them line up waiting for their slice of attention. Especially when they know that some of the guys have girl-friends."

"Like Greyson and Knox." I sink lower in my seat.

"And Steele," Violet adds with a smirk.

The devil himself skates out onto the ice. He glances first to the groupies, then over to where Willow, Violet, and I sit. I raise my eyebrows at him, and he scowls.

"Why'd he want me to come if he's going to be grumpy about it?"

"Why do any of them do what they do?" Violet asks. "I've stopped trying to map out Grey's intentions."

I eye Willow. "What's up with you and Knox?"

Violet nudges her best friend. "Yeah, Willow, what's up with you and Knox?"

Willow scoffs. "We're having fun."

"You're dating," Violet presses. "And...?"

"And we're dating. So?"

"He flirts with everyone when you're not around," Violet points out. "And he's probably more of a jerk than Grey—but..."

"But?" Willow stares straight forward. She's tense, but it seems like more than that. A wake-up call she's not ready for?

"He doesn't act possessive." Violet shrugs. "Steele does. He doesn't want any guy talking to you. And he hasn't so much as glanced at another girl since—"

"You can't say that about Greyson, though," Willow snaps. "He fucking made out with Paris—"

"We weren't together," Violet replies calmly. "He doesn't give a shit about any other girls now. I'm his, he's mine, it's simple. But I'm just worried, Will, okay? I'm worried he's going to hurt you. And..."

"It's fine," Willow snaps, finally looking at her best friend. "I love him, so, there's not really much more we can do about it."

They hold a glare, and then Violet reaches out and puts her hand on Willow's leg.

"You love him?"

"He got under my skin," Willow murmurs. "I haven't told him. I'm not going to tell him."

Love is never a good thing. Not in our cases anyway.

"I'd hate to see Steele in love," I comment, more out of sympathy to change the subject than anything else. I find his jersey on the ice, marveling at the way he moves. Still, I know exactly what he'd do with *love*—and it'd be nothing good. "He's a scary motherfucker as it is."

They both burst out laughing.

I sigh.

Yeah, I get the feeling I'm screwed, too.

———

Steele: You stick around?

Me: I figured you wouldn't want me running off after begging me to watch you skate in circles for hours...

Steele: You thought correct. Come down.

I sigh and roll my eyes. Willow, Violet, and I already came down to the main level. Greyson was one of the first out of the locker room, sweeping Violet under his shoulder. Knox followed, picking up Willow and twirling her around. Then other players.

It made me question whether Steele had slipped past me, although I stayed put mostly out of stubbornness.

With the text, I assume he means the locker room, so I push the door open.

There's water running in one of the shower stalls against the far wall, with just an opaque white curtain hiding Steele's naked body. My mouth waters for the strangest reason, and I'm half tempted to shed my clothes and join him.

My curiosity certainly doesn't stop me from ambling closer.

He's groaning under his breath. Groaning *my name*. I stop breathing and inch closer, until my shoes are on the tile, and the curtain is within reach. I slide it open and stare at Steele's cock. He's stroking it fast, his other hand braced on the wall. Water rushes down over the back of his neck, rolling down his back and perfectly sculpted ass.

Why have I never seen his ass before?

And his chest tattoos. The deer skull with the horns in the center of his sternum. Only the tips of the horns that frame his neck are usually visible with his shirt. There's something I can't make out on his stomach. And the scratches I left on him, too. They bled, and now they're scabbed-over lines. It appears like he was attacked by a wolf or something, four claw marks on each side of his neck dragging down to his chest. In my haste to make him feel a fraction of what I felt, I didn't stop to analyze his tattoos. Even when I ripped off his shirt.

He turns and looks at me, his eyes hooded. "You like to watch, too?"

I bite my lip. My gaze drops back down to where he's jerking himself off. Slower now that he has an audience of one.

"Aspen, do you like watching?"

"I'm debating crawling in there and taking over," I whisper. "But another part of me doesn't want to touch you with a ten-foot pole."

His eyes flash. "And what do you want me to do about that?"

I step back and shed my coat, dropping it over the lip of the stall. I tear off my shirt, too, and toe off my shoes. Socks. Until I'm in my leggings and bra, my chest heaving.

"I won't ever gag you again," he swears. He leaves the

water running and steps toward me. "Was that it? Was that the line?"

I force myself to keep eye contact. "The spreader bar. The gag. The dark. The... combination of the three."

"They're gone for good." His chin lowers, his gaze burning into me. "One day, you'll tell me the whole story."

I shake my head, my lips curling into a sneer. "No, Steele, I won't."

He lunges for me.

I jerk back, but I'm not fast enough to avoid him. He crushes me against the side of the stall, his wet body touching *all* of mine. Soaking through my leggings and bra in an instant. My nipples harden through the fabric, and I struggle to push him off me.

Instead, the only way he lets me go is toward the water.

I inch that way, and he herds me under the stream. Hot water douses me. I tip my head back and let it rinse over my face. I've taken to not wearing makeup lately, and I'm weirdly glad of that fact right now. No one wants streaks of mascara running down their faces.

My hair is drenched in an instant, sticking to my neck and back. My leggings are goners, too. I'll be dripping by the time I get out of here. I reach behind me and unclasp my bra, tearing it off and throwing it at his face.

He catches it and smiles down at the fabric, some secret thought going through his head, then tosses it behind him.

Steele palms my throat, using it to push me back farther. My shoulder blades touch the wall, and the water goes over my head. It hits his chest, little rivers coursing down his body. I stare at him, taking him in.

His washboard abs, the tattoos. His hair is darker wet, and I give in to my sudden impulse to touch him. I run my fingers through his hair, spiking it a bit, and curl my fingers around the back of his neck.

I pull him toward me.

He doesn't resist. He stays still when I press my lips to his once, twice. My nails bite into his skin, and I nip his lower lip.

When he grips my hips, I don't move. He hooks his thumbs in my waistband and drags my leggings and underwear off, guiding my feet out of them and tossing the soaked material away. He rises and picks me up, urging my legs to wrap around him. My back hits the wall again, harder, and the water sprays him in the face.

I reach up and redirect it. I mean, I'd love to see him get blasted by it while he fucks me, but something tells me it wouldn't add to the experience. Not this time anyway.

The head of his cock slides through my center, and I gasp.

He smirks. "Wet already, little viper?"

"Better than being caught masturbating..."

His smile widens. "I'll admit, that wasn't part of my plan."

"What was your plan?" Sue me, I'm curious. But my voice comes out a bit shaky, because he's still dragging his cock between my legs and teasing me into shambles. I hook my legs harder around his hips, locking my ankles and trying to force him closer.

"I was going to..." He leans in and kisses my neck.

I automatically tip my head to the side and give him more access.

His teeth score my throat, and I jump.

"I was *going* to chase you all around the stadium. In the dark. With a mask. And force you out onto the ice where I could fuck you right out in the open."

Goosebumps rise on my skin that has nothing to do with the cooling water droplets.

"A mask?"

He leans back and nods, the corner of his lip curling. "You just got wetter, sweetheart."

Fuck.

I look away, but he pinches my jaw and drags my face back to his. With one hand on my thigh keeping me steady, and his hips pinning me to the wall, he notches at my entrance and slides in without a word.

We both let out little huffs at the contact. I force myself to keep my eyes open, not wanting to miss the lust in his. His cock stretches me, sending waves of pleasure crashing through my body. Not an orgasm—but damn it, I could stay like this for a while.

"Why on the ice?"

"To erase my memory of you standing out there with that fucking twat Knight player."

He pulls out almost all the way and slams back into me. He does it again, slower, and my lips part. He's going slow and hard, setting a pace that my mind can't latch on to. I want him to move faster, but each time he pummels me, I see stars.

"Is this what you imagined when you wandered into the boys' locker room?" He releases my jaw and slips his hand between our bodies. His fingers find my clit. "Getting fucked in the shower?"

"I—" I lose the ability to talk, because my orgasm rolls over me like a tidal wave.

He keeps rubbing my clit, thrusting into me like he's got nowhere to be.

"Fuck, Steele," I groan. My head falls forward, my forehead touching his shoulder.

He holds me tighter, his grip on my thigh bruising.

"That's it," he whispers in my ear. "Come on my cock like the little slut you are. And after I use you some more, you're going to come again. Aren't you, sweetheart?"

Shit.

That does something to me.

He retracts his hand from my clit and pulls out of me entirely, setting my feet on the floor. My knees are still wobbly, but he guides me out of the shower. He points to the bench between the lockers. The one all the guys probably sit on to put on their equipment or whatever.

"Sit," he orders.

I do, facing him. Ignoring the water still dripping off both of our bodies, pooling under us. He steps up between my legs and reaches down, palming my breasts. He pinches my nipples, pulling them until they stiffen even more between his fingers. They were already little rocks from the cold, but it seems like they react even more to his touch.

I arch my back into his grasp.

"I love your tits," he groans. "But right now..." He releases them and fists my wet hair. "Open."

My attention drops to directly in front of me. His cock, which he stroked in the shower, then plowed into me, stands at attention. The head is redder, clear liquid oozing out of his slit. I meet Steele's gaze and shake my head.

"Make me," I say.

He smirks. "Thought you'd say that."

He yanks my hair hard enough to make me gasp. He takes that opening and shoves between my lips, filling my mouth. He hits the back of my throat, and I gag around him. I hold his thighs, my nails digging into his skin. I hope it makes him bleed.

I don't mind it, though. In a way, it feels like I'm spinning out of control. A top let loose on the counter. Except Steele's the one who set me off, and I have to trust that he'll keep me from falling, too. Now that he's learned from his mistakes.

So I stare up at him as he fucks my mouth hard enough to bruise, forcing his way down my throat. He yanks me off him, his fist in my hair, then he uses it to push me forward.

I take the fucking. I suck and swirl when the tip is in my mouth and breathe when he lets me.

What does it say about me that I like this?

He warns me that he's going to come, and I don't even think about it. I yank myself off his cock and manually stroke him before he can stop me. I point him at my chest, closing my eyes when hot ropes of cum coat my skin.

His fingers are still tangled in my hair. I hadn't even realized it, that he let me pull away from him. It would've been easy for him to force my head down.

"This is a familiar sight." He helps me stand.

Yeah, right. Except the last time I had cum on my tits, he left me to deal with it—and all my spilled papers—in the stairwell.

That feels like a lifetime ago.

We go back toward the shower, but before I can get in, he bear hugs me from behind. His body curls over mine. And for a split second, I think, *Aw, this is nice.*

But then he smears his cum into my skin with his palm, dragging it down between my breasts. He swipes two fingers through it, and his hand disappears between my legs. His other arm keeps me captive against him.

His fingers push into me.

I bite back a groan, more confused than anything.

"Should've come in here," he says in my ear, then kissing the spot just behind it. "When is your period due?"

S. MASSERY

I narrow my eyes, looking back at him. "Why?"

"Because I'm just trying to figure out if you're pregnant."

"I'm not."

"You're sure?"

"Yeah, I—" I laugh. "This is ridiculous. I'm getting my period next week. You won't be able to miss it."

He adds a third finger inside me, and I shudder.

"I won't miss it, huh? Someone has a blood kink I don't know about?"

"Fuck off," I groan.

"No, now I'm curious."

I shift, pushing at his arm. Guys are weird about periods, aren't they? I don't need his judgment. "All I meant was that you'll see that downstairs is closed for business next week," I snap.

He goes silent. And almost still, except for those damn fingers twisting me up. My clit throbs, needing attention to come. But he seems content to torment me like this.

Finally, he says, "I'm not sure why you think I'd be repelled by a little blood. I've heard it makes girls more... sensitive."

I exhale. "Maybe."

"Maybe?"

"I don't know."

He chuckles. His chest, pressed to my back, vibrates. He squeezes me tighter, then releases me. Pulls out from my pussy, too, and strides back to the shower. He shuts the water off and collects our clothes, frowning at my wet leggings and bra.

Without a word, he grabs his towel and wraps it around me. I barely manage to grab the edges in my confusion, but he just stalks back to his locker.

The next thing I know, he's throwing a hoodie at me.

I hastily wipe away the water, patting my skin dry and wringing out my hair, then I slip on the hoodie. It covers me to mid-thigh, which is more than I could've asked for. His boxers follow, and I glare at him.

He just smirks and drags his gray sweatpants up his legs, apparently planning on going commando.

"You should go straight home," I murmur.

"I was planning on taking you home," he says.

I lift my shoulder. "Girls will want to ravage you if they see your dick swinging in your gray sweatpants. It's that season."

"What season?"

I roll my eyes. "Gray sweatpants season. Did you buy them with that in mind?"

He faces me and cups his dick through the fabric. "So this turns you on?"

"No." I wrinkle my nose. "Never mind."

He smirks. "Uh-huh."

Great. Just what he needs—more ego.

23
STEELE

As it seems to be the case with every important away game, the fan bus was overbooked. I think the organizers secretly plan it that way, because they're just graduated puck bunnies who would love nothing more than to ride with the team.

I would know. Amanda is one of them.

Whatever job CPU hired her for has kept her out of my line of sight until now.

She sits with a few other girls on the team bus. Coach already informed us that we'd be sharing, and he said it with a distant sigh. Like... it's not unexpected. It would be more unusual if it *didn't* happen.

But then I see Violet waiting for Greyson, and my stomach twists.

What would the odds of Aspen choosing this bus be?

Out the window, I can see the other bus waiting for us to load up. The buses travel together, which means that the fan bus inevitably follows where the team bus goes. Including to the stadium to pick up the team.

After a quick scan to make sure that Aspen *is* ducking me, I spin around and trot right off the bus.

"O'Brien!" Coach hollers.

"Be right back, Coach!"

I head for the second bus. The driver squints at me in confusion, but he opens its doors for me anyway. I pound up the stairs. The students break into cheers when they see me. Every one of them is decked out in over-the-top school colors.

"Aspen Monroe," I call out loudly.

The bus goes quiet.

I spot her toward the back, next to her roommate.

"If you don't come with me right now, I will go back there and carry you out," I threaten.

She stares at me for a long moment, and I wonder if she's going to actually call me out on my threat. But then her lips quirk into a smile, and she rises. She saunters down the aisle, ignoring the stares, and stops right in front of me. Her head has to tip back to meet my gaze, and I lean over her.

She cranes back farther.

"What are you doing, sweetheart?" I ask her loudly. "You're supposed to be with me."

"Is that a rule?"

"When you're my girlfriend, *yes*."

That gets everyone's attention. Murmurs start up behind us, the noise steadily climbing. And Aspen's face gets redder and redder, until she finally sucks that gorgeous lower lip between her teeth and nods.

"I'm taking this one," I tell the driver, perhaps unnecessarily. He doesn't seem to have much authority beyond driving anyway.

I curl my fingers around Aspen's hand and tug her off the bus, quickly crossing to mine.

Ours.

Whatever.

Coach waits by the door, his hands on his hips. "What's this, O'Brien?"

"Sorry, Coach, she's my pregame good luck charm." Hockey players are superstitious, and perhaps Coach the worst of us all. If I say she's what I need to get my head in the game, then she's what I get.

Besides, I'd rather focus on the feel of her instead of thinking about how I'm going to meet her gold-digging mother after this one.

I don't release her hand. Not until I've sat and tugged her into the seat beside me.

What I really want is her on my lap, but Coach would probably yell about that. So, I'll wait until he gets absorbed in his book or movie on his phone, whatever he has planned to keep himself occupied this time, and then I'll have my way with her.

I brought her home after practice on Thursday and left. And then yesterday, it seemed like we were pulled in two opposite directions. I only saw her at lunch, for the briefest of moments.

Not enough.

Coach gives us some spiel about bus safety and how the trip will be four hours. We'll have time to check into our hotel rooms and grab a ridiculously early team dinner, then we need to report to the stadium.

"Why did you want me with you?" Aspen whispers.

"Because."

This is our first big away game, and last year, Greyson made this big stink about Violet being on the bus. Until he put her on his lap. *Then* he played the best game of his life.

Well, okay, the best game of his life thus far. He proved to continue to get better after that game, which I attribute to Violet.

Knox, on the other hand, seems to fluctuate. Willow isn't his good luck charm, that's for fucking sure. Which is why he's sitting up front, closer to Greyson and Violet, and Willow is talking to Miles and Finch with one of the other dance girls. Michelle, maybe?

Their names escape me sometimes.

"'Because' isn't a reason," Aspen argues, drawing my attention back to her.

I shake my head and pull my phone from my pocket, unwinding the earbuds I had already plugged into it. Aspen stares at me as I set it to my pregame playlist and fit the buds in my ears.

With a sigh, she does the same. Hers are the fancy Bluetooth ones, though. I watch her out of the corner of my eye, when I should be focusing on the game ahead of us. She shifts, she flexes her legs. Her fingers tap on her thighs, and it takes me a few minutes to realize she's not randomly tapping—she's playing an imaginary piano.

And suddenly, my playlist be damned, I want to know what she's playing.

I shut off my music and reach for one of her earbuds, plucking it from her ear and putting it in mine. The sweet melody of classical piano fills my head.

She glances sharply at me, and her fingers stop moving.

I glare at her.

She glares back.

I can't exactly tell her what I want—which fucking crazy anyway. So I turn away and pretend to ignore her. But my heart is hammering, and I peek at her again. It takes a moment for her to start drumming again. Her fingers match the notes. Maybe. I don't know much about music, but the timing seems right.

"Can you play this one?" I interrupt.

Her fingers don't stop, though. They dance in place, and she sighs. "I can."

"I want to hear you."

"You did," she says. "And then you drugged me."

I shrug. "You were feeding my dad information. I had to find out a way to stop it."

Her mouth drops open, and she twists in her seat to face me fully. "Are you kidding? *That's* why you did it?"

My brow furrows. "Why the fuck would I kid about that?"

"Because I *told* you that I wasn't giving him anything." She hits my arm. *Hard.*

I glance over the seats toward Coach. His head is down, so whatever. Fuck it. I grab her and haul her onto my lap, adjusting her until she's straddling me. She squeaks in surprise, gripping my shoulders. Her ass settles on my thighs, her knees at my hips.

Her weight on me feels right, somehow.

Like we're a perfect fit.

"I didn't trust you," I say, leaning up to get right in her face. "What was I supposed to do, Aspen, just believe that you were going to keep my image clean for my father? Any little bit of information you gave him could be twisted against me. And trust me, sweetheart, he's been trying to get anything on me to prove I'm a disappointment."

"Is your relationship with him really that bad?" she whispers. "I don't understand why he asked me in the first place, why—"

"Was Crown Point your first choice?"

Her gaze shutters. That wall drops down, and she doesn't answer.

So it wasn't.

"My father manipulates people for a living, Aspen. I have my inheritance, but I've never done what he's truly wanted: to take over *his* business. To become exactly like him. For a while, I was on track to do just that." My fingers find their way under the hem of her shirt, inching up her back. "But then I found hockey."

"And you want to make a career out of it," she guesses.

"Exactly. So, outwardly, my dad is supportive. But on the inside, he's boiling. Itching for a reason to yank me from this school and force me to join his business." I shrug, like it's not a big deal. But it does sting, sometimes, to know that he doesn't really give a shit about what I want. "Dad has an empire. Empires need rulers, succession. And sometimes, I think Dad plans to force me to work for him."

Aspen shifts closer.

My fingers reach her bra clasp, and I unhook it quickly. The band immediately loosens under her shirt, and I slide my hands around to her front. She sucks in a breath when I palm both of her tits.

I wasn't lying when I said I loved them.

They're the best fucking things I've ever seen. Perfect size for my hands, pretty nipples. If we weren't on a bus, I'd push up her shirt and take one in my mouth.

As it is, my fingers will have to do.

My cock hardens between us, but I ignore it. A little tension will do wonders for my game—I think. I'm hoping.

"Steele," she gasps. "What—"

"I just want to see if you'd come like this," I murmur. "You can grind on me if you need to."

Her face flushes. She went with makeup today, dark-blue stuff on her eyelids and dark-red lipstick. I'd love to kiss her senseless, but then Coach would really know that we were up to no good.

"Touch yourself," I say under my breath.

Her eyes flash, and she lifts her head. She's not so tall that she's visible above the headrests of the seats. I can see if I crane my head, but she should be okay. Which means that we're in our own little bubble with no one in our row.

Still... I say it knowing that she'll refuse.

And then she actually fucking does it.

I like that she surprises me. I like that I can guess a hundred different scenarios and she'll pick the least likely, the one that I never saw coming. Of course, there are other ways that I can read her like a book.

For example, the way her breathing hitches when I roll her nipples between my fingers and tug. Or when I palm her whole breast, my fingers digging into her flesh, and her eyes lose focus.

Her hand slides into her jeans, and she fucking touches herself. She tips her head back and lets out a soft moan like a quiet porn star, and I rip my hand out from under her shirt to cover her mouth.

She stares at me, eyes wide, and her hand in her pants moves faster.

My cock *throbs*. I might actually combust just from watching her, and the movement of her body so close to it is the sweetest torture.

I press my hand harder to her mouth, stopping the escape of certain noises that would *definitely* give us away. Her lips slide against my palm, and then her tongue flicks out.

"Fuck," I groan. "You're mine after the game."

I pinch her nipple, and she whimpers.

Her eyes dilate, and she grinds down on my thigh. Her back arches, and her body goes tense as her orgasm overtakes her. I absorb it all and try not to blow my load just from the sight. After a minute, she comes back down to earth.

She pulls her hand from her pants, her fingers wet. She glances from them to me, then smears them across my lips.

Jesus Christ.

I open my mouth, and her two fingers slip in. I close my lips around her digits and taste her, not releasing them until they're clean. I slip my hand out from under her shirt and remove my other one from her mouth. Her dark-red lipstick is smeared a bit, across her cheek. And there's a messy print of her lips on my palm.

I ball my fist, protecting the mark. I'm not going to fucking wash that off until I have to, that's for sure.

Aspen sags against me. She hooks her bra back together, fixing it under her shirt while she leans on my chest.

I wrap my arms around her and hold her against me.

The music is still playing in our ears, and I find that I don't even mind listening to her classical shit.

Eventually, my hard-on goes away. Sort of. There's no way I'm going totally soft with the gorgeous girl sitting on my lap, playing with my hair, but it's not raging to the point of poking her eye out.

"You're supposed to be wearing my jersey," I say at some point. Time has passed, that's for sure, but neither of us have moved. Just her fingers in my hair, twisting it and scratching at my scalp in a way that feels too good to be real.

"You didn't give it to me," she says, picking her head up from my chest.

I smirk at her messed-up lipstick and wipe at it with my thumb. She frowns and lets me do it, cleaning up the dark red until it's contained to her lips again.

Her lip print is still on my palm, though. Right where I want it.

Well... I can think of better places.

But my palm is good for now.

"I brought a spare," I inform her. "And we're sharing a room."

Her eyes narrow. "How?"

Knox and Greyson are the experts. I asked them yesterday, and they said they'd take care of it. Not sure what that means for Aspen's roommate, or where she'll end up. Maybe she'll get a room to herself. Either way, all I know is that my girl will be in my room tonight.

We just have to survive our parents.

Oh, and the game.

24

ASPEN

The hockey team has a dinner together, then they're heading straight to the stadium for a meeting before the game. It leaves all the CPU students who came for the game with about an hour to grab dinner.

Thalia, Willow, Violet—the latter two somehow worming their way into my short list of friends—plus some other dance girls are gathered around in the hotel lobby. They're trying to figure out where we should eat. I've got Steele's oversized jersey in my grip. He gave me the dark-blue one they wear at home games, but I haven't put it on yet.

Because once I do, I'm sure I'll draw more looks. Questionable ones.

More than I already have anyway.

I join the girls, and my phone vibrates in my hand.

Then, from across the lobby, "I see her! Asp!"

That's a voice I would recognize anywhere.

My twelve-year-old sister, Lennox, charges through the hotel lobby and performs an expert flying tackle. I brace at the last minute, scooping her up and swinging her around. She's tiny, especially for her age. Light enough to lift off her feet for a minute before returning her to the floor.

Her arms are locked around my neck, and even when she stands, she doesn't release me. I'm left awkwardly bent over. I pat her arm, then force her hands apart. To cover for the rough handling, I slide my hand through her blonde hair.

Super blonde, almost platinum, like our mother.

"Hi," I whisper.

She beams at me. "I knew I'd find you first."

"That you did."

"Aspen!" Mom calls, striding toward us. "Lennox, I told you not to run off."

Len pouts. "But I was running to Asp, Mom. That's gotta be okay. We haven't seen her in forever."

"It's only been two months, kid."

Two months is a lot. I try not to let that pang of guilt hit me. The one that says I should've gone home to visit or something. Called more. I don't know.

Mom, Dakota, and Stephen join us. I hug Mom first, shake Stephen's hand, then face my fourteen-year-old sister. The grumpy one, apparently. She eyes me like she's annoyed with me for even being here.

I ignore it and drag her into a hug. "Missed you, D."

She exhales. Slowly, her arms come up, and she hugs me back. But just for a few seconds, then she squirms out of my hold.

"How are you feeling?" Stephen asks.

I tilt my head. "I'm fine."

Mom touches his arm, then hugs me again. It's impulsive, but I go with it. Logically, I get why she married Stephen. It's just claiming to be in love that has me confused. She's always claimed love, even over the summer. Dramatic assurances, or displays of affection, left me feeling... untethered.

If she could love him so quickly, what about dropping *out* of love? Could that happen even faster?

The answer is yes, of course. Love is this fragile little thing, wrapped in trust and respect. If one of its shells cracks, the love can break. Or—sometimes it just means that love becomes more jagged.

Fucked-up shards of love, cutting everyone and everything.

That was her and Dad.

"Is this your family, Aspen?" Violet asks from behind me.

I step aside. "Yes, sorry. These are my sisters, Dakota and Lennox. My mom, Mari, and..."

"Stephen O'Brien," he introduces. "Pleasure."

"Same," Violet answers. "That's Thalia, who you might already know, and Willow." Violet's gaze travels over my siblings and then my mom. "We were going to go to the Japanese place down the street. Do you all want to join us?"

"Oh, no, we have reservations at a steak house," Stephen says.

I got used to him being... normal, I guess? Like, over the summer he would wear jeans or shorts and t-shirts, he'd do work in his yard or bike ride with my sisters. Hell, he even took my mother on a fishing trip once, decked out in waders and those wide-brimmed hats.

But now he's completely in his element as *the rich guy*. The expensive, perfectly tailored suit. The haircut that probably cost more than my entire outfit. His gleaming watch. And Mom's dressed in a different manner than I'm used to, as well. She went for black pants and a caramel-colored sweater, with layered necklaces. But her hair is curled, her makeup flawless.

Her demeanor is different, too. Less skittish.

I eye Stephen, chewing over what Steele told me on the bus. That he wants dirt on his own child to get him out of college and out of hockey. To force him on a path he doesn't want. It sounds achingly familiar, and it makes me loathe Stephen just a little bit more.

"Aspen, are you joining us?" Thalia asks.

"We didn't think we'd see you before the game, honey," Mom says, her expression contrite. "We could adjust our reservation—"

"No, no, it's okay." I step back, closer to my friends. "I'm going to have dinner with them. We'll see you after the game."

They nod, and Stephen herds my mom away. The girls follow a bit more slowly, eyeing me with confusion.

"That was awkward," Thalia whispers. She loops her arm around mine. "Are you going to put that on or just hold on to it all night?"

I sigh and shake out the jersey. It smells like him, which is probably the best—and worst—part. After what happened on the bus, the *last* thing I need is to have him on my mind every second, thinking about his hands on me.

Jeez. I need to get a hold of myself.

Slipping the jersey over my head feels like I'm being invaded by Steele from all sides. And it's not unpleasant either. In fact, part of me never wants to exhale.

Did he wear it before he gave it to me?

Or spray it with his cologne?

I wouldn't put either past him. Especially since his smell is so visceral, it drags up every lust-filled thought. And memory.

"Ready," I say, smiling at my friends.

Friends. Plural.

Haven't been able to say that in a while. But for the first time in too fucking long, I feel like it's a hundred percent true.

Me: How's your dinner meeting?

Steele: Coach is giving us a pep talk. *snoring emoji*

Steele: What're you doing? What are you eating?

Me: Our parents made dinner reservations and didn't account for me.

Steele: Don't take it personally, Dad probably doesn't want to catch your looney tunes disease.

Me: ...

Steele: Sorry, too soon?

Me: A hundred years would be too soon.

Steele: So, where'd you go??

Me: Mars.

Steele: Aspen.

Me: Some Japanese place with friends.

Steele: Girl friends?

Me: Well, you scared off Chase, so yeah. All I have left are girl friends.

Steele: I feel exceptionally smug about that, little viper. And for the record, I had grilled chicken and a salad. It was quite boring.

Steele: Where did you go?

Me: I'm eating.

Steele: Should we make it interesting?

Me: Should we make WHAT interesting?

Me: Do you have some food kink I didn't know about? Because I'm gonna pass on that one...

Steele: What? No. The game.

Steele: (Obviously.)

Me: I'm listening...

Steele: Well, the Devils are known for being particularly aggressive.

Me: Are you proposing you get into a fight?

Steele: If it would turn you on, yeah.

Me: What if you lose?

Steele: Baby, I never lose a fight.

Steele: But... are you saying you want me to lose? Or win?

Me: A blow to your pride would certainly help. Shave off some of your ego.

Steele: A blow of something else would be even better ;)

Me: I want to see blood.

Me: Your blood. On the ice.

Me: And if you're lucky, I'll kiss it and make it better later.

25
ASPEN

Part of me thought, *Nah, Steele won't get his hands dirty.*

And yet, the gloves are coming off. Literally.

Steele and one of the Devils are skating in a circle. Both have ditched their gloves. They drift closer to where we're sitting, and I lean forward.

I have no doubt that this is for my benefit.

They've been trash talking each other all night, shoving each other around. Seeking each other out—or maybe they're just assigned to guard each other, I don't know. Either way, the tension between them has been ratcheting up all night.

It's the third period. The CPU Hawks are up by one. But there's still ten minutes left, and a power play by the Devils could seriously hurt our chances of winning.

Basically, from what Violet has said—at this time, anything could happen.

The Devils player throws the first punch. Steele retaliates, hitting back with power that snaps the guy's head to the side. They're right in front of us, and the life in Steele's eyes is enough to make my heart lurch.

I like it and hate it at the same time.

How's that?

Steele's helmet is torn off and tossed aside, and his opponent hammers his fist into Steele's face. Steele shoves him away for a second and spits a glob of blood onto the ice. His face is red, blood coming out of his nose.

Suddenly, I don't *want* him to lose.

I rise from my seat and bang on the glass. I scream, "Fuck him up!"

Steele's brows furrow. He doesn't look at me, but I swear he hears me. He comes back at the guy twice as hard and somehow gets him onto the ice.

The CPU crowd erupts.

We're not on home ice—we're outnumbered by Devils fans. But we sure do make a lot of ruckus. I'm not alone in banging on the glass as the refs separate them. Steele is pushed away, and he skates to the bench.

Someone examines his face, turning it this way and that. The Devils player climbs to his feet and skates off, expression dark.

Steele returns to the ice, skating toward us. He points at me and gives me a full-toothed smile. Even with his mouth guard, his teeth are stained pink with blood.

He steps up into the penalty box beside our section and takes a seat.

I shiver.

"Wow," Willow murmurs. "That was hot. And I mean that in a respectful way."

I snort and take my seat again. "Yeah, yeah."

But on the inside, I'm smiling. Because I got what I

wanted, and I can still see it. Steele's blood left behind on the ice.

Except it backfires, because the Devils score while Steele is off the ice. The home crowd goes nuts, a horn sounding. Their music plays in celebration. It's a little obnoxious, and my heart is in my throat.

They're tied with eight and a half minutes remaining.

What if I cost them the game for this stupid challenge?

I keep looking over at the penalty box. It's just a few feet away, practically taunting me. But Steele doesn't so much as glance over. I get that, too. He needs his head in the game, and my momentary distraction could've cost them.

No, it *did* cost them.

When the power play is up, Steele is released from the penalty box. The Devils are pressing hard, on the heels of their goal. Steele, as a defenseman, charges back into the fray without hesitation. He shoves one of the Devils away from crowding Miles. The other Hawks move around the ice, and Greyson intercepts a pass.

He takes off, chased by Devils and Hawks alike.

The charge lights up the stadium.

It's a one-on-one play, suddenly. Greyson versus their goalie.

He shoots.

Violet screams as it soars over the goalie's shoulder and sinks into the net.

We all leap to our feet. The Hawks zoom toward Greyson, crashing into him in celebration. They slap his helmet, his arm, his back. He's grinning widely; he skids to a halt in front of Violet. He pats his chest, then points at her, and damn it. My heart melts a little bit.

She's feeling it, too, because her face goes totally gooey.

It's kind of sweet and kind of gross.

I refocus on Steele. He's on the bench now, and Greyson joins him. They drink water and exchange words, their attention fixed on the ice. My fingers itch, wanting to... I don't know. I've got restless energy that doesn't have a way out.

"They're up by one," Violet murmurs, patting my leg.

Five minutes left. Then four.

Greyson and Steele hop back over the wall, replacing two skaters who return to the bench, and they rush out with an unmatched fury. Steele body checks a player into the glass, and Greyson steals the puck, passing it long to a waiting Knox.

We jump to our feet again, the whole CPU crowd shouting. Knox to Greyson. To Finch, who gets slammed into the wall by a Devil. The puck soars free, and a Devil reclaims it —only to be met with Steele.

No one is playing nice anymore. There seems to be a frenzied tension amongst the teams as the clock ticks down. The whistle blows, and Willow points. Knox stands in front of Miles, Steele and Tony Rodrigues beside him. He's squared up to one of the Devils players who looks like he might want to start shit.

But he backs down after a long moment, skating back to his bench.

The time gets closer to running out, and I stand. I'm not alone—it seems like that palpable energy is contagious. The players feed off the crowd, and vice versa. Steele comes back out again and plays the last few minutes, and I just take a second to marvel at *him*. Appreciating the way he moves, the way he holds the stick.

I shouldn't do that... but I do.

The buzzer sounds with no more goals. The Crown Point University Hawks held off the Devils. The team flies out onto the ice, surrounding Miles and Knox. They all jump and cheer and celebrate, and I laugh.

"It's going to be a good night for us," Violet says. She elbows Willow.

Thalia giggles.

"Get yourself one of the Hawks," Willow says to Thalia. "Even if it's just for a night, because god damn, they're going to fuck like animals."

I cover my mouth to hide my wild laughter. Thalia blushes, glancing at me. But hey, I don't have anything to add. It's not like I have a habit of seeking out hockey players on a winning high.

Just one, I suppose.

We head out of the stadium and wait by the locker rooms. I'm getting weird looks, but I brush it off. Until a whole group of girls turn their heads to watch me as they pass.

"Do I have something in my hair or something?" I ask Thalia, glaring at the girls.

She glances from them to me, then shakes her head. "I think it's the jersey."

I look down at the dark-blue fabric.

Right.

Forgot about that one.

Violet glances at her phone, typing something. "Grey said to meet them at the pub on the corner of the stadium."

"Oh, good." Willow hooks her arm through Thalia's.

My phone goes off.

Steele: Stay.

I meet the girls' curious gazes. I realize I automatically took a step back.

"Um, I'm going to meet up with you in a few minutes..."

Violet snorts. "You've got our numbers. Text if you need anything."

Right.

They head away from me, and I lean against the wall. The door doesn't open for some time—long enough that I guess there must be some other exit for the players. Or maybe I'm just completely in the wrong place.

But eventually, the door opens and Steele steps out. He has his skates slung over his shoulder, and he drops his bag to the floor. He's got a bruise forming on his cheek, and a split lip that probably contributed to the blood he spat on the ice during the game.

Without a word, he comes in close and cups my jaw, tipping my head back. His brown eyes burn into me, and for the first time, I understand what a fucking smolder is. I squeeze my thighs together, and a blush works its way up my neck.

His thumb sweeps along my lower lip, and then he leans down. He stops a hair's breadth from touching me, his lips hovering over mine.

"Did you enjoy that?" he whispers.

I nod. My nose brushes his, and he exhales.

"So did I." He smirks and rises. He takes my hand. "Come with me."

I follow him through the lower level of the stadium, to the large gates where the Zamboni recently drove through. The ice is clean, free of any skate marks. The Zamboni itself sits against the wall, and I automatically pull toward that.

"They seem fun," I say absently, running my hand over the wrapped side. It has the Devils' mascot on the side and some advertising about tickets to home games. "To drive, I mean."

He raises his eyebrow. "Well. Hop on up."

I purse my lips, waiting for him to crack a laugh. When he doesn't... who am I to object? I set my purse down, and he sets down his bag and skates beside it. He follows me to the little step-up ladder, his hands gripping the railing on either side of my body while I climb up.

A little thrill goes through me when I sit in the driver's chair.

"How does it look?"

"Giant," I murmur.

"This would be an apt time for a 'that's what she said' joke." Steele climbs up after me, stopping on the top step.

I run my hands over the steering wheel, the levers beside the chair. I have no idea how to drive it, and I don't think I'm destructive enough to *want* to do it. Not on my own like this anyway.

"What are you afraid of?" Steele asks.

I meet his dark gaze. He's not as... loud, I guess, as I was expecting. Like even though they're coming off that win, and the energy is still simmering in *my* chest like a live wire, he seems quiet. Contemplative.

And I'm not sure if that's because of me or him.

Or both.

"I'm afraid of a lot," I say lightly. I twist to face him. It's meant to be humorous, maybe, but it falls flat even in my ears. It's the one bit of truth I'll allow myself. That I'm desperately scared of a *lot*, and trying to face it has given me split results.

Sometimes good.

Sometimes fucking triggered.

He motions for me to stand. It puts me right in front of him, my abdomen even with his face. He grips my hips and tows me forward, pressing a kiss to my stomach through the jersey.

"What are you afraid of tonight?" he clarifies.

I shiver. I don't know how to answer that without dragging us out of this moment, and he seems to agree. Because he doesn't ask again. Instead, he works the edges of the jersey up, and his fingers skim my bare skin.

Goosebumps rise on my arms that have nothing to do with the cold, and I put my hands on his shoulders. I don't know what he's going to do, but I think I trust it. Maybe. Trust is one of those fragile things that may or may not break. And he's got it for now—somehow. Impossibly.

Now I just have to hope he doesn't smash it—and me—to dust.

Because that, I won't come back from.

The sight of her in my jersey has me hard for her. Aching. And her sitting on the Zamboni like a princess just does something extra to me, too.

I step up the rest of the way and move her to sit on the hard ridge above the steering wheel. I saw someone sit on that flat top last year at one of our charity events, and I won't lie—I used to climb all over the Zamboni when I was a kid. It's sturdy enough to hold us.

She parts her legs, but I just shake my head and sit in the driver's seat. It's plush, not terribly uncomfortable. After the game, I changed into dark jeans and a dark-blue pullover, intentionally matching my jersey colors.

Now I have Aspen alone, and there are too many thoughts running through my head. Too much energy. I want to claw her shirt off and ravage her, I want to savor her slowly. I want her to kneel between my legs and suck me off. I want to kneel between *her* legs and eat her cunt like I'm starving.

I lick my lips.

She makes the decision for me. She scoots back on the

top, testing its weight. The hard plastic flexes under her, but not enough to scare her. And I doubt it would break even with both of us.

She keeps her eyes on me as she wiggles out of her jeans. Her panties come with it, and she tosses them at me. I catch the pink satin and raise it to my mouth, inhaling slightly.

Smells like her.

Sweet, musky.

Smells like how she tastes.

My mouth waters.

"You're too easy prey," I comment, although my heart is beating out of my chest.

"I'm not prey," she answers, spreading her legs slowly.

It gives me the perfect view of her pussy, which is glistening wet already. And I haven't even touched her.

Her throat works. "I'm the reward."

Fuck.

"How can I argue with that?" I stand and shove my jeans down, kicking them off. I don't hesitate to climb up over her, hovering until she grips my sweatshirt and drags me down.

Aspen touches my cheek. The pain that burrows through the bone is deep and aching. The bruises formed quickly—and no doubt my father will be equally quick to point out my failure. At getting hit at all, at getting lured into a fight.

Not that he needs to know it was *me* goading *him* the whole game, shit talking like my life depended on it. Pushing him into fighting me, fucking finally.

Her thumb touches my lip again, and I try not to wince. She digs her nail into the scabbed-over cut suddenly, and fresh blood wells to the surface. I taste it when I lick my lip.

"There," she murmurs. "Kiss me."

I do.

My blood coats her lips. Her mouth. Her tongue sweeps out and runs along the cut, probing it, and then into my mouth. The coppery taste is different on her. I kiss her harder, my tongue forcing hers out of my mouth and back into hers. They tangle. Our teeth clash. She grips the back of my neck hard and lifts her legs around me, her heels digging into my ass.

I get the silent message.

I shift my hips, adjusting my angle until my cock slips through her slick center. She moans and tears her lips away. She drags her mouth down my jaw, to my neck. Little chills race down my spine.

When's the last time anyone kissed me like that?

She sucks at my skin, marking me, and I let her. My cock twitches, and I can't fucking wait any longer. I slide into her, cursing at the way her cunt grips me. She's wet, she's tight. She's perfect—and she doesn't even know it.

Her teeth score my neck, then she moves lower. Shoving aside my sweatshirt. Kissing a path across my collarbone, and the deer skull ink. Her fingers trace my abdomen, over the tattooed eagle that says, *Be Free*. As if it's that simple.

I grip her by her jaw and tow her back up, burying my face in *her* throat. She gives me a hickey—I'll give her several. My blood leaves a trail on her skin, too. She tastes like sweat, she smells like heaven. Some scent I can't iden-tify. I rock my hips back, pulling out of her for the first time, until just the tip is still inside her. Then I thrust back in hard enough to bow the cold plastic beneath us.

She shudders, her thighs tightening around my hips.

Her fingers slide into my hair.

I raise myself and watch her beneath me as I stroke

deep inside her.

"Pull the jersey up," I order.

She does, and those *breasts*, fuck. She's wearing the barest strip of a bra. It's just lace and underwire, I think. It does nothing to hide the way her nipples harden. I lean down and take one in my mouth through her bra, biting and sucking. The fabric is a barrier that I ignore.

Her back arches, pushing her breast harder into my face. I take it in my teeth and tug, and she cries out.

The noise is sweet.

I fuck her harder, rolling my hips and eliciting a whimper every time I drive back in.

My balls tighten.

I switch to her other breast and slip my hand between us, rubbing her clit with quick, short strokes. I want her to come with me. At the same time, crashing into oblivion together.

I don't know why.

It just feels right.

She gasps and moans above me, her nails raking against my scalp. Tugging, trying to get me to move. My control is fluttering away, just the barest thread still in my grasp. Enough to listen to her directive and kiss her again.

"I'm going to come inside you," I say against her lips. Each word feels like a kiss of its own. "You like that, huh? You like living on the edge with me."

I stroke her clit faster. She makes a noise, a wordless plea. Her eyes shut, and her head tips back, trying to evade me.

I'm not avoidable.

I bite her neck, *hard*, and her whole body jolts. She glares at me through her pleasure, and I smirk through mine. Because I'm about to blow, and she's not there yet.

But then she gasps, and she says, "I'm going to come. Don't stop, don't stop." She chants it, repeating the words.

I have no intention of stopping.

Her cunt tightens around me, an orgasm cresting through her. One more pump, two, and I slam fully inside her as my balls tighten and I come harder than I ever have. She squeezes my cock to death, and her nails dig into my neck, my scalp.

We stay like that for a minute, locked in that embrace.

And then the sound of something vibrating brings me back to earth.

Slowly.

"Phone," Aspen says beneath me, her body limp. She doesn't even seem to mind that I'm still inside her.

My cock is half-hard and slowly losing steam, but I keep her filled for another second.

The vibrating stops. Then starts up again.

It's my father. I know it, she knows it. And it immediately sours my mood. He's out there, probably waiting to introduce me to his new bride. The rage returns like an old ache. But when I pull out of Aspen and see the evidence of what we did, it soothes it.

A fraction.

I accept that knowledge and climb off her, holding out my hand. She stares at it for a second, then takes it. I help her slide to the edge of the Zamboni's top, and I retrieve her panties from my jeans pocket. I pull them up her legs and secure them against her pussy.

"Steele—"

"The thought of my cum between your legs right now is the only thing keeping me from losing it," I tell her in a low voice.

The vibrating stops.

Then starts again.

"Fuck!" I kick my jeans off the Zamboni, my phone with it.

"She's not that bad." Aspen crosses her arms over her chest. The jersey is back in place. Her jeans are on the seat, and I hand them to her wordlessly.

She very well could be that bad.

"She raised you," I allow. "So..."

"Exactly." Aspen stands, shimmying the fabric up her legs. She makes a face. "I don't like the feeling of it between my legs. My underwear is going to be soaked—"

"Good," I snap.

Her eyebrows rise.

"I hope we smell like sex, too," I add. "I hope your gold-digging mother sees right through us, because she does the same to my father—"

Slap.

It hurts worse that she went for my bruised side.

I clench my jaw.

"Stop calling her that," she hisses. "If you knew anything, then you'd just drop it." She pushes past me and climbs off the Zamboni. She fishes out my phone and answers the call, turning away from me. "Yeah," she says loudly. "He lost his phone, so I was helping him search for it. We'll be right there."

Aspen hangs up and turns around, frowning at me. "Well?"

"Well, what?" Why the fuck do I feel like an insolent child right now?

Snap out of it.

"Let's go meet the executioner."

I know she's being sarcastic. But in a way, that's what it feels like.

Lennox and Dakota are beside themselves to meet Steele. They, along with Mom and Stephen, are sitting at a table in their hotel restaurant. The restaurant seems to be doing some sort of late-night service, perhaps to accommodate people who traveled to attend the game. It's surprisingly busy in here.

Len finds us right away, and she jumps up and rockets over to me. She hugs me hard, like I didn't just see her a few hours ago, and then faces Steele.

Dakota is slower to approach but no less awestruck.

I'm pretty sure the bruise on his cheek and split lip doesn't help her budding infatuation.

Their eyes rounded, they take him in.

And then the questions start.

"How do you skate so fast?"

"Does it hurt to hit the glass?"

"What's your favorite movie?"

"Why'd that guy hit you?"

"How do you know when to get off the ice?"

"Why did the ref blow the whistle so many times?"

"Who—"

"Okay," I interrupt, holding back my laugh.

Stephen and my mother are still at the table, talking with their heads bent. So clearly, they're not bothered by the girls' interrogation. But Steele looks vaguely uncomfortable, his gaze darting between the two of them like they're radioactive.

"Youngest is Lennox. The surly one is Dakota."

"I'm not surly," Dakota replies, frowning.

I ruffle her hair. "Right."

"So?" Len asks, still staring at Steele.

"Oh." Steele pauses. He finds his father and my mother, and perhaps draws the same conclusion that I did. He refocuses on my sister. "Um, the ref blows the whistle when one of the players does something wrong."

They nod along.

"Okay, you can ask him more questions next time." I herd them toward the table, dodging a harried server. "We've got to talk to Mom."

"Are you okay, Asp?" Len tugs on my hand.

I pause. "Of course I'm okay. Why?"

"Stephen said you might have to go away." Her eyes fill with tears.

Go away? What the hell does that mean?

Pushing that foreboding aside, I follow Dakota and Steele to the table. Mom and Stephen are already greeting Steele. Mom shakes his hand, and then Stephen does, too. I can't help but feel a pang at that. No hug? He hasn't seen his father in months—since before the summer, obviously. And they've already demonstrated their lack of relationship, what with the whole spying thing.

"Girls, go up to the room and get ready for bed." Mom gives them both pats on their shoulders and steers them past me. She hands them a room key, and they take off without a backward glance.

Steele and I sit across from them. I don't bother looking at him. Really, I just don't want to deal with his shitty attitude toward my mom. He just met her, but he's been judging her for months.

It's not really fair.

"Aspen." Mom reaches across the table for my hands.

I give them to her, offering her a small smile. "Hi, Mom."

"Honey, we're worried about you."

I try to pull back, but she holds fast.

My smile wavers. "What do you mean, you're worried? I'm fine."

Her gaze darts to her new husband. Letting him take over?

He clears his throat and faces me. "We saw the video, Aspen. And frankly, it's alarming. The school recommended you to the counselor, of course. We're happy that you went. Upon further discussion with a doctor friend, however, we think it's best if you had a little more structure."

I slowly retract my hands. "You talked to a doctor? About... the video?"

He frowns. "Yes. And more structure presents itself as an inpatient hospital for an evaluation, and it would simply cut into the semester."

Inpatient hospital?

Because they think I'm crazy?

"I wasn't suffering a psychotic break," I say through my teeth. "I was drugged."

By your son.

Mom cries out at that admission, covering her eyes with her hand. The huge, stupid ring on her finger stares at me.

My stomach knots. And for some reason, I know that she won't be on my side for this. That whatever way Stephen and Steele spun this, it's already locked in.

"You were drugged," Steele's father repeats, as skeptical as the counselor. "Or, more likely, you thought to experiment and suffered the very obvious consequences?" His chin lifts. His expression, his whole demeanor, has shifted. Gone are the days of shorts and t-shirts at home, of the throwaway smiles he'd shoot my way. He made us all feel at ease and welcome over the summer, but it's so far away from here. Now, he's all business. This is just another deal he needs to negotiate.

"Aspen, you are dealing with a lot of pressure. It's only natural that you'd crack." Stephen offers me a small smile, but it's so fucking cold. "We want what's best for you—and right now, that means getting you outside help."

My mouth opens and closes.

I'm over eighteen. They can't do that, right? I mean— he's not even my father. Mom could get me committed involuntarily, maybe. But she wouldn't do that. Even at this moment, when she can't meet my eyes.

A chill races up my spine, and then the sick feeling twists my gut. I'm going to be sick.

Steele sighs. "I don't think that's necessary, Dad."

My heart skips.

"You have an opinion on this?" Stephen focuses on his son.

"I do. I think Aspen's now tied to your name. People on campus know her mother married you. So... if you send her away, that's going to get out. Media slander, campaigns about how you're no better than Snow White's evil step-mother." His gaze flicks to my mom. "Except her real parent is still alive."

His father scoffs.

But... maybe he looks a little unsure.

"What do you propose?" he asks.

Steele puts his hand on my shoulder, and I jump. "We have the extra room in the hockey house. She'll move in so I can keep an eye on her."

I frown.

Mom does, too. "You want my daughter to move into a house with a bunch of..."

"I know them all, Mom," I blurt out. I knock Steele's hand off my shoulder. "It's not, um, the worst idea I've heard."

Although Uncle will probably murder Steele when he finds out.

"Have you heard from Dad?"

Mom stops moving. Stops breathing, really. I wonder if Steele realizes that I just completely freaked her out in five simple words.

"No... I haven't. Have you?"

I narrow my eyes. Do I mention the money? Or Uncle? "Nope."

"How was Spain?" Steele asks suddenly. "Did you have a good trip?"

I've never been so glad to have a change of subject. I let out a slow breath when their attention diverts to Steele.

"It was beautiful," Mom answers. "And congratulations on your hockey game. It was nice to get to watch you play after your father talked you up."

"Where in Spain did you go?" I ask.

"Madrid first, and then we stayed in a small villa on the west coast. The girls got to practice a bit of their Spanish." She smiles.

I almost feel bad for bringing up Dad. *Almost.*

"The game was good," Stephen says. "Your fight was... interesting."

"Scouts like some aggression." Steele shrugs and leans back. His shoulder brushes mine. "Plus, the guy had it coming."

"Well, if you say so." His father picks off some invisible lint from his sleeve. "It's late, and I think we're going to retire to the room."

They rise. We do some awkward version of a goodbye— Mom hugs me while I remain sitting. I don't really hug her back, a sour taste on my tongue. Stephen and Steele shake hands again, and Mom ends up patting his shoulder on the way past.

We watch them go.

"Thanks for coming, asshole," Steele says under his breath.

I sigh. "All that, and we didn't even get a drink out of it."

Steele leans forward and snags the two glasses left behind. They didn't even bother finishing their drinks— there's a finger's worth of an amber liquid in a rocks glass and half a pour of red wine left in Mom's. He hands me the wine, and I roll my eyes. We clink the glasses in a silent cheers and down the liquid.

The wine is dry, but I ignore the bitter taste. It seems to fit how I'm feeling toward Mom right now anyway. Why didn't she say anything? Or stick up for me? The delayed hurt that comes from her silence is worse now than hearing Stephen suggest it for the first time.

"So, a mental institution." Steele sets down the glass. "I didn't see that one coming."

"Oh, you didn't predict that would be his reaction?" I scowl. "Probably didn't think he'd pull my funding for school. So even if I move into your house—which I'm *not*—it would only be for a month. No more CPU for me."

He narrows his eyes. "It was more of an effort to stop him believing you if you tried to convince him of anything *I* was doing. He pulled the tuition money for next semester? Already?"

"Covering your own ass," I mutter. I flag down a waiter. "Two glasses of your top-shelf whiskey, neat. Doubles."

He eyes us, then the glasses in front of us. He nods once and disappears.

"You want to get drunk, little viper?"

I grit my teeth. "Why do you call me that?"

"That's for me to know." He nudges me. "We won't let my father ship you off somewhere."

That's nice of him to say. Too bad, though, because I don't believe it.

We sit in silence until the waiter comes back. I take a sip of the smokey, caramel liquid. It burns a path down my throat, but I appreciate the sting. We sit and drink, and finally, when my limbs feel a little less heavy, I sigh.

"Mom needs your father more than she needs me," I whisper.

He glances at me sharply.

"What?" I finish my whiskey and stand. It doesn't burn anymore. In fact, it tastes kind of good now that my taste buds are numb. "Did you think she just got married for his money? Oh... that's right, you *did* think that. Because we can't have any deeper motive than that."

He stands, too, and takes my arm. I don't realize how much I was wobbling until I stop. Oops.

"Are you going to explain it, then? Since you obviously know."

"Nope. Not gonna tell you." I snort. "We should've drunk at our own damn hotel."

He sighs and follows me out. All the way onto the street. I glance over and realize he's still carrying his bag. And my purse, too. The strap is sticking out of the bag he's carrying, like he shoved it in there without thinking.

Nice.

Maybe.

Unless he was stealing.

Not that I have any money or anything particularly interesting at all in there. Just a few tampons, you know, *just in case*. A compact mirror. That dark-red lipstick I put on earlier and forgot to reapply. Which I actually wiped off between the second and third period, afraid of getting it everywhere when I met up with Steele.

Look at me, thinking ahead.

I smile to myself and walk faster. The stadium is all lit up from the outside. Workers cleaning up, maybe? Hopefully no one witnessed our Zamboni adventure. Wouldn't that be awkward...

Then Stephen would definitely lock me up.

A giggle slips out, and it's like a dam breaks. I can't contain my laughter.

Steele wraps his arm around my waist, keeping me upright. The laughs burst out of me, and tears slip down my cheeks. I can't breathe.

It's not funny.

It's *so* not funny.

"Up you go," Steele grunts, lifting me into his arms. One under my knees, the other across my back. And he's got his bag over his shoulder to boot.

I kiss his cheek.

He stops walking and glances at me, brow furrowed. "What was that for?"

"The lift. And... I mean, I'm glad I get to finish the semester. It gives me a chance to plot my escape." I tuck my head in the crook of his shoulder and neck, closing my eyes.

"Escape?"

"Well, I'm not going to be locked up. This isn't the first time I've hidden from someone, Steele." I wasn't supposed to say that. I press my lips together, but the words are out there.

My bad.

"I'm not even that drunk," I mutter. "It was just some wine and the equivalent of two shots."

"Maybe you're a lightweight," he replies.

"Maybe we should go dance."

"I'll do the horizontal tango with you."

I pout. "Steele. We never get to *dance*. We're in New York. It's time to party and celebrate your win."

He rolls his eyes. "Let me drop my bag off at the room, then we can go find the others."

28
STEELE

There's something more at work with Aspen and her family. Her sisters are probably innocent. Her mother? Guilty as fuck.

Of *something*.

Aspen's snoring. Her head is on my lap, cheek smashed against my thigh. If she shifts again, which she keeps fucking doing, I'm going to poke her eye out with my hard-on.

We found my teammates and the rest of the CPU students who came on the fan bus at a local nightclub. It was, in a few words, *fucking intense*. The strobe lights were on full throttle, swinging across the gyrating bodies and painting the walls in color. The bars were packed, but Violet and Willow seemed to slip through to the front just fine.

They kept a filled glass in Aspen's and Thalia's hands just fine, too.

Greyson and I were supervising. Knox was dancing with Willow... and then someone else... and then Willow again. Not that she noticed. It took me a little while to spot Miles in the shadows, nursing a drink.

Thalia found Finch. Which, honestly, good for them. If they end up fucking, it'll be just another thing to cement Aspen's friend group to the hockey team. Finch isn't a hit-it-and-quit-it sort of guy, and I get the sense that Thalia isn't either. Not that Aspen isn't already stuck with us... Being friends with Violet, especially. She's not going anywhere.

Aspen sure as fuck isn't going anywhere.

I grind my teeth again at the thought of my father's idea. Having her committed to a mental institution for any length of time, on a one-time irrational act, seems extreme. Even for him. I wanted to break his trust in her, not destroy her life.

I run my fingers through her silky hair. I don't know what she does to it, but I love the way it glides through my grip. It's thick and dark and gives her green eyes an even more enchanting appearance. Especially when she tries to use them to guilt me into something.

Like dancing.

Dance, we did. It'll be a long time before I forget the feel of her writhing against me in time to a deep beat. Fully clothed, oddly enough.

She murmurs something and rolls over. Her body contorts, and her shirt rides up to expose her back. Her nose presses into the crease of my thigh and hip.

Yeah, she's definitely about to get poked in the eye.

I shift her onto her own pillow and cover her with the blanket, then resume my internet searching. Her name doesn't bring up much—just some old recitals and concerts that were blurbed in one of Chicago's smaller papers.

Her mom's name doesn't do it either.

I try just "Monroe, Chicago" and hit the search button.

Pages of results, with startling headlines.

Peter Monroe Arrested for Drug Smuggling into Canada.
Then, *Monroe Escapes on Bail from Detroit County Jail.* And,
*Crime Lords Bargain with Authorities to Bring in Peter Monroe
—to No Avail.*

Who is this guy?

I click on the article about his arrest—but it turns out
the case was dropped due to insufficient evidence. And
when he escaped bail in Detroit, he was caught two days
later. Similarly, the charges were dismissed.

This guy has been a nuisance for more than two
decades. But there aren't any articles more recent than five
years ago. Does that mean he died? Dropped off the radar
because he was picked up somewhere? Or maybe he went
into hiding on purpose.

I try various search terms, trying his full name with
Aspen's, or her mother's—Mari, Dad said, although it's
short for Marina.

Actually...

I glance down at Aspen again.

He didn't say she was a Monroe. Although Aspen clearly
took that last name because of her father. I think he said
she was a Saldo?

Dakota and Lennox have the last name Saldo, too.

I guess their mother learned from her mistakes the first
time. Is he even on their birth certificates? It wouldn't help
her with child support, but it *would* give her some distance
from him in any custody battle. Unless he demanded a
paternity test... but something tells me this guy won't want
any form of DNA on file.

Finally, a result comes up that includes Marina Saldo,
Peter Monroe, and Aspen. It's a tiny little blurb, just
covering church activity. It's included in a piece about the

recent happenings of a church in one of the Chicago suburbs.

I scan it until their names pop up.

We extend our hearts and prayers to Aspen Monroe, who joined our One Sacred Church through baptism on Saturday morning. Aspen's parents are Peter Monroe and Marina Saldo. Her godfather is Cillian Monroe. Welcome, Aspen!

There's that name again. Cillian.

He called her.

Godfather... and uncle?

I bite the inside of my cheek and set my phone aside. I've got a million more questions, but I don't think a simple Google search is going to bring up the kind of answers I need.

I'll find a way to make Aspen tell me.

And if she won't... I'll find someone who will make her.

29
ASPEN

My head aches. That's my first thought.

The second is the pleasure between my legs, my pussy throbbing like I'm on the cusp of an orgasm. And then the feeling intensifies, and I whimper. It sweeps through me, obliterating my thoughts. I squeeze my legs together, only to find them held open by two hands on my inner thighs.

I lift my head and squint in the low light.

Steele's between my legs, his head buried against my skin. His grip on my thighs tightens ever so much, like he's ready for me to rip my limbs away. But then his tongue pushes into me.

"What are you doing?" I groan, my fingers sliding into his hair.

He pulls up just a little, kissing my pubic bone. His gaze travels up my body, lingering on my breasts under the t-shirt I don't remember falling asleep in, and finally stops on my face.

"Having breakfast," he says. "I woke up starving."

I collapse back to the bed as he leans back down.

"Steele." I don't know why I'm saying his name.

Everything is too sensitive. My headache lingers, but it's really my hunger to come again that makes my hand return to his hair—to tug his lips back to my clit. He obliges with a grin, his tongue flattening on the sensitive bud.

"Oh God," I moan.

He stops just shy of pushing me over the edge, climbing up my body and shoving my t-shirt up as he goes. He licks my nipple. I drag my nails up his neck and wrap my fingers in his hair. I love that his hair is a little longer in the back and top, because my grip is solid. And I use it to guide him up my body.

Steele growls, going with my pulling but trailing his lips across my skin. Over the shirt that's now caught around my neck, up my throat to my jaw. He shifts his hips, aligning with me, and I make some desperate noise.

He thrusts into me. I'm slick already, but the stretch of his length, combined with my near-orgasm he left me hanging on, undoes me.

My eyes close, and my muscles tremble, riding a cresting wave. Two hard strokes inside me, and I shatter completely.

I cry out. He captures my lower lip between his teeth. The pain slips into pleasure.

What sort of fucked-up person am I to *enjoy* pain?

"I know, sweetheart," Steele whispers, nipping my ear. "I know what you crave—and it's not sex on a soft mattress. You want to be fucked on the ground. Taken from behind like an animal." His voice is hoarse, his movements slowing. "You need dirty, and you need to hurt. You need to be stuffed full of cock that you're not sure you entirely want, like a little slut that Daddy didn't pay enough attention to as a child."

I grip his chin before I can register making the conscious thought to do so. I drag his face closer, his dark eyes boring into mine. Sometimes I feel like he can see right through me... and other times, I want him to look *into* me.

"Maybe I'm a little slut because my daddy gave me too much attention," I whisper against his lips. "Ever think about that?"

"No." He grabs my wrist and tears my hand off his chin. He pins it to the bed next to my head. "No, I didn't. Is that what happened?"

I blink.

Breathe.

His eyes go impossibly darker. "Did he tie you up, sweetheart? Put something in your mouth?" He's stopped moving entirely. There's more, he knows there's more. And he doesn't shy away from it. "He spread your legs. And then what? Did he touch you?"

"I don't want to talk about this," I whisper.

I don't have nightmares about my childhood.

I don't have lingering trauma—unless something like what Steele did to me triggers it. In everyday, ordinary life, I'm fine. Normal. Happy.

"You are going to talk about this, Aspen. Because knowing what happened to you lets me inside you just a little bit more—and I won't stop until I'm buried so deep in your bones that I'm impossible to remove."

I shudder.

What's worse is my body's reaction. My skin prickles, my core tightens. I'm sure he feels the way I clench around him.

"Tell me, and I'll be yours forever. Just let me in, viper."

My gaze slides away from his.

"Tell me, Aspen."

"Soft. Everything was soft and slow," I gasp, trying to break his hold on my wrist. A yank, two—it does nothing. "He'd leave me tied up for hours in the dark, and I'd cry and plead, and nothing ever worked."

I can't believe I'm telling him this.

My wrists wrapped in his silk ties. My legs held open with padded cuffs, each secured to the corners of my mattress. The flash of a camera, sometimes, or just a red blinking dot in the dark. A piece of rubber in my mouth. My tongue would loll against it, and sometimes it felt like I couldn't get a breath in. Especially when my nose clogged, when the tears burned my eyes and panic overrode my senses.

I stare up at him, and part of me wants to believe him. But the other part is sure that he'll run away from me and never look back. "Everything is warped in my memory. His face staring down at me, the flashes of his camera. I don't know what else, but it's not anything a kid should know about, much less be forced to endure. I was six when it started, Steele. *Six*."

He doesn't. Fucking. Flinch.

And for some reason, that pisses me off.

Like he doesn't give a shit that my father is the worst piece of trash on the planet?

I yank at my wrists again, just wanting him *off* me. I thrash with my whole body, harder than I've ever fought him. My hand slips from his grasp, and before I can latch on to reason, I punch him in the face.

He growls and rears back. His cock slides out of me, and the sudden loss creates a newfound ache. *Why* am I so messed up?

I scramble off the bed, falling to the carpeted floor. The hotel room is foreign, dark, and it's hard to get my bearings. Didn't need them up until now. But I spy the open door to the bathroom and rush for it.

Steele slams into me, our bodies hitting the counter next to the sink. He folds me over it and grips the back of my neck. My cheek kisses the cold surface, and a shudder ripples up through my body. He kicks my legs wider and pushes back into me.

I groan, bracing my hands against the wall. "*More.*"

He gives me just that. His fingers on my skin are bruising, and I close my eyes as he takes whatever he wants from me. And then he lets out a noise, a gasp with my name on his lips, and stills fully inside me. He groans with his climax, and the force of his hips pressing mine into the counter. The way he fills me, the lust and pain that seem to mirror each other in my body—it's all too much.

We stay like that for a moment. Connected.

My heart thunders, my pussy pulses.

I want to come, but he didn't make any move toward my clit. Nothing that would give me pleasure.

And fuck if that makes me wetter.

He slips out of me. His hand leaves my neck, but the pressure on my skin doesn't. He keeps his palm on me, sliding down my spine. It stills at the small of my back. My breathing turns ragged when cool air brushes my ass cheeks—and then his lips. His teeth follow a moment later, and I try to jump—but there's nowhere to go to evade him.

He chuckles, nipping my sensitive skin again and then licking it. His free hand cups my other ass cheek, squeezing gently. And then it parts my cheeks, and my body goes hot.

"Steele—"

"Quiet, Aspen." His tone warns not to argue with him.

I shiver at the darkness in it. And he doesn't make me wait long before he runs his finger around my asshole. He spits—the noise is unmistakable—and the liquid hits my ass a second later. He uses it like lube, smearing his spit on my skin and then slowly pushing his digit inside me.

I groan at the sharp sensation.

"I wish you could see how my cum looks seeping out of your cunt right now," he says. "Do you feel it on your thighs, little viper?"

Bite.

I close my eyes.

He kisses and bites his way lower, tilting my hips to get better access. His tongue flicks my clit, and I moan again. Unbidden. Every inch of me is hyper-focused on him. His hand on my back, his other inching deeper into my asshole.

And then he removes his hand from my back, and he thrusts two fingers into me. Hard. My back arches, my breasts pushing into the counter, but I don't lift more than that. He sits back and finger-fucks me, pushing his cum back into me.

I'm trembling with the need to come. The sensations are too much, him filling both my holes with his fingers, fucking my ass and pussy at the same time. It's too over-whelming.

Bite.

The pain draws my focus to a point. A spearhead lancing through me.

"Come for me," he orders, driving me right over the edge.

And I fall.

When my body has stopped trembling, he withdraws. Moves to the sink beside me and washes his hands, his gaze on me. I feel like I'm stuck, unable to straighten up until he commands. Stuck in some space in my head where I do not want control.

He runs his finger up my spine. Along the top of my shoulder, following the contour of my arm. To my bent wrists, my hands still pressed to the wall. To my knuckles. My fingers. When he gently pulls my hand away, my exhale comes out shaky. He guides me upright, then leans down and picks me up.

I rest my cheek on his shoulder, and he carries me back to bed.

The alarm clock on the nightstand reads just past seven, although the blackout curtains hide any trace of sunlight. He lies down with me still in his arms.

"Rest."

I gulp.

He runs his hand up and down my arm and moves me to the side. My legs are still draped over his, even when he rolls to face me. He drags the blankets up with one arm, pulling them up to my shoulder.

"You okay?"

I blink at him. *No*, is what comes to mind. But I'm not sure how to say that.

"Mom left because of Dakota and Lennox," I whisper. Continuing this story even though he's long since stopped forcing it out of me. "It took her until her two younger children were in danger to get us out of there. She didn't believe me, I think. Not that I ever told her outright—but what was I supposed to say? The signs were there, but she never made a move against him when *my* life was in danger."

The old bitterness is resurfacing. I never blamed her for getting away from him. In fact, as it was happening, as we were running, I was grateful. Terrified and relieved. We stayed in shitty motel rooms and cheap, rat-infested apartments while Mom worked two jobs to afford more than that. Hid and feared and tried not to worry that the monster was hunting for us.

Steele leans into me and presses his lips to mine.

Soft.

Slow.

Exactly what he accused me of not wanting earlier seems to be the perfect balm now.

I inch closer and wrap my arms around him. Our chests press together, all the way down to our hips. His tongue sweeps across the seam of my lips, and I automatically open for him. Letting him taste me, tasting him in return.

It's... I don't know. Nice, I guess. In an unexpected way. Like we just went through battle and now he's trying to heal me from the inside out.

And I let him.

That's the strangest part.

I *let* him heal me. I give him all the bad parts—well, not all. There are so many more pieces of me coated in blood and ash that he has yet to see—and he takes them like they're precious.

Gifts, even.

I've seen the demons under his skin, too. They come out to play when I provoke him, when I want to feel what it's like to burn.

But his demons were nowhere near this tonight.

This was all for me.

I let out a whimper in the back of my throat, and Steele pulls me tighter. Slips his leg between mine, until his thigh is nestled against my core. Our kiss breaks off, and we breathe like that for a long moment. His eyes burn into mine.

I open my mouth to say something. A thanks, maybe, or... *something*.

But his alarm goes off with shrill, expert timing, and the words get stuck in my throat.

Time to go back to the real world, Aspen.

30
STEELE

Something has shifted between Aspen and me. I look for her on campus constantly—but not in anger. Not looking for the spy sent by my father. That's over anyway. No, I look for her because I want to see her dark hair fluttering behind her. The sway of her hips as she walks, the curve of her ass. The way her green eyes find mine almost as easily as I find hers.

I stride into the dining hall and grab food, then head to our table. It's been the team's as long as I can remember, in prime placement toward the back of the room. Center. Visible by so many people, but sitting there doesn't feel like we're in a fish tank—not like other places. Like when I sit in class and feel the weight of my classmates' stares.

If I had known hockey would come with a certain level of notoriety, I'm not sure I would've done it. I love the sport, I just hate the attention that comes with it. There are perks, of course. The perks outweigh the weight of notoriety.

My father has been radio silent, so I haven't taken steps to move Aspen into the hockey house. I want her there, but also... I rather like sneaking into her place. Which is exactly what I plan on doing tonight.

She's sitting with her friend, Thalia. Miles and Finch are with them, as well as more dance team girls. Girls I know for a fact have slept with more than one hockey player... including me.

Well, let's hope Aspen doesn't ask about a history, because that would get a bit awkward.

I set my plate down beside hers, sprawling out. My thigh brushes hers, and she glances at me. Then away.

Still shy. She's tried to withdraw once we got back from the away game. Embarrassed, ashamed. My dick is hard just thinking about how that night played out. Besides the earth-shattering confessions she laid on me. Obviously.

"Hey, sweetheart." I use my finger to direct her face toward mine and claim her lips.

She lets out a little gasp of surprise, like we've never done this before. But after a second, she leans into it. Her lips are soft on mine, yielding. She lets my tongue slip into her mouth for a moment. And then I withdraw, smirking at her dazed look.

"Don't hide from me," I order.

She nods vaguely, and I settle into my seat. Greyson and Knox join us, and they both slap my hand in greeting. I grin at them, tuning in to their mid-progress discussion. Something about the best way to get a puck past the goalie.

"Party at our house on Friday," Knox says suddenly, straightening up. "After the game. I forgot to tell you."

I roll my eyes. When is there *not* a party after a game? Although sometimes we take it to Haven, other times there's just too many people. And it's nice to be able to sit on a couch, or watch my teammates make fools out of themselves.

"It's small." Knox is defensive. He glances across Greyson at his brother, then back at me. "Like, fifteen people, tops."

"Who?" I ask.

"Me, you, Miles, Finch, uhhh, some puck bunnies—"

"Your girlfriend?" I bite the inside of my cheek.

Knox waves me off. "She's got a dance thing. She might be around later."

Greyson shifts. He meets my eyes, and I pick up what he's saying. That Knox is taking this bet thing a *little* too far, especially when we know Willow's already in love with him. She just won't admit it, the same way Knox won't give up.

They're stubborn.

And only Willow is going to end up hurt.

I roll my eyes in return and focus on eating my meal. Aspen chats to her friends beside me, but her hand finds my leg under the table. I grin to myself at the contact. Her fingers dig into my jeans, and her palm inches higher... and higher.

I grunt under my breath, not minding that she's being so bold—but also, if she wakes up this beast, she's going to have to suffer the consequences.

Her fingers graze my cock, and it leaps against the denim. I curse the jeans... and then I get an idea.

I grab her wrist and squeeze once in warning, stilling her movements. I finish my food and rise. I tug her with me. My blood is racing, but I ignore it and tell my friends that we'll be right back.

Greyson watches us with a small smirk, but the rest seem unbothered.

Aspen doesn't put up a fight until we get to the stairwell.

The same stairwell where I spilled the contents of her bag everywhere, then came on her tits. The idea of doing that again is kind of alluring... but I have a better idea.

"You want to get me hard, sweetheart?"

She hums behind me, still trying to get her wrist free.

There's a little alcove under the stairwell, drenched in shadows. It's a useless design flaw—they could've made it a closet from the other side or something, but instead it's just empty. I point to the space in front of me.

"Kneel."

She shivers and looks up at me.

My brows lower. "Now, Aspen."

She drops.

It's the most beautiful thing. She goes to her knees in front of me, and I run my fingers through her loose hair.

"Undo my jeans." My voice is no louder than a whisper, but she still flinches. Just a little.

Still, she does it. She unbuttons them, then drags the zipper down. My heart picks up speed, but I flex my hands and try to control myself. She pushes my jeans and boxers down, exposing my cock. It's hard already, bobbing in her face.

I back away from her and lean against the handrail on the wall. I let most of my weight settle and stare down at her.

"Crawl to me."

Her eyes lift to mine, and another thrill goes through me. I like it when she gives in to the side of her that wants to listen to me. That needs extra guidance... and humiliation. Plus, the added thrill of doing this where anyone could walk in...

She inches forward on her hands and knees, her hips swaying. I grip the railing instead of my cock, and she stops between my legs. She reaches out and grasps my length, and I let out a low groan. She strokes me a few times, then her hot mouth is on me.

I run my fingers through her hair again.

The door bangs open, and she tries to pull away.

I tighten my grip and force her down harder. We're hidden here, around the corner. Not that I really give a fuck. Voices reach us, and footsteps pound the stairs heading up.

Aspen pushes at my thighs. I release her, and she sits back on her heels. She glares up at me wordlessly.

"Afraid of getting caught?" I lean down. "You were turned on by watching that night... but what about being the one watched? We've already done that once, too. But it's different when it's unsuspecting, sober strangers, hmm?"

The party was a controlled environment—and we were both caught up in our lust when I fucked her in the basement. I had caught her, after all. That was my reward, consequences be damned. This is more risky, and she knows it.

She groans.

"Okay, sweetheart," I say suddenly, grabbing her by her elbows and forcing her to stand. I turn her around, putting her hands on the railing. "Don't let go."

I unbutton her jeans from behind and drag them down her legs. I dip my fingers through her center, unsurprised to find her dripping wet for me. Kicking her legs wider, I grab a fistful of her hair and yank her head back.

"You're my little slut," I say in her ear.

She whimpers.

I line my cock up and push inside her slowly. Her cunt squeezes me, and I nearly combust on the spot. She's so fucking tight. Her muscles pulse, and her mouth opens.

"I'm not going to last long," I continue. "And then we're going to go back to dinner and you're going to wear my cum like a good little whore."

Her nostrils flare. I lick up the side of her face. Her taste is addicting.

"Just fuck me already."

I smile to myself.

And then I do just that.

I fuck her hard, our bodies slapping together until neither of us can take it anymore. I reach around her and flick her clit. She gasps.

The door above us, the second or third floor, creaks when it opens. Voices echo around us, a conversation between two people. I wrap my free hand around her mouth and continue to fuck her, to work her toward an orgasm. I wonder if she'll make a noise.

The footsteps are coming down, headed toward us and the door.

The thrill of getting caught sweeps through me, and I roll my hips. The new angle gets me deeper inside Aspen, and I almost make a sound. Almost. I lean down and bite her shoulder.

Her fingers scrape my wrist, her nails digging into my skin.

Pain and pleasure burst down my spine, straight to my balls. I let out an exhale and try to hold on. I'm so fucking close—

The doors on the first floor slam shut.

Silence wraps around us, and then it's too late. My balls tighten, and I jerk inside her as I come.

It's relief and bliss.

She follows me, her sharp, staccato cry, muffled by my

hand, still fills the space around us. Her back arches as she comes, her face screwed up.

We stay like that for a second. But like any quick, dirty fuck—we're not meant to linger. I slide out of her and tuck myself back in my boxers, doing up my jeans. I squat and take her panties and jeans and pull them up her legs. Trapping my cum against her pussy.

For a second, I wonder about her birth control. I finally figured it out—she's on the shot. She's still in the safe zone, with a month left before she needs another. I've been tempted to cancel her appointment just to fuck with her...

"Steele." Aspen has turned around and faces me now, her brows drawing down. "What are we doing?"

I scowl. "In what sense?"

"Like..." She motions between us. "I get that you want to tell people we're together. But we're going to go home for Christmas and we'll be *siblings*. There's no way our parents would let anything like this slide under their roof—"

"First," I interrupt. "It's not *their* roof. It's my father's roof. And second, if you think I'm going to stop fucking you just because our parents think it's a bad idea, you've got another think coming. They don't own us, remember?" I cross my arms and raise my eyebrow.

"We can't—"

"So help me god, Aspen, if you finish that sentence..." I shake my head. "You're mine. Okay? Here, there, on fucking Mars. There's nothing you can say or do that's going to derail me from you."

This obsession has gotten out of hand.

I know that.

She knows that.

But I can't stop—and I won't.

Watching Steele play when we're on the same page is *way* different than when I hated his guts. Or when he hated mine. I wear his white away jersey while he slams opponents into the glass, and gets hit a few times, himself. He pushes off one of the players and charges after the puck, and our crowd goes nuts.

It's a home game, and Crown Point never slacks in attendance.

Thalia, Willow, and the rest of the dance team aren't here, though. They have a competition across town. Violet is absent, too. I think she went to cheer on her best friend, since Willow's boyfriend is currently on a warpath on the ice.

Someone drops into the seat beside me.

I jerk, then look over at the beaming face of Chase King.

He's wearing a CPU football sweatshirt and a Hawks beanie, and he's got a beer in his hand. "Mind if I join you?

I shake my head and turn my attention back to the

game. He's in Violet's empty seat—the one that Greyson buys whether or not she can come.

"How are you?" he asks.

"I'm surprised you're talking to me." I watch him out of the corner of my eye.

Really, I'm more curious about what Steele is going to do when he sees who I'm sitting beside. It's only a matter of time before he notices. They're on the other side of the rink for now, fending off the opposing team.

"Eh." He leans back. "You seemed lonely. Wouldn't O'Brien rather have someone you know sit with you than risk anything else happen? I heard what happened with that asshole a few games ago."

I wince.

"So. How are you?"

"There's been a lot going on."

But I'm fine. I'm not going to explode, or implode, or have any sort of meltdown. The past is the past, and it's staying there.

"Uh-huh." Chase nudges me. "I think he's noticed us."

It takes me a moment to locate Steele. He's off the ice, and I scan the bench, only to find him staring at me. Or at least, in our direction. But it sure as hell feels like his gaze is on my face.

Glaring daggers.

"I don't think he takes the same viewpoint as you," I say lightly.

Chase shrugs. "Maybe it'll make him play better."

"Maybe," I agree.

But I've got to admit—it is nice to have a little company. And the anticipation of Steele's fire later on sends a curl of heat straight between my legs. It's made even more obvious how pissed he is when he charges back onto the ice and flattens the first player he comes across.

The crowd *ooh*s at the display of violence.

Chase chuckles. He's not touching me—I don't think he has that much of a death wish—and in the end, the Hawks decimate their opponents. Chase and I follow the crowd out of the stadium, and we wrap around the building toward where the players will exit. A short time later, Steele emerges.

His gaze goes right to Chase, who backs up with his hands raised.

"Take it easy, jackass," Chase says. "I was just making sure your girl was okay. None of her friends were with her."

On that note, he turns and saunters away. Not that it really matters, because Steele consumes my vision. And Steele seems to think the same, because he smiles when he sees me. *Smiles.*

My stomach flips. I'm not sure if the smile is a good or bad thing. Like a shark smiling... it's gotta be bad news. Right?

And I'm the prey he's stalking.

I swallow. He either doesn't notice my trepidation or chooses to ignore it, coming close and taking my hand. He reels me in and plants a kiss on my lips, and for a second I forget my wariness. My whole body wants to be kissed by him.

His lips move against mine, and his tongue slips into my mouth.

I'm a goner.

My knees go weak. He wraps his arm around my back, binding me to him. I mean, it's right out of a movie—and I'm breathless by the time he pulls back.

Steele smirks at me, still holding me close. "You wear my jersey well, little viper."

I blush.

Blush, like a teenager.

I shake it off as best I can, and we head toward the parking lot. Greyson waits by his truck. Steele hugs me from behind, holding me back as Knox, Finch, and Miles all pile in the back. I narrow my eyes, but Steele just smirks and swings up into the passenger seat.

He pats his thighs. "Climb aboard."

"We don't have all night, Monroe," Greyson calls.

I grimace and step forward, letting Steele manhandle me onto his lap. He rearranges my limbs to his liking, gripping my hips.

"No funny business," Greyson warns, glancing at his friend.

I snort and elbow Steele. "Yeah. No funny business."

Steele drags my back flush to his chest. His lips touch my ear. "Nothing funny about it."

Oh, great.

I keep my gaze on the road as Greyson drives us to the hockey house, where the party has clearly already started. He parks on the front lawn and hops out, and the rest of us follow. There are already a million people spread out across the front porch and in the house.

"Fucker," Steele calls to Knox. "You gave Erik a key, didn't you?"

Knox grins and jogs past us. "Obviously."

People are noticing our arrival. Well—I suppose with Greyson's parking job, it would be unrealistic to assume otherwise. But they cheer and whoop, lifting their cups toward the hockey players.

Steele lurks behind me. Knox, Miles, and Greyson lead

the way, accepting congratulatory pats on their shoulders and backs. Within seconds, girls have pressed red cups into their waiting hands.

Like royalty.

I wrinkle my nose.

Someone tries to give Steele a cup. A girl with rather impressive cleavage, her breasts on the verge of bursting out of her neckline. I glare at him over my shoulder. He winks at me and rejects it with a quick shake of his head, saying something to the girl.

Whatever he says makes her face go red.

She disappears back into the crowd. The music is loud, the bass vibrating in my chest. The furniture has been pushed aside in the living room, leaving a space for dancing. Beyond it, the kitchen looks packed with people pouring themselves drinks.

I scan the party, taking note of Greyson in the corner, greeting some football guys. Of Knox already dancing with someone. And Miles shoving his way toward the back door. My curiosity toward the younger Whiteshaw brother is piqued.

Steele steps up beside me, distracting me from my musing. He puts a cup in my hand—where it came from, I don't know—and takes a sip from his own. He watches me steadily over the rim. It feels like a dare. Or a promise.

I don't know what it means—but there's a part of me itching to break free. My heart skips, and I take a sip.

Cold beer slips down my throat. I lower the cup, but Steele puts his finger under the bottom. Tipping it back up. I finish the cup, and he tosses it away. Then wraps his hand around mine and pulls me toward the dance floor.

32
MILES

My mood is black. I've retreated to the back deck, overlooking some morons in the yard below who are trying to start a fire. They've been at it for too long, building and rebuilding the logs after each failed attempt. Inside, Steele and Aspen are practically having sex on the dance floor. He's got her right where he wants her, like a spider with a meal caught in its web.

Good for him, right?

Greyson got his girl. Steele is on his way to securing his —if he doesn't scare her away before that happens. My brother... well, fuck him.

I curl my fingers around the blade of my knife, digging another notch into the railing. It's being replaced over the summer, and my marks will be gone. So it doesn't matter that I'm keeping track of how many times I lose my temper. It doesn't matter that there are more lines in this railing than ever before, because soon, it'll be like it never existed at all.

It being so many things. My temper, my demons, my lack of control.

My brother and I rarely fight. We hardly ever disagree about the important things—well, one important thing: hockey. The rest we let roll off our backs. I think my parents like it that way. They raised us to be best friends, and it stuck. Except for the past year, when my anger and vitriol has been growing and morphing into some beast I don't understand. Something directed at *him*.

"Hey, stranger."

I glance over my shoulder, already frowning.

Willow closes the sliding glass door behind her and steps up next to me. Her gaze flicks to the knife, the tip still buried in the wood, then up to my face.

"How was the competition?" I force the words out, because I don't want her questioning me. I don't want her kindness or friendliness or compassion. So better to keep the attention on her, exactly where it belongs. She deserves the spotlight anyway.

She lifts one shoulder. She's still dressed in her competition outfit, the tight dark-blue cropped shirt with silver lettering across her chest, the dark-blue shorts. High socks and silver shoes. It's all ridiculous how much school spirit she's forced to have.

Good thing blue is her color.

The only thing seemingly undone is her hair, which is pulled into a messy braid that hangs over her shoulder. Strands have fallen out, framing her face.

"It was fine. We didn't win."

"You'll get 'em next time," I mutter. Because I don't know what else to say.

She shrugs. "Maybe."

"Why are you out here?"

Last I checked, Knox was dancing, and it wasn't with

her. But that was before I retreated out here. It was either stay inside and punch him, or... not.

I chose the latter.

Above all, he's my brother. Fighting him would do neither of us any good. So I pick him over everything else, even when he's being a dick.

For a split second, I hope she didn't see him. I hope she didn't have to witness Knox being a narcissistic asshole. But then my common sense overrides, and *my* inner asshole wins out. Because fuck that—she should see all of him, not just the pretty parts he keeps polished for her.

"It's hot inside," she lies.

I exhale.

One day, Willow Reed will grow a fucking spine—but that day isn't today.

"I'm bored," I say, straightening.

I'm sure as fuck not going to stand out here and commiserate with my brother's girlfriend. Not when I've wanted her from day fucking one. Not when seeing him treat her like garbage—and her *let* him—makes me angry enough to stab another line in the railing.

Someday, she'll admit her feelings out loud, and my brother will stomp all over her heart.

And all that'll be left for me is broken little pieces.

But you know what?

That's all I deserve.

33
STEELE

"Easy," I murmur, guiding Aspen up the stairs.

Her eyes are mostly closed. She's been getting progressively less responsive for the past hour, and now her muscles are failing her, too. She stumbles and puts more of her weight on me. She mumbles something, but I can't make out the words.

Eventually, once we're out of sight of the party, I swing her up into my arms and carry her the rest of the way. I balance her and unlock my door, then set her on the bed. She flops a bit, her body relaxed. She doesn't so much as shift.

I lock the door and reposition her on the bed, her head on the pillow. She looks like a sleeping angel like this, her dark hair fanned out, her lips slightly parted. Her eyes flutter. I pull the blanket up over her and flick off the light, then sit beside her.

After a while, she falls into a deeper sleep.

The drugs I put into her drink grab a deeper hold of her mind.

"Aspen." My voice is loud.

No response.

I turn my bedside lamp on, and she doesn't react to that either. My heart picks up speed, and I take a deep breath. I've been planning this for so long, practiced for even longer. I'm not the sort to get nervous—but I am *ready*.

I push the blanket off her. With slow, sure movements, I unbutton her jeans and yank them down. Over her hips, past her thighs. I toss the denim to the floor and go for her panties. Dark purple. Satin. A thong, no less. I smirk as I drag them down, too. The strip that sits against her cunt is damp. It makes me wonder what sort of wicked plans she had for us tonight.

She probably didn't see *this* coming.

I run my finger up her center, noting with pride that she's wet. She doesn't react to the intrusion of my finger, or my thumb resting on her clit. I stroke her, finger-fucking her, until I *do* get a reaction. Her cunt clenches on my fingers, and her body goes rigid. Not as powerful as when she's awake, but I'll take it.

I pull away. My jersey is still on her torso, her nipples poking through the fabric. I push it up and expose her breasts, undoing the bra and maneuvering it off without removing the jersey.

Then my true task begins.

In the corner of my closet is a box of supplies.

Ordered from a local shop, along with a quick lesson. The box is also filled with practice material. I made sure I could do it without issue before I'd even attempt it on Aspen.

And still, there are risks.

What I should've done was bring her to a shop.

Had a professional do it.

But she'd never agree—and the thought of someone else seeing her in this state is unthinkable.

I set out a towel and lay out my supplies, then take the cheap disposable razor and clean the area. She's already shaved—or waxed, maybe, I don't know—so my job is easier. I turn on my overhead light and glance up at Aspen's face.

She's so fucking peaceful. Beautiful.

And *mine*.

With a small smile, I get to work.

I wake up to weight.

And intense pleasure.

I groan and shift, trying to bring my arms down. They're stuck over my head.

Blank fear hits me for a moment, until I force my eyes open. Steele is over me, thrusting into me like he's trying to wake me up. His cock stretches me, hitting a spot inside me that feels *too* good.

The pops of pleasure are addicting. Thrilling, even.

"That's one way to wake a girl up," I mumble. My mouth is dry. The more aware I become, the more I feel like something is wrong. Beyond Steele initiating sex before I was even awake...

He leans down and slides his arm under me, gripping me to his body. He buries his face in my neck, groaning and panting. "You came before you woke up," he says in my ear. "But I think you want to come again, don't you, sweetheart?"

How long has he been...?

My head swims, and I screw my eyes shut tighter.

I try to move my legs, to drag them up higher, but they don't move.

"Breathe," he groans in my ear. "Fuck, you feel so good."

"Stop," I say, trying to fight against him.

He's just... everywhere. In me and around me. He's all I can smell and see, and my heart is going to pound out of my chest.

"No." His teeth scrape my neck, and then his lips are on mine. His tongue in my mouth as suffocating as a gag. He pulls back and looks down at me.

The light is on. The one on his nightstand.

"You thinking of what your father did to you?" His eyes bore into mine. "Because newsflash, Aspen. I'm. Not. Him."

He punctuates each word with a thrust, and my eyes roll back at the feel of it. He shifts again, his movements getting softer.

There's heat on my pubic bone. I don't know why it catches my attention, but I focus on it for a second—until Steele's fingers close around my nipple.

My back arches as much as I can—but we're practically smashed together anyway. He kisses a path down my jaw, my throat, to my other breast. He sucks and licks at my nipple, and shocks of energy flutter straight to my core. He twists the other one, tugging on it.

Pain.

Pleasure.

I close my eyes and yank on my wrists again. "Tell me what you did."

"Drugged you," he admits to my chest. "Fucked you. *Claimed you*."

The words bounce around my skull.

"You're so fucked up," I whisper.

"I know."

His hand leaves my nipple and runs down my body. Over my curves, over my hip. He touches my clit just the way I like, and I curse him in my head for knowing my body so well. Like he really does own it.

He brings me to the cusp of an orgasm and then pulls away.

Entirely.

His cock slides out of me, his fingers leave my clit. He's right over me, there but *not*. Not touching me at all.

"I need something from you, Aspen," he says.

"What?" I gasp. I pull at my wrists, my legs.

Useless.

He touches my clit with the lightest brush, and I shiver. Goosebumps rise on my skin.

"Tell me that you're mine, body and spirit. That you're going to let me *all the way in*."

My brows furrow.

Haven't I done that? Haven't I said I was his? And every time I do, bad shit happens. He can claim me all he wants, but this—*drugging* me—is going too far.

This is too much.

"You can't torture me into agreeing to be yours," I argue. "And every time you hurt me, it makes me hate you more."

He smiles. "Hate? Your body has already admitted to enjoying what I do to you, little viper. It's just a matter of your mind following... and if that means breaking it, I'll do that."

I shake my head.

He leans down and kisses my pubic bone, and I wince.

Why does that hurt?

I try to straighten enough to see it—stupid boobs,

stupid stomach getting in the way—but the way he has me restrained, I can't see it.

My heart thumps. Skips.

He moves lower. His tongue dances around, tasting me. My labia, my slit. His tongue pushes into me, and I try to get away. It's all the sensation I want, but not where I need it. He continues to play with me until I'm squirming against the bindings.

"Please," I whisper.

His tongue flicks my clit, and I gasp.

I'm right at that edge.

"Please, Steele, I'll—" I press my lips together and squeeze my hands into fists. "I hate you," I chant.

I hate you.

I hate you.

I hate you.

Over and over.

He backs away from my clit and sweeps lower. He kisses my inner thigh.

I'm going to lose my mind.

"I hate you, *fuck*, I hate you so much," I continue. "I don't want anything to do with you. I don't want to see your stupid face. Your touch makes my skin crawl. *God dammit*," I yell. "Get off me, you ogre."

I thrash. He wraps his arm around one of my thighs, keeping me contained.

It's pointless to fight him, but—

"You're wetter." His finger dips into me. "The fight turns you on, but I know you're only lying to yourself."

He climbs up my body and thrusts back into me. *Hard.* I groan at the contact, but then his hand is wrapped around my throat, and his lips are on mine. Everything about this is aggressive. Like he's stoking some fire in me, even when I can't move.

Fuck that.

I bite his lip.

Blood coats my tongue. Then his, as he forces his tongue into my mouth.

I bite that, too.

I feel unhinged, feral. He bites me back. My lips, my jaw. We fight with our teeth. His hand at my throat captures my pulse, my breath. One squeeze and he could cut off my air, or the blood flow to my head.

He could make me pass out with just a twitch of his fingers.

Or kill me.

He lifts his head and stares down at me. His lips are red with blood. His tongue darts out and probes the wound. Another drop of blood oozes out, then drips down onto my cheek.

"Tell me again," he whispers.

"No."

He tsks. Rolls his hips. "Do you think I like torturing you?"

"I think you enjoy it, yeah."

He shakes his head and climbs off the bed. I track him, licking my lips. His cock bobs in front of him, pointing in my direction. He gets back on the bed, but this time, he swings his leg over my face.

I shudder.

"Make me come, and maybe I'll do the same," he says.

He lowers his dick to my mouth. I open automatically, but I'm not prepared for him to thrust in as powerfully as if he were taking my pussy. The tip hits the back of my throat, then slides even deeper.

I choke around him.

His balls hit my face.

The humiliation is enough to strangle me—if we forget that I'm already suffocating on *him*. He pulls out, inch by inch, and I widen my jaw enough so I won't bite his dick off. I inhale sharply through my nose, and then he's filling my throat again.

My hands twist helplessly above me. There's no way to help myself here—he's making me take all of it.

And fuck if that's not turning me on even more.

His fingers part my pussy lips, and I make some deep noise in my throat. A cry and a moan. Tears prick my eyes at his continued invasion down my throat. He gets into a rhythm that lets me take quick, shallow breaths. And after a minute, I suck and swirl my tongue around his shaft. Tasting him and myself.

And then his mouth is on me, and stars spark behind my closed eyelids.

He ravages me. Touching everything but my clit, while his own pace increases. His thrusts get jerkier, his control unraveling.

Fuck.

Fuck.

Fuck.

He sucks my clit into his mouth.

At last.

The sensation decimates me. I lose it, everything pulsing inside me. My heart feels too big for my chest. He thrusts his fingers inside me, giving my cunt something to clench around. I scream around his cock, uncaring that my teeth scrape his length. That my throat is probably giving him some great vibrations.

Suddenly he pulls back until he's only filling my mouth.

He comes. Not down my throat, not on my face. Or my chest. It shoots across my tongue, his cock jerking with the force of it, and I automatically block my throat. It fills my mouth and drips out the corners of my lips, down my face.

I haven't swallowed by choice since the summer. By choice.

And I'm not about to start now.

Except he's suddenly spinning around and clamping a hand over my mouth, his face *right there.*

"You want me to leave you here until tomorrow morning? Bound up like the little slut you and I both know you are? Then spit it out. I fucking dare you, Aspen. Spit it out and I'll treat you like a cheap whore. Maybe take some pictures while you're tied up like this, or put a pretty gag in your mouth." He glowers at me. "Swallow it and I'll let you up."

Not much of a choice here, is there? My eyes are still blurry with tears from the intense throat-fuck, and as I blink, they fall. They roll into my temple, my hairline.

He lifts his palm away from my lips, watching me closely.

I suck in a breath through my nose and weigh my odds.

I believe every threat he's issued.

That's my problem, isn't it?

So I ball my fists and open my throat. And I fucking swallow.

"Good girl," Steele croons.

He undoes my legs first, then my wrists. Quick, like he knew I wasn't going to fight him on this. I pull my arms in, tugging his jersey—which has been around my neck this whole time—down over my breasts.

I feel... bare.

Bruised.

He helps me stand, then walks me to the bathroom. The hallway is dark, the rest of the house relatively quiet. There's still music playing downstairs, and a light coming from the bottom of the staircase. No one's up here, though, it would appear.

I don't even know what time it is. Just that it's dark out.

For a second, I'm delusional enough to think that he's going to let me use it alone. Instead, he follows me in and flips the lock behind himself, sitting on the edge of the tub. He watches me closely.

"I have to pee," I say.

He shrugs. "Go on, then."

"Can you look away?"

"No."

I glare at him.

He glares back.

But the urge in my bladder is more pressing than anything else, so I sigh and sit carefully on the toilet. I focus on my knees, waiting for my muscles to unclench long enough to go. It's weird, with him in the bathroom like my own personal... prison guard.

That's not normal, right?

And then my body cooperates. I close my eyes until I'm done.

It's only then that I feel something odd between my legs.

Not like, *in* me, but...

I stand and lean over to examine myself. There's a bandage taped just above my pussy. Over my pubic bone, which felt like it was burning earlier. I stare at it, then glance at Steele. He's watching me with an intensity that makes my stomach flip.

"What did you do?" My voice is shaky. Raspier than usual.

I peel away the tape carefully, lifting the bandage.

Dark lettering sits on my skin.

In my skin.

I swipe at it and let out a hiss of pain. The skin is sensitive, red around the letters, even with the oily substance coating it. I look over at him again. I need my phone. My brain isn't working, isn't computing what the letters mean upside down.

"Tell me this is some sort of elaborate prank," I whisper.

He shrugs. "If it'll help you sleep at night."

"Steele."

"Aspen."

"I—you—"

He rises and turns me around, facing the sink. I stare at our faces in the mirror, even as he tips me forward and dunks my hands under the warming water. He squirts soap into my palm, then guides my hands together. It suds, and his fingers move between mine. Guiding my movements.

He rinses both of our hands, and then he manually turns me around again. He kneels, even with my hips. He lifts the bandage back up and pats the tape into place.

"Keep it covered," he orders. "For at least twenty-four hours. Then clean it with an unscented soap and water. No scrubbing. Aquaphor or unscented lotion to keep it hydrated after that."

Tattoo care instructions.

What the fuck?

"What does it say?"

He looks up at me, frowning. Still on his knees before me. "It says you're mine."

P roperty of Steele O'Brien.

That's what the fucking tattoo says.

I pull my underwear up with an exhale, trying to keep calm.

After he let me up, I went home. It was four in the morning, but I just couldn't be around him anymore. Simple as that. I was lucky to find my phone on the way out, deader than a doornail. No one was on the streets on my walk back, and even Uncle wasn't waiting for me in my apartment.

I fell asleep promptly, only waking when the sun streamed in through my window. I showered, somewhat disgruntled at the extra care I had to pay to the *tattoo* while washing.

Now my phone is alive, and the first thing I see after dressing is an email from the music theory professor I had met weeks ago. William Wilcox. I snatch it up and unlock my phone, scanning the email.

. . .

Ms. Monroe,

Thank you for your patience while I worked out the finer details on my end. If you are still willing, we would like to have you come in and audition for the open pianist position in the Crown Point Orchestra next week. As you may know, I hold a position on the orchestra's founding board. Our members are looking forward to meeting you.

Sincerely,

Professor William Wilcox

Holy.

Shit.

It's happening. There's an audition piece attached to the email for me to learn.

I leap up and spin in a circle, suddenly realizing that I haven't played the piano in four days. How the hell did I just—*forget*? Did Steele blindside me so much that I forgot my one true love in life?

I need my sheet music. I need to get back to practice *immediately*. Plus learning this new piece, which I have to perfect in a limited amount of time.

"Oh my god." I can't find it.

My whole binder of music is gone.

I drop to my knees and look under my bed, my stomach in my throat.

Not here.

Where's the last place I saw my music?

When's the last time I had it?

I scramble around my room, yanking open my closet doors. The bag of money stares at me, reminding me that I still have to figure out next semester's financial situation, and also somehow return this blood money to my dad, without actually giving it to *him*.

I'd like to keep up my no-contact record, thank you very much.

Besides the eyesore bag of cash, there isn't much else in my closet. Just clothes and some storage bins. None of which hold my binder of sheet music.

"Fuck," I mutter.

I have a music class that requires a final performance. It's what I've been working on since the start of the semester. Technically difficult pieces of composition that have tested me at every turn.

Yes, I could reprint them. But then I'd lose my notes, and it would be like starting over.

From scratch.

The thought of walking onstage and performing anything less than perfect is nauseating.

With sudden clarity, I know exactly who took my sheet music.

Steele.

I stand in the middle of my room and shake out my arms. I'm too hot. My skin is tight, my muscles locking up. My stomach rolls like I'm going to be sick.

When did he come in here and snatch it?

And why was I *so* blinded by him that I let him?

The last thing I'm going to do is go begging for my music back. I'm not pathetic. I will not cower in front of him like I've done to every other imposing asshole. My mother instilled that in me. The fear. The way she thought every man was a version of my father.

So I don't understand why she married Stephen O'Brien without hesitation.

I don't understand how she trusted him above anyone else.

How she let my sisters live under his roof, knowing what men are capable of doing.

"I'm home," Thalia calls, the apartment door slamming closed behind her. "Are you here?"

My eyebrows rise. Truth be told, I should've kept a closer eye on my roommate at the party. Should've kept track of her after she arrived with the rest of the dance team.

Well, didn't Steele say he drugged me?

So maybe my friend should've kept better track of *me*.

I hate that immediate accusation. It's not her fault, it's Steele's. The guy who calls himself my boyfriend, and now apparently my keeper. I want to go out into the living room and watch her make a cup of coffee, see the rosy redness of her cheeks that might belie the kind of night she had.

But instead, I can't move. A sharp loneliness rises, closing my throat. The echo of the counselor asking who I had resounds in my head. Besides Thalia, who else do I have to talk about what's happening to me? What Steele is doing to me?

I hurry out of my room and into the common area, stopping short at the sight of Thalia.

On the counter.

Kissing my uncle.

For a moment, all I can do is stare. His tattooed hands are on her waist, his fingers digging into her sweatshirt. Her arms are around his neck.

I stumble backward. One step, two, and then I'm spinning and rushing back to the safety of my room. I close my door and press my back to it, covering my eyes.

Dramatic, maybe, but *what the fuck*? Is that the first time they've done that?

Or is it a regular thing?

Without thinking, I cross to the window and remove the bar that's held it shut after Steele's intrusion. I shove the glass upward and then unhook the screen. I get that out of the way, setting it against my dresser, and stick my head out.

It's not so far a drop.

I cannot picture for one more moment the sort of debauchery that's happening in this apartment. I thought she was with Finch! Apparently, I had it very, very wrong.

That, over everything else, drives me to swing one leg out. I straddle the windowsill and eye the drop again, then move my other leg out.

"One, two, three," I whisper, heaving my body out on *three.*

Strong hands catch my hips and lower me down.

I look up, only half surprised to see Steele in front of me. I was too busy staring at the ground to see who was approaching, and now he's got ahold of me. When my feet touch the grass, he lets go. Still standing too close, though. All I would have to do is sway forward and my chest would brush his.

"What are you running away from?"

I blow out a breath. "What makes you think I'm running away?"

"Sensible ladies use the front door."

"What makes you think I'm sensible?"

He smirks. "Certainly not your way of exiting your apartment, that's for sure." He leans down. "Or maybe it's the way you like to fuck that gives it away."

I smack his shoulder, belatedly remembering my anger. "You stole my music."

His eyebrows rise. "Did I?"

"Yes, and I'm mad at you for it." I glance up at the window. The top is out of reach to close, which is a minor inconvenience.

Whatever.

I brush past Steele and step onto the sidewalk, striding quickly toward school. He doesn't follow. Not immediately. And a quick glance back shows him stretching upward to close my window for me, his shirt riding up and revealing a slice of his abs.

My cheeks heat, and I whip back around.

Soon enough, he's at my side. A step behind, like a hulking shadow that I can't remove. I ignore him. The tattoo keeps drawing my attention, the ache of it like a sunburn. My panties irritate it, and I bite the inside of my cheek to keep from lashing out.

"I like you mad," he says. "But something else has you riled. Nothing I've done would make you go out the window. Even stealing sheet music. Which I did not do."

I ignore that observation. I really don't want to talk about it anyway. We get to campus in silence, and I go straight to the music hall. There's a printer I can use to get this audition piece printed, and then I'll be well on my way to rehearsal. Then I just need to perfect it and schedule my audition.

Easy.

He keeps up with me while I do just that, snatching the pages still warm with ink the moment they come to a rest in the tray. I reach for them, but he blocks me with his body. He flips through the pages, then faces me again. Still holding those damn papers like they're not the most important thing right now.

This is my future we're talking about.

"Give them back." I hold out my hand.

"What will you give me in return?" His eyes dance.

No. "Nothing, Steele. I'll give you all the cold shoulders you could ever imagine—and none of my fight."

His smile fades. "What's really wrong?"

"You're what's wrong," I snap, reaching again for the pages.

He lets me have them this time. They slip harmlessly through his fingers.

I press them to my chest. My heart is beating furiously, and I don't know what to do to stop it. How to calm down around him. I just want to hit him and yell at him and—

"Aspen," he murmurs.

"You branded me like some—some—" I shake my head. *Not doing this.*

I go to a practice room, my ID unlocking it with a soft click. I try to close him out. I *do* close him out, for all of three seconds. Until he taps his ID against the pad and the door gives him admittance, too. I forgot he did that before. The day he drugged me, he just strolled in.

My brows furrow. "You don't play an instrument."

"This school loves hockey," he counters. He pulls the shade on the door's vertical window. "I don't need to play an instrument to be allowed access if I ask for it."

I humph. "I don't want you here."

"And I don't want you upset with me." He inches closer, fingering the strap of my bag. Dragging it down my arm and tossing it aside.

"Who says you can fix it?" I let him take the sheet music

out of my hands, too. "Maybe my anger just needs to burn for a while."

"It's not anger." He frowns. "I could make you mad, if that would help? Instead of what this is. I think it's disappointment. Are you upset?"

"Cute, but no. I need to practice. I need the rest of my music back." I lift my chin. "Now, maybe if you weren't completely obsessed with hindering me at every step—"

"I already told you I didn't take it." His head tips. "Someone else, then?"

I groan. It's him. I know it's him. There's no one else it *could* be.

"I'll take care of it," he adds.

Yeah, right. "It's not as easy as reprinting it. If it was, I would've done so already."

"Okay." His gaze drops lower. "How's your tattoo?"

"It's been less than twelve hours." I step back. "It's fine."

"Feeling okay?"

I don't like the concern in his eyes. The weight of it sits on my skin and makes me think he actually gives a shit. Everything he's done since our parents got married has been an act. Not coming home from Crown Point for the summer. Making my life hell on repeat. The softer things that any normal person would perceive as him *changing* or becoming *good*—lies. Manipulations.

"It's fine," I repeat.

My ass hits the piano, compressing keys. The notes fill the small room. I had hardly realized I was backpedaling until now, and suddenly, I can't go anywhere. He's right in front of me, with no signs of letting me free.

Instead, I watch him undo the buttons of my jeans and drag the fabric down. He pushes me back again, making me sit on the piano. The notes sound bitter, clashing. It matches my thrashing heart.

He lowers my panties and stares at the black ink lettering.

I close my eyes.

"You know what went through my mind when I did it?" He traces just below his work, eliciting goosebumps to rise on my body.

"No."

"I thought, 'Now her daddy won't be able to take pictures of her. Now she's safe, because she doesn't belong to him anymore. She belongs to me.'"

A lump forms in my throat.

"You belong to me, Aspen. You did the moment you drew the joker at the party, although neither of us fucking knew the gravity of it." His lips touch down just over my pussy.

My fingers find their way into his hair. It's soft, and I drag my nails across his scalp before gripping his locks. He lets out a breath when I force his head to tip back, and his eyes laser onto mine. He registers my tears at the same moment I do, because I blink and suddenly his face is blurry.

"Oh, baby." He rises and drags me against him.

A hug.

Takes a second to register it for what it is.

An all-encompassing hug, his arms around me, his hands hot on my back. My head tucked under his chin. I don't know the last time I was hugged like this.

I close my eyes, and a foreign feeling washes over me.

For the first time in a long time, I feel *safe*.

And that scares me more than anything.

I unlock Aspen's apartment door and slip inside.

The interior is dark, which makes sense. It's the middle of the fucking night. But I couldn't sleep, and all I want to do is curl up next to Aspen. To smell her familiar scent and feel her curves. To make her moan delicious, dirty things in a half-sleep daze...

Too late, I register the moving shadow. It detaches from the wall and flies at me, and I barely have time to get my hands up before I'm slammed into the wall.

I let out a grunt. It hurts, but I've taken worse hits at practice. I shove them off me and duck, automatically driving forward. My shoulder buries into his stomach, and we rock back. His fists bound into my sides. His punches are hard enough to crack my ribs—and if I can't play, then I'm fucked. So I release him and stagger backward.

He comes at me again, this time taking us to the floor. We crash into the stools against the kitchen island, bringing them down with us. We roll, and suddenly, hands are around my neck.

Squeezing.

I grip his wrists and glare up at the stranger. I can make him out now, the dark tattoos that crawl up his skin, all the way up his neck. His eyes are so cold.

"Uncle!" Aspen screams. "Stop!"

She's suddenly beside us, slapping his shoulder.

He glances up at her.

My vision flickers.

"Let him go," she demands. "It's *Steele*."

His fingers loosen, and blood rushes back to my brain. I gasp, furious that I was just brought to my back by this asshole.

My mind is slow to supply his name. And then it does, a lightbulb flickering to life inside my head: Cillian Monroe.

Her uncle stands and pushes Aspen back. Thalia is in the entrance of the hallway, a robe wrapped around her.

I leap to my feet, too pissed to be caught lingering on the floor. The room wavers, the floor pitching. I steady myself on the kitchen island and ignore how my head swims.

Fuck.

"Are you okay?" Aspen shoves past her uncle and stops in front of me, her hands fluttering between us like she doesn't know where—or if—to touch me.

"Peachy," I mutter. My mood sours, and I focus on the man over Aspen's shoulder. "Cillian Monroe, I presume?"

He inclines his chin. "And you're the asshole who's been making my niece's life a living hell?"

I go to deny it, then pause. Because, frankly? Yep, I'm guilty of that.

"Who else has access to their apartment?" I tuck Aspen to my side, my arm over her shoulders. She must've been sleeping in just a long t-shirt. Thick sweatpants hide her legs and pool around her ankles. On second thought, the t-shirt might be mine.

That makes me absurdly happy.

"No one," Cillian answers, his eyes narrowing. "Why?"

"Someone stole Aspen's music binder from her room."

Besides, my old set of copied keys didn't work the other day—which meant someone changed the locks. I obviously fixed that problem and promptly made a new set before Aspen even noticed the apartment key was missing from her ring.

No, the bigger issue is that someone thinks they can just come in here and take what doesn't belong to her.

"You've been camping out in here," I continue, glancing at Thalia. Could the roommate be behind it? Why else would Aspen have gone out her window this morning? Only if someone was in her living room or kitchen, making things awkward.

The more I think about it, the likelier suspect she becomes.

Thalia can't meet my gaze, and Aspen winces.

Her uncle's gaze moves to her. "Is that true?"

"I thought..." She shrugs, her expression sheepish. "I'm sure it'll turn up."

I grunt.

"This isn't really a two a.m. conversation, is it?" Thalia asks. "Seriously. *Men*." She comes over and rights one of the stools. Then the other. She glares at us over her shoulder, then heads toward the bedrooms. "I'm going back to sleep."

"Sweet dreams," Cillian calls. Sarcastic. Ish.

My nose wrinkles.

Aspen lets out a huff and takes my hand. Her fingers lace with mine, and she yanks me along with her after Thalia. Down the dark hall to her bedroom. She locks the door behind us and leans on the painted wood, her hand resting on the knob.

"What are you doing here?"

"How long has your uncle been sleeping over?" I counter, touching my throat. I don't like people getting the upper hand on me. My skin crawls, and I shift my weight. Part of me wants to drag her out of here and back to my place, where I know it's safer. Maybe not for her when she's solo, but for *us*. And my ego that she values so much.

"What was your plan?" She toys with the hem of her shirt.

"Maybe I came to watch you sleep." I glance at her bed. It looks like a nest more than anything, with more blankets than usual.

But any plans of curling up beside her have shifted. Now, I want to make her scream with her uncle and roommate on the other side of the door.

Mmm. Yeah. Option B it is...

"Come here," I order, crooking my finger at her.

She pushes off the door and moves toward me. I hook my fingers in the front of her sweatpants and drag them down a few inches, revealing my handiwork. The tattoo stands out against her pale flesh, and I drop to my knees to see it better. It's healing nicely—thanks in part to somehow keeping my distance from her this week. A little bit of torture... but better that than get it infected.

Plus, seeing my name on her skin gives me a certain thrill.

"Steele." She grips her sweatpants at her hips and keeping them up. "We can't."

"Nonsense." Although it is a bit peculiar of her. I ignore it and order, "Sit and spread your legs, sweetheart. Show me my pussy."

She sucks her lower lip between her teeth.

"I have my period," she mutters.

Oh.

"Yeah, I just got it tonight. So you may as well go home—"

"Asp?"

She pauses. "What?"

"Shut up and get in bed."

It surprises her. I clench my fists at the idea of any boy making her feel worthless when she's bleeding. What's a little blood anyway? I happen to like the stuff.

She finally moves back and crawls onto the bed, lying on her side. I follow her, glancing at her bedside table. It's got what I would expect to be normal items—a glass of water, a small bottle of pain relievers.

"What happens when you get your period?" I ask, gesturing at her abdomen. "Cramps?"

"Yeah. My lower back spasms sometimes, and everything gets sore." She bites her lip again. "And..."

"And?"

"My nipples."

I try not to smile at her low voice. Sounds like she's almost embarrassed. "What about them, sweetheart?"

"They get sensitive. Sometimes to the point of hurting."

I nod once. "And what hurts right now?"

"My back."

I kick off my shoes and roll her onto her stomach. She lets out a squeak but quickly goes still when I push the shirt up her back. I run my hands along either side of her spine, my fingers digging into her muscles ever so gently.

She groans.

"That's my girl." I continue to massage her back, paying attention to her lower back. She's got knots, from stress or her period, I don't know, but she seems to sink into the mattress with every touch. "Let me help you."

After a while, her breathing evens out. I stretch out beside her and pull the blankets up and over us, angling my body toward hers. And while I know I'm a sucker, part of me enjoyed helping her, making her feel a little better.

So with that in mind, I try not to think about what's coming.

I moan before I'm fully conscious. Pleasure twists through me, eradicating the awful cramps that have been lingering in my lower abdomen. And then I'm more aware of what's actually happening. The weight pressing on my hips, the hand around the back of my neck.

I force my eyes to open and stare up at Steele. He's watching me, leaned over a little while his fingers move across my clit. And then my shock gives way to horror.

"Steele, I'm—"

"Shh," he whispers, thrusting harder into me. "I've got you."

My eyes roll back. I reach up and loop my arms around his neck, dragging him down harder against me. Our chests are flush, skin sliding against each other, but he doesn't relent on my clit. Everything about it is slow and purposeful, like he enjoys stoking this fire within me.

I'm burning up.

His lips finally touch mine, and I open my mouth to him. His tongue takes possession, and another whimper comes out. I lift my legs and hook them around his hips, and he suddenly slides even deeper. The stretch of his length inside me is glorious. It's like he's never fucked me before, every part of me is hypersensitive.

He breaks off the kiss and trails his lips lower, down my throat. He sucks my nipple into his mouth. My back arches automatically, and I gasp. The sound echoes in my ears.

"Oh, god," I cry when his teeth scrape my skin. His tongue flicks at my nipple. He matches the movements with his fingers on my clit.

It doesn't just bring me to an orgasm—it shoves me into it.

I cry out again, louder, as it rips through me.

His pace quickens. His fingers leave my clit, dragging up my body. He palms my other breast, squeezing and kneading it as he pumps inside me faster. Harder. Each slam rocks my bed against the wall, the headboard knocking. I lift my hips to meet his thrusts.

And then he explodes with a growl, his mouth dropping my nipple. He buries his face in my neck and comes inside me.

We're still for a handful of seconds, until reality filters back in.

I shudder. I'm on my period.

I had a tampon in—which is really not advisable for sleep, but sometimes it's just *that bad*. I shove Steele off me and sit up. The sky is lightening, enough that I can see exactly the sort of mess we made.

Red coats the insides of my thighs and speckles the towel under my ass. He sits back on his heels, and I stare at his dick. Which is still half hard and pointing at me. And streaked with blood.

I close my eyes.

Horrified. A little disgusted.

"Hey." He grips my chin. "Look at me."

"This is—"

"Did it feel good?"

I swallow around the lump in my throat and crack my eyes open. Did it feel good? "Yeah..."

"Good. Then don't be ashamed, because I don't give a fuck if you're bleeding. Your pussy is mine in all its states." He releases my chin and pulls me up. "I took your tampon out, by the way. In case you were worried."

Wow. Just when I thought I couldn't be more embarrassed.

He leads me out of the room and straight into the bathroom. I watch my bare feet as he locks us inside and turns on the shower. While the water heats, he comes back to me. Runs his hands up my sides and over the outsides of my breasts. His thumbs skate over my nipples.

There's blood on his fingers. The ones that were touching my clit...

"You want me to prove how much I don't give a fuck?" There's a challenge in his voice.

I don't answer. I can't.

He lifts me and sets me on the counter, then spreads my legs. He pushes two fingers into me, curling them. Rubbing my G-spot with expert pressure. He pulls them out and pushes them back in. Then he kneels.

My heart goes into my throat.

His gaze is locked on the tattoo, but his mouth descends lower. He sucks on my clit without hesitation. He adds a third finger inside me, and I groan. The sound of the water hides it, at least, but I can't hide my fascination with him. Or the fact that he truly seems to be enjoying this.

He's hard again. He palms his dick with one hand. Not stroking, though.

"Put me in the shower and fuck me again," I say on a groan, giving in and digging my fingers into his hair. My hand seems to have other ideas than my mouth, though, because I press him harder to my core.

He snickers and flicks my clit with his tongue, then sucks harder. His teeth scrape it. He travels higher, his nose brushing the sensitive tattoo. The one that proclaims me *his*.

For the first time, I feel it.

Like he owns me.

I shudder at the realization. I've let him inside me in more ways than one, and the vulnerability in that rocks through me.

All my life, I've learned to never trust a man. I barely trust my uncle—he's inserted himself into my routine now, thanks to Steele—but Mom never trusted anyone except us. We were always on the run, always looking over our shoulders.

So why would I open myself up to hurt?

But Steele has broken me wide open, and he's feasting on my insides.

"Stop," I whisper, tugging his hair. "I can't do this."

"You can," he growls. There's blood on his lips, his chin. Not that he seems to care—and it makes him look more like a warrior than anything else, fresh from battle. "You can and you will, Aspen. You're going to come on my fingers. And then I'm going to put you in the shower and wash the blood from us, and I'm going to worship your body again."

I close my eyes.

"You want to know why, little viper?" He twists those fingers inside me, finding some new way to elicit a moan from my lips. "Because obsession and love are the same fucking thing. And I've been obsessed with you from the start."

He dives back down before I can respond.

I'm pretty sure he just told me he loves me.

But my mind has blanked.

I come, just like he promised.

And I'm sure the rest will follow, too.

38
STEELE

"I think Aspen has a stalker."

My announcement is met with silence.

Greyson and Knox exchange a glance, then focus on me. Greyson is no doubt remembering last year, and Violet's troubles. Miles seems more concerned, his brows drawing down. Jacob, a graduated senior from last year, also occupies our couch. He's got a few days off and decided to join us. Coach asked him back, I guess. But he's gracing us with his presence.

"Her sheet music was stolen," I add. "And I'm thinking I fucked up with the website. It probably led to someone trying to get in touch with her. When that didn't work, they escalated. I don't know."

For the last four days, I've been scouring campus, around her apartment building, the whole freaking neighborhood, for signs of disruption. Or an outsider lingering around Aspen where they shouldn't.

Instead, I've found absolutely nothing.

Knox frowns. "Has she said she thinks she has a stalker?"

"No." I cross my arms. We've got hockey practice soon, and it's rare to find everyone all together nowadays. "I just feel like something is off."

"So, what's the plan?" Greyson grabs his bag and swings it over his shoulder. "How are you going to catch a phantom stalker?"

"I'm working on that," I grumble.

But it means more watching Aspen. Which, all in all, isn't a bad pastime. I just know if someone wants to take her from me, they're going to have a hell of a fight on their hands.

"Let's head over," Greyson urges. "We'll mull it over on the ice, yeah?"

The others climb to their feet and get their stuff. I'm glad that they didn't outright laugh, even if they don't believe me. I'm not even sure I'm right—I just know that when Aspen thought I took her music binder, it felt wrong. Like someone wanted her to suspect me.

Well, why wouldn't she?

My love comes out like torture—it's luck that I found someone who enjoys that sort of thing. Humiliation, pain. The desperate sort of shame I crave.

I've always known there was something wrong with me. Something fucked up in my brain that just wouldn't let me have a normal relationship. Having sex with girls, sure. Most of the puck bunnies who followed the team even let me do some out-of-the-box stuff. Or, *in* the box, maybe. Tie them up, spank them.

Aspen understands.

She and I are cut from the same cloth. We need the same things.

But if the stalker wanted her to suspect me, it means they want to frame me. Right?

Which means they have a vendetta against me as well as her.

I pile in Greyson's truck with the other guys, Miles and Jacob and me squashed in the back together while Knox claims the front. In no time, we're parked at the stadium and heading inside.

"Maybe move her into the house," Knox suggests. "She might like it more now that you're regularly fucking and not trying to make her cry."

I huff. "I didn't want her to cry."

Knox rolls his eyes. "You know what I mean."

"That was the original plan anyway, wasn't it?" Miles eyes me. "I don't give a fuck, by the way. Have her stay. We both know you're going to end up moving out anyway."

I grumble. Having her in my bed would solve a lot of problems. But there's no way she'd go for it—she already balked after I told our parents she'd move in with me. Which is why she hasn't... and I haven't made her.

Not sure why.

Maybe I like her independence.

It hasn't stopped me from staying at her place every night this week. Massaging the backaches away, giving her toe-curling orgasms that stave off the cramps. Being generally... I don't know. Boyfriend-like.

I wouldn't even call myself her boyfriend. We're together, sure, but *boyfriend* is too weak a word for what I am to her. And what she is to me.

"If something bad happens, I'll never forgive myself," I say under my breath. I don't want to voice the rest: that I *know* something bad is going to happen. As surely as I know the sun will rise tomorrow morning. I can feel it in my bones.

Greyson sits beside me, clapping me on the shoulder. "It's not going to come to that."

Yeah.

Maybe.

"You could put a tracker on her phone," Greyson suggests.

"Or under her skin, maybe?" I open my phone and reveal the tracking app—similar to the one he uses to keep tabs on Violet, but a little more... *more*. The tattoo isn't the only thing I gave her when I drugged her at the party last week.

"Dude." Greyson leans in for a better look. "That's ballsy."

I shrug. "Rhodes gave me the tech."

We both look across the locker room at Jacob, who's standing in the doorway with his skates already on, talking to one of the juniors. Unlike us, he's forgoing the pads today—I think his role is purely demonstrative.

"He's all sorts of fucked up after that professor left," I say. "He's got access to quite a lot because of his dad, and he said he can't find any trace of her."

If anyone is a stalker, it's Jacob Rhodes. Not that I blame him—his obsession with his professor last year ran *deep*. Until she up and disappeared without so much as a trace. It left him not quite sane, but I think that's why the NHL wanted him. Because he became ruthless on the ice, and recruits took notice.

Anyway, it worked out for him, minus getting the girl.

"So even if something happens, you can find her," Greyson assures me. He finishes lacing his skates and rises. "Let's go put on a show for our fans."

I sigh and rise. Miles is almost done with his full pads—the gear goalies wear always cracks me up—and Knox is helping him secure the last pad on his leg. He's got his helmet under his arm, a water bottle in his grip. I grab my stuff and follow everyone out.

We set our bottles on the bench. I stuff the mouthpiece past my lips and fit it to my upper teeth, then step out onto the ice. Coach is already out with Jacob, standing near the penalty boxes. There's already a ton of pucks on the ice, waiting for our warm-up. I palm my stick and head toward them with Greyson, picking off a few and sending them flying toward Knox.

Our warm-up has always been seamless. Before games, before practice, we do the same thing. Shooting drills, passing. Stretching. The rest of our team comes out onto the ice, and we cycle through shooting. Miles takes his position in the goal.

A cheer goes up from the stadium when he stops one.

I cast a glance in that direction, frowning.

It's not unusual for the diehard fans to show up to practice, trying to get players to notice them. I secretly think they'd like us to lavish them with attention, although a wink or a smirk works. The glass doesn't hide their reactions from us either. Especially if they're close enough.

I do a double take.

Aspen sits off to the side, her feet on the back of the seat in front of her. She's not looking at the ice, but she's impossible to miss. Her dark hair is fanned out over her shoulders. She's wearing her jacket and a fuzzy blue scarf.

She's alone.

Why did she come?

"O'Brien!" Coach yells. "Get your head out of the clouds!"

I snap to attention. Most of the team is staring at me

from near the wall. Coach must've given an order while I was fixating on Aspen—no surprise there.

Jacob claps me on the back. "No worries, Coach," he calls. "O'Brien can help me demonstrate this move."

I raise my eyebrows at him, but he just grins. It's a bit manic, and I have a feeling this is going to hurt. With a sigh, I go where he points me. Miles stays in the goal, at the ready. I flex my fingers and adjust my grip on my stick.

Sometimes being a defender sucks. Jacob was the starting defenseman with me last year, so he knows the ropes.

Now, he winks and controls the puck in front of him, then comes charging at me. I bite my mouth guard and skate forward to meet him. He dips his shoulder and slams into me, knocking me flat on my back.

It happens too fast.

One minute he's in front of me, the next he's faking a shot at Miles and then putting the puck in the net.

Silence from the rest of my teammates.

And then Jacob looms over me, and he offers his hand.

I swat it away and rise on my own. I punch his arm.

He skates out of reach, grinning at me. "What's wrong, O'Brien?"

"You asshole," I hiss, tearing off my helmet. It rolls away on the ice. I drop my stick next and shed my gloves. "What the fuck was that?"

I glance over at Aspen again. She's staring at me.

Jacob shoves me. I whirl back around, surprised that he's even in my face.

"Get your head in the game."

"It's fucking practice." I swing at him.

He grabs me by the front of my practice jersey and

yanks me closer. He shakes me back and forth like a freaking rag doll.

I punch him as hard as I can.

His head snaps around, his grip loosening.

Coach is suddenly between us, pushing Jacob away and forcing me in the opposite direction. "Are you out of your goddamn mind?" he screams at me. "Get out of my fucking sight. *GO!*"

I circle around Coach, too pissed to even say anything, and collect my helmet, stick, and gloves from Knox. I hurry off the ice and into the locker room, throwing my helmet into my locker with a short yell.

Fuck.

I pull out my phone and text Aspen.

Me: I'm hunting you tonight, sweetheart. Better run.

Me: Don't think hiding will work—I'll find you either way.

I let out a slow breath and crack my neck. My undershirt is soaked with sweat for no goddamn reason. But the thought of finding Aspen, of chasing her down, eases some of my anger. Tamps it, however temporary.

"I just want to know that you're okay." My sister's voice is quiet, hushed.

If I didn't know any better, I'd say she was hiding.

I bite my tongue against asking about it, choosing to believe that Mom wouldn't have a problem with Dakota talking to me. Or Len, although I haven't heard from my younger sister in weeks.

My heart pangs. I miss them more than I want to admit. Seeing them in New York for just a blip of time wasn't enough.

"I'm okay," I assure her. "How are you guys? Where—"

"Mom said I'm not allowed to tell anyone where we are," she whispers. "I heard her arguing on the phone..."

"With who?"

"Uncle Cillian. I think he wanted to know where she was, and she wouldn't say. And then they started talking about you." Dakota lets out a breath. "It's just freaking me out a little, you know? Stephen hired us bodyguards."

"What?" My spine snaps straighter.

"There are three of them, and they're with us all the time. They kind of freak me out. This whole situation does. I don't like taking all my classes online."

She's quiet. Sensitive. More than I ever was—but then again, I learned to be tough from a young age. All Dakota was told was that our lives were being uprooted and we were constantly afraid. Lennox was too young when we started running from our father. She doesn't know any better.

"They're coming back," Dakota says in a rush. "I've got to go."

She hangs up before I can get a word in edgewise, and I'm left staring at my phone screen. I've got two messages from Steele almost twenty minutes ago.

I left the stadium after he was kicked out. The fight was explosive and short-lived, and I have no idea what set Steele off. Maybe it was me?

Coming to his practice was a dumb idea anyway.

But now I scan his texts, and a chill sweeps through me.

Steele: I'm hunting you tonight, sweetheart. Better run.

Steele: Don't think hiding will work—I'll find you either way.

That chill is replaced with excitement. Anything to block out the pang of missing my family. I look around, aware that I'm just standing on the sidewalk halfway between the stadium and my apartment. I'd been taking the scenic route while I talked to Dakota... and part of me doesn't want to go back and risk interrupting whatever Thalia has going on with my uncle. *If* there's anything going on. I mean, maybe I just interrupted a misguided first kiss, never to be repeated.

I can kind of see the allure. My uncle's a big, tattooed,

dangerous guy—I also will get sick if I think about it too much. The thought of *talking* to her about it turns my stomach.

I shut off my phone, not bothering to answer Steele. He might be tracking me down right this very moment. The sun has set, and the streetlights are flickering on. Instead of going to my apartment, I head toward campus. There's a forest on the other side, a few walking trails carved through it and lined with woodchips. It's all very meticulously maintained by the city, with the exception of proper lighting.

Anyway. A proper hunt needs a proper atmosphere, in my opinion. I unwind my scarf from around my neck and stow it in my jacket pocket, then resolve to move faster. Goosebumps rise on my arms and race down my spine.

I cast a furtive glance behind me, almost unsurprised to see someone following me.

Of course he found me.

Unless it's not Steele... he mentioned the possibility of a stalker the other day, when his search for my music came up empty. But I'm not sure who the hell would stalk me. I glance back again, and the person walking is gone.

My heart skips.

I pick up my pace, heading for the forest trails.

All of a sudden, someone comes around the corner— and I smash into them.

"Whoa." Hands grab at my arms, keeping me upright. "Aspen?"

My gaze lifts, locking on to Chase King. He eyes me, his brows furrowed.

"Are you okay?" he asks. "You look like you saw a ghost."

"I'm fine." I step out of his hold. "Um, I... I just thought I saw something, and it freaked me out."

"Where are you headed?"

"Campus," I lie.

He falls into step with me, turning back the way he came. "I'll escort you."

You're going to get wrapped up in something you don't want any part of, I almost say. There's a new lump in my throat, though, and I can't seem to push out the words around it.

"O'Brien treating you okay?"

I glance sharply at him, then straight ahead again. "We're a good match, I think."

"Uh-huh."

"Am I interrupting something? Were you headed somewhere?"

He's got his bag slung over his shoulder. Unlike me, who bundled up as much as I could to sit in the cold arena, he's only wearing a sweater over a shirt and jeans. And he seems completely unruffled by the bite in the air.

Winter is coming fast, and it's all the more apparent after the sun sets.

"I was just going home," he replies, shooting me a glance. "Even though Crown Point is pretty safe, I don't like the idea of you wandering out alone."

"Thanks," I murmur.

We reach campus, and Chase only pauses at the huge doors to the Administration building.

"I'm good from here," I tell him. "I appreciate your... kindness."

He smiles. "Anytime."

Nodding to himself, he ambles off the way we came. I watch him for another beat, then lift my gaze and scan the area. Students mill around, of course, but there's no one out of place. No dark gaze that makes my heart pound faster.

No Steele O'Brien.

I hurry inside, toward the auditorium. At this time of night, I might get the whole place to myself for a moment —which means I can play on the baby grand on the stage. I slip into the back of the darkened auditorium and scan it. There's no one here, as far as I can tell. And it takes my eyes a minute to adjust to just the dim emergency lighting.

Still, I can play the piano in the dark. Something simple to calm my nerves.

Steele won't find me here—not when I should be running scared.

I slip down the aisle and up the side staircase, dropping my bag at the edge of the stage. I shed my coat, too. My fingers don't tremble when I pull out the bench and take a seat. The ivory keys are barely visible, but I know them by heart. I find my place and play a single note. It rings through me, unlocking the desire to do this permanently.

My audition is coming up next week. Between Steele and classes, I've spent far too many evenings locked in the practice room trying to get the audition piece perfect. Memorized.

I do have it memorized now, and I run through it without thinking.

"It feels hollow."

I almost jump out of my skin at the voice that comes from behind me.

Steele.

His hands drop on my shoulders, and I almost flinch again. Those hands wander, down my arms, along my sides. My hips.

"Where's the passion?" he asks in my ear.

My heart is rioting.

His fingers slip under the hem of my shirt, dancing along the waistband of my leggings.

"Play it again," he orders. "But... put your heart into it."

I suck in a breath and begin again. As I start, his hand slides into my leggings. Under my panties. He cups my core, and two fingers push inside me. Slow. So slow.

My notes falter.

Without commenting, I start over. Putting my *heart* into it, because god knows where else my heart may end up at the end of the night. In Steele's grip, if he has anything to say about it.

His fingers curl, pressing to my G-spot. I can barely think, but somehow, I continue playing. Putting more feeling into it, more expression that I'd been afraid to insert before. The rise of a crescendo, the fury that this section of music demands. His thumb presses on my clit.

I gasp, my back arching. My shoulders meet his.

He's kneeling behind me, wrapped around me like an octopus. Feeling every reaction in the dark like he's playing *me* as much as I'm playing the music. Absorbing me. His head touches my back, and his thumb moves. Just a little brush past my clit, strumming a deep chord inside me. He works in time with the music, winding me tighter and tighter. My muscles tense, on the verge of coming out of my skin, when the piece ends—and Steele withdraws.

"Oh, god." I sag back against him.

His chuckle rumbles through me. He paints my lips with my own arousal, then rises.

"This is hiding." His voice is so dark, it curls deep inside me.

I shift around, facing him.

"I want you to run." He lifts his arm, pointing toward

the stage exits. Where black curtains hide the doors into the back hallways, and another door that leads outside beyond it.

I rise, the adrenaline pumping through me as we stare at each other. It's hard to make out his expression like this, even though he's only feet away. I lick my lips and bolt past him. I'll collect my coat and bag later.

He reaches for me, and his fingers slip through my loose hair. I let out a yelp and put on a spurt of speed. I don't like running. In fact, running is probably one of my least favorite things. But *this*, the idea of being prey he's hunting down, turns me on way too fucking much to care about the searing in my lungs.

It's all just adding to the experience.

I burst outside and head back toward the woods. That's where I originally wanted to go before Chase intercepted me. Now, though, the sidewalk is clear. I scramble across the street and onto the woodchip path. Bits kick up behind me with every step. My breath comes out in sharp pants.

Yeah, okay, so maybe being part of the *experience* isn't all it's cracked up to be.

I glance behind me.

He's jogging. *Slow*, keeping me in his sights.

Fucker.

There's a curve on the path, a dip, and he'll lose sight of me momentarily. An idea ticks through my head, a scenario flashing before my eyes.

It might work.

I round the bend, my stride carrying me down the short hill, and I dive off the path. I creep between trees and skid to a stop, pressing my back to one of the thick-trunked trees. My heart is hammering almost too loud to hear anything else, and I cover my mouth to mask my breathing.

There's nothing. The woods are too dark and silent around me. The rushing in my ears blocks out every other, more subtle, noise. Steele might've moved past me, or maybe he stopped.

I peek around the tree, but all I can see are shadows.

After another few seconds, I leave my position and creep back the way I came, parallel to the path but still firmly in the shadows. The glowing lampposts lend little light—their dim tops barely create a five-foot radius around each one.

The back of my neck prickles.

I turn around, and Steele is right behind me—

Wearing a fucking mask.

I scream and sprint away from him. Fallen branches and brush scrape my legs as I pass, but holy shit.

I don't like masks.

Where did he even get a mask?

It was one of those *Scream* ones, the white long face almost glowing in the darkness. I run faster than before and burst back out onto the path. I'm heading back toward campus, but I don't even give a fuck if someone sees me running for my life.

Suddenly, something catches my ankle. I go sprawling and barely catch myself on my forearms. The impact jars me, my teeth clacking with the force. Hands flip me over and roughly yank down my leggings before I can register what's going on, and I stare up at the mask.

I know it's Steele.

It has to be Steele.

But there's some part of my brain that refuses to register it as him.

I scream and thrash, catching him in his side with my knee. It doesn't even slow him down. He restrains my legs under him, my leggings twisted to imprison my calves. He yanks them up, nearly folding me in half, and grips my ankles with both hands.

My fingers dig into the woodchips under me. I try to claw into the dirt to scramble away, but he's got too much leverage.

And when he thrusts into me, I cry out. His cock hits deep inside me, and my vision flickers. He's got his arms banded around my legs, immobilizing me. Keeping them pressed to his chest even as he leans over me.

I can't move except to try and squirm away—but even that does nothing. My thighs held together makes him feel bigger, and each stroke causes an involuntary tremor to run through me.

And then I see the mask again, and the terror grips me all over again.

It's not even rational.

I just fucking *hate* masks. I reach for it, for him, and he bats away my hand. A growl slips from under it, and my chest tightens.

His pace ups until he's ramming into me without restraint. I groan at every hit. I'm still sensitive—my period only stopped yesterday. Everything is burning up.

And then he goes still, groaning and coming inside me.

"Holy shit," someone says.

Not masked Steele.

I tip my head back. Chase, upside down from my point of view, stands on the path with a girl under his arm. The girl looks horrified, but Chase seems mildly intrigued. And even more so when he registers *me*.

"Aspen?"

I can't move. I don't really know what to do—I feel a bit

like a deer caught in headlights. Well, a deer being ravaged by a mountain lion caught in headlights...

Steele grunts, sliding free of me and pulling up his pants. He shoves my leggings back into place, manhandling me until I'm covered. Then he drags me upright and tosses me over his shoulder before I can so much as open my mouth.

His shoulder digs into my stomach, and he strides past Chase silently.

No threats.

No revealing himself.

I shudder and keep my gaze focused on the ground. Better than meeting Chase's eyes after he just caught us...

Holy shit, why does that turn me on even more?

"You like being scared, sweetheart?" Steele asks, slapping my ass.

I grip the back of his shirt.

"Or was it the eyes on you at the end that did it? Watching our little performance."

"I hate masks." I press my lips together. I shouldn't have admitted that—now he's just going to bring it out more often. "Where did you even get that thing?"

"Halloween shop."

We missed Halloween this year. He and I stayed in my apartment while Thalia went out. It's for the best, though, with my inability to deal with masks. Still, apparently he found the time to go out and buy this one.

He chuckles, then jostles me. "And you definitely didn't hate it fully." A second later, he passes me the mask behind his back.

I take it, running my fingers over the smooth white plastic. It's not as scary when I hold it. Or when I press it against my face and look through the eyeholes.

Never mind that I'm still slung over Steele's shoulder.

"Are you going to put me down?"

"No."

I scoff. "Why not?"

"Because I'm going to take you back to my room and ravage you the proper way, and I don't want you running away again." He snorts. "You were a proper catch."

"I tripped," I grumble.

"On the wire I set across the path."

I press my lips together, contemplating that. I mean, *really?* There's no way—

"You don't like running," he continues. "I figured you were going to try to circle back around eventually. And even worse than running is crashing through the dark off the path."

Jeez.

"Fine," I huff. "Take me back to your place, you caveman. But I better orgasm at least twice."

His fingers find my ass again, digging in. "Yes, ma'am."

40
ASPEN

"Did you borrow my Crown Point sweatshirt?" I march into Thalia's room and eye her pile of laundry.

She glances up from her textbook, frowning. "No, I don't think so. You can't find it?"

I shake my head, but I can't look away from the laundry. Because it reminds me that I've had some other items go missing recently. The bottle of my favorite lotion. A lipstick I wore a few times in the past few months. My best black jeans.

"Maybe you left it at Steele's," she suggests. She's sitting cross-legged on her bed, the textbook on her lap, computer open beside her. A notebook and highlighters surround her. It's Saturday, and she mentioned doing all her homework before the game tonight.

Which is smart, because if the Hawks win, we're definitely going drinking.

And drinking usually leads to the two H's—hookups and hangovers.

"I might've," I say slowly, shaking my head. I don't

remember bringing that stuff over, but maybe he thought he'd pack them to tempt me into staying longer.

A sweet sentiment, if a bit demented.

Actually, that sums up Steele pretty nicely.

"Has my uncle been staying here still?"

Thalia shakes her head. "He left a note for you on the kitchen island. Sorry, I read it. He had to head back to Chicago this morning. It said he would be in touch."

Weird.

I shift my weight, suddenly worried that his rapid departure has to do with my dad. If he was causing more chaos in Chicago that required his immediate attention.

My stomach swoops.

Thalia points to the empty space on her bed. "Want to join me?"

I shake my head. "Going to do lunch with Steele. Like an actual date."

Her jaw drops. "He's capable of chivalry?"

"Oh, shush." I head back to my room and search for something else to wear, because clearly my CPU sweatshirt isn't going to miraculously appear. I find a black sweater instead and brush out my hair. I leave it long and loose, pulling it forward over my shoulders, and pair it with shiny black leather leggings. Plus some gold jewelry, and I appear more put together than I feel.

Steele strides in as I'm applying mascara.

I glance at him, truly not even surprised that he just let himself in. Boundaries like knocking seem beyond him. He drops a kiss on the top of my head and flops on my bed. He's dressed in dark-gray slacks and a light-blue button-down shirt and sports jacket, unbuttoned. He looks *hot*, but I try not to think about that.

After the finishing touches of my makeup are done, I

face him and plant my hands on my hips. Asking him about my sweatshirt is on the tip of my tongue. And really, I *should* ask him—

"When you wear lipstick, all I can think of is smearing it on my dick," he says.

I roll my eyes. "You've got to feed me first."

"I'll feed you, all right..." He rises, a devious expression flickering across his face. "Come here."

A shiver overtakes my body. "Steele."

"Aspen," he replies. "Do you want to do it here, or under the table at the restaurant?"

My mouth drops open, shocked that he would go there.

But also...

"Naughty," he breathes, stepping into my space and wrapping his hand around the back of my neck. His fingers digging into my skin sends more tingles down my spine. He leans in and captures my lips with his, his tongue infiltrating my mouth without warning.

I love the dirty, open-mouthed kisses he gives me when I manage to surprise him.

He releases me after a minute, once my toes have curled in my sneakers and my hands have found their way into his hair. Now he's got my lipstick across his lips, just as I'm sure it's all over my face, too.

"Fix your lipstick, sweetheart. Then we'll go." His voice is rough, low.

Turned on.

Me, too, babe, me, too.

We drive to the restaurant, which is one of the fancier restaurants. It's on the point that overlooks the lake. Crown Point gets its name from this exact spot. It's clear today, and warmer than usual. It's been chilly for the past few weeks, but now the sun is shining, and there's no need for jackets.

Which is a fabulous break from the past week.

The restaurant has a wall of windows to maximize the lake view, and of course our table is right against one. The white linen tablecloths go all the way to the floor. There are wine glasses and water glasses on the table, as well as two sets of knives and forks.

"This is excessive," I mutter.

Steele shrugs. "Dad used to take me to places like this all the time. After..."

I wait, but he seems to be done talking.

I lean forward. "After what?"

"After Mom went away." He looks down, scanning the menu. "Dad didn't cook, so it was either go out or starve. And he wouldn't be caught dead at a fast-food place."

This is the first time I've heard him mention his mother. "What happened to her?"

His dark eyes lift, crashing into mine. And for a second, I see exactly what he must be feeling—misery, hurt, anger. And then it's gone with a blink, like it was never there before.

"I'll take you to meet her tomorrow, if you want."

My mouth opens and closes. It doesn't really answer any questions, so I nod mutely. He nods back, satisfied with that casual agreement. Like it's not a big fucking deal or anything.

What am I going to say to her?

Hi, Steele's mom, I'm his new stepsister and also dating him...

That would go over well.

The waiter approaches, and I stare down at the menu. Everything is expensive and fancy, and I freeze up.

Steele's foot runs up the inside of my leg. He orders for us both, snapping his menu closed and handing it over. I follow his lead, then shake my head. I don't know what that was.

"What's wrong?" he asks.

"I shouldn't be spending my money on this sort of stuff. I have to figure out how to pay for next semester—"

He snorts. "If you think I'm letting you pay for lunch, you've got another think coming." He glances around, then crooks his finger. "Now, I think you're ready for your appetizer... don't you?"

I swallow and follow his gaze around. This section of the restaurant is empty—for now. So maybe that's why I don't hesitate to slide off my chair and to my knees, crawling under the table. My heartbeat is thundering in my ears, a dull rushing sound. I push the tablecloth up, letting it pool around his waist and revealing his lower half.

His stance widens, his legs parting to let me get closer. His erection strains against the zipper of his slacks. I undo the button and drag the zipper down slowly, reaching in and pulling his cock out of his briefs. I run my hand over the length of it, my thumb brushing the oozing slit.

"Aspen," Steele warns from above.

I smile to myself and rise on my knees, leaning over him. I lick him, taking my time. Savoring the *appetizer*, as he so nicely put it. Since he's not about to reach under here and force me to choke on it—I'm going to enjoy this the way *I* want to... and if that includes a little torture, so be it.

He should know all about torture.

When my mouth closes over him, he makes a noise under his breath. A rumbling in his chest. I try not to smirk —no time or room for that, with my mouth filled with *him*. My lips wrap around his shaft, and I swipe my tongue across his slit. I taste the precum before I suck hard.

Desire and lust rush through me, going straight to my core. I rock my hips in time with the motions of my mouth. My tongue dances under the ridge of the mushroom head, tracing patterns and veins. I take him deeper, forcing him to the back of my throat, and then I pull back again.

I take his balls out, too, cupping them gently.

He shifts, and suddenly his foot is nudging between my legs. Giving me something to grind on—an inch of relief. Something to hold me over.

I lick his shaft, then lower. I drip spit on his balls and take one in my mouth. His thighs tremble, his legs spreading even wider. I repeat until his cock is twitching in my mouth. My jaw aches, but I don't stop.

Not even when something touches down on the table over my head, and Steele murmurs something about me being right back.

Our food arrived, maybe, or drinks.

I grind harder on his foot, chasing my own pleasure as well as his. The leggings are barely in the way, the fabric sliding between my legs. The tattoo still smarts when I rub too hard, but I think I like that little dose of pain.

"Aspen," Steele says under his breath. "You're driving me crazy."

Good, I think. *Because same.*

I take him in my mouth, gagging around his length when he touches the back of my throat again. I can barely get him halfway into my mouth without him forcing it. I use my hand to stroke the rest of him, down to the base and back up. I grip him tighter.

He flexes his foot, pressing up into me, and a rising tide of a climax rushes through me. I hum around his dick, my eyes closing. I can't control the noise that comes out of me, a low moan that is a surefire giveaway of what's happening here.

He knocks on the table twice.

A second later, his cock jerks. His balls lift and pulse in my palm, and his cum fills my mouth. I swallow it down, then keep my mouth around him. My eyes are still shut, and I stay like that. Perfectly still.

Because I don't want it to end?

Or because I don't want to be seen crawling out from under the table?

After a minute, though, I pull away. He slides a white cloth napkin under the table, leaving it on his thigh, and I take it with shaking hands. I wipe my face and dab under my eyes, surprised that they watered so bad. Tears track down my cheeks.

I didn't even go that hard...

Didn't I?

I pat his dick and balls dry and tuck him back into his slacks. I left the streaks of dark-pink lipstick behind, though. I do the button and the zipper and run my hand down his thighs. My hands stop just above his knees, and I bow my head forward to rest against him.

My face burns.

"Come on out, sweetheart," Steele says softly.

He's going to have to tow me out of here.

And then his chair is scooting back, and the tablecloth lifts. He offers me his hands.

I take them both and let him guide me out, again between his legs. I use his thighs as support to stand, but I'm not on my feet long. He pulls me down on his lap, cinching his arms around me.

"Kiss me," he orders.

I lick my lips.

"Aspen," he warns. "Kiss. Me."

My eyes close, and I lean toward him. His lips touch mine. Part them. His tongue sweeps across my lower lip, and his teeth follow. A quick nip, and then he's done. He leans back and touches my chin.

I crack my eyes open again, meeting his gaze. He seems... *proud*. Or content, maybe?

"Tell me, Aspen, is your lipstick on my cock?"

I bite my lip, then nod.

His smile wins out.

"Good," he says. "It's going to stay there through the game."

My heart skips, but he's already putting me back on my feet and motioning for me to take my seat. It's a good thing it's close, because my legs wobble on my way to my chair.

There's a glass of red wine in front of my place setting, and a basket of bread between us. I reach for the bread, instantly ravenous, but Steele pushes my hand away. He tears off a piece and spreads butter across the surface with his knife. He tilts his head, then points to the seat next to him. It has a better view, arguably... and also puts me closer to him.

So I slip into it, and he makes quick work of putting my drink in front of me.

Then he holds out the bread to me.

I lean forward and bite into it. It's warm and flavorful, and it bursts across my tongue. I groan and close my eyes, savoring it.

"That good, hmm?" He takes a bite of it.

I open my mouth when he bumps my lips with the bread again, and we finish the piece like that. I take a nervous sip of my wine, absolutely shy for no good reason.

He still makes me nervous.

"What were you and Jacob fighting about?"

Steele lifts his shoulder. "I wasn't focused."

"But you're going to be focused tonight, right?"

"Of course."

I fiddle with my fork. "Because I could not go—"

"Absolutely not." He eyes me. "If you even think of not going, I'll spend the whole game looking for you and wondering where you are. And then I'll definitely be distracted."

I crack a smile. "Okay, okay, just checking."

Our food arrives. I hadn't paid attention to what he'd ordered for me, which is why I'm surprised to find *exactly* what I would've wanted. An open-faced turkey sandwich drizzled with gravy and cranberry, with a side of roasted potatoes and veggies. He got the same for himself.

We dig in without further conversation, until both of us have taken the edge off our hunger.

"When is the audition?" Steele asks.

"Tuesday."

So close, and yet it feels like each hour until then will drag. I've also reprinted my sheet music and started the laborious process of recreating every stupid notation on them. It's not as good as it was, but it'll do. And I still have time before the final performances in December.

"Where is it?"

"The orchestra shares a space with Crown Point Ballet, so it's in that building."

Something unexpected crosses his features.

Worry?

"What's wrong?" I set down my fork.

He shakes his head. "That place just gives me a bad vibe. But your professor is going to be there. It's not like your stalker is a professor."

"Yeah, well." I make a face. "He's not my stalker, and he's not my professor, he just happened to hear me play that one time. I got lucky that they were looking for someone. Anyway, if I land this gig, then it'll help me put some money toward next semester. I might have to take it off..."

"You're not taking the semester off." He drops his silverware, staring intently at me.

"I will if I can't scrounge money to pay for it, since your father cut me off—"

"He may have cut you off, but I haven't." He eyes me. "Don't freak out."

I narrow my eyes. "Why would I freak out?"

"Because I took care of it for you."

My jaw drops.

He smiles and shakes his head, going back to eating his food like... like that's nothing. But I'm not smiling. In fact, it feels more like the whole floor has dropped out from under me. He did *what?*

"Close your mouth, sweetheart," he murmurs.

My teeth grind together. "What do you mean you took care of it?"

He ignores me.

"Steele."

"I paid for it."

"*Why*?" I screech. My face heats, and I glance around. The lunch service has been slowly filling up, and more than a few tables look our way. I lower my voice and lean toward him. "Why would you do that?"

He finally meets my gaze, and it's as fierce as mine. "Because you are *not* leaving me."

I reel back.

"Me being in school is just to satiate your need to have me close, then?"

"For fuck's sake," he growls.

He grabs my hand and drags me out of my seat, tossing a hundred dollar bill down on the table. I gawk at it for a moment—long enough for him to remember my purse on the back of my chair—and then we're moving. We weave through the tables. And then we're outside.

We wrap around the building and get on a footpath that leads to the point. I follow helplessly along behind Steele. The concrete path turns to gravel, then just worn dirt. It pitches upward slightly, ending in a grassy knoll. We crest it, and only then does he stop.

We're at the point, and he still hasn't released my wrist. He does whip around, though, and gets in my face. I stare up at him, for a second confused about why *he's* the angry one.

"I want you to do whatever the fuck you want," he snaps at me. "If that's play piano, then great. If that's graduating with a degree in art or chemical engineering or fucking astrology, *whatever*. But just know that you're going to be taken care of no matter what. I'm going to the NHL. I'm going to make a shit ton of money—I already *have* a shit ton of money, Aspen. Thirty thousand dollars to keep you in school and with a meal plan is a drop in the bucket. I'd give you more if it helps. I'd give you all of it if I thought for a second that you cared about that."

My mouth opens and closes.

"I know you don't, though." He grasps my upper arms, keeping me steady. "I know you don't care about money. You care about safety. You care about surviving. But, sweetheart..." His voice cracks. "There's so much more than that for you."

Tears fill my eyes.

I wipe them away hurriedly, then glance around. I

have the notion to do something reckless after that admission. He wants me *happy*? I don't know what that means. I play the piano to escape—but what if there's nothing to escape from? What if my life is good and full and... carefree?

The way I want that so bad it hurts is a reminder to myself—and a warning.

Good things don't come to people like me.

I pull away from Steele and approach the edge of the point. There's another, lesser-used path that curves down and around, to a jumping point. I heard Thalia and the dance girls talking about it one day at lunch. They never did it, but they mentioned how the hockey boys would for initiation.

Suddenly, I want that, too.

A baptism by ice.

I head down the path without a backward glance. I take off my sweater first, letting it flutter out of my hand to the grass. Then my shoes, which I pause to remove my socks and leggings, then stick back on my feet. Until I'm just in my underwear and shoes.

"Aspen—" Steele's words are snatched away on the wind.

If they can do it, I can.

Right?

The jump-off point is plastered in *Do Not Jump!* signs. *Danger! Rocks below!* Yet as I peer down at the murky, blue-green water, I can see where the rocks aren't.

So I just need to aim for that.

Steele catches my arm.

"Let me be reckless!" I swing around, ready to shove him away.

But he's stripped, too. Even his shoes.

My gaze trips over his tattoos, his abs. His hand trails down my arm, and his fingers lace with mine.

Together, his grip says.

But he doesn't move until I do.

Two running steps, and then we're airborne.

41
STEELE

I squeeze Aspen's hand as we plunge over the edge of the cliff. I suck in a deep breath and cast a quick glance at her, and then we're crashing through the surface. The water is cold, but not as bad as it could be for this time of year. It sucks us down quickly, pressing in on all sides.

We both kick, surging back toward air. Her hand slips from mine, but it's no matter. I feel the heat of her in the water, only inches away. I shake my head, sending water droplets flying everywhere, and reach for her.

She slicks her hair back and wipes her eyes. Her makeup is still intact—barely—and I groan at the thought of the water rinsing her lipstick off my cock.

I know. I shouldn't be thinking of *that* right now.

But then I decide that we can just have a repeat performance since it was her idea to jump. Her fault if it gets washed away.

I find her waist and haul her closer, until her chest bumps into mine. We're both treading, our legs avoiding kicking each other.

She tips her head back and eyes the point.

Then she laughs.

Laughs, and it's goddamn music to my ears.

I kiss her, intent on swallowing her happiness. Maybe it'll help me be less miserable.

She's still smiling against my lips. Her hand loops around my shoulders, and her legs wind around my hips.

"You shouldn't have jumped," she admonishes quietly. "You have a game in a few hours."

I shrug off her concern. I wasn't going to let her go on her own, that's for fucking sure. I gesture toward the spot we've climbed out before, and she unwinds herself from me to swim in that direction. We pass over some rocks—the ones the signs warn about—and get to the ledge.

Aspen tries and fails to hoist herself up.

I swim up behind her and grip her hips, giving her a boost. She pivots and sits on the ledge, her lower lip caught in her teeth. I hop up, too, and then climb to my feet. The path back to our clothes cuts back and forth, and it's a little rocky. If I hadn't been wearing dress shoes, I would've kept them on.

She had the right idea.

I help her stand, then propel her in front of me. Water sluices off her body. Her nipples are visible through her bra, and I try not to think about the tattoo just under the hemline of her panties. I pull my briefs away from my dick, eyeing it.

The lipstick is still there.

I don't know why I care that much. But her going under the table at the restaurant shows her daring, and it gives me a thrill all my own.

Because she's *mine*.

Fuck, she doesn't even argue that point anymore.

Finally, we get back to the jump spot and locate our clothes. I don't bother putting my stuff back on—we're both soaked, and I don't really have another outfit planned for today. I bundle it all up and watch as Aspen comes to the same conclusion about her leather leggings: that there's no way they're going on wet legs.

"I've got a towel in the back of my car," I say, urging her with me.

We pick up a faster pace and hurry through the restaurant parking lot. She seems keenly aware that people can see us through the restaurant windows.

Hell, they might've seen us jump.

I snatch the threadbare towel and wrap it around her. She takes it gratefully, tossing her clothes and purse into the trunk. I snap it closed and get the heat cranking in the car.

We'll be at my apartment in minutes.

Aspen shivers beside me, wrapping her arms around herself. I put my hand on her thigh and leave it there until we're parked in front of the hockey house. The guys are home—I spot Erik's truck, too, which is irritating.

He ogled Aspen enough at the party, I don't need him seeing her in her soaking-wet underwear now. I eye her as we climb out of the car, then grab her and throw her over my shoulder.

"Hey!" she squeals, almost kicking me in the face.

I smack her ass with my free hand, the one not securing her against me.

She lets out a huff and goes limp. Her ass really is gorgeous, her cheek reddening from my palm without much prompting at all. Her chest brushes my back, and I groan.

My dick twitches.

"Our stuff—"

"I'll come back for it," I tell her, striding toward the house.

Anything to get her off the sidewalk, where *anyone* could see her. I stroll in the front door and kick it closed behind me, sparing only a glance at the guys in the living room.

Erik and Jacob are both there with beers in their hands. It appears my teammates are refraining, waters and sandwiches in front of them.

"Whoa," Erik calls. "What happened to you—"

The rest of the guys eye us, too. Aspen lifts her head just enough for Erik to get a look at her, and then she flips him off.

I chuckle. "We jumped off the point."

"It's freaking November," Erik says, his eyebrows shooting up. "And you have a *game*—"

"It's fine," I interrupt. I keep moving, around the corner and up the stairs. Straight to the bathroom, where I deposit Aspen. Her expression is pure lust.

"You keep eyeing me like that, and everyone downstairs is going to hear you," I warn.

She shrugs, holding my gaze. "Let them listen." She gestures to the door. "I dare you to leave it open."

Oh, she'll be the death of me.

Still.

Challenge accepted.

I point to the counter. She slides her panties off and kicks them away, then hops up on it. She spreads her legs without prompting, giving me a view of her gorgeous cunt. She's already wet and glistening for me. The tattoo is perfect.

Property of Steele O'Brien.

The rush that goes through me is indescribable. Those words are unavoidable—there's no one who will try to fuck her and not know that she's already claimed by another. No asshole would survive that anyway.

I've never killed anyone before, but I know in my bones that I would for her.

Without hesitation.

I step up and run my finger through her center, catching that moisture and gauging how responsive my little viper is going to be today. Her eyes flutter, her lips parting. I take her hands and position them on the edge of the counter, allowing her fingers to curl around the lip and hold on to it.

She makes a small noise when I drop to my knees in front of her.

This is one of my favorite parts. Tasting her. Making her scream and writhe. Driving her absolutely fucking crazy. I get an up-close view of the tattoo, and my heart beats harder. Never mind my cock, which is straining to get out of my wet briefs.

I lick and suck and finger-fuck her until her head falls back, and then I pull away. Dance around her clit, pay attention to her inner thighs. She's panting hard, her muscles clenching around my fingers. She wants to come, but she hasn't begged for it yet. She hasn't opened her pretty mouth and let loose the cry I know is coming.

So we repeat this until every swipe of my tongue sends a tremor through her muscles. A ripple down her legs and up her abdomen.

"Please," she finally says. "Please, Steele, just fucking give it to me."

I chuckle, sitting back on my heels. I look up at her, at her wet hair, her ruined makeup, her hard little nipples poking through her bra. I slide one finger inside her. Slow.

She groans and lifts her hips.

"Fuck me," she cries. "Please. God, I'm begging."

A flutter soars through me.

"That's right, sweetheart," I agree, leaning forward and running my nose across her clit. Inhaling her musky scent. "I am your god."

She moans, but it ends on a whimper when I pull away again. When my finger slips out of her. I rise, pushing my briefs down. It frees my aching cock, my balls ready to unload my cum. We both look down at my lipstick-streaked length, and I shake my head.

We'll have to redo it later.

I unclasp her bra and yank it off.

The bathroom door is wide open, but whatever. Her tits are perfect, heavy globes. Every curve of her is a thrill to explore.

I palm both of them, digging my fingers into her flesh. Her mouth is still open, her chest heaving, and her eyes go wide when the head of my dick slides through her slickness. Over her clit, then down. It notches at her entrance without much effort at all, and I push in an inch.

My muscles ache, too, and it takes all my willpower not to thrust into her as hard as I can. She clutches my upper arms, her throat working as she swallows her gasp.

This is about edging her until she breaks.

"Oh, god," she whimpers again, reaching for me.

I let her grip my neck and bring me down to her. Our lips touch. She's breathing too hard to do much more than that. Her legs wrap around my hips, her heels pressing into my ass. What she wants is extraordinarily clear.

But… the thought of torturing her a little longer is too good to resist.

I rock forward the smallest amount. An inch, a millimeter. She stretches around me, and her mouth opens when I withdraw again.

"Beg," I whisper against her lips. "Beg for your orgasm, Aspen. And make sure they can all hear you."

Her nails bite into my neck, and her gaze bores into mine. Her green eyes to my brown.

And then she opens her lips and does just what I ask.

"Please," she cries, *loud*. "Please let me come, Steele. I need to come on your cock."

I inch forward, then back. Torture for both of us. My hands tighten on her breasts, my thumbs coasting over her nipples. It evokes another shiver.

"I can't take it anymore. *Fuck me*." Her voice rings between us, like she's screaming to the heavens and not me, inches away.

I grip my dick and stroke my length. I'm still inside her. *Barely*.

Working her up has had the same effect on me, and I shudder when my balls tighten. My abdomen tightens, too, and pleasure races up my spine. I come inside her like that, with just my tip lodged inside her sweet cunt. I force myself to keep my eyes open, even as my knees go a little weak.

She bows forward and watches it happen, too. Watches my dick twitch and cum ooze out of her almost immediately after I slip out.

I immediately replace my dick with my fingers, pushing the cum back into her. "You look so pretty filled like this. You take me so fucking well, Aspen. You did so good."

I lean down and kiss her chest. Then higher, up her neck. I capture her lips last, plunging my tongue inside her while my fingers plug my cum in her pussy.

"Gorgeous," I say against her lips, then I pull back. I take her hands and help her off the counter, leading her naked down the hall and into my room. I close the door—because the fuckers downstairs definitely heard her, which is what we wanted. But I don't need them to see the aftermath.

She gapes at me. "You're not going to finish the job?"

"I finished." I wink at her.

There are some of her clothes in a drawer, and I open it for her. "Underwear. No bra."

She narrows her eyes at me. When I don't budge, she lets out a sigh and steps up, choosing a very basic, almost boring pair of panties from it. She doesn't ask me where they came from—the answer is, *her dresser, duh*—and instead bends over and drags them up her legs.

I get dressed, too. Barely. A new pair of black briefs and dark-gray sweatpants.

"Good," I say. "Now, will you leave my pussy alone while I go down to the car and get our stuff, or do I need to tie you up?"

Her glare is all I need. She backs up a step at whatever expression crosses my face, but it's too late. I lunge for her.

We hit the bed, her under me, and she's immediately fighting to get me off. I capture one wrist and twist her, folding her arm behind her back. Then the other one. I use my weight to keep her down, and it only takes a little stretch to find one of my discarded ties on the floor.

I knot it around her wrists and flip her onto her back—and subsequently, her hands.

"Stay," I order, smirking to myself.

She blows out a breath, her dark hair fluttering away from her face.

If looks could kill...

Ah, well. Good thing they can't.

42
ASPEN

I struggle on the bed for approximately eight seconds.

Eight seconds is a lot of time, and also no time at all. It makes me realize that I can't do shit with my hands behind my back, besides roll off it and land on my knees. I press my face into the comforter and close my eyes.

My body is electric. It seems to crackle under my skin, threatening to detonate me from the inside out. And it all comes down to the pulse between my legs. The insistent need for Steele that he's denied me.

"You okay?"

I roll my head to the side and eye Steele. He's got my clothes and his in his hands, along with my purse. He sets everything on the bed and hauls me into his arms. He sits and cradles me on his lap, then undoes the tie around my wrists.

I lick my lips. "Why'd you do that?"

He eyes me. I bring my arms in front of me and cradle them to my bare chest, when all I want is to satiate the desire wrecking me.

"Why didn't I let you come?" he clarifies.

I nod, my gaze averting.

He smooths away my damp hair from my face and tucks it behind my ear.

"Because I want you to think about me whether I'm in front of you or not." His lips press to my temple. "I want you to ache like I do, with your eyes on me the whole fucking game. And every time I glance your way, I want you to feel it *here*."

He cups between my legs, over my underwear.

Even that is too much. My legs fall open wider, a silent plea for him to just... ignore what he wants and give me what *I* want.

"Tonight," he promises in my ear.

I groan. But then he's standing, depositing me on my feet. I shake my head and get dressed slowly. I face the mirror, and horror overtakes me.

My hair looks like *that*?

My makeup is salvageable. The mascara and eyeliner held up surprisingly well, but my hair is a tangled and clumped mess.

"Any chance you have a hairbrush and detangling spray?"

Steele frowns.

I'll take that as a no.

I open my purse and dig for my phone. My brows furrow when I don't immediately see it. I take out my wallet, random receipts from the week, Chapstick, a pack of travel tissues...

"Did you see my phone in the trunk? Or... in your car at all?"

"I didn't, but we can check again." He opens my purse wider, like that's going to make it appear. I mean, it's wishful thinking, for sure.

I let out a sigh. "I just wanted to see if Thalia would bring my makeup bag to the stadium. Do we have time to swing by my apartment?"

He glances at the clock, and his frown deepens.

"Oh, no—don't worry about it, then." I shove everything back in my purse. "I'm gonna head home, and then I'll meet you there. Okay?"

"You know I don't want you traveling alone," he says in a low voice.

I roll my eyes. "I don't have a stalker. If I did, Uncle wouldn't have left."

Besides, clearly Steele's been the one taking my stuff. The drawer he just showed me is evidence enough. And I don't mind—I get it, even. He's trying to make me stay with him by any means necessary, and that includes slowly relocating all of my favorite things to his room.

I smooth my hands down the front of Steele's crisp collared shirt. He hasn't put on the jacket yet, but he still looks so fucking hot in the shirt and slacks. Like... delicious.

"I've got to touch up my lipstick, anyway," I add. "For later."

His worry fades. *Slightly*. We go downstairs, slipping undetected past the guys in the living room, and scour his car for my phone.

Nothing.

"It may have fallen out at the restaurant," I offer. "Do you mind calling them? I'll hook up with Thalia, and you can get in touch with me through her. Or any of the other girls."

Steele nods, his brows still drawn together. Not entirely letting go of his concern.

I rise on my toes and loop my arms around his neck.

"Kiss me," I order.

His lip curls at the corner, and then he leans down to meet me. Our mouths part, tongues sliding against each other. That delicious heat I always feel when he kisses me now packs a bigger punch, and I groan into his mouth. Hungry for *more*.

He pulls away, chuckling when I try to follow him.

"Go home," he laughs. "And tell Thalia to text me when you're with her so I know you're okay."

I wave him off. *Because walking two blocks is going to kill me.*

Crown Point, or at least this neighborhood, is surprisingly calm for the impending game day. The weather is taking another turn, the temperature dropping, but not enough for me to freeze to death. The sun is still out, although low in the hazy, periwinkle sky. It'll be completely dark by the time the game starts.

My skin prickles when I'm halfway home.

I glance over my shoulder, but no one is there. I shake it off and continue, my gait a little more rushed. Because okay, even if I *don't* have a stalker, I don't really love the idea of ignoring instincts. Right?

Right.

I make it to my apartment in record time, locking myself in.

"Thalia?" I call. "Are you still home?"

Silence.

I groan and drop my purse on the island, double-checking her room just to make sure. Her door is propped open, her bed perfectly made. And no trace of her.

Great.

I go into the bathroom and perform some life-saving miracles on my hair, somehow managing to make it curl and shine without rewashing it. Sure, it may *smell* like lake water mixed with detangling spray. If anything, it'll help keep over-rowdy assholes at bay.

Not that I've ever had to worry about that.

I remove my makeup and start over, then reach automatically for my phone to check the time. Grimacing to myself, I retrace my steps into the kitchen. The digital clock on the stove informs me that I have an hour till game time.

How I wasted so much time is beyond me.

Focus.

Back to my bedroom for my shoes—

A breeze ruffles my hair. I stop and stare at my open window. Confusion hits me first, then the fear.

Something moves behind me.

Some*one*.

Before I can turn around, a black fabric bag descends over my head. And with it, the smell of something chemical. I fight the inhale and try to push it off, but the edges go tight against my throat. My fingers scramble uselessly.

My head swims. My knees buckle.

Whatever is on the bag goes straight to my head—and lulls me into the darkness.

43
STEELE

I finish my stretches on the ice and return to the locker room. I drop my helmet on the bench beside me and grab my phone from my bag, checking my messages for the hundredth time.

Nothing.

I glance across the room at Greyson, trying not to go to Worst-Case Scenario. Maybe Aspen didn't link up with her roommate yet. Or Thalia forgot. Or maybe she doesn't have my number, and—

"You okay?" Miles sits beside me, kicking his legs out wide. His gaze is on his brother, who's fooling around with Finch in the middle of the room.

"Aspen hasn't checked in. She lost her phone."

Miles whistles. "First her sheet music, then her phone. Hope she didn't blame the latter one on you, too?"

I scowl. "No."

"Did you check the stands?"

"I didn't see her."

My phone goes off in my hand, and I scramble to unlock it.

Dad: We're coming to the game. Suite 12. See you after.

I stare at it for a moment, confused. They were doing some sort of tour of Europe last I knew—which wasn't that fucking long ago. He said they'd be gone for the month—including Thanksgiving. Which was fine by me.

Dad: Where is Aspen?

A chill goes down my spine. I rise, striding down the hall to the rink. I stand at the edge and look out at the crowd, then up at the row of glass-walled suites. They're reserved for the rich and important. Sometimes scouts get them. Greyson's dad usually has one permanently held for him and his entourage.

Suite 12 is lit up, but it seems empty. I only know what number it is because a few upperclassmen locked us in there when we were freshmen. Like a hazing thing, or whatever. We stayed there all night—it was either that or break the door down and face damages.

That's how Knox and I bonded. And later, Miles. Then Greyson, when he came along, slid seamlessly into our friend group.

Anyway, suite 12 is all the way at the end of the row across from the benches, over section 112. I stare at its darkened windows, then down at my phone.

Me: Are you already here? Aspen should be on her way soon.

I pull up the tracking app and check her location, but she's still at her apartment. I shake my head and blow out an irritated breath.

Me: She's at her apartment.

Why is she still there?

She knows how important it is that she be here, and the

game is going to start any minute. There's a new tightness in my chest, and the doubt creeps in.

What if this was all too much for her? She could be packing to leave right now. Disappear with her mom, my dad, and just... leave Crown Point.

What if she regrets everything?

"O'Brien!" Coach claps my shoulder.

I almost jump out of my skin, wheeling around to face him. He raises his eyebrows at me.

"Sorry, Coach," I say quickly, moving past him. Back to the locker room.

The lights around the rink dim as I get to the door, and the music begins to hype up the crowd.

Maybe Aspen fell asleep. Maybe she's changing her clothes.

Or maybe her stalker got her.

No. If that was the case, they wouldn't still be in her apartment. No sick fucker holds a girl hostage when her roommate could come home at any time.

"Okay, guys." Coach claps to get our attention.

I sit beside Miles and focus on him. Well, I try anyway.

"We're facing our toughest competition yet," Coach warns. He takes a second to meet all of our gazes. "But you've prepared for this. You're *ready* for this. So go out there and play your damn hearts out and make Crown Point proud."

We all jump to our feet, jostling each other. I pull my helmet on and slip my mouth guard in, elbowing Miles. I leave my phone in my bag, hoping that Aspen is just running behind. But also knowing that she might not be.

We take the ice. My stick feels foreign in my hand, and I look down at it. The tape is all wrong, the stick too short.

Whose stick did I grab?

I hurry to the bench. We've got an equipment manager on hand who stays at the back, and I hop up to pass him the foreign stick.

"What the hell are you doing, O'Brien?" Coach barks at me.

The equipment manager hands me my backup stick, and I wave Coach off. My mood sours further when the game starts. I can't seem to concentrate on what's happening—and as a result, our opponents are skating circles around me.

Someone checks me into the wall. My face rebounds off the glass, my teeth cutting into my cheek. Blood fills my mouth, and I shove off it to chase after them. I spit the blood out as I charge. Another of their teammates has the puck, so I change my angle and slam into them.

It's a move similar to the one Jacob performed on me at practice, and it works great... until I realize that he passed the puck before I fucking touched him.

The more distracted I get, the angrier I get.

How could she do this?

I scan the seats again, where I *know* she sits. My gaze lifts to suite 12, but all I see is a woman in a dress. Aspen's mother, maybe.

There's a roar from the crowd, and then the shocked quiet that follows a goal from our opposition. I whip my head around, only to find Miles climbing back to his feet. He scowls at me, and I understand that this was my fault.

A horn blows.

I skate for the bench and jump the boards, taking a seat before anyone can say anything. I squirt water into my mouth, flushing out the taste of blood.

Fuck.

Coach stops behind me. "What is your problem,

O'Brien? I haven't seen you play with your head so far up your ass since you were a freshmen."

I stiffen. "I just need a minute, Coach."

"See that's all that it is," he snaps.

He retreats to his spot, clipboard under his arm. He watches them restart, but my gaze goes to the stadium. Specifically, to the fan section. I go row by row, double-checking that Aspen isn't there. Then the suite again.

Without my phone, I don't know if she left her apartment—but I do know that this is unacceptable. Part of me wants to storm back to the locker room just to check. If I were Greyson, he would've snuck his phone out here and put it with his water bottle or some shit. I grit my teeth and remain still.

Greyson drops into the seat next to me.

"Spill," he demands.

"Aspen's not here."

"And you're worried?" Greyson looks across at where Violet and Willow sit.

"Of course I'm fucking worried." I shoot a glare filled with loathing at him. It's misguided, obviously. He didn't do anything wrong. But I'm boiling already. I *told* her what would happen if she didn't show up. "And pissed. And lost."

He sighs and pulls out his phone.

See? Fucker always sneaks it into the bench.

He taps out a message, then stows it again. "There."

"What did you do?"

"Violet's going to find Aspen's roommate, and we'll get an update."

Fat lot of good that'll do. Still, it's more than sitting here stewing will do. I hop up, suddenly eager to be back on the ice. To hit something, or someone.

I catch one of the defensemen's attention, and he skates

toward the bench. He goes through the door, and I hop over the wall.

My attention is on the puck. The moving players. I skate closer to Miles, who spares me a glance. I nod back at him, then Rodrigues. We're not going to let another puck get close to our goalie. We both drift forward, finding guys to block.

The crowd cheers.

Greyson, always a fan favorite, has the puck. Rodrigues and I follow as Greyson passes to Knox. Then Finch. Back to Greyson, who shoots almost faster than my eye can follow.

It sails past the goalie just before Greyson gets knocked on his ass.

I rush forward and shove the asshole away from Greyson—but that just seems to fuel the fire. We're swarmed by half the team—and ours doesn't fucking hesitate to dive in either. For a moment, we're just a mass of packed bodies trying to cause a little damage.

Someone yanks me back, sending me sliding on my skates out of the melee. Miles is systematically pulling out our starters, somehow finding Greyson and Knox next. Rodrigues is already out of the body pile, wiping his bloody nose on his sleeve. The refs are blowing their whistles and breaking up the rest of it.

It takes me a second to find my stick and register the pain in my face. I didn't lose my helmet or my mouth guard, though. Surprisingly. My cheek stings where I must've caught an errant fist or elbow.

It does nothing to soothe the rushing emotions inside me.

We all leave the ice while the refs sort out who's to blame. I sit next to Greyson and grab for my water. He does the same, furtively checking his phone.

"She found Thalia," he informs me. "But neither of them have seen Aspen. Your dad was going to her apartment to check for her."

I clear my throat. "Thanks."

He claps me on the shoulder. "Don't worry about it. Focus on the game."

44
ASPEN

Something hits the floor in front of me. It's heavy, judging from the way the impact makes the floor under my feet tremble. I can't open my eyes, though. They weigh a million pounds, like the rest of me. It's bad enough my awareness came back first—the inability to move is *killing* me.

A hand touches my face, and my eyelid is lifted. I get a blurry view of a basic, almost-empty room, and then my eyelid is lowered again.

Silence.

So much silence, it's never-ending. I strain to hear anything outside of my shallow breathing—the breathing of another, maybe. Footsteps. A ticking clock.

Eventually, whatever held my muscles hostage ebbs away. My system burns through it slowly, my fingers first twitching back to life, then my ability to swallow. My eyelids flutter, and I force my eyes open all the way.

There is a body on the floor in front of me.

Someone in a suit, curled away from me in the fetal position.

"You're awake."

The voice—familiar and terrible, with a rasp that rivals mine—draws my attention to the doorway. I shudder, then immediately regret it. I shouldn't show fear.

My father steps forward, his green eyes locked on me.

I get most of my features from him. My eyes, my dark hair. My complexion, even. My sisters are blessed to share more of my mother's physicality. Her blonde hair and golden skin, always sun-kissed even in the dead of winter.

"You've grown up into a stunning young woman," he says.

I wet my lips. I don't trust myself to talk, or... try to bargain for my freedom. I look around more. The room really is simple. I'm not tied to a chair or bed, not like I originally expected when my limbs were too tingly or numb to get a lock on. Instead, I'm positioned in an armchair like I had fallen asleep watching television, or something equally... *normal*. My legs are pulled up under me, my arms at my sides. I think my head was left to rest against the back cushion.

"Come with me," Dad says, offering his hand.

I stare at him without comprehending.

Where we are, how I got here. *Why* I'm here. And the man on the floor—

"Don't look at him, babydoll." Dad jars my thoughts. He takes my feet and puts them on the floor, then picks up my hands. He tugs me upright, holding my arms as I wobble. "You're like a kid learning to walk again."

My stomach twists. I know all about how he treats kids. *Me* as a kid. His grip on me is firm and unrelenting, and he leads me through the doorway, into a kitchen and dining room area.

Actually...

I squint at it, then glance back over my shoulder. If there wasn't a wall dividing the two, it would be an exact replica of my apartment. And the hallway is positioned in the same spot, too.

"Go on." Dad suddenly releases me.

"Wh—" I clear my throat. "Where?"

He gives me an odd look. "To your room."

Um…

He shakes his head and points. "The door on the left."

"Okay," I whisper. I walk on unsteady legs down the hall, running my hand along the wall. There are picture frames that I refuse to look at, although I catch a passing glimpse of one: my parents and me when I was barely three months old. All smiling.

That was before, of course. Before my father fell in with the wrong people, then turned further into the world of child pornography. That has to be it, right? That explains the camera flashes in my memory.

The more I don't want to think about it, the more my brain wants to suck me back there.

The door on the left is painted eggshell blue. I touch it, running my fingernails down one of the grooves, then grasp the handle. Turn the knob, open the door.

Should be just that easy, but I can't do it. My limbs get stuck.

There's something bad on the other side of this door.

Something I don't want to know.

I glance back down the hall, to where my father stands. His arms are by his sides, loose, relaxed. That's always the persona I knew him to exude.

My knees buckle, and my weight opens the door for me.

I practically fall inside. My knees hit the plush blue carpet first, and I can only stare at the familiar color. There was a rug like that in one of the apartments we lived in, in the room I shared with Dakota and Len when I was maybe nine or ten. We'd roll around on it, giggling about pretend, alien invaders trying to shoot us out of the sky. Because on it, we were fighter pilots. Civilization's last hope.

My throat closes.

It's the same layout as my apartment bedroom, but so, *so* different.

There are three beds. A double bed against a window with an achingly familiar comforter, maybe torn right off my real bed, and a set of twin bunk beds opposite it. The closet doors are open, clothes from my apartment. The CPU hoodie I was missing, a few sweaters and t-shirts. I stagger toward it, rifling through the clothes.

There are smaller-sized items, too. Things that would fit my sisters.

I wheel around and go to the dresser, yanking it open.

It's filled with kid things. Underwear and sleep shirts and shorts, play clothes.

There's a makeup bag on top of it. Without thinking, I overturn it. My makeup—*my makeup*—spills out. Spills everywhere. Tubes of mascara and lipstick roll off the dresser. My eyeshadow palette clatters to the floor and shatters.

"Careful, Aspen!" Dad tows me away from the shards of glass and plastic, almost lifting me completely off my feet.

I kick and squeal, unnerved at how easy he carries me away. His arm banded around my waist gives me no leniency.

He tosses me down on the double bed, his expression fierce. "You can't destroy your stuff like that."

He's *angry*. But not just that—disappointed.

"What is this?" I have to ask.

Dad squints at me. Confused. "This is ours, babydoll. Just temporary, of course, while I get your sisters and mother. We'll set up at a bigger house back in Chicago, get you your own room. But we're going to be a family again. That's all I've wanted."

I can't do this.

I sit there and stare at him, my mind turning over the horrors of a reality I'd live out if he succeeds. What he would do to my fourteen- and twelve-year-old sisters. Or me.

How many debts does he have?

How many mobsters want him dead?

My mind goes to Steele. Just picturing his face gives me an ounce of room in my lungs for air. I suck it in greedily, and I snap out of being coy, or scared, or fucking *weak*. I didn't survive all that shit with him just to turn around and bend my head for my father. Not when he's talking about ripping my sisters away from their lives. And what, kidnapping my mother along with us?

I rise from the bed. "You can't do that. I have a life. A good life. And so do my sisters, and my mom. Are you seriously so delusional to think that any of us will last? You're trouble incarnate."

He retrieves a brown paper bag out of the closet, from the top shelf, and tosses it at me. "Why didn't you spend this?" His voice rises, his face reddening. "I gave this to you —my brother passed it along. And yet I found it untouched in your closet while you took handouts from some other man?"

I flinch. "I don't want *anything* from you."

Dad stares at me. The seconds tick by... and his expression morphs.

From a sympathetic, caring Dad, straight into the face of a madman.

"Foolish girl," he whispers.

Ah.

Ice trickles down my spine. I should've remembered that when he went quiet was the worst. The deep, dark monsters that lived under his skin never made much noise —but they always made an impact.

He leads me out of the room and back toward the kitchen. There's a piano on the wall that divides the kitchen and the living room. And my music binder sits on top of it.

"I went through so much trouble for you," he growls. "You ungrateful child."

He pulls a matchbook from his pocket and snatches the binder. He marches to the sink and holds the binder so all the pages fan out.

My heart goes into my throat. All those carefully written notes, my handwriting cramped between the bars of music. All the practice and rehearsal that went into it.

He strikes the match and sets it to the pages, and all my hard work goes up in flames.

I lunge for it, but he drops the burning music into the dry sink basin. The pages blacken and curl, and I let out a ragged noise. He comes around and drags me closer, forcing me to watch up close.

Tears burn my eyes. The smoke gets in my nose, scratching my throat. I blink, and the tears drip down my face.

"This is why you should listen to your father, babydoll," he says in my ear.

He drags me back into the living room and throws me in the armchair I woke up in. He positions himself right in front of the man curled on the floor, a grim smirk over-taking his face.

Evil. Now and always.

He kicks over the suited man in front of me, and my throat closes all over again.

Steele's dad.

He's unconscious, but he lets out a low wheeze at the kick to his ribs. Dad crouches and pulls something from his jacket pocket. A length of cord, which he uses to tie Stephen's wrists together. He lets Stephen's hands fall to his chest, then slaps him.

Stephen's eyes crack, barely glancing off my father and coming straight to me. "Are you okay?"

I nod quickly. I mean, I'm not—but for his sake, I can be.

But Dad has more things in his hands. A clear plastic bag, a mostly used roll of tape. I stare at him in confusion, until he snaps the plastic bag open and drags it over Stephen's head.

Stephen immediately bucks, trying to get it off, but Dad moves fast with the duct tape. He loops it tight around his neck, then sits back on his haunches.

"Every action has a consequence." Dad eyes Stephen with disdain.

Steele's father is trying to get the tape off his neck, but with his hands bound he's not making much progress.

Dad rises. "Will you help him, Aspen? Because he's going to die tonight, one way or another. But I'm feeling charitable, so I'm going to leave the method up to you."

He leaves us. The door slams behind him.

Immediately, I launch out of the armchair and fall down beside Stephen. I go for the plastic, my nails biting into it. It's heavy, and for all my tugging doesn't even rip. His face is getting redder, and the bag is filling and deflating against his mouth and nose with every rapid breath.

I rip at the tape, too, joining his efforts. His movements are getting weaker, slowing down.

"No, no, no," I whisper.

His eyes shut, and he sags fully into the floor. I get through the tape just below his ear and yank it away, enough to unwind it and get the bag off. He's not breathing.

How the fuck would I ever tell Steele that I let his dad die?

I slap Stephen's cheek. My next step would be CPR— but figured I'd try a shot of violence first. Right? I don't know. I only know that CPR should be done in time to that song about living. Or believing. Anyway, my slap is successful.

Stephen sucks in a ragged breath and shoots upright.

I grab his shoulders to steady him.

"Are *you* okay?" I ask, mirroring his first question to me. I untie the rope binding his wrists, tossing it away from us.

He takes a few deep breaths and rubs his throat, then seems to shake it off. "I'm okay. Thanks. How are you? How long has he..." The concern flashing across his face is touching. "Has he done anything?"

"If redecorating this apartment with clothes and stuff he stole from me, remaking everything to be perfect for us to live with him, is 'anything', then..." I shrug and cross my arms. "How much do you know?"

Stephen sighs. "Your mother was forthcoming after our... rather sudden wedding. When we met, it was love at first sight. Or maybe lust, I don't know. Getting married felt like diving into the ocean headfirst."

"Terrifying and dangerous?"

"*Fun*, Aspen."

He smirks, and *damn it*, it reminds me of Steele. They must have the same mouth structure. A pang goes through me, and I look away.

"We jumped off the point today."

Shouldn't have said that.

To our parents, we're stepsiblings. We're supposed to be doing that brother-sister bonding thing, or whatever. At the very least, Steele was supposed to move me into his house to keep watch and make sure I didn't go crazy.

Although drugging me was his fault.

"Mari was furious with me for threatening you with hospitalization," Stephen says in a low voice. "And I was planning on apologizing about going that route the last time we saw each other."

That's... nice. And a little belated on my mom's part, but I would understand it more if he just sprang it on her at that hotel restaurant. She's never been great at standing up for herself—or me. The fact that she said anything at all means she trusts him.

I go to the windows and peer out.

It really is an exact replica of my apartment. I'd even be convinced we were on the same street.

Wait.

I lean into the window, my forehead touching the cold glass. I recognize the cars down there. We're high up, probably on the sixth or seventh floor, but—

Shit.

He's been in my apartment building this whole time?

My stomach swoops, and I pivot. I eye Steele's dad, then the door.

"How do we play this?" I ask. "There's a fire escape in the room down the hall on the right. We could go out—"

Stephen shakes his head. "And he'd meet us at the

ground level, probably with a gun. That's how he got to me. I was checking your apartment, and he followed me in. Said he'd shoot me if I didn't go with him upstairs. I figured he was going to kill me on the roof or something, dead either way," he confesses. "But he just hit me over the head... And then I woke up in here."

Shit.

"Listen, Aspen." He takes my hands. Both of them, pressing my palms together. His hands are warm and dry, and that alone screams of confidence. "Whether or not I make it, your family will be okay. Your mom is getting everything in my will, you and your sisters have inheritances in trusts—"

"Why are you telling me this?" I try to pull my hands away. "That's—"

"Listen to me," he snaps in a low voice. "I will *not* let this man ruin your life again. So I'm going to distract him, and you're going to go to the fire escape. Or out the front door. And scream bloody fucking murder until you get free —and don't stop running until you find my security at the stadium."

"Why didn't you bring security *here*?" I look at the window again, then back at him. "I can't do this. I can't let you just... sacrifice yourself. He'll kill you."

"When I don't return, they'll move your mother and sisters to a secure location. We did this to keep them safe from *him*, but I didn't think he'd find you here. Your uncle assured me that you'd be safe."

I scoff. "Cillian? My father's brother? He left a few days ago—he went back to Chicago—"

The door opens, and the words die on my tongue.

Dad's upped the stakes on us.

Now, he has a gun.

"Mr. O'Brien, we need to escort you to a safe location."

Coach and I stop our conversation and eye the unfamiliar man in our locker room. He's wearing all black, with an earpiece in one ear. There's a gun on his hip, a radio on his opposite side, and a Kevlar vest strapped over his black shirt.

Coach folds his arms. "And you are...?"

"Security for Mr. Stephen O'Brien, sir. He went to go pick up his stepdaughter and hasn't checked in within our designated timeframe. It means going through Protocol Orange." The guy actually looks a little apologetic. "I realize this is half-time, but my orders are non-negotiable."

"Let me see your credentials," Coach snaps, glancing at me. "Hockey doesn't have a fucking half-time, you idiot. We've only got one period left. The *most important* period."

The man hands over his identification. His neck is getting red.

Coach scans it, then dials some number on his cell. "Mrs. O'Brien."

I jerk—then realize that he's calling Aspen's mother, not mine. I turn away sharply and press my fingers into my eyes. Damn, that hit a little too hard. But then the true realization hits: Dad went to go get Aspen, and neither of them came back.

My stomach sinks.

All thoughts of Aspen leaving me, or choosing to skip the game, goes out the window. There's no fucking way that my father wouldn't check in with his security, especially knowing the protocols. Stuff he probably created to keep everyone safe.

Which means it was Aspen's stalker.

"This is Coach Roake," he continues. "Can you confirm the security company that your husband employs? Uh-huh. Okay, excellent. Thank you, ma'am." He hangs up and eyes me. "Well? Go get changed into street clothes."

I nod and hurry inside, brushing past my friends. Greyson, Knox, and Miles all fall silent when they see me, but my throat is closing. I don't have words to tell them that something bad happened to my girl.

Something I could've fucking prevented if this day had gone any different.

I remove my pads and skates in record time, snatching my phone from my bag and pulling up the tracker.

She's still at her apartment.

My brows furrow.

That doesn't fucking make sense.

"Tell us," Greyson demands.

When I look up, all of the team has cleared out except my three best friends.

So, quietly, I tell them what I just found out. Which is painfully little.

"Listen, if you go with the security, they're just going to try and keep you safe."

I nod along, because... well, no shit. And then I see what Greyson's really driving at: they're not going to search for my dad or Aspen. They might call the police, or track his phone...

The locker room door bangs open, and two girls storm in.

Violet and Thalia.

The former goes straight to Greyson. He takes her hand and kisses her knuckles, then starts unstrapping his skates.

"Wait," I protest. "What are you doing? You have a game—"

"A game we're up by four in," Miles interrupts. "All the second string goalie has to do is keep the puck out of the net for twenty minutes." He begins to undo his pads, too.

I watch helplessly as they all start changing, and my gaze goes to Thalia.

"Here," she says, thrusting the phone at me.

I take it. There's an open call line, the seconds ticking away.

"This is Steele."

"Steele," a man replies. "Cillian Monroe here. I was called away on urgent business to Chicago, which I believed had to do with my brother. However, I've now learned that this was a diversion."

My chest tightens. "What sort of diversion?"

"The sort where he orchestrates an elaborate plan to get Aspen, her mother, and all her sisters all in one place."

I'm going to be fucking sick.

"I've been detained in Chicago," he continues. "Temporary, but definitely my brother's doing. If you can get out of the city—"

"I can't. He has her already."

Cillian swears. "And her mother? Her siblings?"

"Not yet." I grip the phone tighter. "Please, give me anything you can to help us. I need to get her back."

And to his credit, he does. He outlines what her father might do or be capable of. That he probably has a weapon.

"The hardest part would be finding her," he finishes.

"That's not a fucking problem. Thank you for the help." I hang up and toss Thalia's phone back to her.

"Here's the deal."

All eyes swing to me.

"I'm pretty sure Aspen is being held hostage with my father... by her dad. A psychotic asshole—I'll fill you in on those details on the way. They're either still in the apartment, or he discovered the tracking implant and left it there." I slide my shoes on and gesture to Thalia. "Keys?"

She holds them out to me.

"Great. Now, you and Violet—distract that security guard. We just need time to get out of the locker room."

The girls both nod in affirmation. Greyson won't want Violet anywhere near this mess anyway. I find Miles, Greyson, and Knox all standing at the ready, and take a deep breath. As quickly as I can, I explain the shit I've discovered about Aspen's dad. The people he was tied up with in Chicago, the way even the crime lords wanted him gone, that he did some sick and twisted shit to Aspen when she was a kid. I don't go into detail about that.

I won't.

Can't.

But the rest is free information that might help us figure out who we're dealing with.

"He might be looking to establish himself here in Crown Point or take Aspen away from here—I don't know what his goal is, and I don't fucking care." I slam my fist into my palm. "She's mine. No one gets to take her from me."

"Let's go," Greyson says.

He reels Violet in and kisses her forehead, then we all move to the door. The girls slip out first, and their voices drift back toward us. They get softer, and Miles peeks out first. He motions for us to go—so we all book it out into the hallway.

The padding on the floor meant to protect our skates now muffles our footsteps. We get around the corner, and Knox shoves open the exit door. As a unit, we hurry to Greyson's truck. It's always unanimous that he drives, mainly because I think he'd have a stroke if he deigned to sit shotgun—or worse, in the backseat—of anyone else's car.

Unless he had access to Violet, in which case...

I claim the front seat, earning a glare from Knox, and the two brothers hop in the back. Greyson takes off like a shot, but he doesn't go toward Aspen's apartment.

"What are you doing?" I'm about ready to yank the wheel.

He gives me an irritated sigh. "I called in reinforcements. We just need to get them."

"*Them*?"

Greyson doesn't say anything else. Not until we screech to a halt in front of the hockey house, and Jacob comes trotting out with a huge duffle bag. He forces Miles to scoot into the middle seat and sets the duffle on his lap.

As soon as the door is closed, we're off again.

"Anyone know how to shoot?"

I crane around and stare at Jacob. "You're not serious."

He shrugs. "Okay, no gun for you."

Jesus.

"This guy is bad news, right?" Jacob eyes us. "So he's probably expecting police trouble, if anything at all. Which means we need to think *not* like the police, and more like..."

"Thieves," Knox supplies.

Jacob grins. "Yeah."

He hands me a crowbar from his bag. Fuck knows where he got it, but he seems to have more than one. Knox gets one. He gives Miles a metal pipe. I grip the cold weapon, adjusting to its weight. It's only a little thinner than a hockey stick.

Greyson parks half a block down from Aspen's apartment. He holds his hand out for the keys, motioning for us to stay put.

Yeah fucking right.

I ignore him and step out onto the sidewalk, my grip on Thalia's keys like iron. I tuck the crowbar into the back of my pants. I unlock the door and step into the large entryway. There's a staircase off to the side, a row of mailboxes, and then their apartment door.

If I had my stuff, I wouldn't have needed Thalia's keys. But my set is on my dresser at home, left there like an idiot because I didn't drive to the stadium.

Jacob, Knox, and Miles are right behind us, walking through the silent lobby. We reach her door, and I stick the key in. Turn it.

There's no audible click of the lock or the weight of the deadbolt sliding open.

It was already unlocked.

A sinking feeling takes over me, and I slowly open the apartment door. It's completely dark. As one, we move into the unit. Jacob passes me a flashlight, and I click it on. The brilliant light sweeps across the living room and kitchen. I spot her purse on the kitchen island, balanced on the edge.

Greyson and Jacob go down the hall and split off, checking the two rooms. Miles peers into the bathroom, while Knox sticks by me.

I recheck the app. She should be here.

"O'Brien," Jacob calls from the entrance of Aspen's room.

I hurry to join him, and my stomach twists at the sight. Her room has been trashed—her bedspread and pillow are missing, half the clothes torn out of her closet. The bar that we put in her window, to prevent it from being opened from the outside, is on the floor.

"Oh, god." It slips out before I can stop it.

"Give me your phone," Jacob demands.

I hand it over without hesitation, staring around at the wreckage.

He fiddles with the app, then nudges me. "The tracking implant has a heat sensor. If it goes below ninety degrees, it sends you an alert. And since it's still active, it's still working."

He hands my phone back.

I stare at it. She's moved a bit, but the pulsing dot is still *here*.

My head tips back.

Well, *here* could be... up, too.

"She's on another floor." Holy shit. He's been here the whole time. "Guys." I burst back out into the main room with Jacob hot on my heels, and we rejoin the other guys. "She *is* here. Upstairs. On another level."

We head back into the hallway and go for the stairs. Miles mumbles something about calling the police, and his brother agrees with him. I think I might, too. Especially since we're walking essentially unarmed into an unknown situation.

Suddenly, a sound rips through the stairwell. The *crack* is louder than anything I've heard, worse than the sound of a puck hitting the glass during a game. We automatically look at Jacob. His dad is a police chief, after all. He'd know the difference between a firework and...

He nods once, his expression dark.

It was a gunshot.

"We need to call the police," Knox says. "This is out of our control—"

Jacob grabs for me. Miles might, too. There's a flurry of motion behind me as I lunge forward, up the steps and out of their reach.

They can call in the fucking National Guard—it won't be in time to save Aspen.

But I can. And I will.

"Come here," my father orders, motioning to me with the gun.

My brain has stalled out. I glance at Stephen, but he's gone white in the face. It takes me a long moment to get my legs to work, and I stumble across the sparse living room. I stop out of arm's reach, although really—if he wanted to hurt me, he wouldn't have to reach. He could just shoot me.

Dad pulls a phone from his pocket.

Everything about him is soul-crushingly familiar. All the details I wanted to forget about him are still there, exaggerated by a hundred. It makes me realize that my memory did its job and dulled him. And the real him is so much worse.

"I got you a new phone, babydoll." He tosses it to me.

I fumble for it and stare at the sleek model in my hand. It seems brand-new, an upgrade from mine.

"I moved your photos over so you wouldn't lose them," he continues. "There are some safety features on this one, of course. Only approved numbers you can call, app restrictions."

He stole my phone. My music. My clothes.

"Did you watch Steele and I jump—"

"Steele," Dad spits. "You shouldn't be messing around with boys like him."

Stephen clears his throat. "Messing around—"

"Fucking." His gaze snaps to Steele's father. "Your child and mine have been *intimate*."

My stomach knots, but Stephen doesn't react. He just stares impassively at my father with blood trickling down his temple—courtesy of a little mouthing back on my part.

Another thing I needed to pay for, he said.

"Now." Dad focuses on me again. "Call your mother and tell her we need to see her. That everything is fine, but you need her help."

I stare at the phone. It lights up, revealing the same lock screen I had. I swipe it open, and it's the same passcode. Same everything—the configuration, the wallpaper. Some apps are missing, and there's no Wi-Fi.

"If you do anything other than call your mother, I'm shooting him." Dad lifts the gun, aiming it at Stephen.

"No," I whisper.

I can't call her. I won't drag her into this, and I *definitely* won't bring my sisters anywhere near his madness.

"Aspen." Stephen has his hands up, some sort of surrendering instinct when looking down the barrel of a gun, but his voice is steady. His expression isn't panicked. Instead, he seems oddly calm. "Don't you dare call her."

I nod.

The phone falls out of my hands.

Dad lunges for me. He wraps his hand in my hair and yanks me backward, and I crash into his body with a sharp exhale. The gun rises in slow motion, and my heart skips.

He's going to shoot Stephen.

Without question.

He's just doing exactly what he threatened, like he's done all along.

I lurch sideways, ignoring the searing pain through my scalp, and shove at his arm. The gun goes off. It's so fucking loud, the *crack* rattles in my skull. I scream without looking at Steele's dad. The last thing I want to see is him dead. To see that I failed.

I kick at my father, batter at him with my fists, my elbows. Everything I have. I fight harder than I've ever fought before, urged on by wild defiance and horror.

He smacks me in the face with the butt of the gun. The force cuts my cheek against my teeth. The pain explodes across my skin, and the taste of blood spreads across my tongue. I let it pool in my mouth. He's still got hold of my hair, and he uses it to swing me back toward him. My chest hits his again.

I spit at him.

He closes his eyes on instinct, protecting them from the bloody saliva. My hair slips through his fingers, free at last, and I push away from him. I go straight for the door, knowing that he'd rather follow me than finish anything with Stephen.

It's safer if I lead my monster father away.

I catch sight of someone against the wall as I pass, and my heart kicks.

Dad is in pursuit—but the moment he comes through is when my savior acts.

Steele swings a metal bar down. It collides with Dad's forearm with a mighty *crack*. Bones probably broke, and his hold on the gun loosens. It drops out of his hand as he turns on Steele, roaring with pain.

Steele swings again, his expression determined.

I've stopped running.

Stopped moving entirely.

Dad jumps at Steele, knocking away the hooked bar like it's nothing. Like his arm isn't in screaming agony. They go down, and I cover my mouth.

What do I do?

Dad punches Steele in the face, straddling his chest.

No.

My gaze drops to the gun.

Before I can register what I'm actually doing, I crouch and pick it up. There's no safety on it—it's one of those small double-trigger handguns. I pull back the slide and check that it's loaded.

Of course it is. Dad wouldn't have just put one cartridge in.

Steele bucks, blocking Dad's hits with his forearm and slamming his fist into Dad's side. Hard, repeatedly. But it's not much good, when Dad so clearly has the upper hand. And in fact, it seems like whatever control my father was maintaining has snapped, too. He stops hitting Steele and wraps both his hands around his throat.

"Hey!" I scream.

Dad glances over at me, but he doesn't so much as let up the pressure.

"Get off him." I hate how wobbly my voice is.

Dad's lip curls. "This will all be over soon, Aspen. Just close your eyes. Call your mother."

Just close your eyes, babydoll. His voice echoes in my head.

And suddenly I'm six years old again, my hands being dragged up over my head. My body immobilized. The flash of the camera, the silence. It all echoes in my head. But more than that—it's the helplessness. The panic wells up inside me, freezing me from the inside out.

What can I do against a monster who's everywhere? He's the shadows. He lurks in the corners of my mind, in my darkest memories.

"Aspen." It's a gurgle. Steele's choking. Suffocating.

And it snaps me out of my nightmare, back into reality.

Steele has a hold of Dad's wrists, but he can't seem to break his grip. And there's no way I can imagine a world, a *future*, without Steele O'Brien in it. And right now, Dad's killing him.

The six-year-old inside me is screaming, and it echoes and echoes and echoes.

I squeeze the trigger.

47
STEELE

Bang!

Aspen's dad slumps off me, and I gasp a breath I thought I wouldn't get. I rip his hands away from my neck and scramble backward. For a split second, I thought I was going to die. My throat burns, my body aches. Like I went through a pulverizer. My face is hot, pulsing with pain.

But then I see what happened to him. He's gaping like a fish out of water, struggling to breathe. Blood flecks his lips, and there's blood soaking his shirt. It's hard to see where it's coming from with his leather jacket.

"Oh, god," Aspen moans.

I look at her.

The gun in her hand.

She just fucking saved my life—by shooting her own father.

She drops to her knees, setting the gun down by her side. Her gaze is locked on her dad. He hasn't made any move to get up, but his attention is on her, too. Even as he gasps for air, and his breath whistles.

They're in a staring contest.

I will *not* lose her to him.

I crawl across the floor to her, blocking her view of him. I grip her cheeks and force her to focus on me. It takes me a second to realize my hands are bloody, and it now paints her skin, too. Her wide-eyed stare bores into me.

"You're okay," I tell her.

It hurts to talk. To breathe, really.

She shakes her head. "I killed him. I-I killed him, Steele, he was going to kill you, and I just picked up the gun and pulled the trigger—"

I drag her into me. All the worry and fear eases when our lips touch. She sags against me, gripping my shoulders. She needs me to save her.

I know that now.

So when I pick up the gun, *I* don't hesitate. I leave her kneeling on the floor and push myself up, going back to her father. He looks up at me, then at the gun. And he fucking smiles.

"She picked a winner," he says, his words gurgled.

I'd bet anything that she nicked his lung. And I'd love to see him drown in his own blood, but it'll take too long. The paramedics, the police—everyone will be here soon. Already, the sirens are drawing closer.

I will.

I aim at his chest and squeeze the trigger. It kicks in my hand, but it lands true. I do it again, just to make sure. And again. Until the gun is only dry-firing, out of bullets, and utterly fucking useless. I toss it away from us and go back to Aspen. I'll deal with it after, if I need to clean it, or... whatever you're supposed to do with a deadly weapon that belongs to a career criminal.

"Your dad," she whispers. "He—"

Oh, fuck.

I pick her up. Because I'm not leaving her to stare at her dead father while I go see about mine. She winds her arms around my shoulders and buries her face in my neck.

"I don't want to see."

"Okay, sweetheart," I murmur. I stroke her hair. "It's okay."

I go into the front room. There's just an armchair in here, nothing else. A wide row of windows, similar to Aspen's living room, but without any curtains or blinds. The overhead light is harsh, illuminating my father on the floor.

He's got his suit jacket off and balled up, holding it to his left leg. He used his tie as a makeshift tourniquet just above it. There's a puddle of blood under his thigh, and his face is white with pain.

But the relief that comes across his expression—and then the fear when he latches on to Aspen.

"Is she—"

"She's okay." I drum my fingers against her arm. "And so is he. Look, sweetheart."

She lifts her head and stares at my dad. Then the blood.

But maybe it's too much for her. Or everything just catches up, because her eyes lose focus. They roll back, and she goes completely limp in my arms.

My phone buzzes. I set her down in the armchair and scan the text.

Miles: Police and EMT are pulling up now. They'll be up in a minute.

I relay that message to my dad, then send one final text to Greyson.

He nods, then glances at Aspen. "Is her father...?"

"Dead," I confirm. "I'd be fucking surprised if he wasn't."

"Listen to me, Steele. You're not to say a word to the police. Go to the hospital with Aspen and get checked out, but if they try to question you, give them our lawyer's number and do *not* speak without him present. Same with Aspen. You've got to protect her."

I grit my teeth. "Of course I'm going to protect her." *I love her.*

He nods.

The apartment door opens, the police sweeping into the room. We go still and let them finish their check, and then the paramedics arrive. I spot one checking Aspen's father's pulse, and she glances up at one of the officers and shakes her head.

Two more come to us, checking first my dad, then Aspen.

Things seem to pass in a blur after that. They load up Aspen, still unconscious, onto a stretcher. And my dad on another. I follow them downstairs, ignoring the police. Knox, Miles, and Jacob are standing on the other side of police tape that's stretched across the sidewalk and street.

I'm glad they didn't come up with me. What if they had been hurt?

What if Aspen's dad had heard us enter and just shot us on sight?

I climb into the ambulance with Aspen and hold her hand. It's cool and limp in my grasp, but the monitor they hooked her up to shows her steady pulse. There's a police officer sitting beside me, his expression carefully blank.

But all that matters is that she's alive.

"Your sister?" the paramedic asks.

My lip curls before I can stop it. "Soon-to-be wife," I reply.

"Oh, I'm sorry. Your father—"

"It's complicated," I mumble.

Aspen wakes up as we're pulling into the hospital bay. She tries to jackknife upright, but the straps around her chest and legs hold her fast to the stretcher. It only serves to panic her, though, and she fights it blindly.

"Hey, hey," I call, squeezing her hand. "You're okay. Breathe."

She finds me and goes still.

I lean forward and press a kiss to her temple. She's got my bloody handprints on her cheeks like a goddamn warrior. Her breath catches when my lips brush her skin, and the heart monitor over her head increases tempo.

"We're at the hospital to get you checked out," I tell her.

Her cheeks redden further.

The doors open, and there's more flurry of activity as they unload her. I hop out and follow her inside the emergency department. She gets her own bed with curtains for walls. The police officer explains that they need to collect our clothes and swab for gunshot residue. All of which Aspen and I don't fight.

They suspect us of the murder, of course.

A nurse returns with fresh clothes for both of us, as one of the officers disappeared with ours. There's another posted just outside of the curtained off area around Aspen's bed.

I shrug into the scrubs and hold Aspen's hand until they return. They take care of Aspen first and foremost—as they should. But eventually, once the testing is done, the nurse eyes me like she wants to say something. Her brows are furrowed.

"What?" I snap.

"Let me check out your hands. And your face."

I glance down at the hands in question. My knuckles have seen better days... the fight at the hockey game didn't help either. But my face feels terrible. My left eye is swelling a bit, and every time I swallow, I taste blood. My lip is split, the insides of my cheeks shredded.

Sighing, I let her examine them. She nods to herself and disappears around the corner, coming back with a tray and wheeling stool a second later.

I sit on the edge of Aspen's bed and let the nurse clean out my knuckles and wrap them.

When she's done, she looks to Aspen. "The doctor will be over to check you in a few minutes. Your father's been taken into surgery."

Aspen's face goes white.

"You mean my father," I interrupt, squeezing her hand again. "The gunshot wound in the leg?"

She dips her head. "Yes, of course."

"Thanks," Aspen whispers to me.

Detectives arrive, as does our lawyer. We all agree to give statements here, as opposed to going to the police station. I get the sense that it's not exactly normal, but it's the middle of the night. We're exhausted. And by some stroke of luck, the security team notified police of both Aspen and my father's disappearance.

It's all on record.

The detectives make each of us run through it a few times separately, sitting in a cramped conference room with a camera trained on me. Being apart from her eats at my insides, but the lawyer, a sturdy looking man who takes *no* shit from the detectives, gives me a look. It translates to, *keep calm or else.*

Can't help but agree with that.

So we follow the police directions, and what feels like hours later, we're cleared to leave the ED by both doctors and detectives.

I'm a strange mix of wired and exhausted, and I know Aspen feels the same. We're in foreign clothes, with blood still in our hair and on our skin. The feel of the gun going off in my hand seems ingrained in my muscles.

Aspen's mom and sisters are safe and sound at a hotel nearby. Dad got out of surgery about an hour ago, and while Aspen's mom got to see him briefly, she didn't want to leave the girls alone with the security team for too long.

My friends wait for us outside, under the floodlights of the hospital. My friends hug me, patting my back. Jacob shakes his head at me, his eyes saying I'm a stupid fuck— but he would've done the same freaking thing if he could get his professor back.

We all would for our girls... even the lost ones.

Greyson catches my eye and nods, reading my mind. He opens the back door for us.

I hoist her into the backseat, then join her. I wrap my arm around her shoulders, not willing to be separated from her for even a moment. She sits between Jacob and me, trembling like a leaf. The other guys will ride back with Willow and Thalia, so Greyson doesn't even worry about waiting. He takes off away from the hospital, flying through the quiet, dark streets of Crown Point.

The clock on the dash reads 3:05 a.m.

Greyson parks at the hockey house. Jacob hops out and gives us a wave before heading straight to his vehicle. I toss a nod at Greyson and Violet, too, before shepherding Aspen inside. They're going to head home. And soon enough, Knox and Miles will be returning here.

For now, though, it's quiet. Empty.

We go up to my room, and I close us in. She stands in the middle of it with her arms wrapped around her middle. The scrubs the nurse gave her are loose and baggy, but at least they're free of blood. One of the nurses in the emergency department helped clean the blood off her face, and cleaned up my face, too. I can feel it in my hair, on my neck.

All in all, a fucking traumatic night.

I go to her and run my fingers through her hair. Stroking it away from her temple. She has a bruise forming on her cheekbone, just a shadow under her skin. But my chest tightens all the same.

If I hadn't killed the bastard, I would want to now.

"He's gone," I assure her. "No more demons haunting your step."

48
ASPEN

Steele takes my hospital-acquired shirt off slowly. I raise my arms to help him, and he drops it to the floor beside him. His gaze roves over my bare skin, and goosebumps rise on my arms at the attention.

His bruises are darkening, and I can't help but reach out and touch his throat. The beautiful throat my father tried to crush—

"Shh," Steele whispers, shedding his matching shirt and tugging me into him. He binds his arms around me, and I tuck my head under his chin. "We're safe."

"I know we are." I hug him back. "But for a second, I thought..."

I didn't have hope.

"Look at me, Aspen." His finger under my chin brings my head up, and I meet his dark gaze. "There's no one who can tear us apart."

"I love you."

A weight lifts off my chest. Spectacularly. The expression on his face is nothing short of awed, and he presses his lips to mine. My aching, tired body suddenly comes alive. I wind my arms around his neck and kiss him harder. His lip starts bleeding again, and I flick at it with my tongue. Tasting the metallic taste of *him*.

He groans into my mouth.

All the teasing from this afternoon, that felt like a lifetime ago, comes roaring back. His hands are all over me. Coasting down my spine, slipping up my ribcage. Palming my breasts. A silent inspection. I'm doing the same to him, fumbling with the drawstring of his scrub pants and dragging them down while our tongues tangle.

I pull back and drop to my knees, gripping his cock in my fist. I take him into my mouth, earning a low groan above me. I want to choke on him instead of memories. Drown out every bad thing with the taste of Steele.

Still, I don't get very far until he's pulling me up. He shoves my pants and panties down, helping me balance as I kick them off. He lifts me into his arms and carries me out of the room. Into the bathroom where so many delicious memories are already stored.

I kiss his jaw. He's got a little five o'clock shadow coming in, and it's rough on my lips. I drag my mouth across the scruff, toward his ear. He's still holding me when he starts the shower.

Steam fills the room, and he sets me on my feet. He points, and I step into the shower. The hot water is a godsend against my skin. He follows behind me, and his hands are all over me again. He cups my breasts and pinches my nipples, tugging and rolling them until I arch my back and lean more heavily on his chest.

"You're so fucking gorgeous." His voice curls in my ear, while one hand dips down between my legs.

The hot water pounds against my chest, but it isn't hot

enough to mask the flash of fire traveling under my skin from his touch.

His finger runs through my center. "If I ever let you walk out of my sight without coming at least twice..."

"Oh my god."

He slides a finger into me, pumping slowly. It's joined by a second one. The heel of his palm grazes my clit with every pass, and my legs fall open wider. I close my eyes and shift my hips, jerking forward for more traction. He lets me chase my pleasure like that, and my first climax rolls through me like thunder.

He withdraws only when my trembling stops. His dick is still hard, pointing at me, but he shakes his head and points to the shampoo. I dunk my hair under, soaking it through, before trading places with him. I squirt the shampoo into my hair and scrub it into a lather.

Steele watches me, his eyes dark. I step forward and reach up, rubbing the soap into his hair, too. It comes away streaked with pink at first.

I don't react. Just put more shampoo in my palm and continue washing his hair. I'm so close to him, my breasts are mashed into his chest.

"Tip your head back," I murmur.

He does as I direct, and the water rinses him. I keep running my fingers through his hair, scratching his scalp in a way that makes his lips part slightly. And then he's moving, spinning both of us in the tight space so I have my turn under the water.

We take care of each other that way. Until we're both clean... well, *everywhere*. And then he picks me up and puts my back against the wall, notching himself at my entrance. He kisses me again, no less fiercely.

"Tell me you love me again," he says, pulling back an inch. His nose brushes mine.

I smirk. "Why?"

"Because we almost died, and I would've never heard you say it. So now I need to hear it as much as possible." He mirrors my expression, then pushes himself into me. So. Slow.

I might combust on the spot.

I dig my nails into his shoulders, and I put my mouth at his ear.

"I love you, Steele O'Brien."

"Marry me," he responds.

He jerks his hips forward and fills me completely. It's unexpected and completely satisfying, stretching and hitting the spot inside me that has been desperate for him since the prior afternoon.

"Asshole," I gasp in his ear.

He catches my hand and kisses my ring finger. "Say yes, Aspen."

"This is a knee-jerk reaction to almost dying," I reply. "You don't—"

"I've never been more sure of anything. You know you're my soulmate. Deep down, we're the perfect fit—and nothing is going to change that." He presses another kiss to my ring finger. "See your future with me—then reach out and take it."

All that I was going to say, to protest, dies away.

Really.

Why should I deny myself this?

"Yes," I whisper.

His lips crash into mine. I *feel* the ecstasy in how he kisses me, capturing this moment. I kiss him back with the same fierceness, needing to be a hundred percent closer to him. His tongue sweeps across my lower lip, and he sucks it into his mouth. His teeth scrape it. I let out a low groan, my core clenching around him. I tear my lips away and kiss down his neck. The tender skin of his throat.

"I love you," he says. "I'm not a wordsmith. Not even close. But I'm so fucking obsessed with you, I can't stand it. I love you. I'll love you forever."

I cup the back of his head and pull back just enough to meet his eyes. To see not only the heat but the *warmth*. Gone is that cold man who stared me down a few months ago, who threatened to make my life hell—and followed through.

"Forever," I agree.

I lift my hips to meet his thrusts. The water is getting cooler, but neither of us reach to turn it off. Our bodies are burning up as it is.

He lets go of my hip and slides his hand between us, rubbing my clit.

My eyes roll back, my head touching the cool tile. It's his turn to put his lips all over my throat, biting and sucking as he works me higher. His movements are getting more frantic. Chasing the high of release. I groan when he pinches my nipple again. It's like shooting fireworks under my skin.

I orgasm like that, crying out and clutching him closer. His mouth covers mine, absorbing the sounds. And only a few seconds later, he stills inside me and comes with a groan.

Forever with Steele O'Brien.

I smile. My legs are weak, and my knees almost buckle when he puts me down. He keeps his arm around my waist and shuts off the water, then sets me on the edge of the tub. I watch him find us towels—two fluffy ones for me, and one that he wipes down his chest with and then ties around his waist. He barely seems focused on himself, though, instead kneeling on the bathmat in front of me.

He takes one of the towels and wraps it around my torso. The other he keeps in his hand. He lifts my foot and dries my leg. Then repeats with the other one. He spreads my legs and inches closer, wiping that towel up to the apex of my thighs. Not touching my pussy, though. I can feel his cum leaking out, and he stares at it for a long moment.

"So damn gorgeous," he mutters, almost to himself.

Then he continues. Dries my arms, pats at my face. Takes special care around my cheek, the cloth barely touching it. He pulls out a shower caddy from under the sink, and I jerk.

It's filled with all of *my* stuff. My products.

"Replicas," he murmurs. "They were delivered last night after you left, because I don't want you feeling like you can't get ready here. I didn't steel your stuff, little viper."

My heart skips. Surprisingly thoughtful of him—but he's full of good intentions when he wants to be. I eye the hairbrush. Damn, he even got the brand of hairbrush right —and it's my favorite color.

"I still want to know where you came up with that nick-name," I reply, trying not to focus on the stuff in front of me. And the way I'm reacting to him. *Again*.

He rips the tag off it and grins at me. "My dad called you Asp on the phone one time over the summer. A nickname he probably picked up from your sisters or mom. An asp is a viper. It felt appropriate."

A laugh bubbles out of me.

With all the horrible things that happened in the past twenty-four hours... yeah, I've lost it.

I can't stop laughing. Tears leak out of my eyes, and I can barely suck in a breath. He went off of my sisters' nickname for me and created a whole new one.

Steele chuckles along with me, his hands on my thighs.

And once the laughter has subsided, he kisses me.

"I thought it would take some time for you to even smile," he says against my lips.

Yeah, well...

All that, and I didn't even see my father's body. Not really. Not after Steele shot him—and even then, I was more focused on my protector. On the way his forearm muscles clenched and his hand kicked up a bit.

The ringing noise of the gunshots, the smell of burning gunpowder.

"I just can't believe he's gone." All the time in the hospital, sitting on that bed while they did bloodwork and checked for a concussion, and whatever else they had to do, it felt like a dream. Or an echo.

Steele turns me at an angle and sits behind me. With slow, methodical movements, he brushes out my hair.

Something I'm totally capable of doing, but... it's nice to not think about it. It actually feels kind of good, and I tip my head back to give him better access. He squeezes the extra water from my hair and repeats the process, and then his fingers are moving against my scalp.

I exhale and close my eyes.

"Do you want to talk about it?" His voice is... unsure. For maybe the first time ever.

"No."

But then... well, I end up telling him about my dad, after all. The bad stuff doesn't come to mind right away. What *does* is the good stuff. Walking hand in hand to get ice cream from the shop on the corner. Him swinging me around in our tiny backyard, and the weightlessness that came with it. The giggles I couldn't contain.

Sitting with him and my mother, who was really pregnant and tired and sore all the time, at the dining room table and learning how to count cards in Blackjack. Just in case I ever found myself in a casino and down on my luck, even though I was only six going on sixteen.

Going to an amusement park when I was twelve, flinching away from him when he tried to hold my hand. But he always just held it tighter, until I stopped fighting.

Finding myself watching his gaze turn to Dakota, who was six when I was twelve, and getting violently sick at his contemplative expression.

It feels good to get them off my chest, and Steele absorbs all of it silently. He's moved from massaging the memories out of my head to relieving the tension in my neck. Then lower, his fingers pressing firmly into the muscles in my shoulders.

"I miss who he could've been," I say softly.

"I know." He kisses my shoulder blade.

When we emerge from the bathroom and tuck into his room, I'm unsurprised to find the sky lightening. Dawn, and *tomorrow*, can't be stopped by anything.

Not even trauma.

"Sleep," Steele orders, guiding me to the bed. "I'll keep your nightmares away."

He sheds his towel, and I do, too. I lie on my side, my back to the wall, and he wastes no time climbing in with me. He pulls me close, until we're aligned, our chests touching. My nipples harden. Steele slips his knee between my legs and wraps his arm around me in a full-body hug. I tuck my face into his neck and try to breathe.

And soon enough, I'm lured into sleep.

49
ASPEN

It's been a month since my abduction ended with the death of my father.

A month of police interviews, of legal jargon I scarcely understood, of being haunted by the fact that I could go to jail for something my lawyer—a fancy-suited man I'd never be able to afford on my own—calls self-defense.

But as of twenty minutes ago, the case is closed. There was sufficient evidence to support our story, including a testimony from Uncle about the depravity of his brother, of the crimes he committed against our family in my childhood—and the threat that was posed with him reemerging into my life. That, along with the bruises on Steele's face and neck... it was a no-brainer. Even if it took a while for the system to process.

It's been a month, and it feels like a year.

"Ready?" Steele asks me.

I meet his gaze in the mirror and try not to bite my lip. All traces of his fight with my father have healed over. He doesn't even look haunted. Not like me, when I wake up in the middle of the night with my skin crawling and night-mares stuck behind my eyes. Playing an endless loop of bloodshed.

I envy him that.

But he wakes up with me. Night after night. Sometimes he's awake before my dreams release me, and he's already between my legs when my eyes fly open. Soothing me in a way that makes me feel not broken.

Our parents and my sisters have been staying in a rented house in Crown Point. They both agreed that my sisters needed some closure surrounding my kidnapping, and the best thing for everyone was for them to be able to see me, and for some stability. So they've been enrolled in the public schools here in town.

And traveling around the country to avoid a madman wasn't really necessary anymore.

Mom didn't claim my father's body at the morgue. Uncle didn't either. So there he sits, in a metal box... rotting.

It's no less than he deserves.

Also, our parents don't know about the engagement. No one does. Steele asked me to keep it quiet, although he hasn't been shy about telling his friends—and random people at the bars, and hockey games—that I'm his future wife. But that he proposed, and I accepted? Still a secret. Not even Thalia knows.

There was another revelation I learned, about a week after the incident. Steele pulled out a brown paper bag from his closet, and I almost threw up. He took a little joy in dumping the sixty thousand dollars on the bed. He had Greyson sneak into the apartment ahead of the police and EMTs, after it was safe to do so, and collect the money. How he knew my dad would've thrown it in my face was a question I didn't want to ask.

But when he mentioned depositing it slowly, over the course of a year or so, into my accounts, I froze up. I didn't want *anything* in connection with my father. That much hadn't changed.

So he arranged an anonymous donation to a charity that fights child pornography and abuse, and he gave me the heartfelt, handwritten thank you card a few days after it was done.

Finally, Dad's money went to something *useful*.

Steele kisses my shoulder. He's been more free about affection. Touching me whenever he can. Picking up my left hand and running his finger across my ring finger. I asked him what he was thinking, once, and he simply said he was picturing the type of ring that would sit there.

"Or tattoo," he added, smiling at me.

I frowned at that one.

Besides the *Property of Steele O'Brien* tattoo, I think I'm done with needles and ink. Unless he drugs me and doesn't give me a choice, in which case... Well, maybe I'm just waiting for him to force it. There's something thrilling about that.

"I'm ready," I assure him. I put on the last finishing touches of my outfit: small gold earrings and a gold chain necklace, with a little crystal pendant that presses against my sternum.

We head to his car, then ride in relative silence to the CPB building. My heart is in my throat for more than one reason.

First: my callback audition for the Crown Point Orchestra.

Steele accompanied me to the first one, sitting outside the room while I played the piece I had been working on. And then we snuck into an office and fucked on the desk... you know, just for the experience.

But they want me back. And I've prepared a secondary piece for them, something of my own choosing. *Passion*, Steele had mumbled in my ear on that desk. *You need to bleed for the music, don't you?*

I had forgotten. My nerves got in the way, along with everything else.

It wasn't enough that I could play it well—I had to feel it.

And second: after the audition, we're going to meet his mother for the first time.

I'm not sure what has me more stressed.

Steele opens the door for me, then follows me into the theater. The full orchestra is set up with chairs and music stands onstage, although it's empty. There's a row of people —the board that will have to vote to hire me—sitting toward the middle of the front section of chairs in the audience.

Steele slips into a seat in the back and winks at me.

I take a deep breath and continue down, smiling at Professor Wilcox when he spots me. I stop at the top of the stage.

"Hello, Aspen," the professor says.

"Good morning," I greet them.

There are five of them. Three men, two women. They don't look *mean*, but they do look... disinterested. So I guess it's my job to make them interested. Right?

I had forwarded the piece I was going to play to Wilcox last week. I don't bother to explain *why* I picked it. It was a personal choice after the last month. I wanted to show something that was sad and soulful and heartbreaking.

I'm playing 'Once Upon a December' from *Anastasia*. It's easily recognized and almost felt like a cliched choice at first. But at the same time, this piece has resonated with me lately. On the same level that Clair de Lune resonates with *Twilight* fans. The magic is in the composition. And my goal is to pour every ounce of passion and need into this performance.

"When you're ready," one of the women says.

"Thank you," I murmur.

My throat is tight, and I head for the baby grand piano. It's in excellent condition, concert-ready, with a gleaming black top that's lifted open for best sound quality. I adjust the bench and discreetly wipe my palms on my thighs. Now is not the best time for sweating hands. I run my fingers over the keys, positioning them to start. My foot hovers above the pedal.

And then I wait. And I sink into what this piece means, what this opportunity means.

I'm not doing it because I'm desperate for a job.

I'm not doing it because I have no other options.

I'm doing this because I love playing the piano, and I've had dreams of being in an orchestra ever since my uncle took me to a ballet when I was ten. I think he took me there because my parents wanted me out of the house—but it doesn't matter. I fell in love with it, the same way you fall in love with a person. Almost without noticing it, until you go home and it's all you can think about.

My parents got a small keyboard to practice on after a month of begging. And upgraded to an electric piano that fit in our living room six months after that. A million hours in lessons and practice, and every bad thing that ever happened to me in my room was let out through playing.

Remembering that, acknowledging that my trauma has come out a hundred times over through the piano... I take a deep breath.

And I begin.

50
STEELE

My dazzling viper hypnotized the room. And me, too. My heart is filled watching her play. Her whole upper body moves with it, leaning forward slightly over the keys. Her hair pulled away from her face, the ends left loose down her back. She chose a long-sleeved purple dress that accentuates her body while remaining modest.

Not my favorite word—*modest*—but I understand it in this regard.

The theater swells with the music she's creating. The notes seem to almost tumble over each other, each one clear and precise and melting into the rest. I lean forward in my seat, unable to take my eyes off her.

But then I do, because I need to remember this. I start recording only a minute or two into Aspen's performance. I zoom in on her slight smile, and the way she's not even looking at the keys. Her chin stays lifted, her gaze lost in some memory—or just focus as she recalls the piece. There's no sheet music in front of her, nothing except the great expanse of the piano.

I angle my camera toward her hands and resist the urge to creep closer.

Pride swells in my chest when, after several more minutes of soul-rocking playing, her fingers linger on the keys and the sound fades off into silence. I wipe a tear away. Her pain and loss was so very powerful.

She did that.

Aspen pulls her hands back into her lap and looks down for a moment, her throat working. I end the recording and research where to buy a piano.

I mean, it should probably wait until we have a house... but do I *really* want her to spend time in a cramped little practice room when she could be playing in *our* place?

No, no I don't.

Besides, I've been working on getting us an apartment. Knox and Miles know I plan on moving us out. Aspen has been a good sport about sharing a house with two other guys. Thalia moved in with one of the dance girls. Neither one wanted to linger in that apartment.

No one blamed them.

Aspen's been having nightmares, though. She wakes up terrified. Sometimes she moans and jerks in her sleep before she snaps out of it. But they're easing. Every night, I'm there to coax her out of her fear. And I never want to be anywhere else.

"Ready?"

I jump to my feet, closing my browser and stuffing my phone in my pocket. Aspen gives me an odd look, but I just shake my head and hold out my hand to her.

Next stop... my mom's.

Aspen holds my hand on the drive there, chattering about the piece, the judges, the rush she felt. "I really felt like the passion was there this time. It was a *good* audition, don't you think?"

"It was brilliant."

"Well." She pauses, her face turning red. "Thank you."

I bring her hand up to my lips, angling for her fourth finger.

The drive is about an hour, out of Crown Point and south on the closest highway. We pass the exit for my hometown, which is no doubt familiar to Aspen, and then drive another thirty minutes.

Mom is in a smaller town, tucked out of the way, in a gorgeous mansion that's been converted into apartments.

We pull into the parking lot, and I see the confusion that crosses Aspen's face. I shrug it off and park, then go around and open her door. I wrap my arm around her waist and cinch her to my side, hurrying her into the building.

After signing in, we go down a hallway and into a huge, airy common room. There are plush chairs set around low tables, a few couches. The ceiling is two stories above our heads, with the second story banister open and allowing that floor to overlook the common room. The windows go all the way up, too, letting in a ton of light.

"Steele…"

I glance at Aspen and bite my tongue. We continue toward one of the far corners, where there's always a chessboard set up.

My mother's favorite spot.

She's seated right where I would expect her to be. There's a glass of water in front of her, near the board but off to the side. All the pieces are set up for a game to begin. Her hair is in a braid, dark brown with streaks of silver in it. Her glasses are perched on her nose, the decorated chain looped behind her neck. And she seems to be focused on the pieces, although she hasn't reached out to move any.

Perhaps she's waiting for an opponent.

"Hi, Mom." I touch her arm.

She smiles up at me. "Oh! Hi, darling."

"Care to play?"

She focuses on the board again and nods. "Yes, of course. I'm quite good, you know."

I crack a smile, although my heart is pounding. "I know. You've beat me a few times. Mom, this is Aspen. She's my fiancée."

Mom's gaze goes to my girl.

"Nice to meet you," Aspen says.

"Pleasure." Mom beams. "I wasn't expecting company today! But please, sit."

I drag another chair over for Aspen and take the one opposite Mom. I've got the white pieces, so I move my pawn forward first.

"Are you enjoying the cooler weather?" I ask.

Mom hums and pushes forward one of her pawns. "The snow is nice to watch. They've got me knitting scarves for all the ladies. Keeps me busy." She leans toward Aspen. "Some of them are real nice about it, but other ones..." Her nose wrinkles.

Aspen lets out a surprised laugh.

We continue to play chess, not thinking especially hard about the opening. And for a moment, I allow myself to relax.

Then Mom's attention lands on me, and she says, "My son and I used to play chess together."

My stomach knots, and I force a smile. "You must've taught him well."

Mom nods. "He's playing hockey at his high school.

Wonderful thing, that sport. Although I wish he would focus more on his science classes."

"Are you talking about Steele?" Aspen asks.

"Yes, yes. My eldest boy." Mom's smile wobbles. "Do you know him?"

"I do," Aspen answers. Without hesitation. "You raised a great guy."

My mom visibly brightens. She shuffles more upright and reaches for Aspen's hand. "Tell me about him. It's been a while since I was able to go see him play."

Aspen scoots her chair closer to Mom, not letting go of her hand. "He's in college now, but he's going to be graduating in a few months. He's still playing hockey." Her gaze finds mine. "He's got kind eyes. A protector's spirit."

Mom pats Aspen's hand with her free one. "You *do* know my son. He's always trying to protect me. College, you said?"

"Yes, ma'am." Aspen's voice lowers. "Can I tell you something?"

"Of course."

She looks at me again, then back at my mom. Her tone is conspiratorial as she says, "I'm going to marry him."

"Well." Mom's throat works. Her eyes fill with tears. "Isn't that just the most amazing thing. Did he give you a ring?"

"Not yet."

Mom scoffs. "*Men.*" She hooks her thumb under the collar of her sweater, pulling out the thin chain... and the ring on it. With surprising dexterity, she gets it off and thrusts the whole thing at Aspen. "Try this on."

My throat is tight. Aspen unclasps the necklace and slides the ring off, and her brows furrow.

It's the ring my father got her when they were freshly

out of college. Barely twenty-one themselves and ready to take on the world—or so the stories go. A single round diamond set with silver prongs. There used to be an engraving on the underside, but time has worn it away. I know, because I used to rub her ring between my index finger and thumb. A comfort thing when Dad dropped me off here to visit.

I go to Aspen and go to my knees in front of her, gently taking the ring from her hands.

"Let me."

She takes a shuddering breath—and I'm right there with her.

"Aspen Monroe." I take in her big, beautiful green eyes that are filling rapidly with tears. "Will you marry me?"

"Oh!" Mom exclaims.

Aspen nods frantically. I take her left hand and slip the ring on her finger, and holy shit.

It's a perfect fit.

Aspen grabs my face and kisses me hard, just for a second. It tastes like her tears. Then she's out of her chair and hugging my mother.

Mom hugs her back, patting it softly. She's bewildered, but she doesn't pull away or shout in fear. No dramatic reactions at all. And after a moment, Mom makes a shushing sound, soothing Aspen.

When my girl withdraws, she swipes under her eyes and blots at her face with her sleeve.

Mom's gaze bounces from me to Aspen, then back to me. She frowns.

"What's that look for?" I ask her, grinning.

She rolls her eyes and points to the board. "It's your move."

That it is.

"What happened with your mom?" I spin the gorgeous ring around my finger, then pause to stare at it again. Then focus back on Steele. My mind has been a freaking ping-pong ball since we left the assisted-living home.

And now we've got about an hour's drive.

"Early onset dementia. They discovered it when I was in high school."

Steele glances at me, then holds out his hand. I put mine in his, eager for the contact. As much as I might need grounding, he probably needs it more. So I lace our fingers together and squeeze softly, letting him take my hand back onto his thigh.

"Mom was still... with it, you know? She knew us, our faces. But it was other things that were slipping. And for a while, she went through some dramatic mood changes. Screaming at my dad, flipping us off. She'd have meltdowns or violent outbursts randomly, set off by things that felt huge to her but really weren't. It was a lot to deal with." His jaw clenches, the muscle ticing. "When she had a day or two of clarity, she and my father both recognized that this couldn't be good for our family long-term. So Dad put Mom in the assisted-living place. She toured it, of course, and agreed to it... And then, a few months later, Dad told me that they were getting divorced."

I gasp.

"Just like that?"

Steele shrugs. "I don't know. He never told me much about it—just that they both decided it wouldn't be fair to him if she was..." His jaw works again. "An empty shell."

"She's not an empty shell." I hold his hand tighter.

"It doesn't matter. It was done. Dad pays for everything anyway. He promised to give her the best life he could, and... I mean, she stays in a pretty nice place. She never says anything bad about the other residents or the nurses."

"Thank you for introducing us," I whisper. I unbuckle my seat belt and shift onto my knee, leaning over the center console to kiss his cheek.

He smirks. "You're not going to be thanking me when I tell you where we're headed next..."

"And here I was about to blow you..." I reach down and brush my finger over his zipper. "So maybe you'll just take me to bed instead of whatever evil plan you've made."

Steele groans, his cock stiffening under his slacks in record time. "You've done it now."

"So... home?"

I undo the button and drag the zipper down, navigating him out of his pants. His cock springs up, already hard for me. I don't wait for him to answer, just licking my lips and descending on him. He hits the back of my throat, and I pull back slightly, inhaling through my nose.

His hand comes down on the back of my head, pushing me back down. He's muttering above me. The whine of the engine goes harder, his thigh flexing as he steps on the gas. It feels dangerous and a little nuts—no pun intended—to be doing this.

But I love the rush of adrenaline that comes with the risk.

He controls my pace, choking me on his dick and then letting me breathe and suck and lick at his tip. Then back down. I hold on to his hip with my left hand, and his thigh with my other. Balancing myself.

"I'm gonna come," he warns on another groan.

I fucking love the noises he makes.

I lock my lips around his head and run my tongue over his slit. My hand curls around his base, pumping and twisting.

"Oh, fuck," he growls above me.

The car swerves ever so slightly, and suddenly my mouth is flooded. I swallow hard, sucking and pumping him. There's another jet of cum, and he lets out a shaky exhale. The taste of him lingers on my tongue, and I sit up. I wipe my chin with the back of my hand. I glance at the road, checking that we're not in danger of crashing into anything or going around a sharp curve, then drag his face toward mine. Our open mouths smash together, our tongues sliding and fighting for space.

I release him after a second and fall back in my seat, laughing.

"Holy shit." He shakes his head. "You're just as crazy as me."

I eye him. His combed hair, which needs some messing. The dark-purple dress shirt tucked into his black pants— which I now realize he somehow perfectly matched to my dress.

"So, home?" I ask lightly.

He shakes his head. "Not a chance."

"Where, then?"

"Well, *first*... we're making a pit stop. But then, we're going to a party."

Uh-huh.

"Buckle," he orders.

"Yes, sir," I grumble. But really, no complaints here. I did my big risky move—I don't need to keep asking fate to wreck us.

We drive for another twenty minutes. Music plays, distracting both of us from conversation. He's been inching his hand up my thigh for the last fifteen, and his pinky finally grazes the edge of my panties.

I keep staring out the window as he slips his finger under the thin fabric.

"You're wet," he says.

"Hmm?" I pretend to notice him for the first time.

He chuckles and withdraws, licking his pinky finger.

My face heats. Even now, it makes me squirm. After everything we've done...

He flicks his blinker on and takes the exit into a rest area. It's one of the smaller ones, with just a gas station and convenience store attached. The rest area backs up to dense woods, and Steele aims for the tree line. He parks far away from anyone else, then unbuckles.

I do the same.

"Take off your panties," he orders in a quiet voice.

I lift my hips and drag them down, pulling them off over my shoes. He takes them and hooks them on the gear stick to the right of the steering wheel.

"Now put your back to the door."

A shiver goes through me as I do, twisting my upper body. He grabs my left leg and guides it over the console, spreading my thighs. My dress falls between my legs, hiding my pussy from him. Not that it will deter him. He drags my ass across my seat, getting me closer, and shoves my dress up to my ribs.

"I'll never get over this tattoo," he admits. He checks his watch and grimaces. "We're going to have to be fast. Can you do that for me, sweetheart?"

I open my mouth to reply, but he's already leaning down to kiss my lips. My *other* lips. And what comes out of my mouth instead of words is some nonsense sigh.

He wastes no time, going directly to my clit. I gasp and buck when he tongues my sensitive bud. All of his focus is *right there.*

His grip on my thighs keeps my legs spread wide. He growls and laps at me, then sucks it into his mouth. Hard.

I tip my head back, hitting it on the window, and cry out. My hips won't stop moving, not that he gives a shit. In fact, the more forcefully I try to press my pussy into his face, the harder he treats my clit. Until he scrapes it with his teeth and flicks just the tip of it with his tongue—and I fucking shatter.

I scream his name, digging my nails into the seat. He continues to lick me, going down farther and plunging his tongue inside me. Absorbing the way my muscles immediately clench at him. It pushes my pleasure on and on, a rolling wave of bliss, until I've completely sagged backward.

"Wow," I murmur.

He smirks at me, picking up my leg by my ankle and pressing a kiss to it. Then he puts it back where it belongs and restarts the car. He tugs the front of my dress down, covering me before he pulls back out onto the highway.

I can't even move for a long moment.

We've gone maybe ten minutes before I sit up and snag my panties, where they're still hanging from his gear stick. He chuckles, glancing at me while I wriggle them back in place. Then fixing my dress in the back, too.

Jeez.

And then I realize where we're going.

The restaurant on the point.

I eye Steele, who just smiles at me.

"What?" he questions. Sounding *way* too innocent for the shit-eating grin that's overtaking his face.

I scoff and climb out of the car. Quick hair and makeup check in my reflection, confirming that the blow job tears didn't ruin my eyeliner, and his hand on the back of my head didn't cause unnecessary sex hair, and then I'm ready. I loop my arm in his and let him lead me inside.

We go through the main dining room and into the room we ate lunch in that day... the day when everything went to shit. My footsteps automatically slow, and Steele glances down at me.

"Don't chicken out on me now, little viper."

The nickname gives me a modicum of resolve. I throw back my shoulders and march with him down the steps and around the corner.

To where our parents wait.

I slam to a halt.

While we've seen more of them, Steele and I have avoided seeing them *together*. As in, Mom will bring the girls to see me at school between classes, or we'll go to a movie together, but Stephen and Steele don't attend. Or Steele will go over their house and watch my sisters for an hour or two, but it's always when I have class or practice.

The few times I've seen Steele's dad has been awkward. I don't know what to say to him. My dad told him Steele and I were intimate, and I don't know if he's just been choosing to ignore it or forgot—or thought it was a lie.

I drop Steele's arm like it's on fire, but he just laughs and puts that same arm around my shoulders.

"You're not getting out of this one," he says in my ear. "You think you can marry me and not tell your mother?"

I wince.

I mean... *yeah*, sure. He has a point. But I also was just hoping to avoid the whole messy situation by waiting until Steele was famous, we were graduated, and living in some fancy house in the city of our choosing before getting married.

Obviously, Steele wouldn't want to wait that long—and I don't think he believes in cowardice.

"Hi, honey," Mom calls, circling around the table and hugging me.

It's too similar to the last time we did this, just the four of us. When they threatened to lock me up...

"Aspen." Stephen reaches to hug me, too. He wraps his arms around my shoulders.

I tense up.

He releases me quickly and steps back. Mom is just releasing Steele from her embrace, too, and we all take our seats. Me across from Mom, Steele on my left across from his father.

Steele picks up my hand by my fingers and sets them both on the table. Showing off the glittering diamond on my finger.

"Aspen and I are getting married," Steele announces.

Neither of them look fucking surprised.

I narrow my eyes at my mom, and she has the good grace to look guilty.

"Well. Your uncle may have been, um, keeping tabs on

you. For me," she adds. "Not that we didn't trust you, Steele, but... well."

Ridiculous.

Ridiculous.

It's so ridiculous, it's almost funny.

No, actually, it *is* fucking funny. I cover my mouth to try and hide my giggle. But as soon as the first one slips out, the whole dam breaks. And suddenly I'm laughing so hard I can't breathe. Tears fill my eyes, and I snort. Then laugh harder.

Steele is laughing, too.

Because we started this train wreck of a relationship with *spying*. Steele's dad asking me to look after his son, and the vitriol that followed. Of course they wouldn't trust us to follow through on that—they hardly trust us at all.

Eventually, my giggles subside. Steele still has a hold of my hand, although he releases it so I can snap out my napkin and dab at my eyes.

"You guys are messed up," I tell them. "We're adults."

Stephen inclines his chin. "We just want what's best for our children."

"Yeah... but you don't try to guide us into better decisions or trust us to tell you. You just watch from the sidelines until we fall on our asses. And then you try to punish us for it." I eye Steele, deciding not to bring up the whole drugging thing. It's water under the bridge between us, even if it might still be a sore spot between his father and me. And that counselor who I ditched. *Whoops.*

He's nodding along. "Dad, you were so willing to dismiss Aspen after I sent you that video. But the whole thing was fake. I spiked her drink with a hallucinogenic and filmed it to discredit her. And you fell for it. Not only that, but you tried to get her to leave CPU and derailed her whole career... for what?"

I'm just surprised Steele admitted it. But maybe he's willing to shed light on his own devious nature if it shows just how ineffective our parents' meddling has been.

Shame fills Stephen's expression, and his attention flips from Steele to me. "My son is right. I used you as a tool, Aspen, and I'm sorry for that. The night with your father proved just how badly I was fucking things up between us. I shouldn't have done that—and I'll rectify it immediately."

"No need," Steele murmurs. "I took care of it. I love Aspen. I knew her before I found out she was the daughter of the woman you married. I knew we were going to be together when I first laid eyes on her. That's why we went to Mom, and she gave us her ring."

For the first time, Stephen goes completely still. His gaze lands on the ring, and his lips flatten. There's a second where I think he might go toward anger, but instead... his whole face softens.

"I'm so fucking proud of you," he says to his son. "And for the record, I support your decision to pursue hockey as a career. I don't know if I understand it, exactly. It's still a violent sport. But you're good at it, and you seem happy. That's what should've been most important to me all along."

Oh, great. Today just seems to be the day for tears, because my vision goes blurry for the thousandth time.

"I'm sure your mother would say the same," he adds.

And I'm crying.

Steele wordlessly pulls me onto his lap. I automatically tuck my face in his neck, and he strokes my hair.

"She's had a long day," he offers as way of explanation. He tells them about my second audition. And how his mother was today—because I guess some days are worse than others, and we got a good one.

I stay there until our food is ordered. Then, shyly, I slip off his lap and clean myself up in the ladies' room. By the time I'm done, most of my makeup is gone. But you know what?

Good riddance.

I rejoin them and smile at my mother, who smiles back at me. She's holding hands with Stephen, much the way Steele held my hand on the table. She looks happy and relaxed. Steele leans over and kisses my cheek, and neither of our parents bat an eye.

I got so used to worrying and fearing for all of us that this relief feels almost strange.

But I never want to let it go.

ASPEN

TWO YEARS LATER

"This is nuts," I murmur.

Steele grins and holds out his hand. I take it, of course, and squeeze his fingers. He pulls me out of the car and onto the sidewalk. He's been talking about this *surprise* for a month but refused to tell me exactly what he had planned.

I would've been fine with not knowing, except he kept bringing it up—and that's what piqued my curiosity. His excitement.

Now we're parked on the street outside a popular tattoo shop on the downtown strip of this little tourist town. It was a bit of a drive from Boston. But now, this is obviously a massive hint at what the surprise is going to be—I'm just not sure whether the appointment is for him, me, or both of us...

"Excuse me," a woman calls, marching down the street toward us. "Are you Steele O'Brien?"

Steele smiles politely at her and nods.

"Oh, my gosh. Can I get your autograph?" The woman, no joke, fishes a small notebook out of her purse. She flips to an empty page. "We're going to your game tomorrow night in Boston! My family is going to freak out. What brings you to our quiet town?"

He takes the notebook and offered Sharpie, although he doesn't answer her question.

"We see so many famous people visiting," the woman says to me. "I like to always be prepared. There's been an influx of visitors lately."

I grin and eye Steele. One thing CPU hockey didn't adequately prepare him for was the amount of fans he would amass. Nowhere near the level of Knox or Greyson, though, who also went into the NHL after college. Scrolling social media, I'm guaranteed to see a video montage of at least one of them, set to some sexy music.

Steele doesn't find it as funny. The tips of his ears are red, and he poses for a picture with the woman. And then she's gone, and I'm left smirking at my husband.

"Shut it," he grumbles, taking my hand and practically dragging me into the tattoo shop.

"You never know who you're going to run into," I tease him.

We moved to Tennessee shortly after Steele was signed. Even still, we're never actually home. If he's traveling, I'm traveling. He says his goal is to get on a team with one of his friends. They've been spread out all over the league at this rate.

Coach Roake was on one of the late-night talk shows the other week. Apparently, no other college team has had as much success getting their players into the NHL as he had. It was almost cute, watching Coach sing their praises.

The bell above the door chimes, and warmth envelops us.

A tattooed man comes out and greets us. He's surprisingly gorgeous—not that I'm, you know, looking. He's just got that tortured appearance. Starving artist meets... success.

"Welcome to Starlight," he says. "You're Steele and Aspen?"

"Yep."

"Saint Hart," he introduces, shaking our hands. "Ready to get started?"

I dig my heels in. "Wait. Sorry." I glare at Steele. "Are you going to tell me what we're doing?"

Steele snickers. "Yeah, little viper. I'm getting you tattooed on me."

I narrow my eyes at him, but he seems unbothered. And he follows the tattoo artist back into his studio without hesitation.

I mean, really. Why would he hesitate? He's covered in tattoos. Another one wouldn't make a difference. Even if it's supposedly representing *me*.

Steele sits where Saint directs him, and I take one of the chairs off to the side. Positioned so I can definitely see what sort of madness Steele has come up with. But then I decide that maybe I'm better off not knowing, and I head back into the front lobby area. There's a white couch with a low coffee table in front of it, and a spread of magazines that feature Starlight.

All in all, the vibe of this place is cool. I can see why magazines would be interested in featuring it—and his work, hung in gold picture frames set against the dark paint.

"Do you want to see the stencil?" Steele calls.

"Nope."

"What if it's on my dick?"

I snort, keeping my gaze on the wall of art. "Then you're shit out of luck on getting laid this trip, huh?"

Steele groans.

I smirk to myself. Except, I wouldn't put it past him to get a snake tattooed on *his* snake.

Gross. But also...

With that thought in mind, I hurry into the room—and relax when I see the purple stencil on Steele's forearm. His other arm is covered in tattoos that I love to run my fingers over. The rose, the trees, a wolf. And the deer skull on his sternum. He has more, of course, but the deer skull is my favorite. For no other reason than it's a nice place to trace with my lips, and I love the morbidity of it.

Still. Even though the placement of the tattoo is better than what I expected, it takes me a minute to work out what it is.

A snake, winding down and ending with its teeth sunk into Steele's wrist.

I shake my head and sit beside him while Saint prepares his tattoo machine and ink. Just a little cup of black.

"A viper," Steele explains.

"I can see that." My cheeks heat. "Wouldn't a tree have been more... apt?"

He laughs. "You're not a *tree*. Your venom went right to my heart." He catches my hand and brings it to his lips. He kisses my knuckles. "And I wouldn't have it any other way."

I shake my head, drawing my legs up onto the chair.

To be fair, it's kind of surreal to see an artist like Saint Hart do his thing. The hum of the tattoo machine is almost kind of lulling—especially since it's not going in *my* skin.

But the longer I watch, the more I think I want one of my own.

Five hours—and a few breaks—later, and Saint wipes down the tattoo for the last time. He had Steele change positions a few times, since it wraps all the way around his forearm, and now he cleans all of it.

Steele rises and checks it out in the mirror. He started smiling when the tattoo began, and now it widens into a full-on grin. He ducks into the bathroom, and I glance at Saint.

I bite my lip.

But Saint just smiles faintly. "You want one, too?"

I nod.

"He already booked you an appointment following his."

"That asshole." It's hard not to laugh, though. "Did he tell you what I might want?"

"Something about a wedding ring?"

I lift my left hand. I *have* a wedding ring. The thin little band perfectly accentuates the engagement ring that came from his mother.

"He's delusional," I inform the tattoo artist. I tell him what I want instead, and Saint nods.

"Give me some time to draw that up."

Steele reemerges, and Saint puts a waterproof wrap over his tattoo. It'll stay on for a few days to help with the healing process.

"Ready to go, baby?" Steele wraps his hand around the back of my neck, drawing me toward him.

I let him kiss me. His lips against mine never fail to elicit a flutter of butterfly wings in my chest—or maybe it's just anxiety for what I'm about to do.

The first tattoo I got—from *him*—I wasn't awake to receive, or to feel the pain. Although I didn't love how long it took to heal, and the sunburn feeling that came with it, I can't deny that I probably got off lucky.

"You don't want me to use my appointment?" I ask against his lips.

He pauses. His eyes open, and he pouts. "How'd you know?"

"Because I told Saint I wanted a tattoo, and he said I already had a booking." I push at Steele's chest.

Not that he lets me get very far.

"What are you going to get?" he asks, his gaze already roving my body. Like he can pinpoint exactly where it's going to be.

I shake my head. "Nope, I'm not telling you. And in fact, you can wait on that couch. Out of sight."

He doesn't argue—surprisingly. He seems excited that I'm doing anything at all.

Saint comes back, Steele leaves, and we get to work.

The design is perfect and simple, the first iteration the best. He places the stencil, double checks that it's what I want, and begins.

The first prick of the needle is the worst, but I relax into it after a while. He works quietly, not making any small talk. Which is fine by me. My heart is in my throat the whole time.

"Done," Saint says quietly.

I jerk out of my thoughts and climb to my feet. I examine my shoulder blade in the mirror, grinning to myself. Because it's gorgeous.

A pair of hockey skates, with rolls of sheet music sticking out of the top. The faint lines of the sheet music, the tiny notes, convey what the papers are exactly. Along with the beads of water on the skates, and the shading, it's absolutely perfect.

"Do you want to call your husband back?" Saint asks me.

I bite my lip. "No. Can we cover it?"

He pauses, then nods. He puts a bandage over it, taping it to my skin. It's not like the waterproof one Steele got—so that way when he rips it off to see it, it's not permanently unprotected.

"Well?" Steele asks, striding back into the room.

Just in time for me to pull my shirt back into place.

"Where is it?" His gaze roves over me. "Hmm, little viper?"

I smirk and go to him, putting my hand on his chest and reaching up to kiss his lips. He obliges for a second, but his curiosity is too great.

I inch around him, and now there's nothing between me and the door.

"Tell you what," I whisper. "If you catch me... I'll let you see it."

His eyes darken.

"Don't forget to pay Saint," I add on a laugh. I back away from him until I hit the door. Then I push through it and step out into the cool evening air.

"Fuck," Steele says behind me. "Take my card. We'll be back!"

I grin and take off running with my husband hot on my heels.

Just the way we like it.

THE END

What's coming next?

Secret Obsession
Miles Whiteshaw.
He's a hockey god... and she's the one he can't have.
Coming June 28, 2023
Pre-order: http://mybook.to/secretobsession

BONUS SCENE
The Group Chat Part Two

Was Saint Hart intriguing?
Get to know him better in my *Sterling Falls* series, which is now complete!

ACKNOWLEDGMENTS

I feel like I think this at the end of every book, but I'm just going to say it again: what a *journey*. From Steele and Aspen's crazy start to their heartwarming ending, I loved every minute of the joyride I was on along with them.

First, I have to thank y̲o̲u̲. You took Brutal Obsession and made it my best seller, and it's been amazing watching that book soar. Giving Steele his happily ever after, with Miles, Jacob, and Knox to follow, has been the best these past few months. (Even when Steele is being difficult.)

Second big thank you is to my reader group, SMassery Squad. They helped me pick out some tropes, very similar to how we did Brutal Obsession, and even helped me choose Aspen's name! If you want 'in' on helping me with stuff like that, plus early teasers and news, come join the party on Facebook!

To my Patreon supporters, thank you so much for your continued faith in me and excitement for my work. You ladies are wonderful.

And without my team, I'm not sure where I'd be. From my cheerleaders to my editing and design teams, I'm so thankful for everything you all do for me.

I'm looking forward to more hockey in the year to come!

ALSO BY S. MASSERY

DeSantis Mafia

#1 Ruthless Saint

#2 Savage Prince

#3 Stolen Crown

ABOUT THE AUTHOR

S. Massery is a dark romance author who loves injecting a good dose of suspense into her stories. She lives in Western Massachusetts with her dog, Alice.

Before adventuring into the world of writing, she went to college in Boston and held a wide variety of jobs—including working on a dude ranch in Wyoming (a personal highlight). She has a love affair with coffee and chocolate. When S. Massery isn't writing, she can be found devouring books, playing outside with her dog, or trying to make people smile.

Join her newsletter to stay up to date on new releases: http://smassery.com/newsletter

Made in United States
North Haven, CT
13 August 2024

56036057R00264